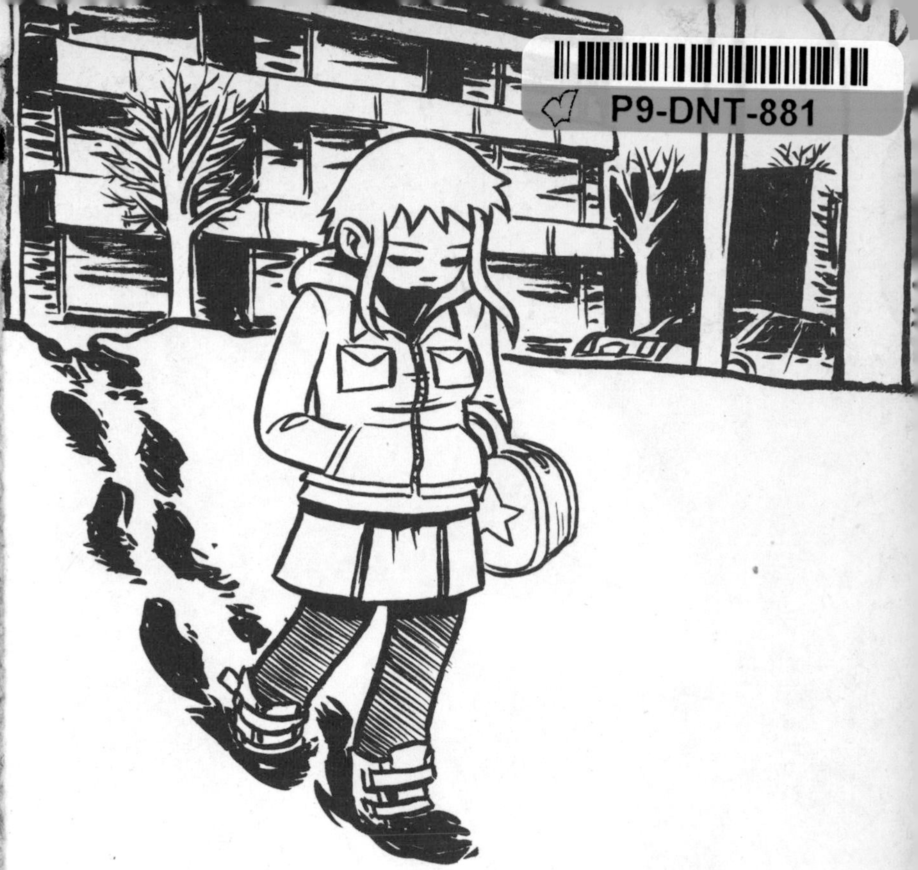

BRYAN LEE O'MALLEY'S

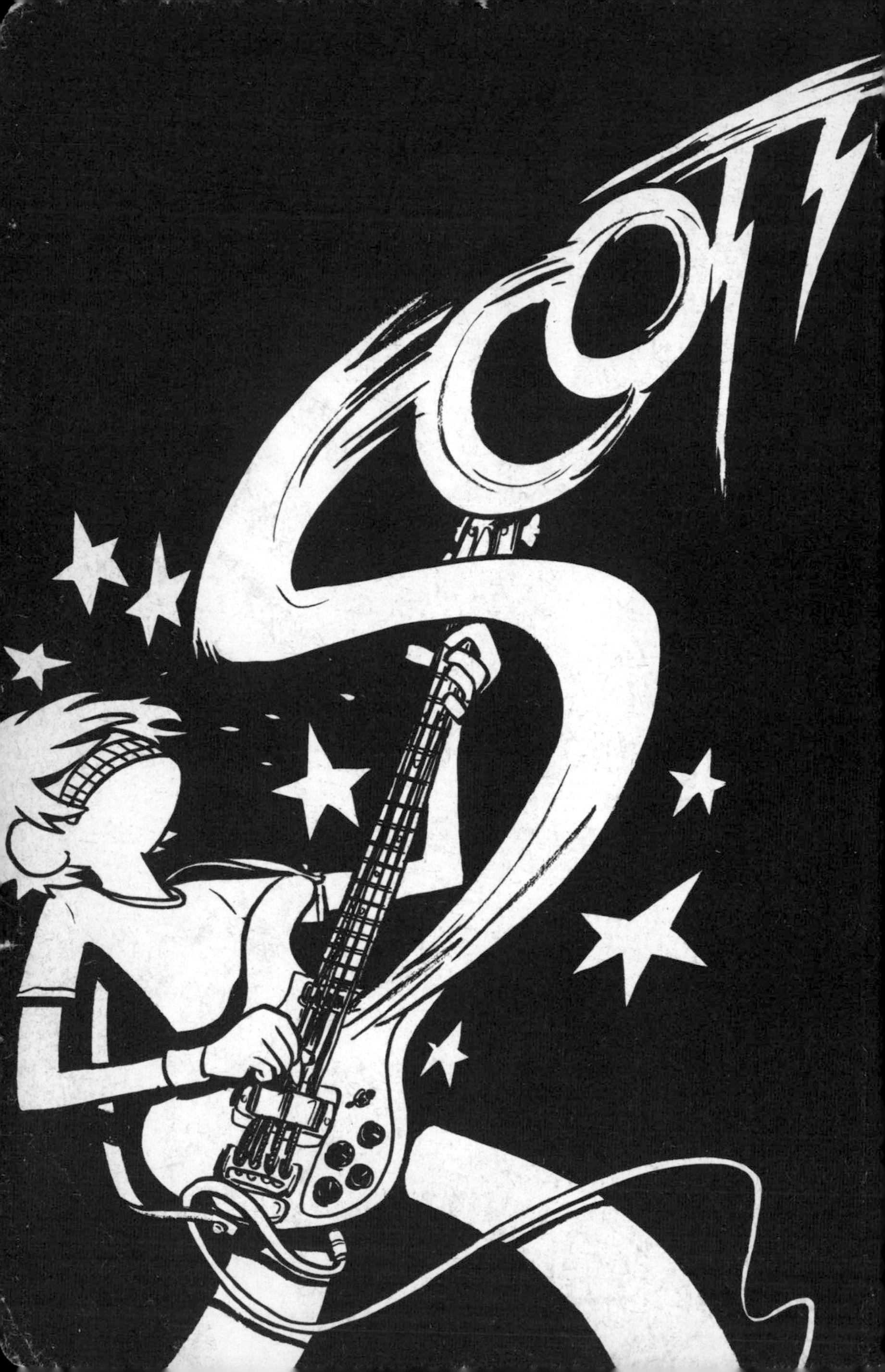
SCOTT

BRYAN LEE O'MALLEY

LOVED BY ANIMALS

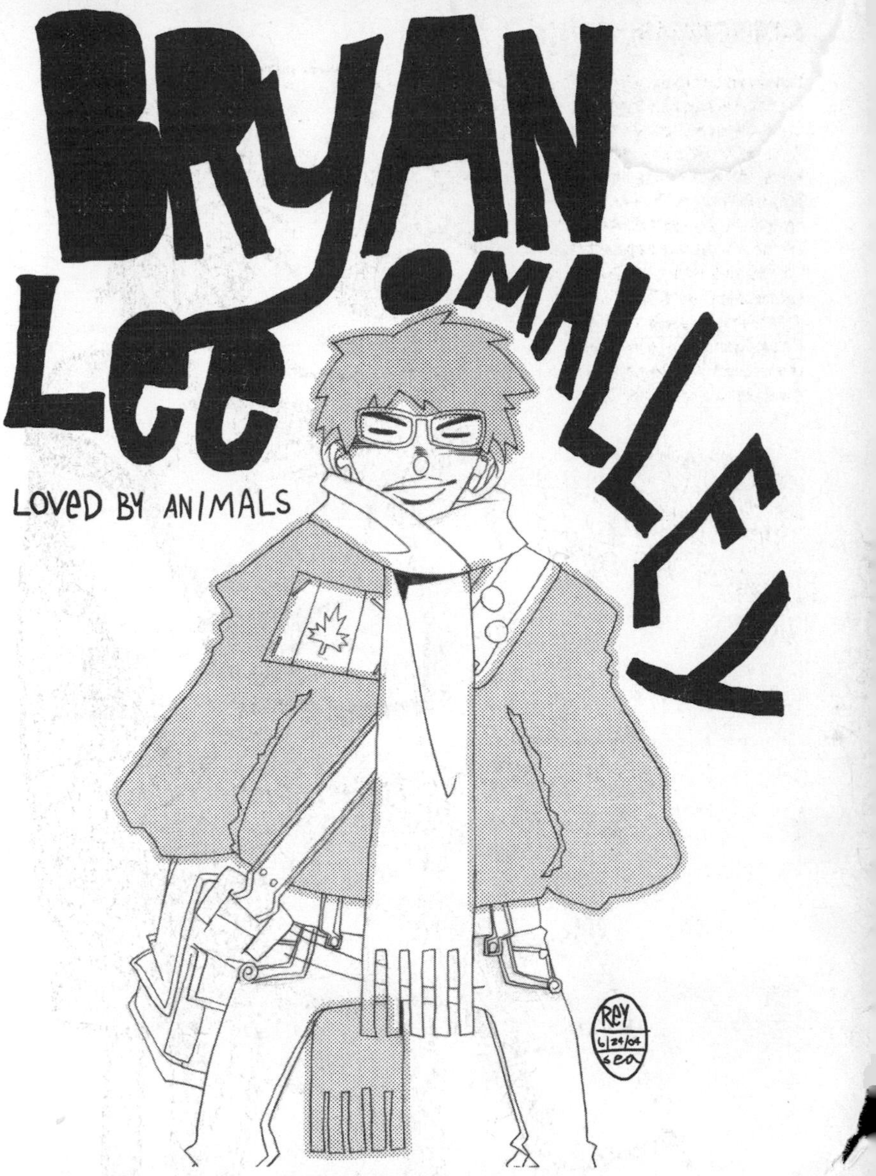

REY
6/24/04
sea

Illustration of the Author by Corey S. Lewis The Rey

BRYAN LEE O'MALLEY has been alive since 1979. He currently lives in Toronto. He plays some guitar and keyboards, but is pretty bad at bass. His first book was called LOST AT SEA. His second book is this one. You can learn more about him at WWW.RADIOMARU.COM.

OTHER BOOKS FROM BRYAN LEE O'MALLEY & ONI PRESS...

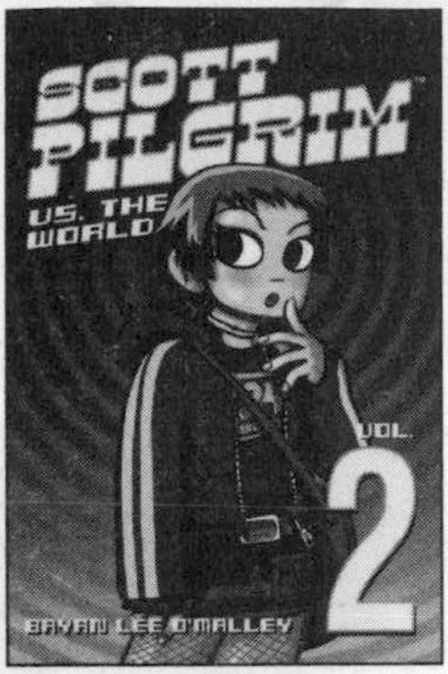
SCOTT PILGRIM
VS. THE WORLD
VOL. 2
BRYAN LEE O'MALLEY

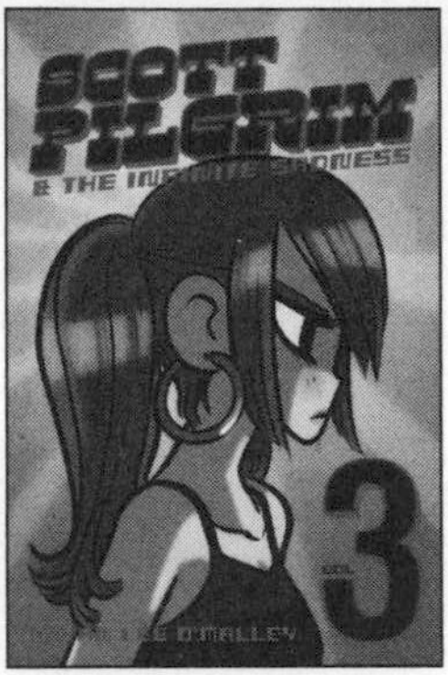
SCOTT PILGRIM
3

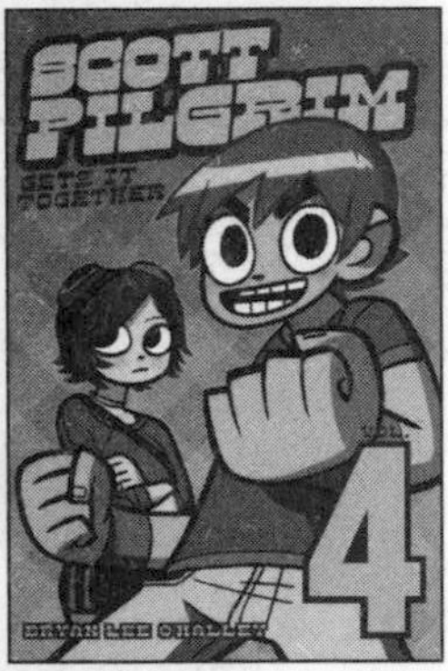
SCOTT PILGRIM
GETS IT TOGETHER
VOL. 4
BRYAN LEE O'MALLEY

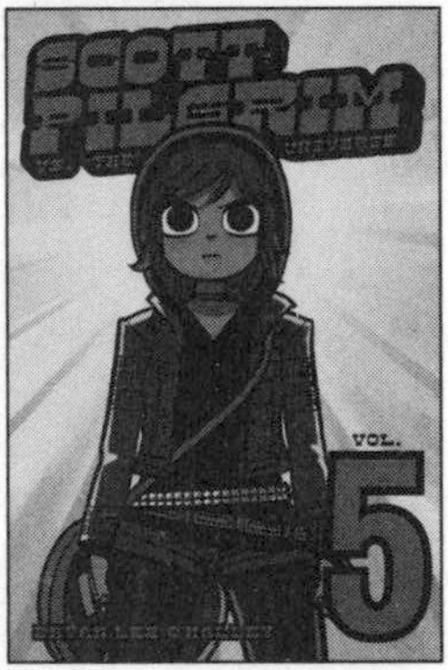
SCOTT PILGRIM
VOL. 5

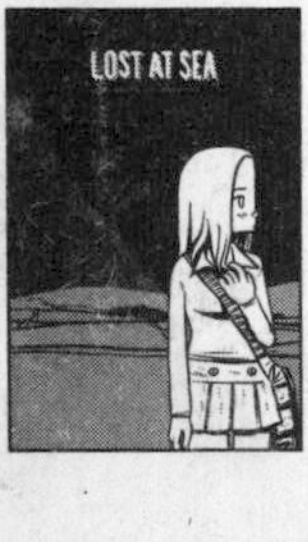
LOST AT SEA

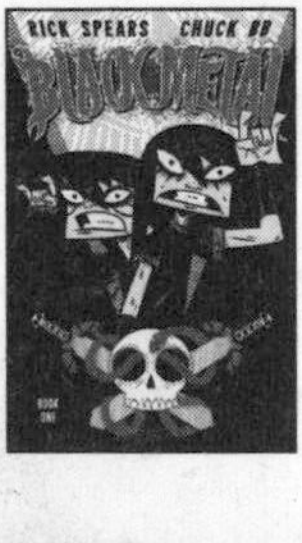
RICK SPEARS
CHUCK BB

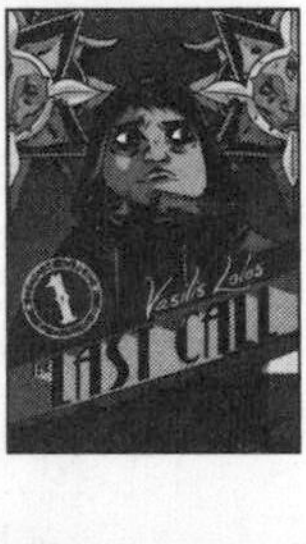
Vasilis Lolos

SCOTT PILGRIM, VOLUME 2:
SCOTT PILGRIM VS. THE WORLD
By Bryan Lee O'Malley
200 pages, digest, B&W
$11.95
ISBN 978-1-932664-12-6

SCOTT PILGRIM, VOLUME 3:
SCOTT PILGRIM & THE INFINITE SADNESS
By Bryan Lee O'Malley
200 pages, digest, B&W
$11.95
ISBN 978-1-932664-22-5

SCOTT PILGRIM, VOLUME 4:
SCOTT PILGRIM GETS IT TOGETHER
By Bryan Lee O'Malley
200 pages, digest, B&W
$11.95
ISBN 978-1-932664-49-2

SCOTT PILGRIM, VOLUME 5:
SCOTT PILGRIM VS. THE UNIVERSE
By Bryan Lee O'Malley
184 pages, digest, B&W
$11.95
ISBN 978-1-934964-10-1

LOST AT SEA
by Bryan Lee O'Malley
168 pages, digest, B&W
ISBN 978-1-932664-16-4
$11.95 US

BLACK METAL
by Rick Spears & Chuck BB
160 pages, digest, B&W
ISBN 978-1-932664-72-0
$11.95 US

THE LAST CALL
by Vasilis Lolos
136 pages, digest, B&W
ISBN 978-1-932664-69-0
$11.95 US

For more information on these and other fine Oni Press comic books and graphic novels, visit www.onipress.com. To find a comic specialty store in your area, call 1-888-COMICBOOK or visit www.comicshops.us.

www.onipress.com

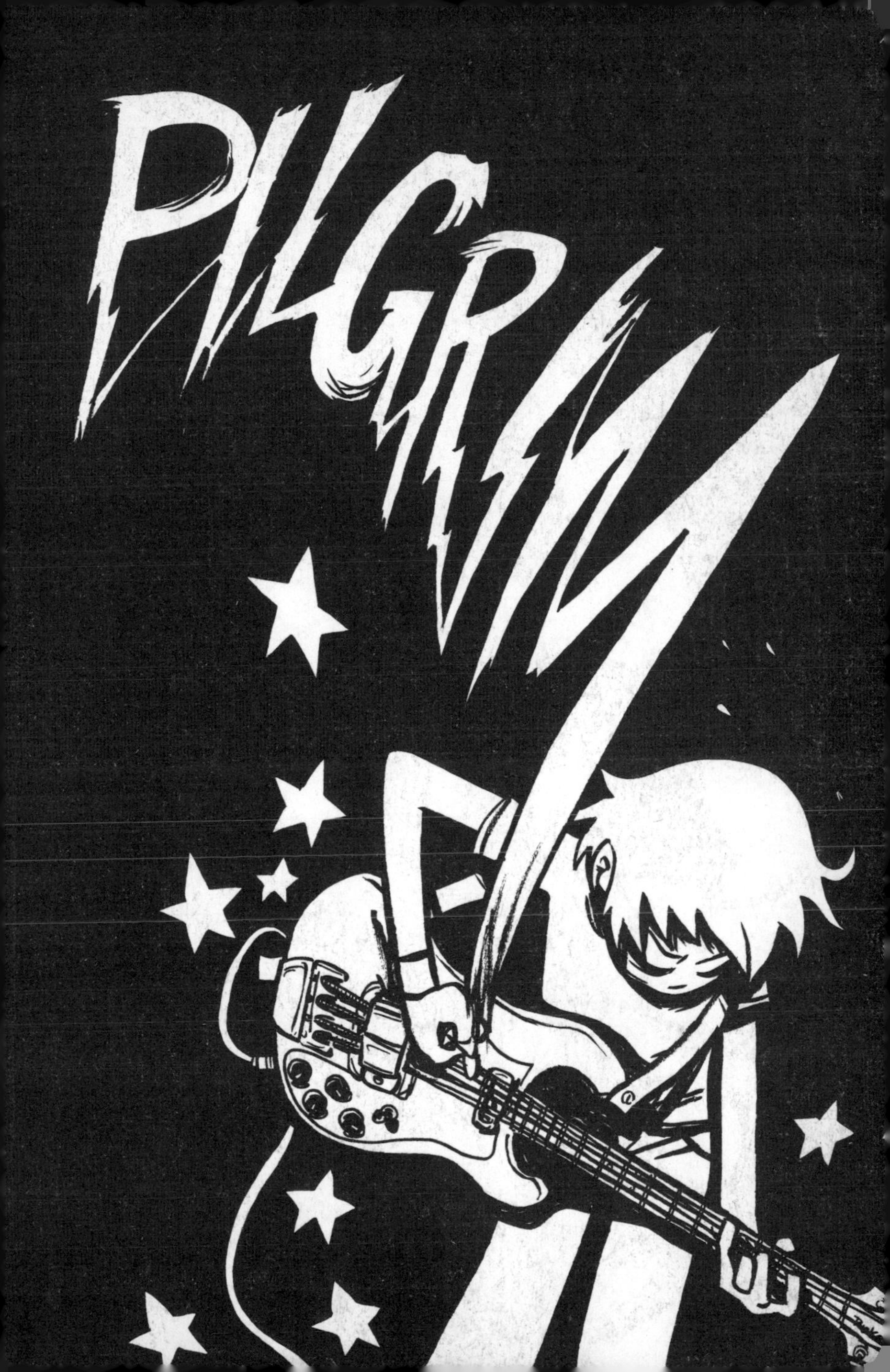
PILGRIM

edited by James Lucas Jones | design by Bryan Lee O'Malley & Keith Wood

Published by Oni Press, Inc.
Joe Nozemack, publisher | Randal C. Jarrell, managing editor | Ian Shaugnessy, editorial intern

ONI PRESS, INC.
1305 SE MARTIN LUTHER KING JR. BLVD., SUITE A
PORTLAND, OR 97214
USA

www.onipress.com
www.radiomaru.com

First edition: July 2004
ISBN 978-1-932664-08-9

10 9
PRINTED IN CANADA.

special thanks to
  Hope Larson
  Christopher Butcher
  Carla, Amanda, Catriona & Lynette
  James Lucas Jones
  AND YOU.

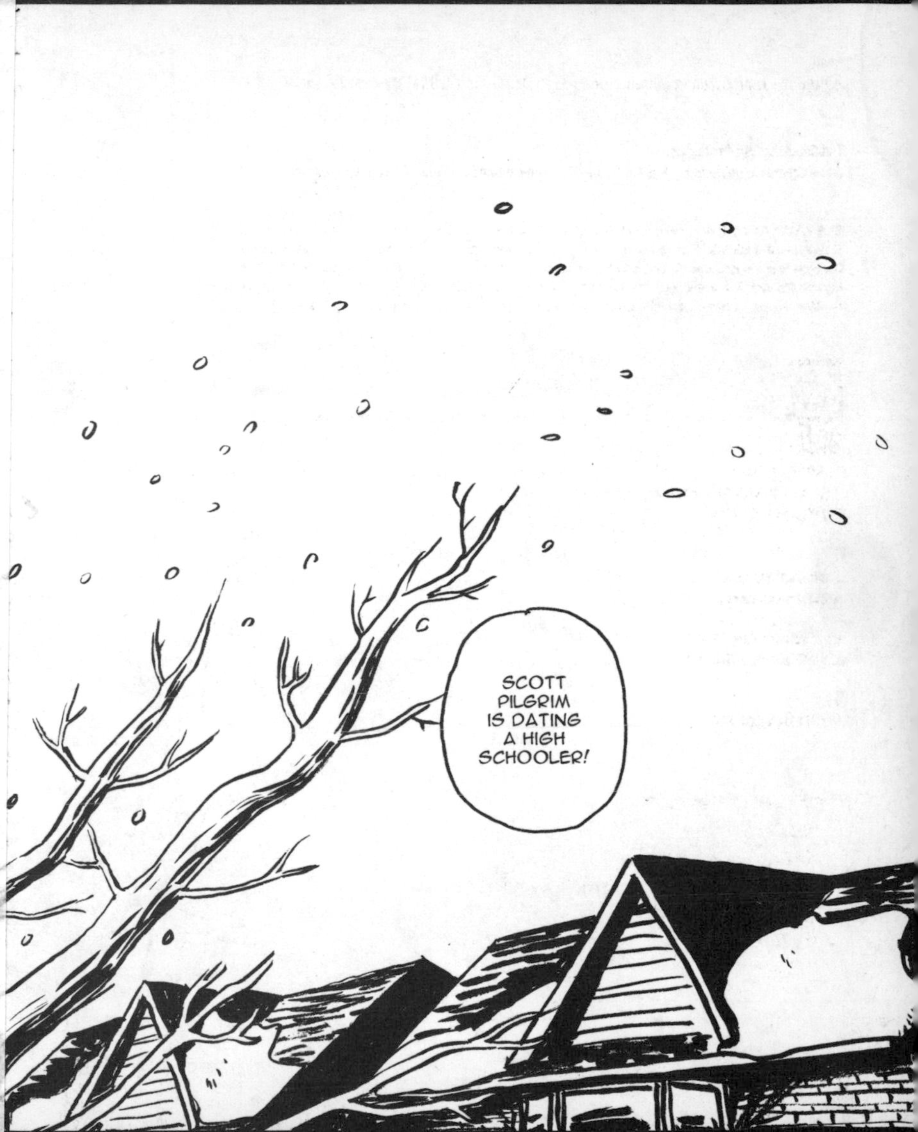
SCOTT PILGRIM IS DATING A HIGH SCHOOLER!

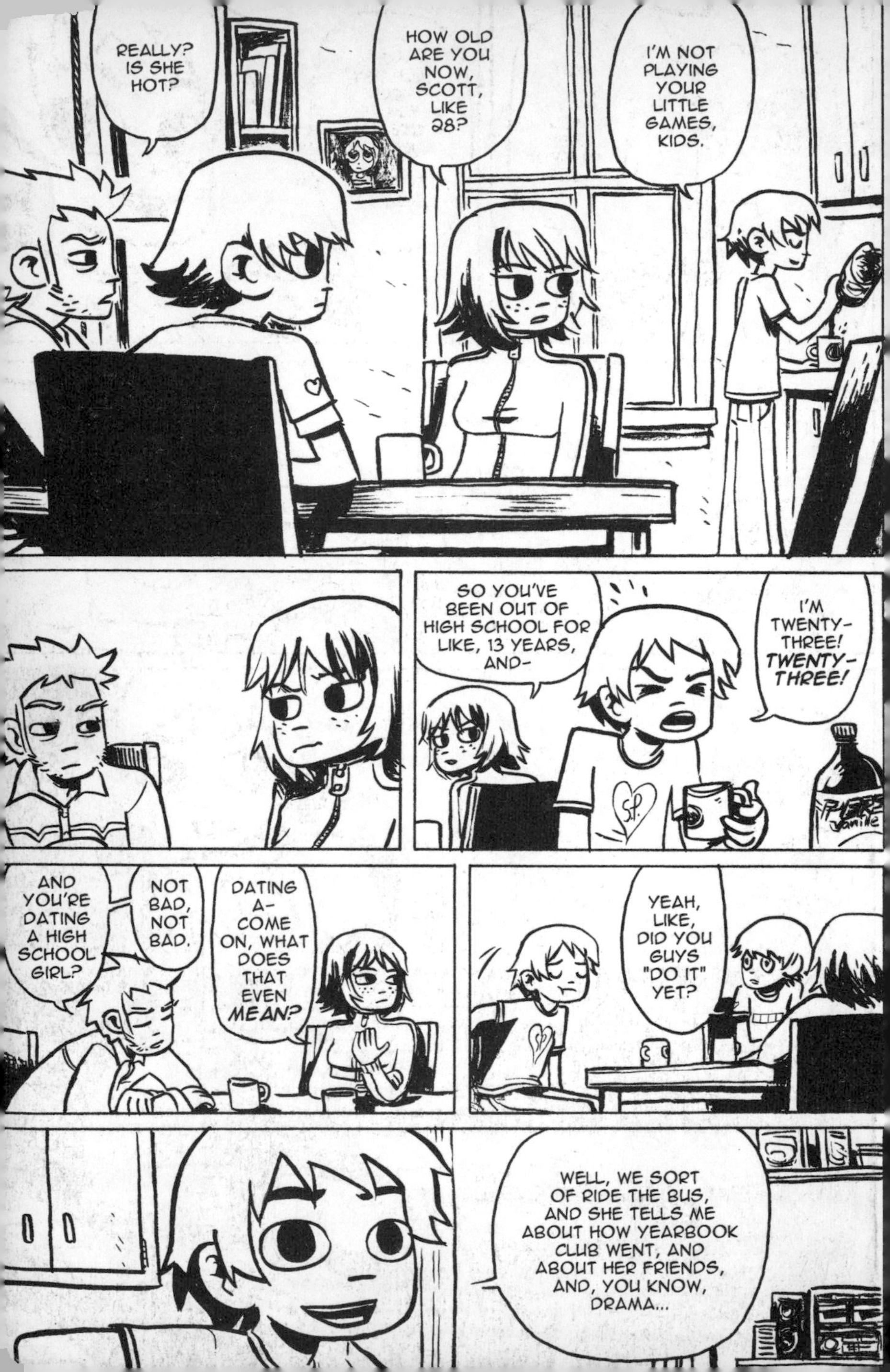
REALLY? IS SHE HOT?
HOW OLD ARE YOU NOW, SCOTT, LIKE 28?
I'M NOT PLAYING YOUR LITTLE GAMES, KIDS.
SO YOU'VE BEEN OUT OF HIGH SCHOOL FOR LIKE, 13 YEARS, AND-
I'M TWENTY-THREE! *TWENTY-THREE!*
AND YOU'RE DATING A HIGH SCHOOL GIRL?
NOT BAD, NOT BAD.
DATING A- COME ON, WHAT DOES THAT EVEN *MEAN?*
YEAH, LIKE, DID YOU GUYS "DO IT" YET?
WELL, WE SORT OF RIDE THE BUS, AND SHE TELLS ME ABOUT HOW YEARBOOK CLUB WENT, AND ABOUT HER FRIENDS, AND, YOU KNOW, DRAMA...

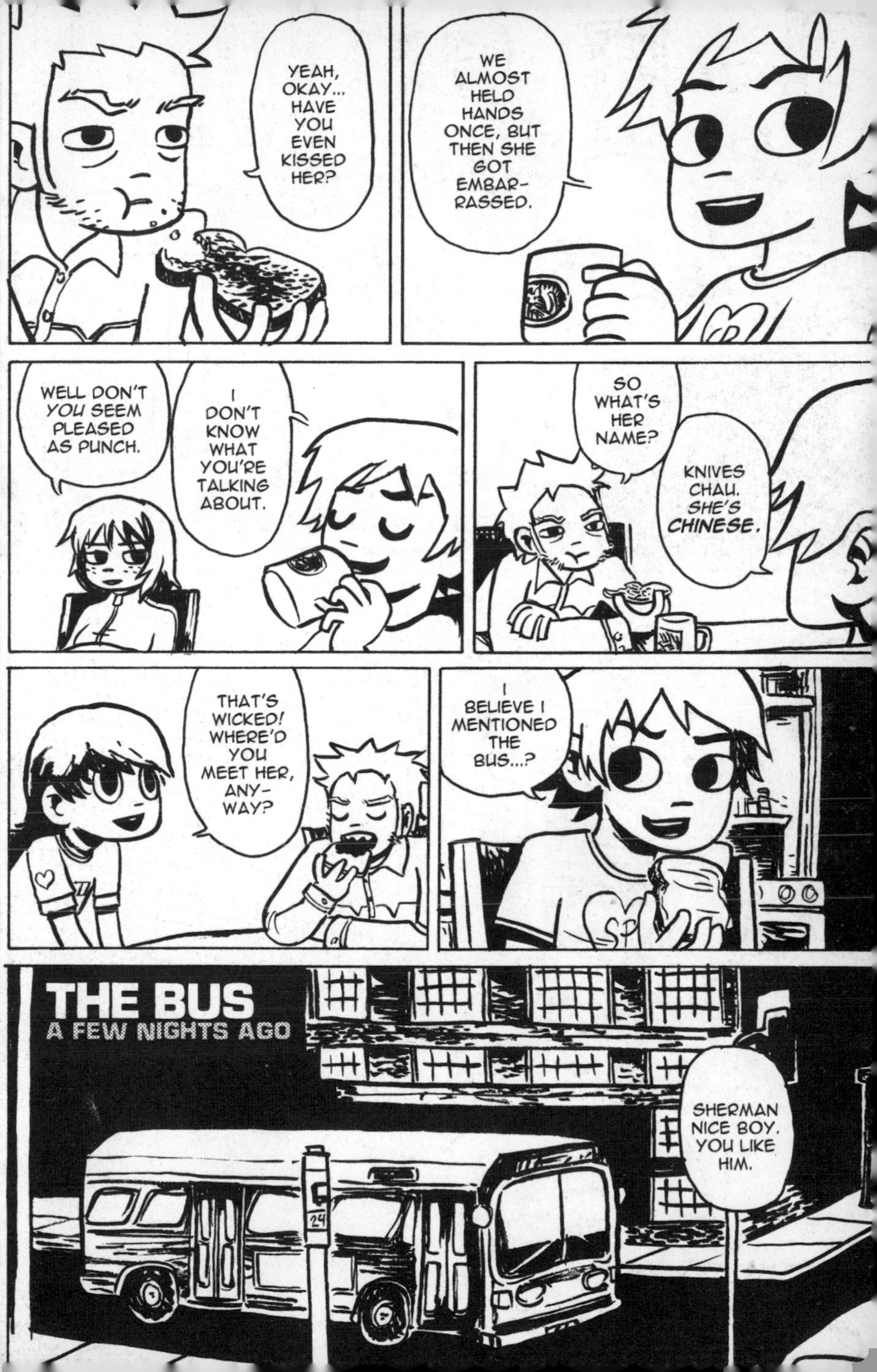
YEAH, OKAY... HAVE YOU EVEN KISSED HER?
WE ALMOST HELD HANDS ONCE, BUT THEN SHE GOT EMBAR-RASSED.
WELL DON'T YOU SEEM PLEASED AS PUNCH.
I DON'T KNOW WHAT YOU'RE TALKING ABOUT.
SO WHAT'S HER NAME?
KNIVES CHAU. SHE'S CHINESE.
THAT'S WICKED! WHERE'D YOU MEET HER, ANY-WAY?
I BELIEVE I MENTIONED THE BUS...?
THE BUS
A FEW NIGHTS AGO
SHERMAN NICE BOY. YOU LIKE HIM.

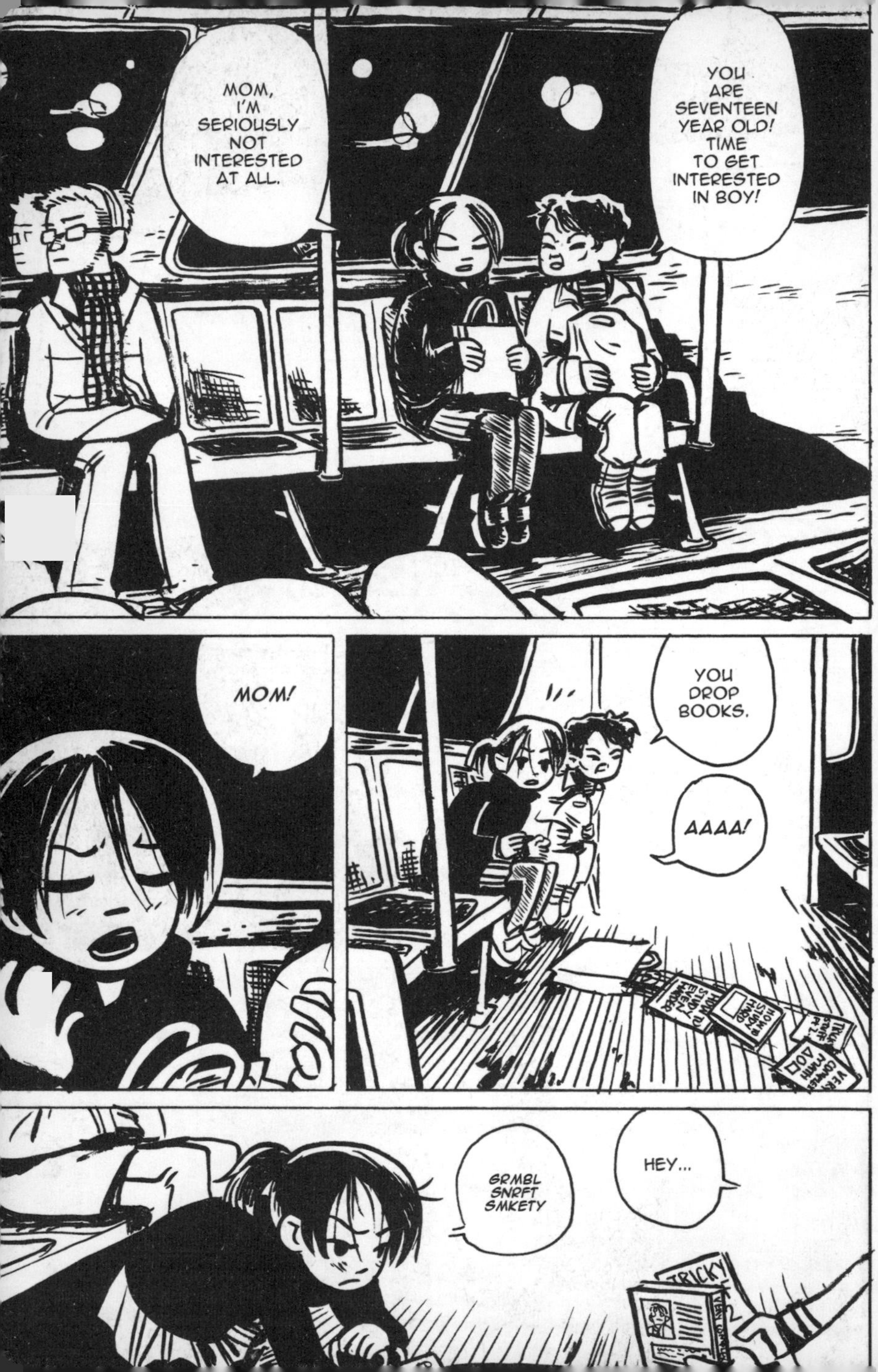
MOM, I'M SERIOUSLY NOT INTERESTED AT ALL.
YOU ARE SEVENTEEN YEAR OLD! TIME TO GET INTERESTED IN BOY!
MOM!
YOU DROP BOOKS.
AAAA!
HOW TO STUDY EVEN HARDER
HOW TO STUDY HARD
TRICKY STUFF PT. 1
VERY COMPLEX MATH
HEY...
GRMBL SNRFT SMKETY
TRICKY

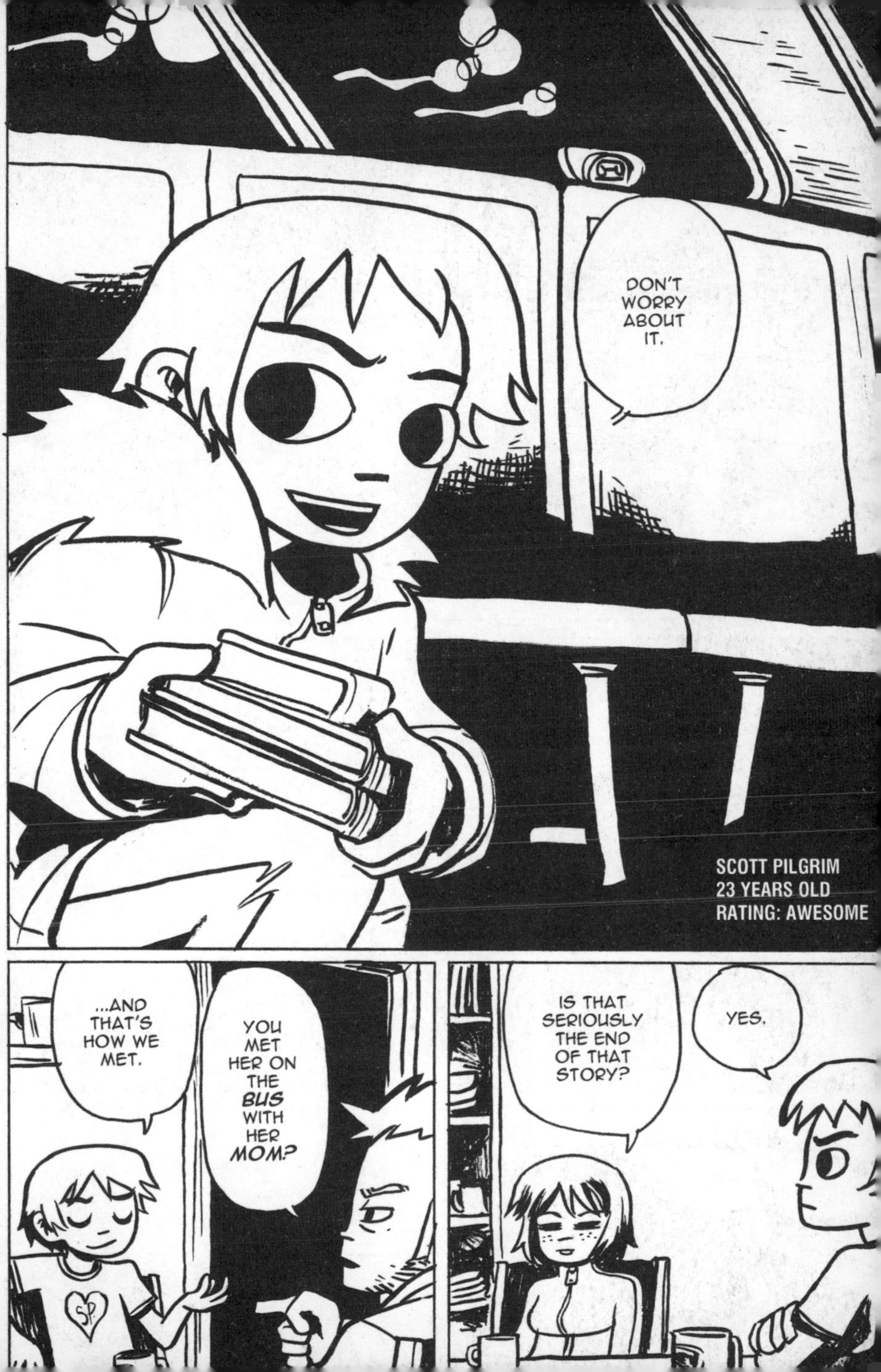
DON'T WORRY ABOUT IT.
SCOTT PILGRIM
23 YEARS OLD
RATING: AWESOME
...AND THAT'S HOW WE MET.
YOU MET HER ON THE *BUS* WITH HER *MOM?*
IS THAT SERIOUSLY THE END OF THAT STORY?
YES.

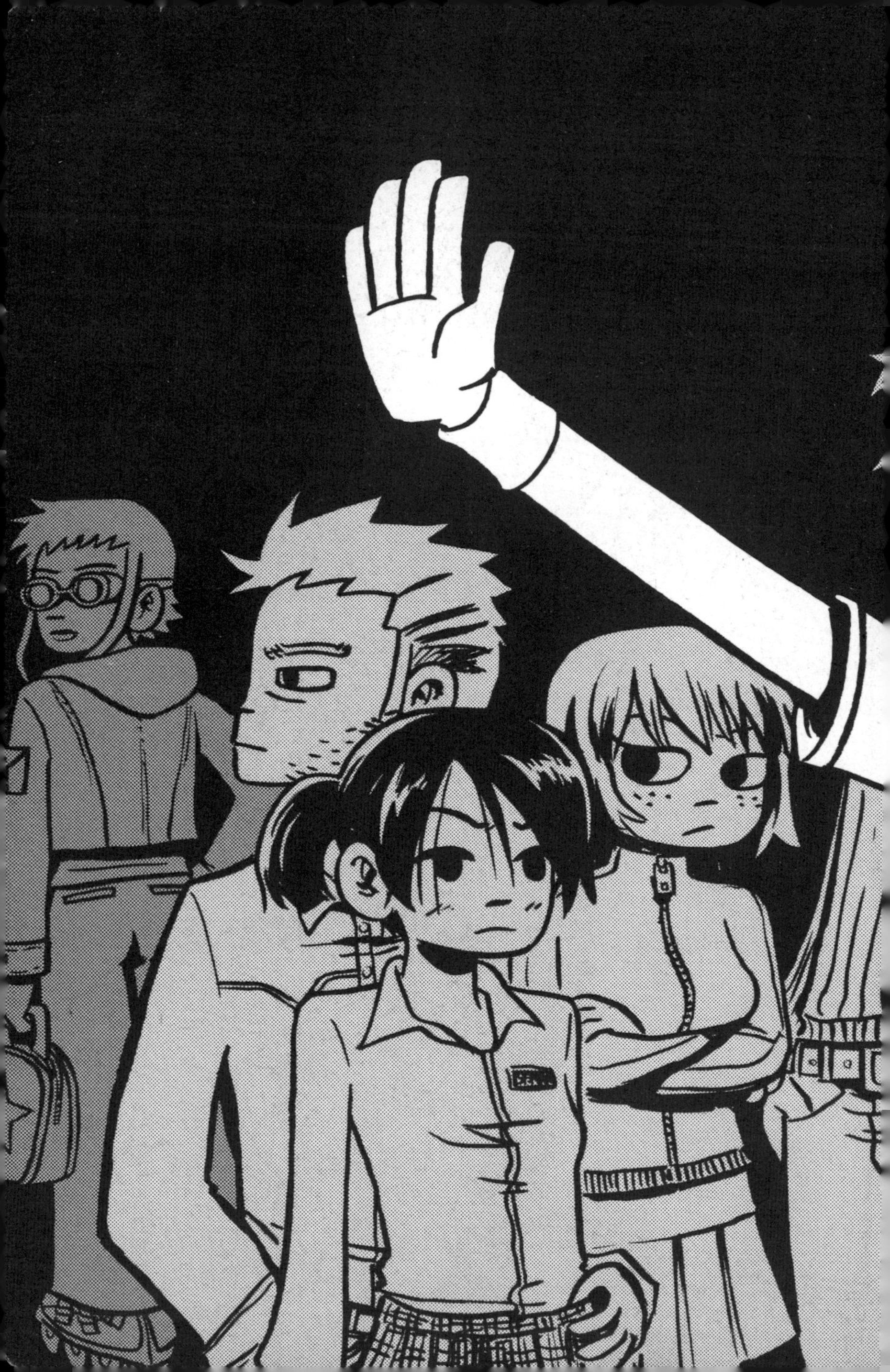

1

DATING A HIGH SCHOOLER

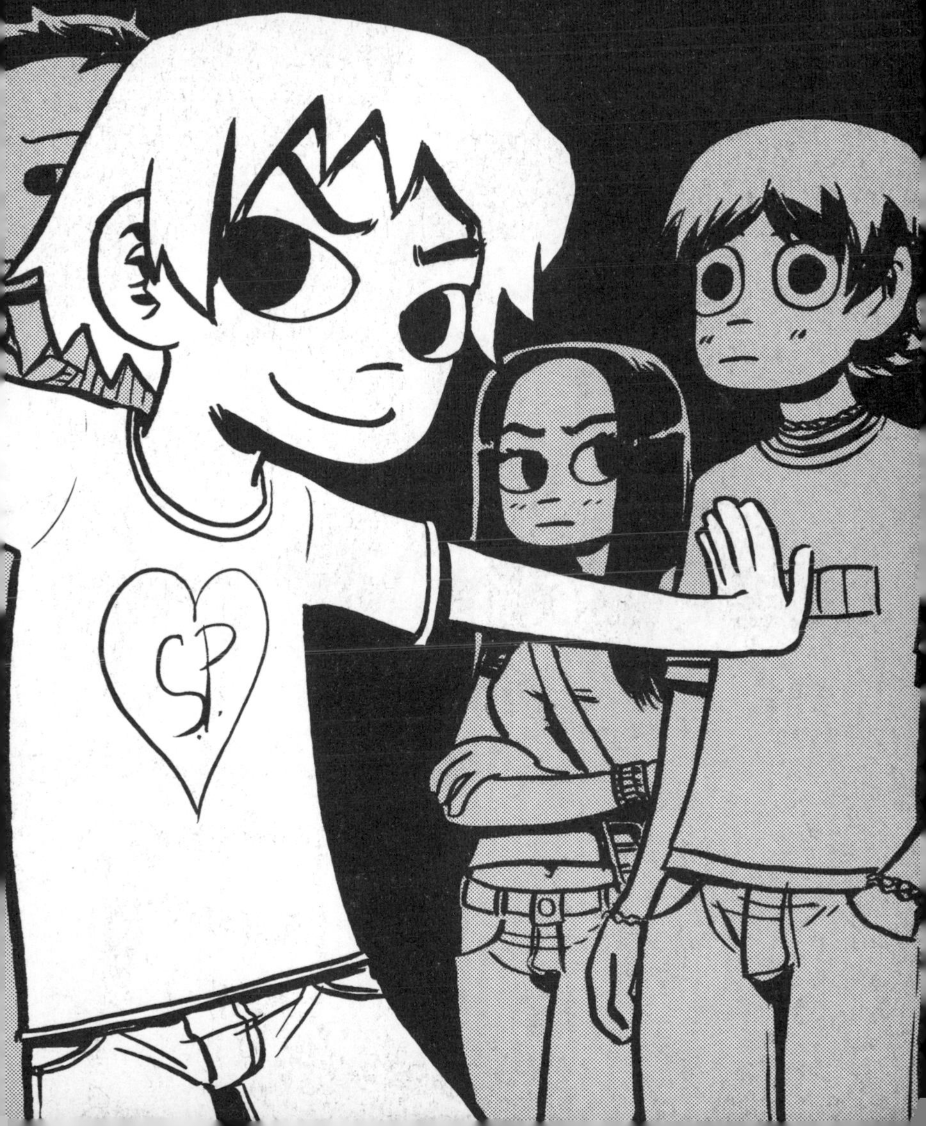

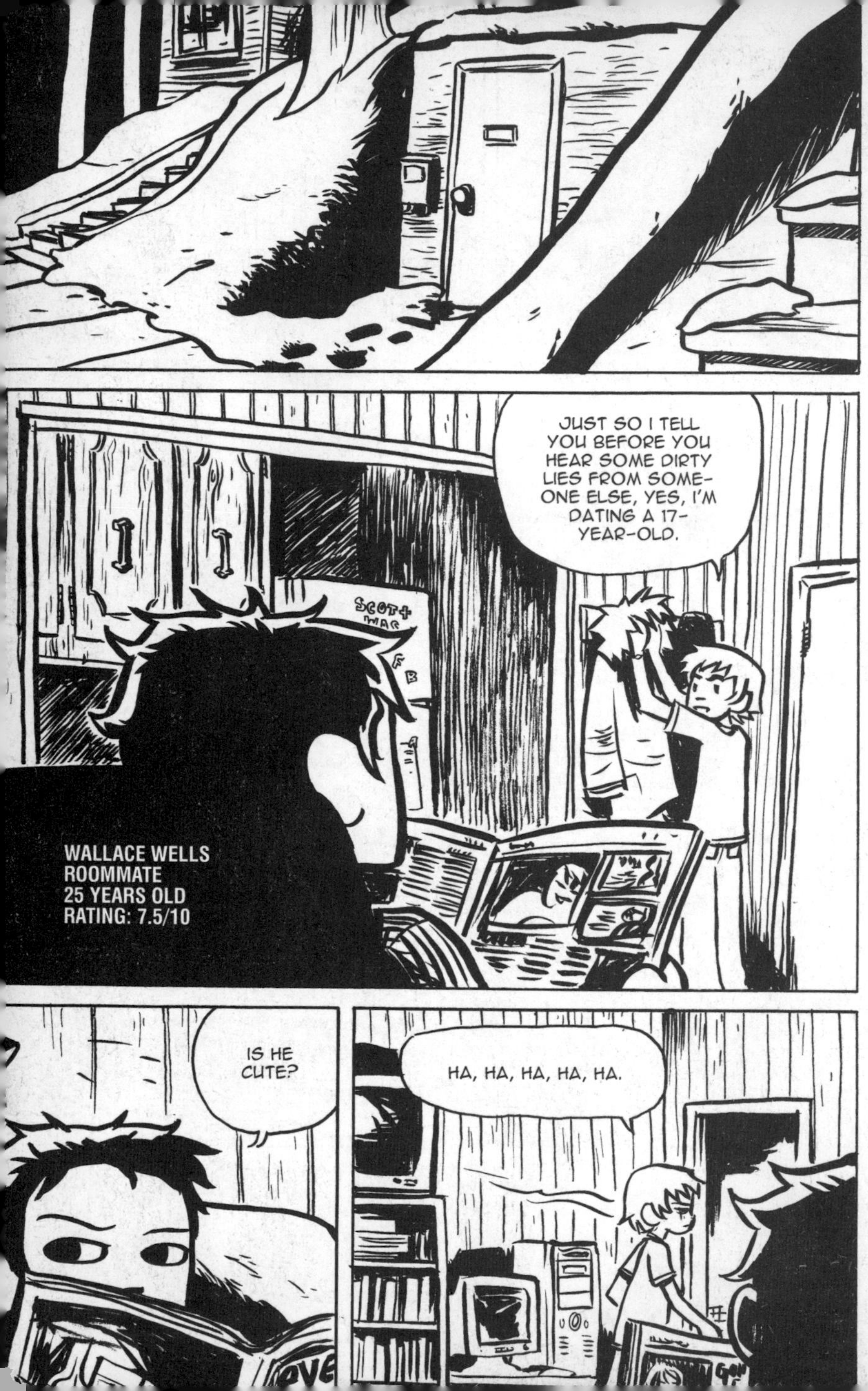
JUST SO I TELL YOU BEFORE YOU HEAR SOME DIRTY LIES FROM SOME-ONE ELSE, YES, I'M DATING A 17-YEAR-OLD.
WALLACE WELLS
ROOMMATE
25 YEARS OLD
RATING: 7.5/10
IS HE CUTE?
HA, HA, HA, HA, HA.

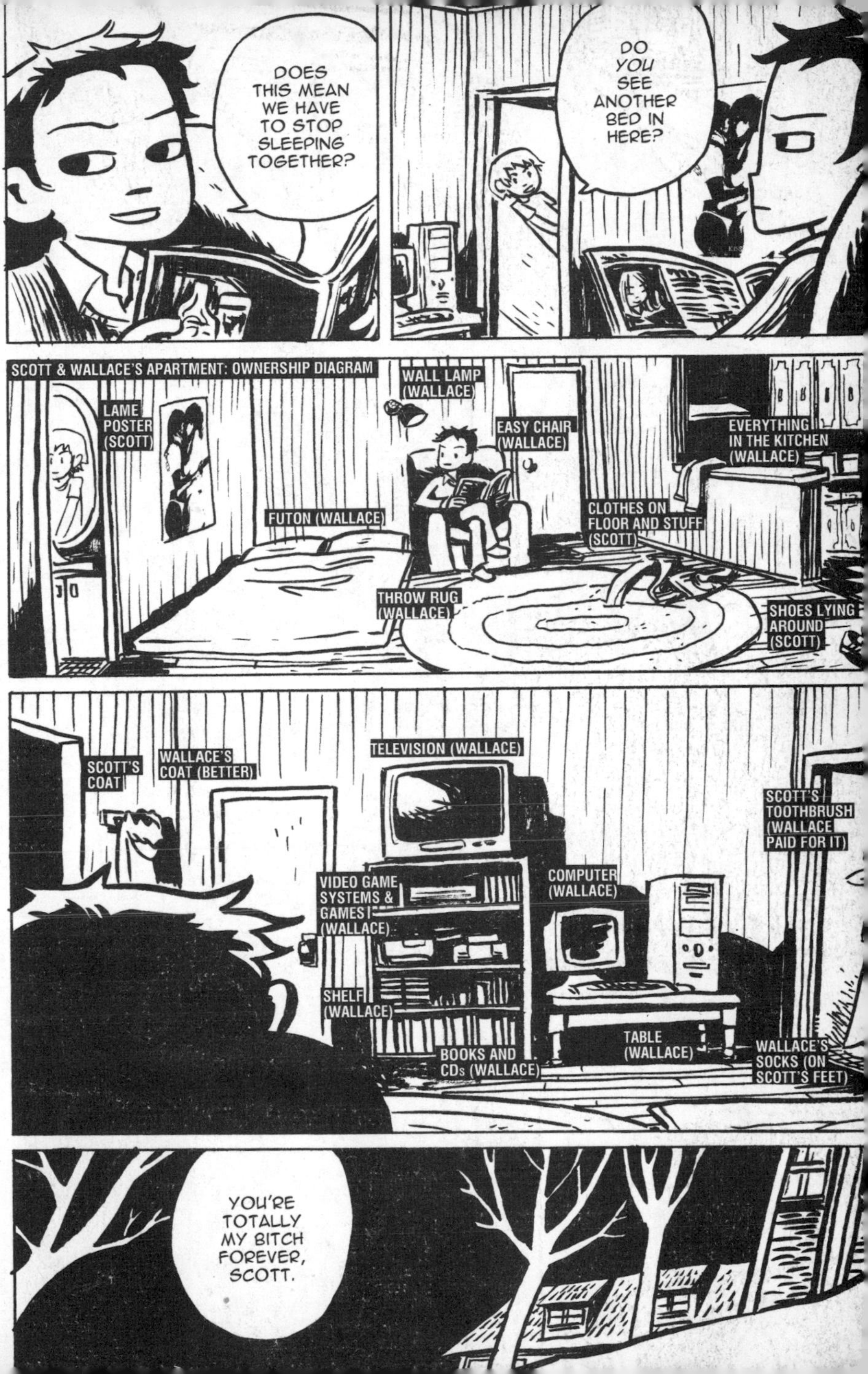

DOES THIS MEAN WE HAVE TO STOP SLEEPING TOGETHER?
DO YOU SEE ANOTHER BED IN HERE?
SCOTT & WALLACE'S APARTMENT: OWNERSHIP DIAGRAM
WALL LAMP (WALLACE)
LAME POSTER (SCOTT)
EASY CHAIR (WALLACE)
EVERYTHING IN THE KITCHEN (WALLACE)
FUTON (WALLACE)
CLOTHES ON FLOOR AND STUFF (SCOTT)
THROW RUG (WALLACE)
SHOES LYING AROUND (SCOTT)
SCOTT'S COAT
WALLACE'S COAT (BETTER)
TELEVISION (WALLACE)
SCOTT'S TOOTHBRUSH (WALLACE PAID FOR IT)
VIDEO GAME SYSTEMS & GAMES! (WALLACE)
COMPUTER (WALLACE)
SHELF (WALLACE)
TABLE (WALLACE)
BOOKS AND CDs (WALLACE)
WALLACE'S SOCKS (ON SCOTT'S FEET)
YOU'RE TOTALLY MY BITCH FOREVER, SCOTT.

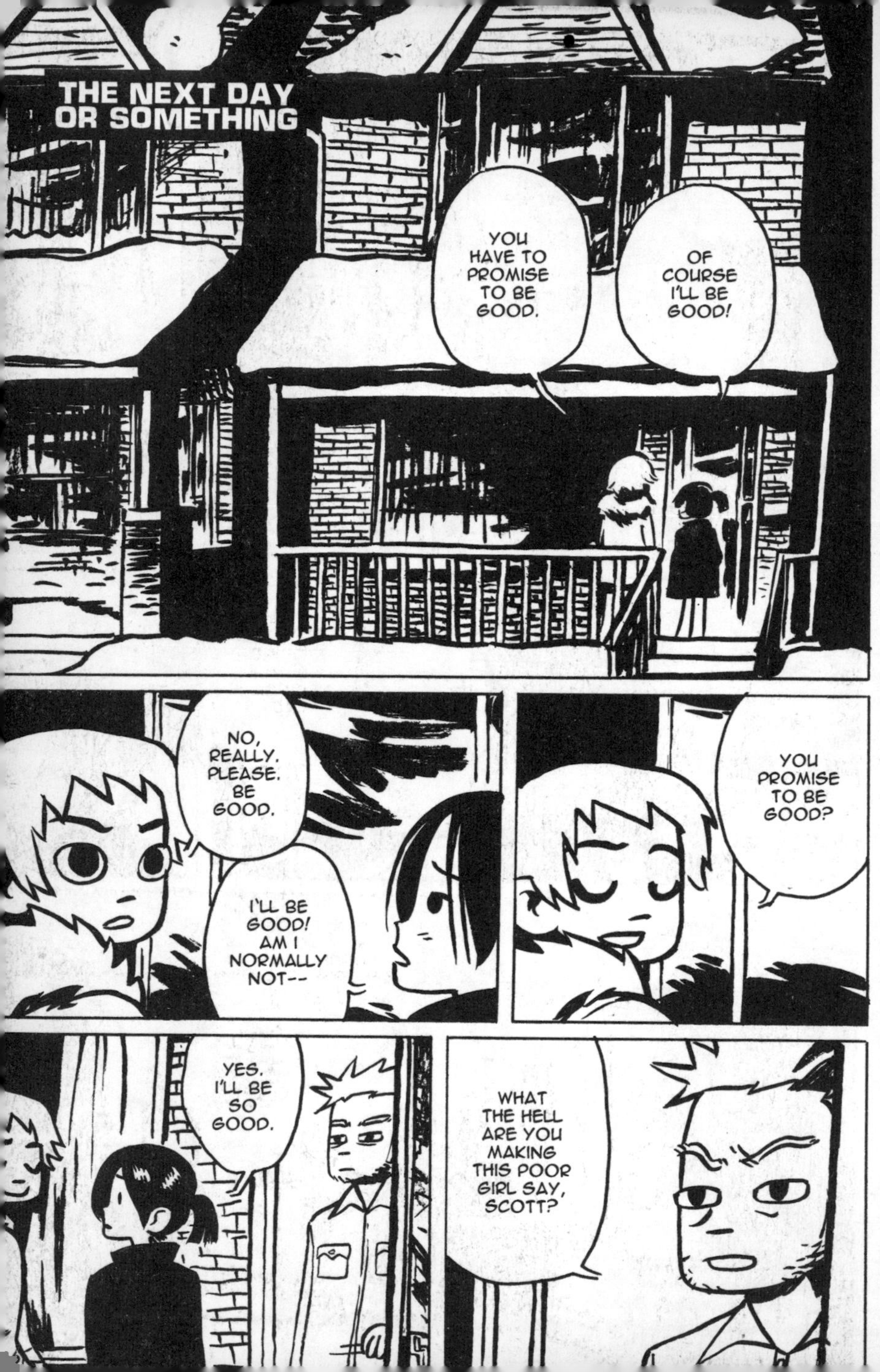
THE NEXT DAY OR SOMETHING
YOU HAVE TO PROMISE TO BE GOOD.
OF COURSE I'LL BE GOOD!
NO, REALLY. PLEASE. BE GOOD.
I'LL BE GOOD! AM I NORMALLY NOT--
YOU PROMISE TO BE GOOD?
YES. I'LL BE SO GOOD.
WHAT THE HELL ARE YOU MAKING THIS POOR GIRL SAY, SCOTT?

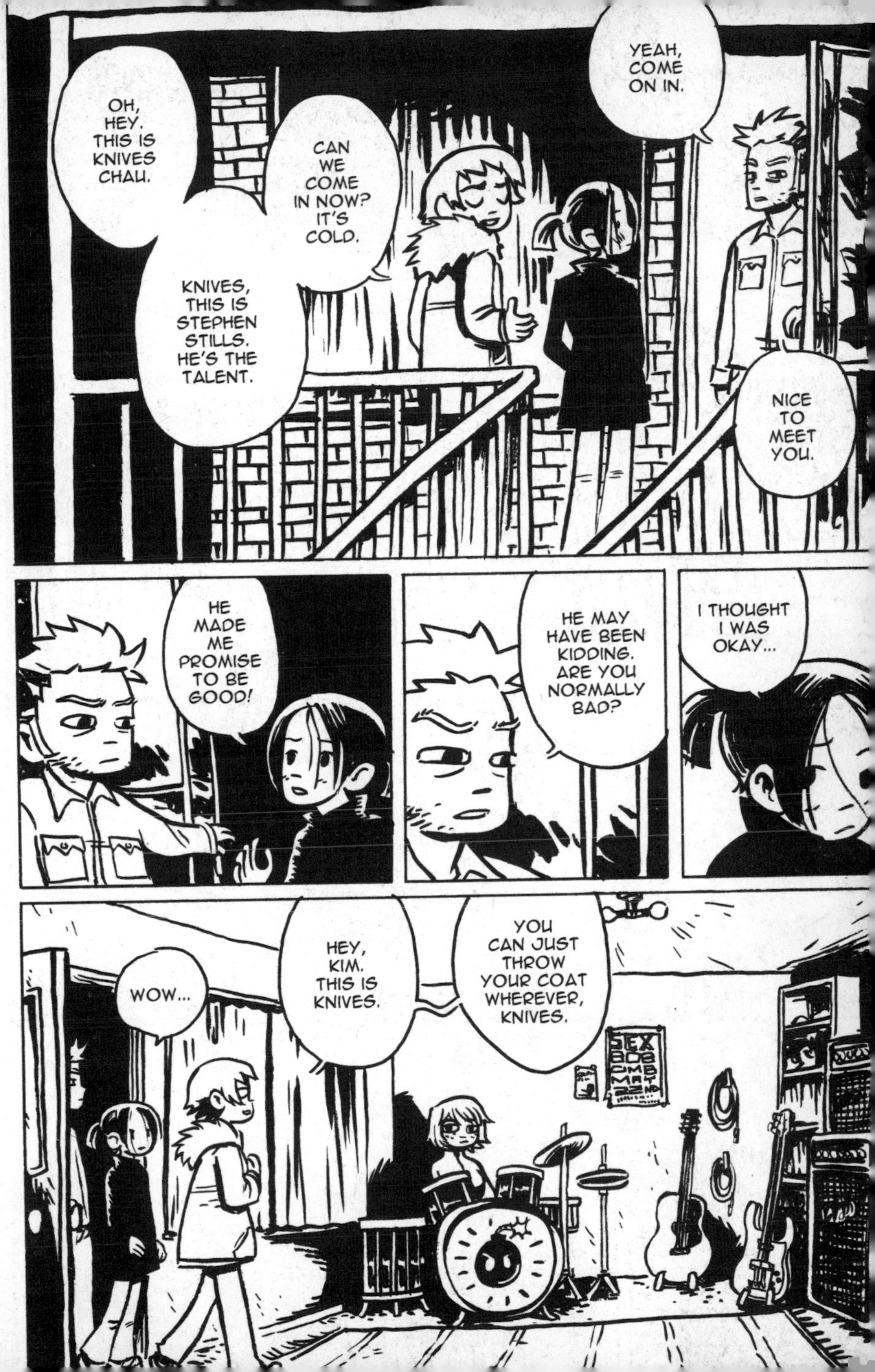
OH, HEY. THIS IS KNIVES CHAU.
CAN WE COME IN NOW? IT'S COLD.
KNIVES, THIS IS STEPHEN STILLS. HE'S THE TALENT.
YEAH, COME ON IN.
NICE TO MEET YOU.
HE MADE ME PROMISE TO BE GOOD!
HE MAY HAVE BEEN KIDDING. ARE YOU NORMALLY BAD?
I THOUGHT I WAS OKAY...
WOW...
HEY, KIM. THIS IS KNIVES.
YOU CAN JUST THROW YOUR COAT WHEREVER, KNIVES.
SEX BOB OMB

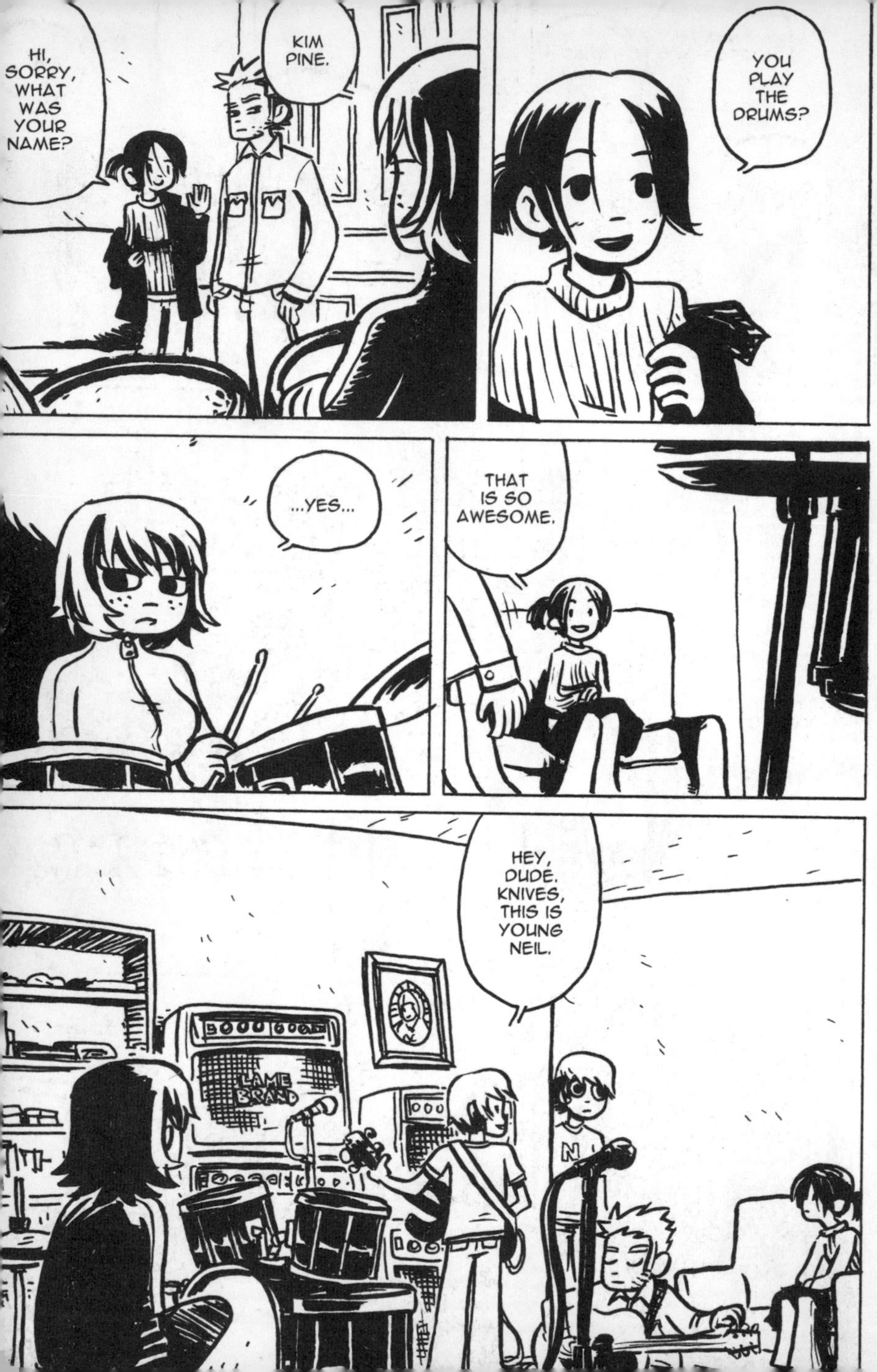
HI, SORRY, WHAT WAS YOUR NAME?
KIM PINE.
YOU PLAY THE DRUMS?
...YES...
THAT IS SO AWESOME.
HEY, DUDE. KNIVES, THIS IS YOUNG NEIL.
LAME BRAND
N

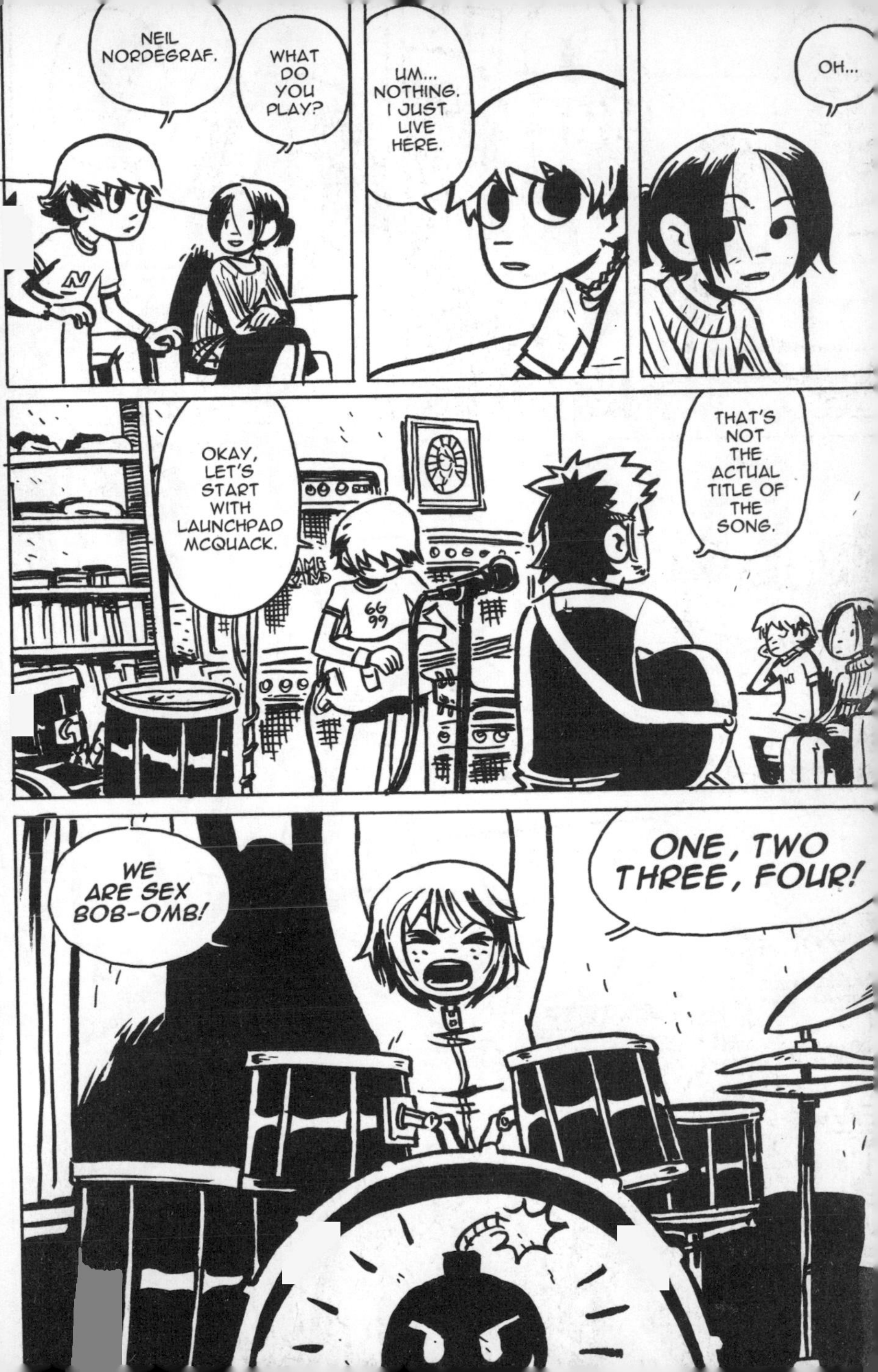
NEIL NORDEGRAF.
WHAT DO YOU PLAY?
UM... NOTHING. I JUST LIVE HERE.
OH...
OKAY, LET'S START WITH LAUNCHPAD MCQUACK.
THAT'S NOT THE ACTUAL TITLE OF THE SONG.
WE ARE SEX BOB-OMB!
ONE, TWO THREE, FOUR!

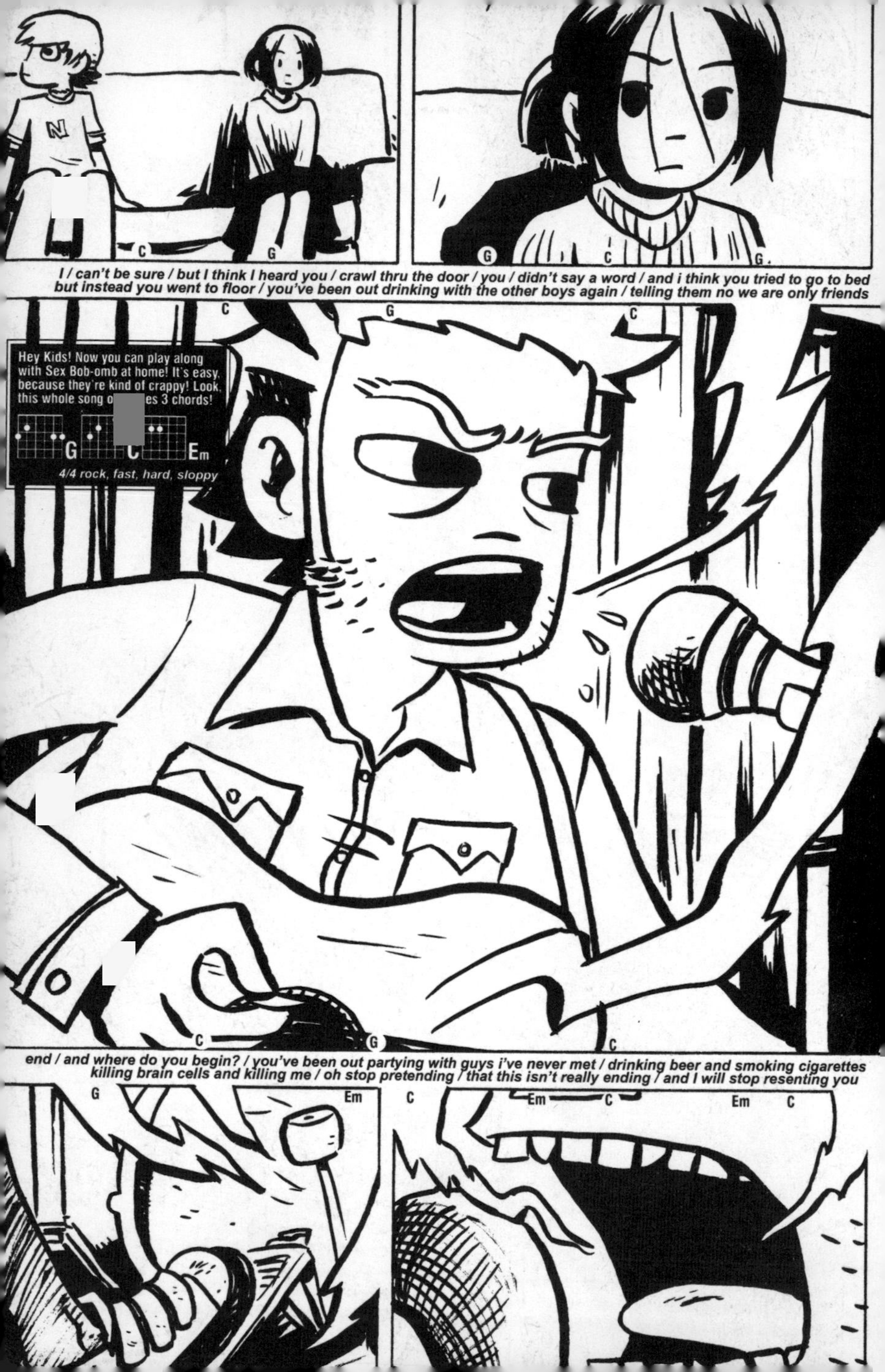

C G G C G
I / can't be sure / but I think I heard you / crawl thru the door / you / didn't say a word / and i think you tried to go to bed
but instead you went to floor / you've been out drinking with the other boys again / telling them no we are only friends
C G C
Hey Kids! Now you can play along with Sex Bob-omb at home! It's easy, because they're kind of crappy! Look, this whole song o es 3 chords!
G C Em
4/4 rock, fast, hard, sloppy
C G C
end / and where do you begin? / you've been out partying with guys i've never met / drinking beer and smoking cigarettes
killing brain cells and killing me / oh stop pretending / that this isn't really ending / and I will stop resenting you
G Em C Em C Em C

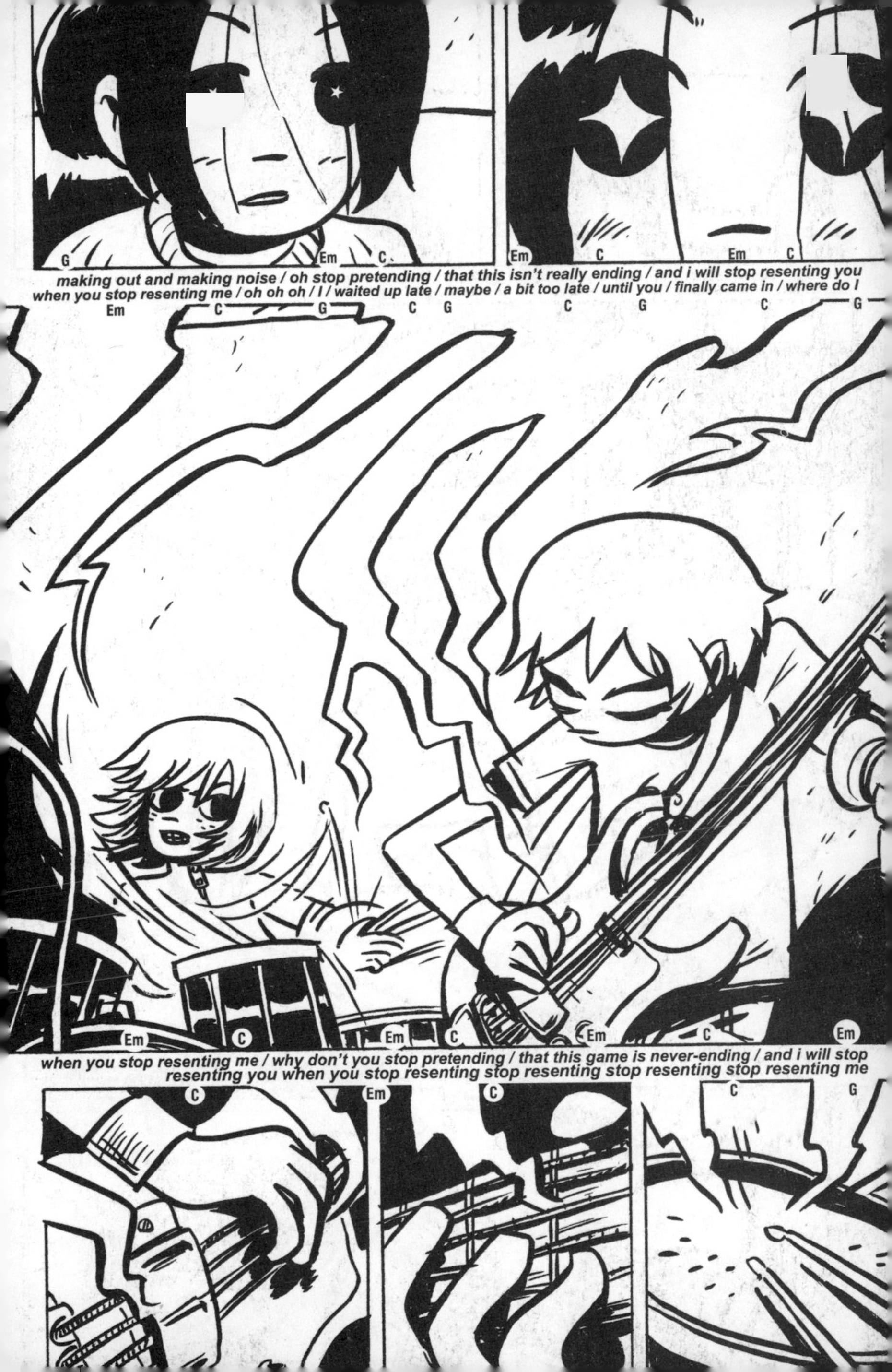
making out and making noise / oh stop pretending / that this isn't really ending / and i will stop resenting you
when you stop resenting me / oh oh oh / I / waited up late / maybe / a bit too late / until you / finally came in / where do I
when you stop resenting me / why don't you stop pretending / that this game is never-ending / and i will stop
resenting you when you stop resenting stop resenting stop resenting stop resenting me

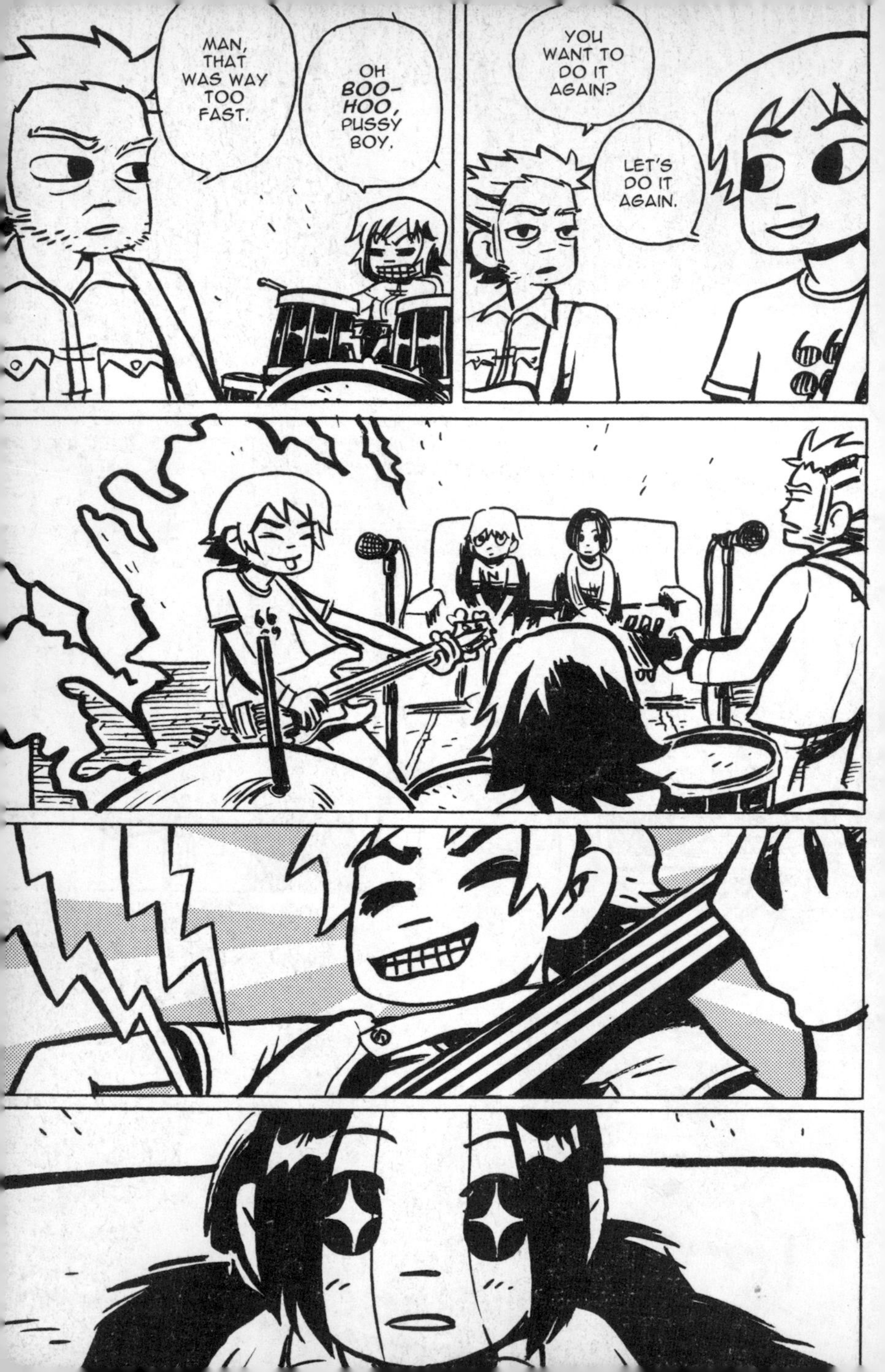
MAN, THAT WAS WAY TOO FAST.
OH BOO-HOO, PUSSY BOY.
YOU WANT TO DO IT AGAIN?
LET'S DO IT AGAIN.

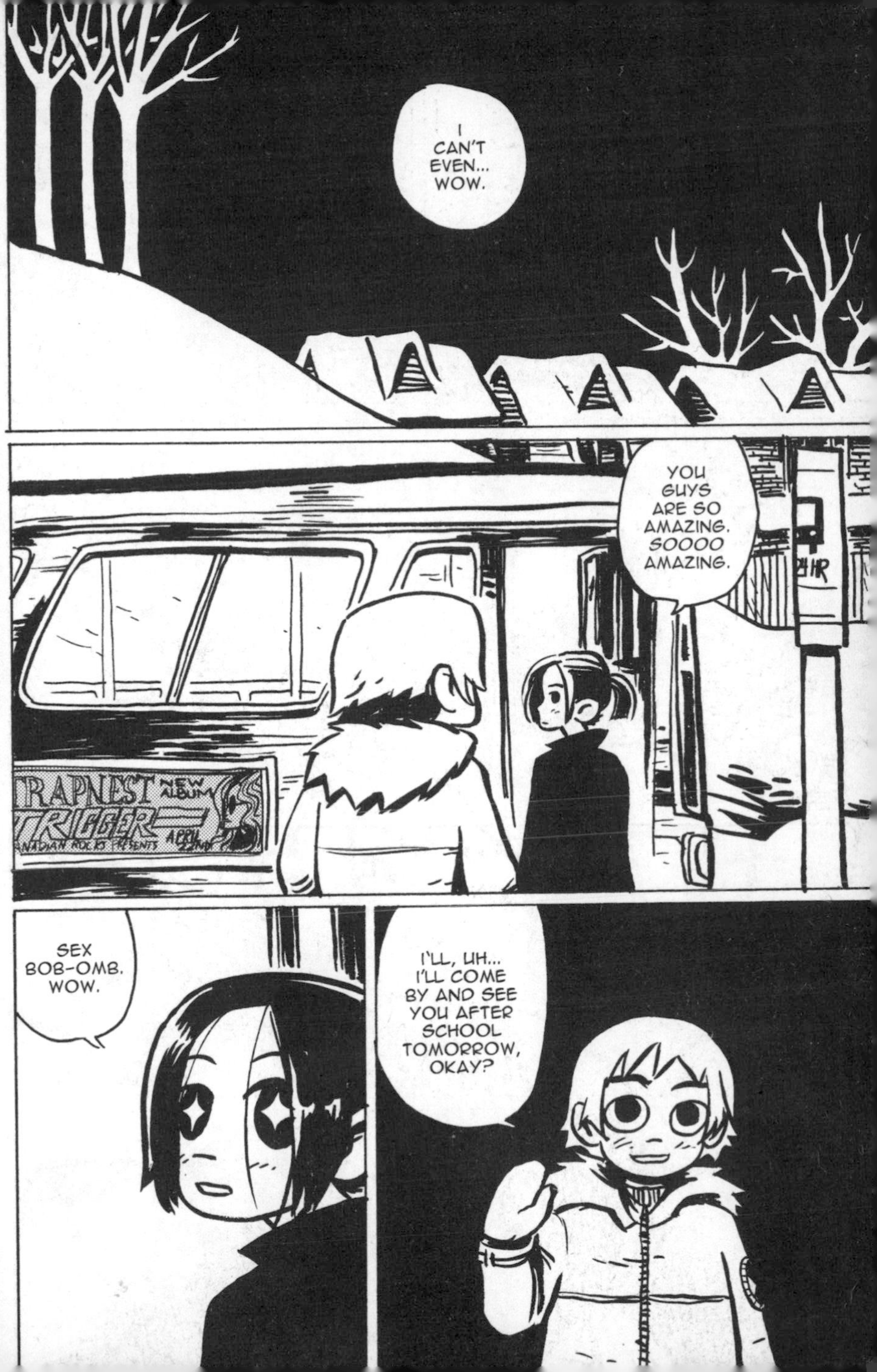
I CAN'T EVEN... WOW.
YOU GUYS ARE SO AMAZING. SOOOO AMAZING.
NEW ALBUM
SEX BOB-OMB. WOW.
I'LL, UH... I'LL COME BY AND SEE YOU AFTER SCHOOL TOMORROW, OKAY?

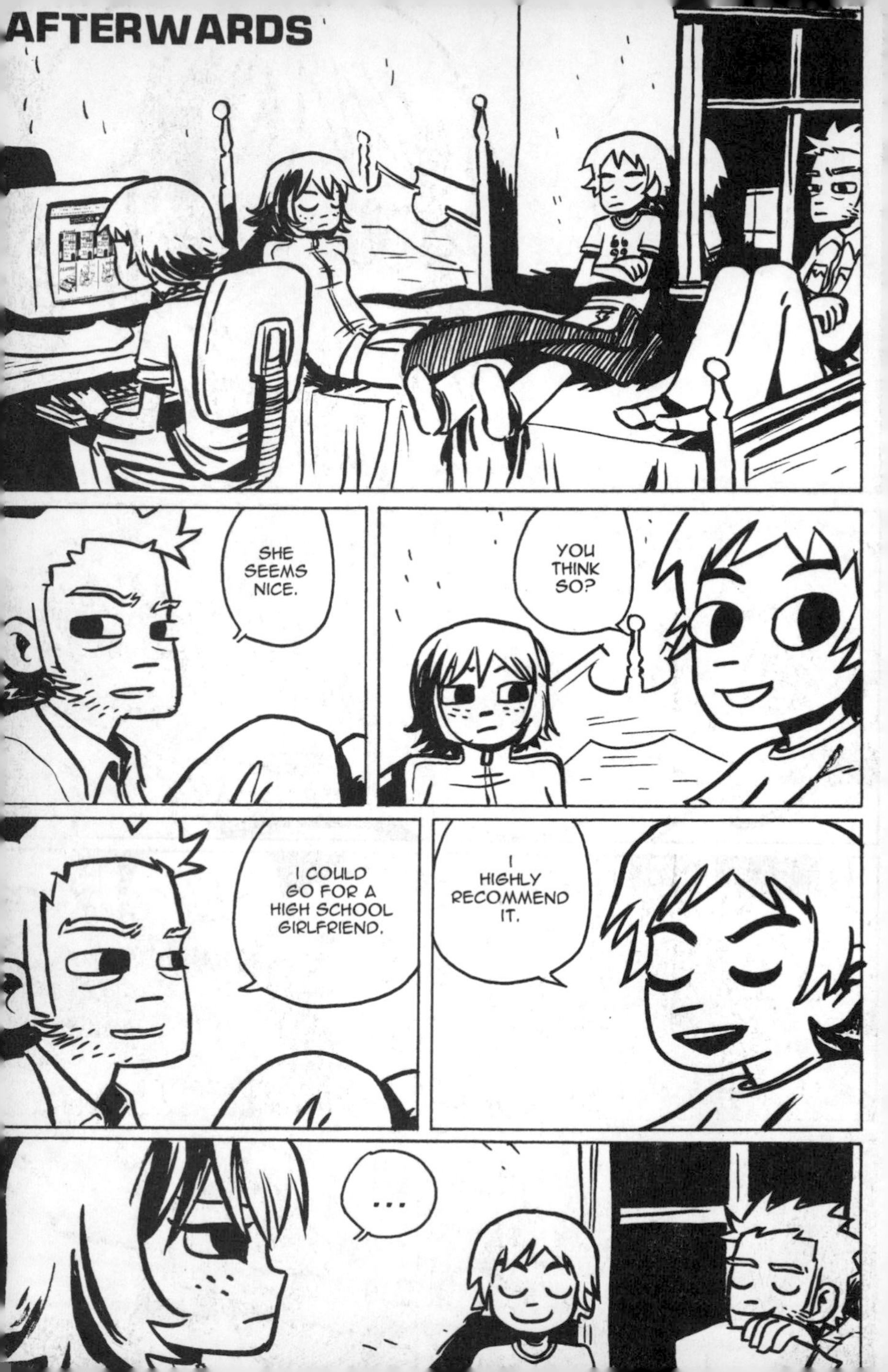
AFTERWARDS
SHE SEEMS NICE.
YOU THINK SO?
I COULD GO FOR A HIGH SCHOOL GIRLFRIEND.
I HIGHLY RECOMMEND IT.
...

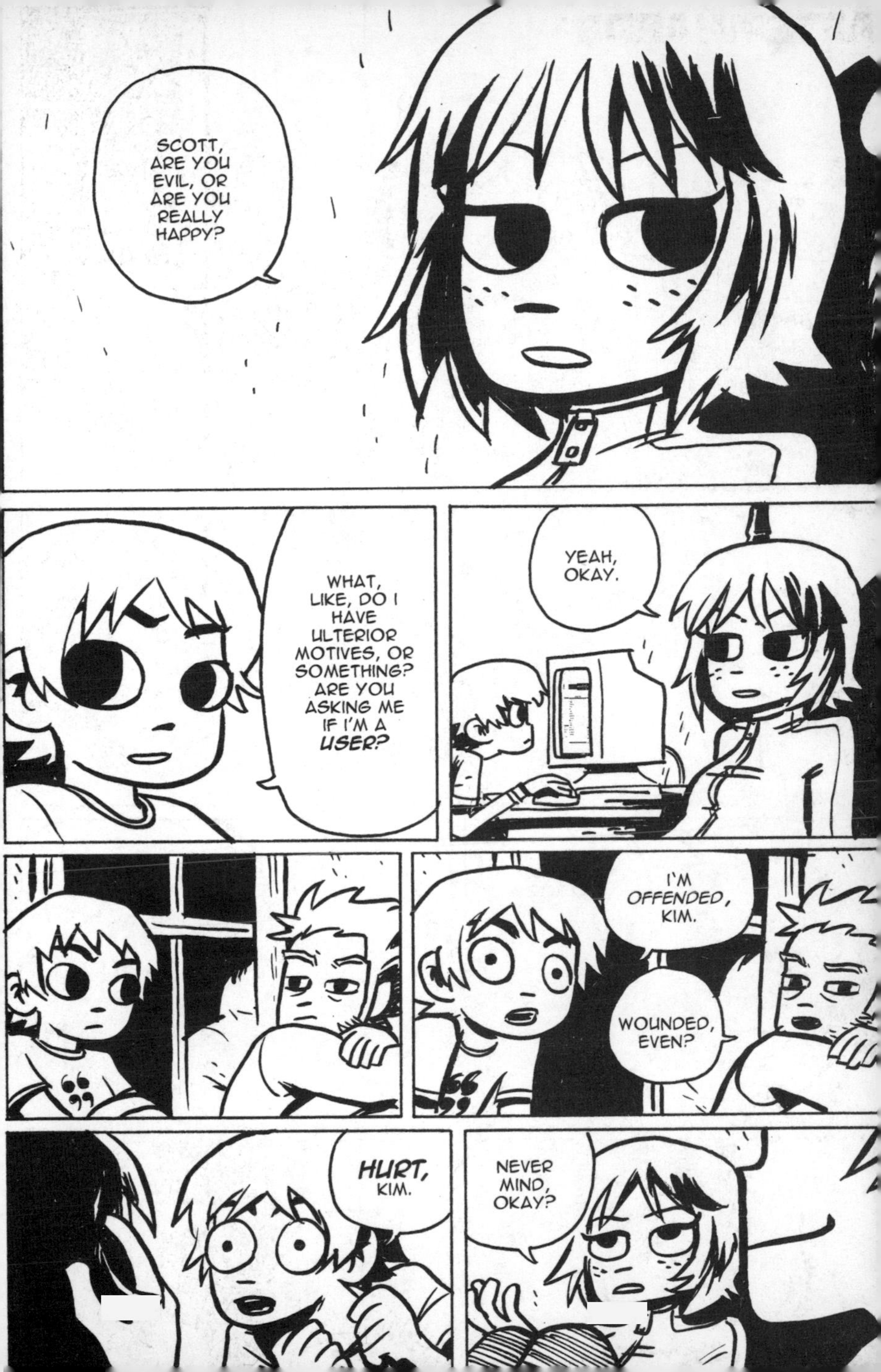
SCOTT, ARE YOU EVIL, OR ARE YOU REALLY HAPPY?
WHAT, LIKE, DO I HAVE ULTERIOR MOTIVES, OR SOMETHING? ARE YOU ASKING ME IF I'M A USER?
YEAH, OKAY.
I'M OFFENDED, KIM.
WOUNDED, EVEN?
HURT, KIM.
NEVER MIND, OKAY?

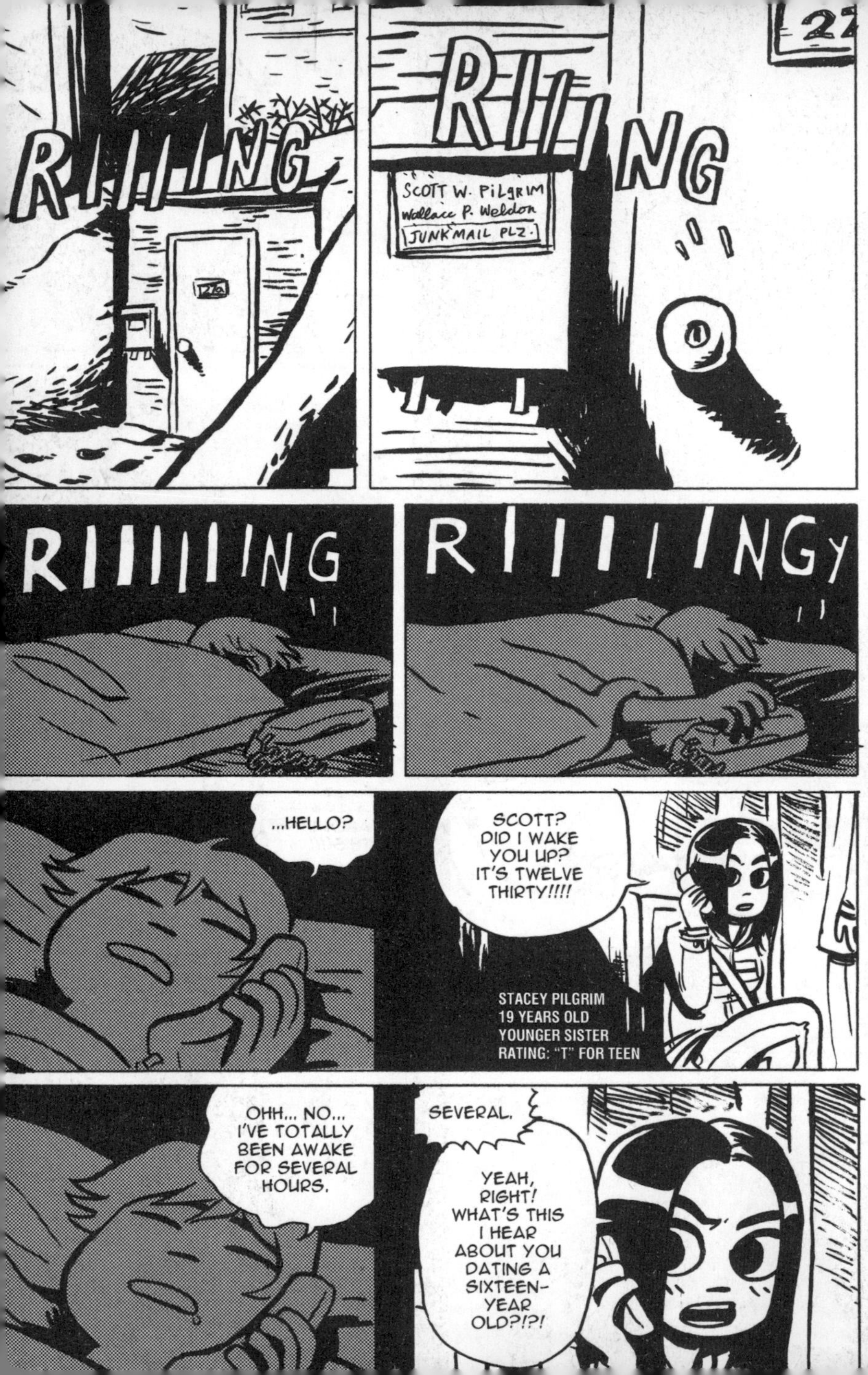
RIIIING
RIIING
SCOTT W. PILGRIM
Wallace P. Weldon
JUNK MAIL PLZ.
RIIIIING
RIIIIINGY
...HELLO?
SCOTT? DID I WAKE YOU UP? IT'S TWELVE THIRTY!!!!
STACEY PILGRIM
19 YEARS OLD
YOUNGER SISTER
RATING: "T" FOR TEEN
OHH... NO... I'VE TOTALLY BEEN AWAKE FOR SEVERAL HOURS.
SEVERAL.
YEAH, RIGHT! WHAT'S THIS I HEAR ABOUT YOU DATING A SIXTEEN-YEAR OLD?!?!

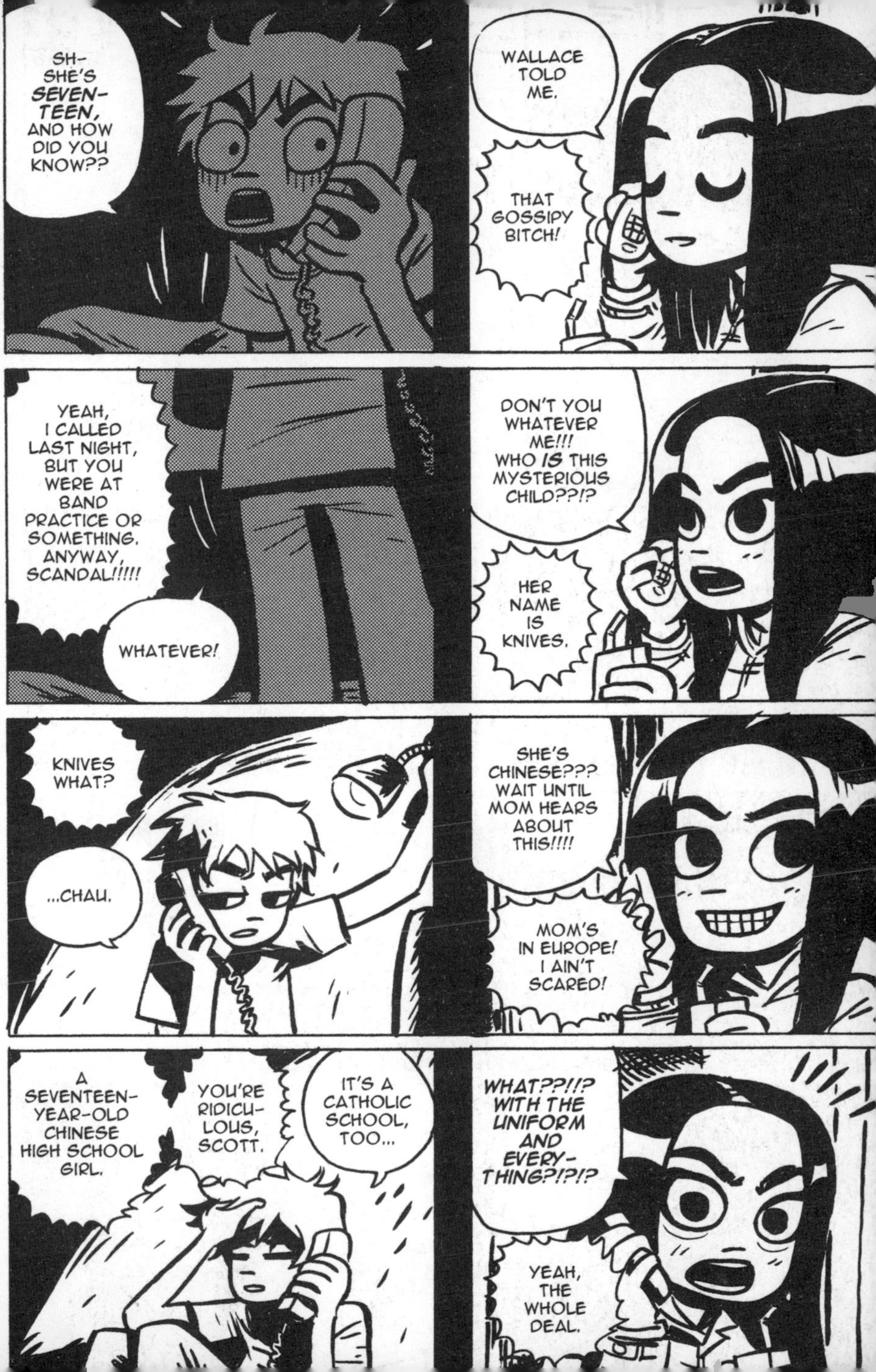
SH- SHE'S SEVENTEEN, AND HOW DID YOU KNOW??
WALLACE TOLD ME.
THAT GOSSIPY BITCH!
YEAH, I CALLED LAST NIGHT, BUT YOU WERE AT BAND PRACTICE OR SOMETHING. ANYWAY, SCANDAL!!!!!
WHATEVER!
DON'T YOU WHATEVER ME!!! WHO IS THIS MYSTERIOUS CHILD??!?
HER NAME IS KNIVES.
KNIVES WHAT?
...CHAU.
SHE'S CHINESE??? WAIT UNTIL MOM HEARS ABOUT THIS!!!!
MOM'S IN EUROPE! I AIN'T SCARED!
A SEVENTEEN-YEAR-OLD CHINESE HIGH SCHOOL GIRL.
YOU'RE RIDICULOUS, SCOTT.
IT'S A CATHOLIC SCHOOL, TOO...
WHAT??!!? WITH THE UNIFORM AND EVERYTHING?!?!?
YEAH, THE WHOLE DEAL.

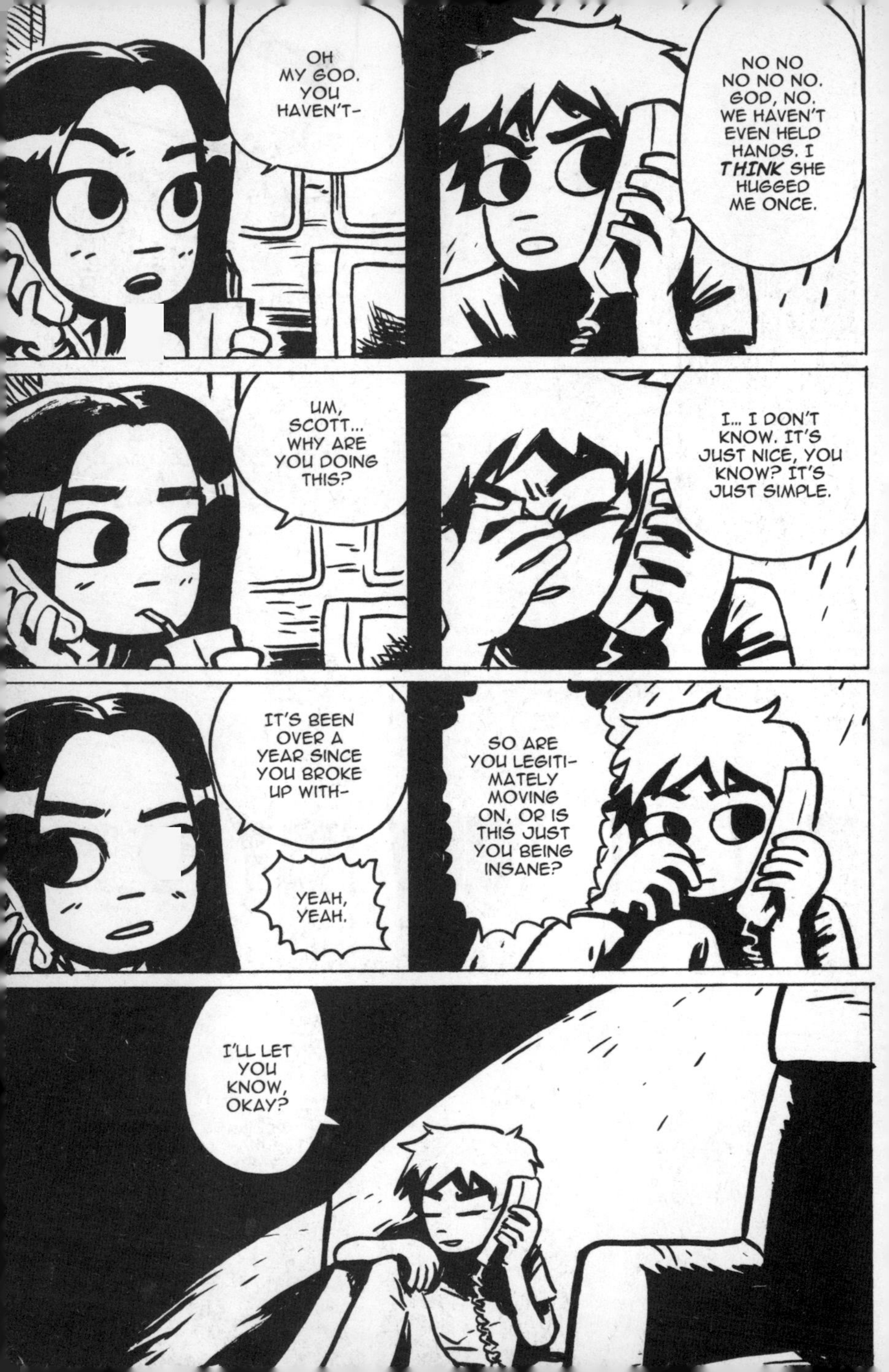
OH MY GOD. YOU HAVEN'T-
NO NO NO NO NO. GOD, NO. WE HAVEN'T EVEN HELD HANDS. I *THINK* SHE HUGGED ME ONCE.
UM, SCOTT... WHY ARE YOU DOING THIS?
I... I DON'T KNOW. IT'S JUST NICE, YOU KNOW? IT'S JUST SIMPLE.
IT'S BEEN OVER A YEAR SINCE YOU BROKE UP WITH-
YEAH, YEAH.
SO ARE YOU LEGITI-MATELY MOVING ON, OR IS THIS JUST YOU BEING INSANE?
I'LL LET YOU KNOW, OKAY?

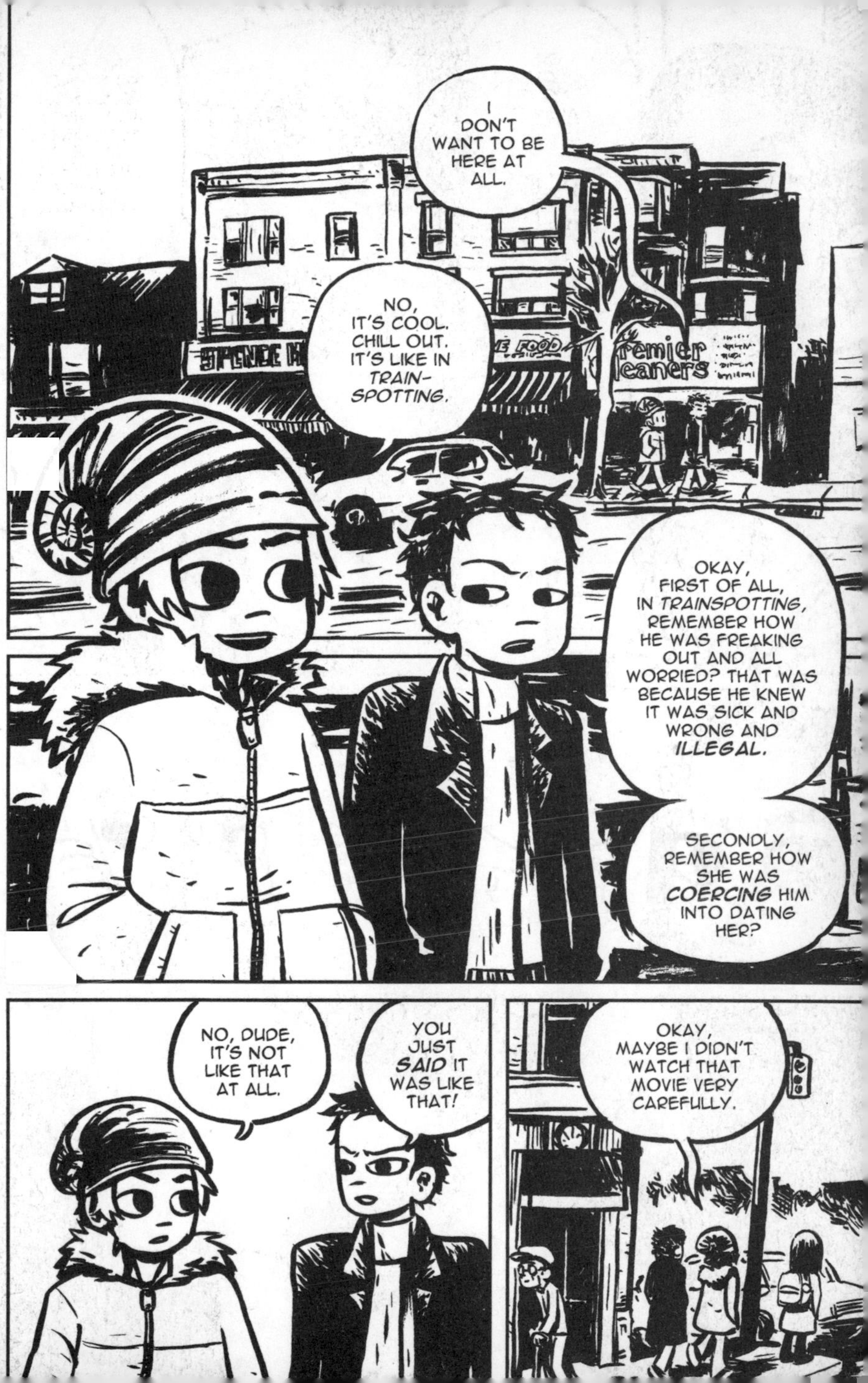
I DON'T WANT TO BE HERE AT ALL.
NO, IT'S COOL. CHILL OUT. IT'S LIKE IN *TRAIN-SPOTTING.*
OKAY, FIRST OF ALL, IN *TRAINSPOTTING*, REMEMBER HOW HE WAS FREAKING OUT AND ALL WORRIED? THAT WAS BECAUSE HE KNEW IT WAS SICK AND WRONG AND ***ILLEGAL.***
SECONDLY, REMEMBER HOW SHE WAS ***COERCING*** HIM INTO DATING HER?
NO, DUDE, IT'S NOT LIKE THAT AT ALL.
YOU JUST ***SAID*** IT WAS LIKE THAT!
OKAY, MAYBE I DIDN'T WATCH THAT MOVIE VERY CAREFULLY.

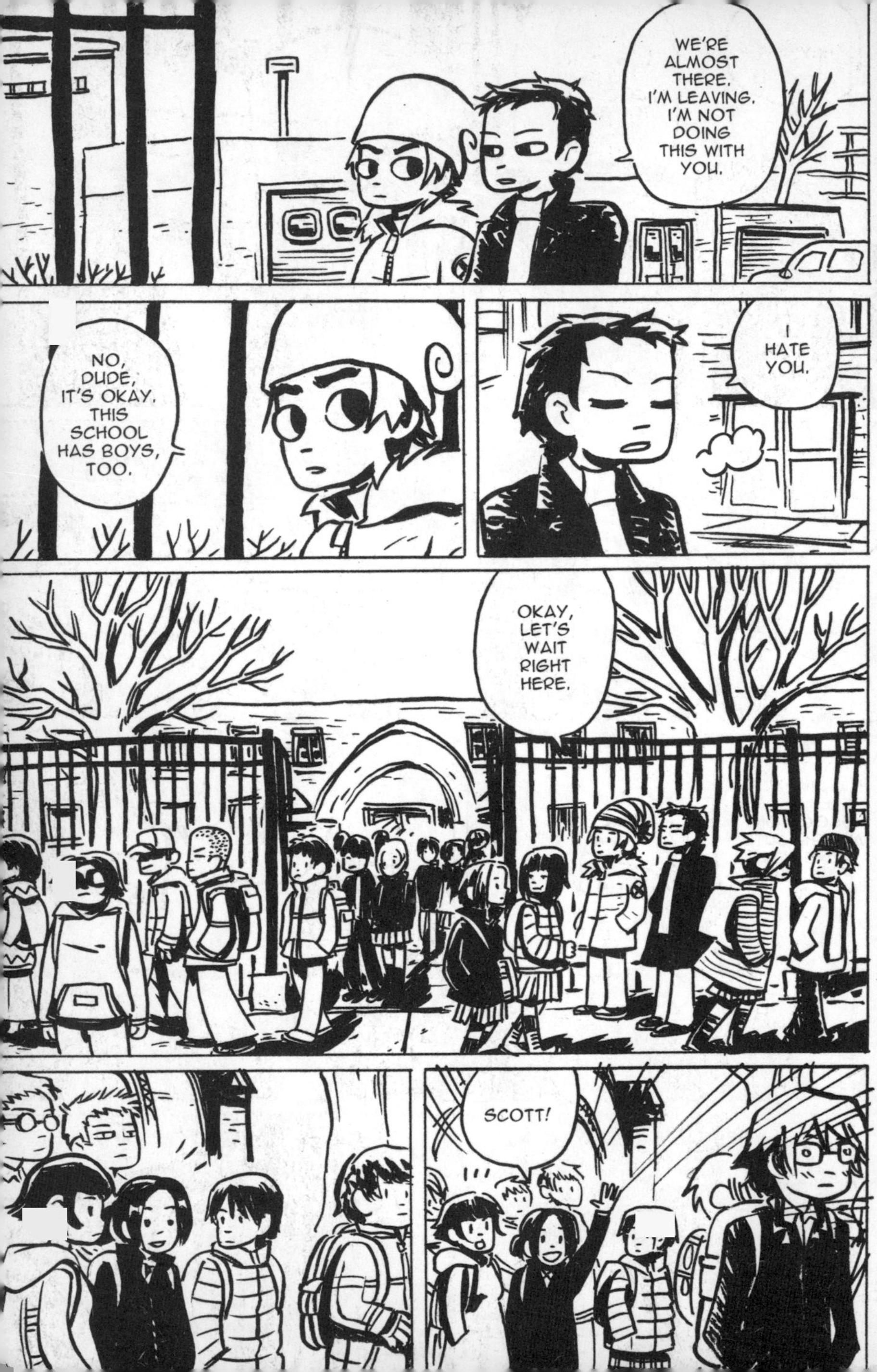
WE'RE ALMOST THERE. I'M LEAVING. I'M NOT DOING THIS WITH YOU.
NO, DUDE, IT'S OKAY. THIS SCHOOL HAS BOYS, TOO.
I HATE YOU.
OKAY, LET'S WAIT RIGHT HERE.
SCOTT!

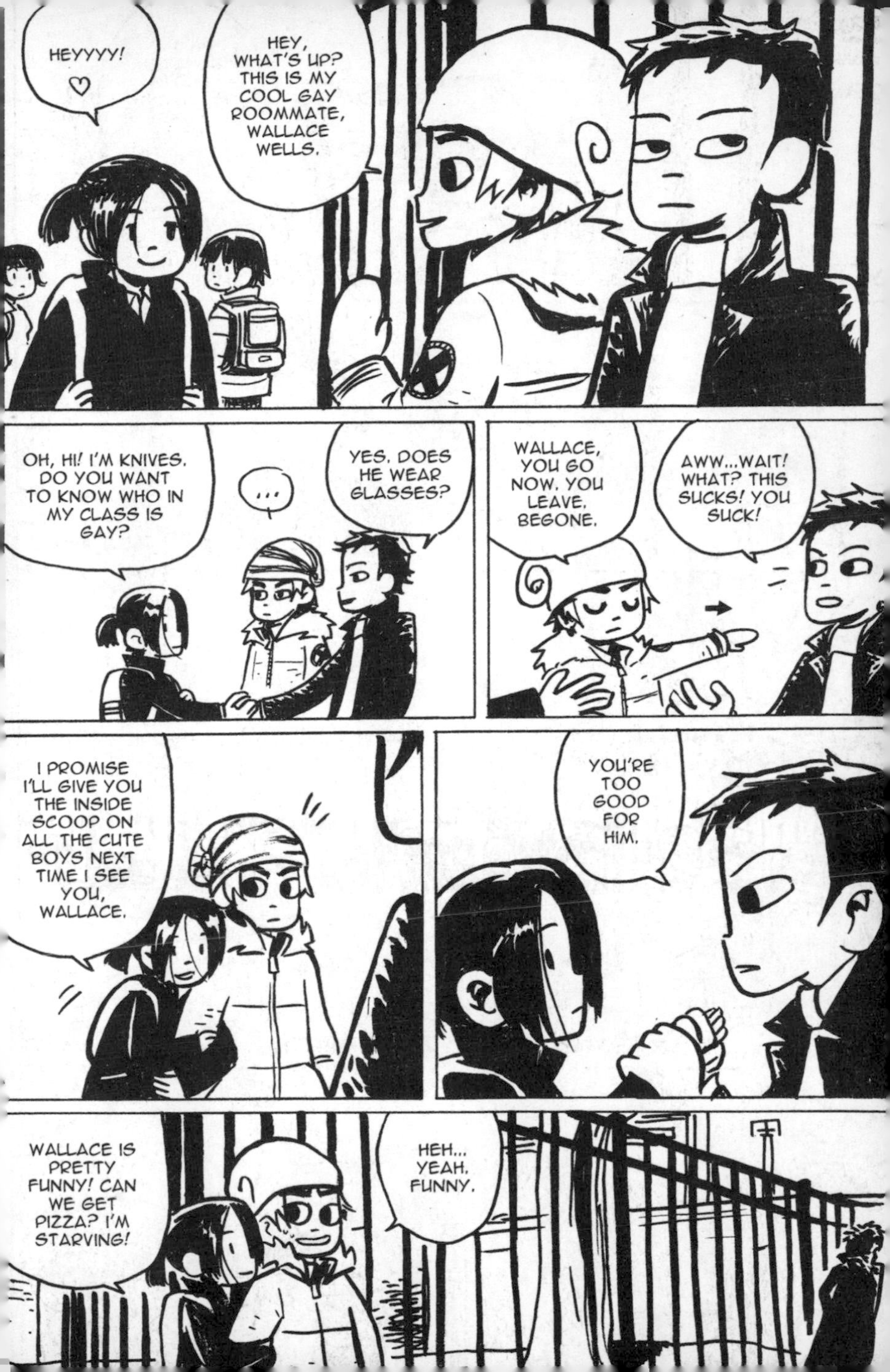
HEYYYY! ♡
HEY, WHAT'S UP? THIS IS MY COOL GAY ROOMMATE, WALLACE WELLS.
OH, HI! I'M KNIVES. DO YOU WANT TO KNOW WHO IN MY CLASS IS GAY?
...
YES. DOES HE WEAR GLASSES?
WALLACE, YOU GO NOW. YOU LEAVE. BEGONE.
AWW...WAIT! WHAT? THIS SUCKS! YOU SUCK!
I PROMISE I'LL GIVE YOU THE INSIDE SCOOP ON ALL THE CUTE BOYS NEXT TIME I SEE YOU, WALLACE.
YOU'RE TOO GOOD FOR HIM.
WALLACE IS PRETTY FUNNY! CAN WE GET PIZZA? I'M STARVING!
HEH... YEAH. FUNNY.

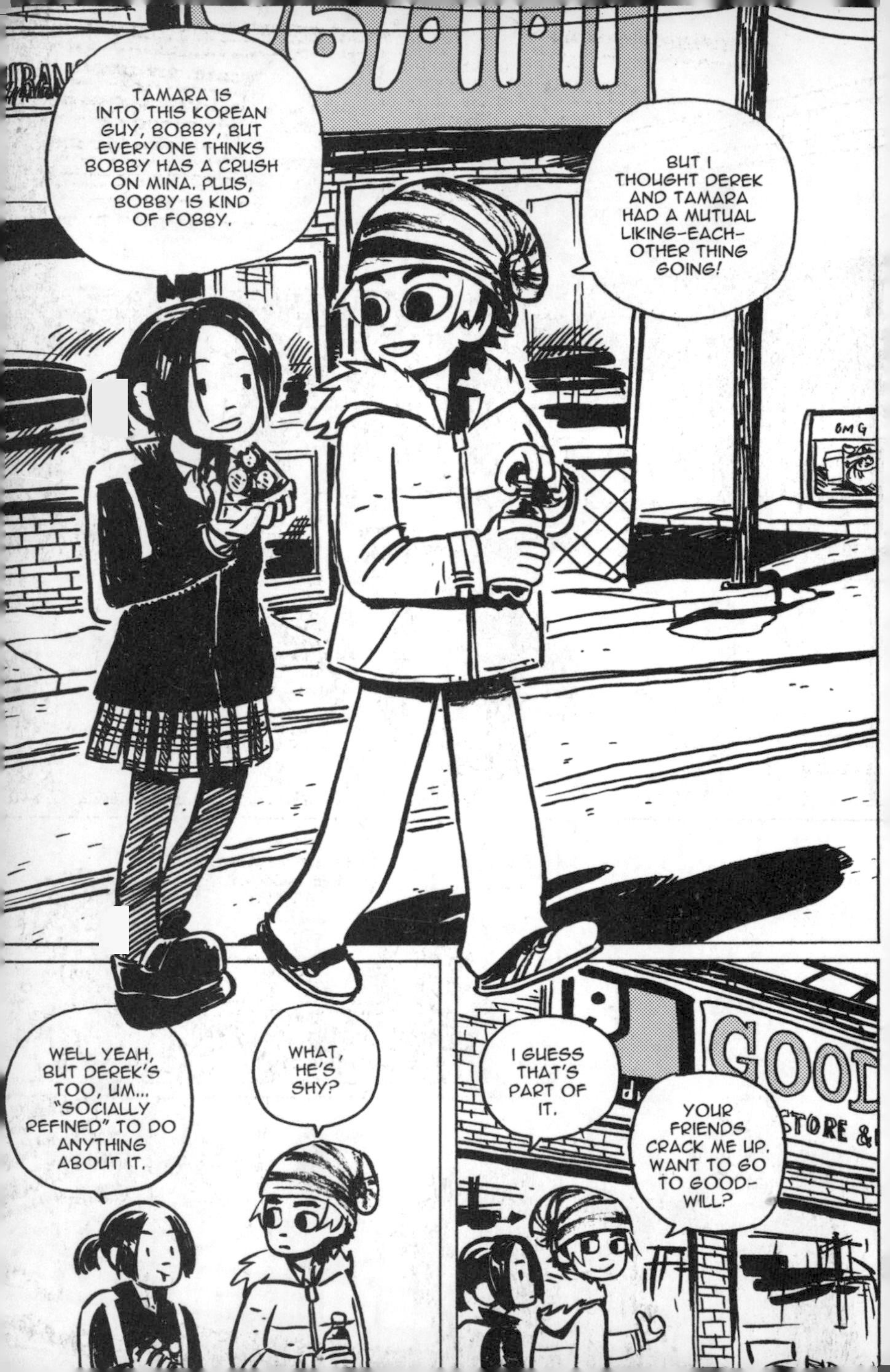

TAMARA IS INTO THIS KOREAN GUY, BOBBY, BUT EVERYONE THINKS BOBBY HAS A CRUSH ON MINA. PLUS, BOBBY IS KIND OF FOBBY.
BUT I THOUGHT DEREK AND TAMARA HAD A MUTUAL LIKING-EACH-OTHER THING GOING!
OMG
WELL YEAH, BUT DEREK'S TOO, UM... "SOCIALLY REFINED" TO DO ANYTHING ABOUT IT.
WHAT, HE'S SHY?
I GUESS THAT'S PART OF IT.
GOOD
STORE &
YOUR FRIENDS CRACK ME UP. WANT TO GO TO GOOD-WILL?

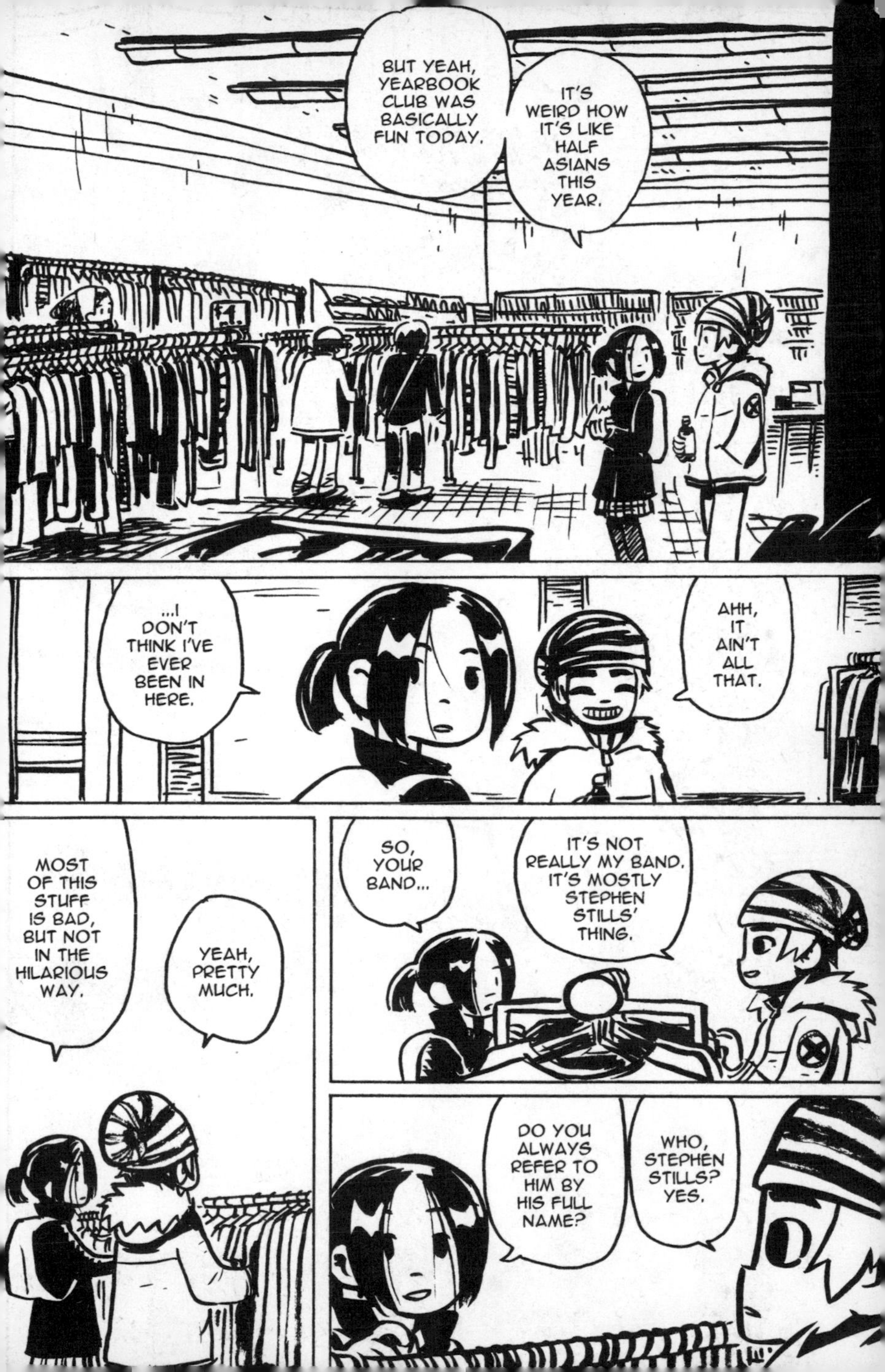
BUT YEAH, YEARBOOK CLUB WAS BASICALLY FUN TODAY.
IT'S WEIRD HOW IT'S LIKE HALF ASIANS THIS YEAR.
...I DON'T THINK I'VE EVER BEEN IN HERE.
AHH, IT AIN'T ALL THAT.
MOST OF THIS STUFF IS BAD, BUT NOT IN THE HILARIOUS WAY.
YEAH, PRETTY MUCH.
SO, YOUR BAND...
IT'S NOT REALLY MY BAND. IT'S MOSTLY STEPHEN STILLS' THING.
DO YOU ALWAYS REFER TO HIM BY HIS FULL NAME?
WHO, STEPHEN STILLS? YES.

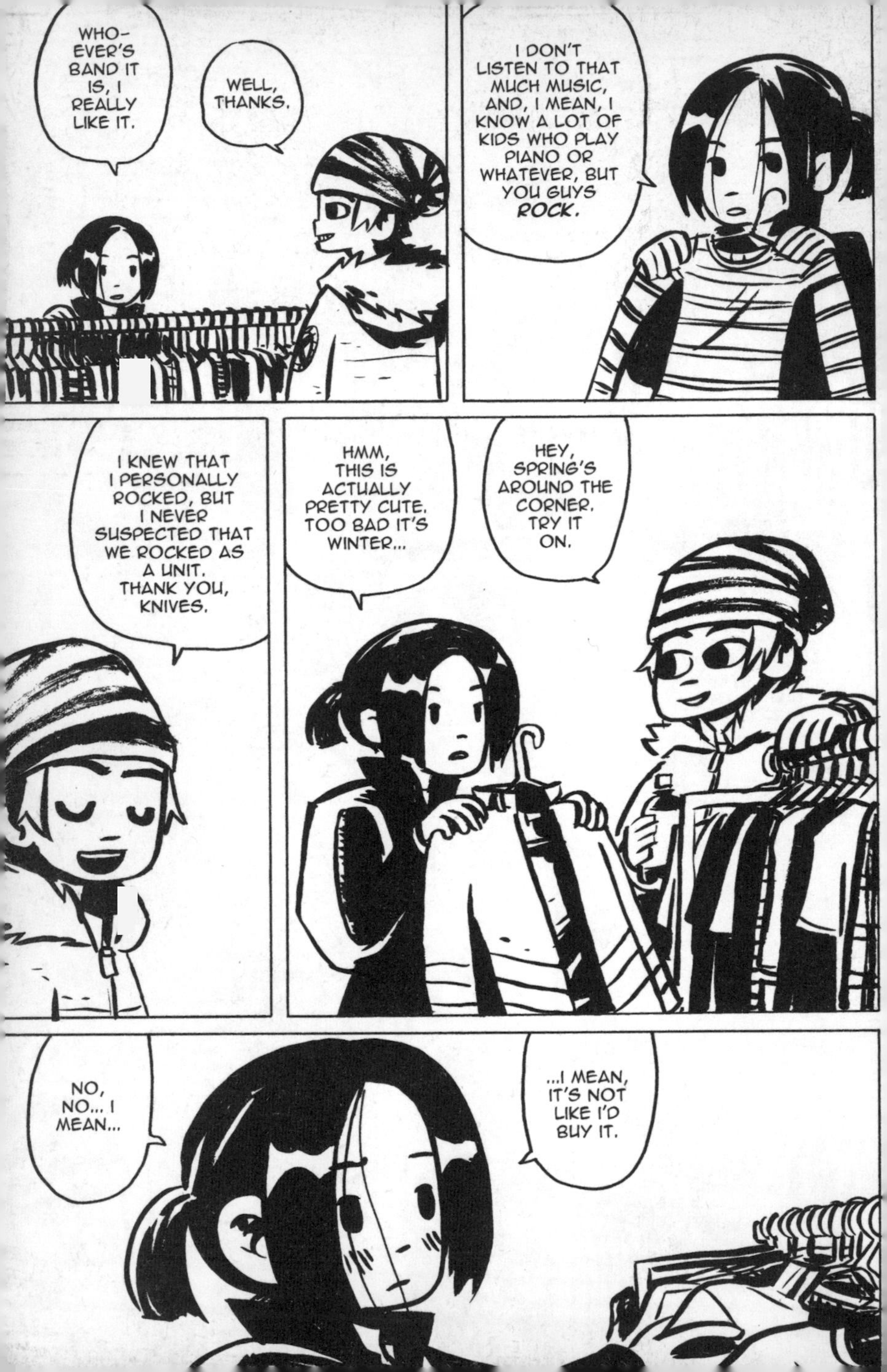
WHO-EVER'S BAND IT IS, I REALLY LIKE IT.
WELL, THANKS.
I DON'T LISTEN TO THAT MUCH MUSIC, AND, I MEAN, I KNOW A LOT OF KIDS WHO PLAY PIANO OR WHATEVER, BUT YOU GUYS ROCK.
I KNEW THAT I PERSONALLY ROCKED, BUT I NEVER SUSPECTED THAT WE ROCKED AS A UNIT. THANK YOU, KNIVES.
HMM, THIS IS ACTUALLY PRETTY CUTE. TOO BAD IT'S WINTER...
HEY, SPRING'S AROUND THE CORNER. TRY IT ON.
NO, NO... I MEAN...
...I MEAN, IT'S NOT LIKE I'D BUY IT.

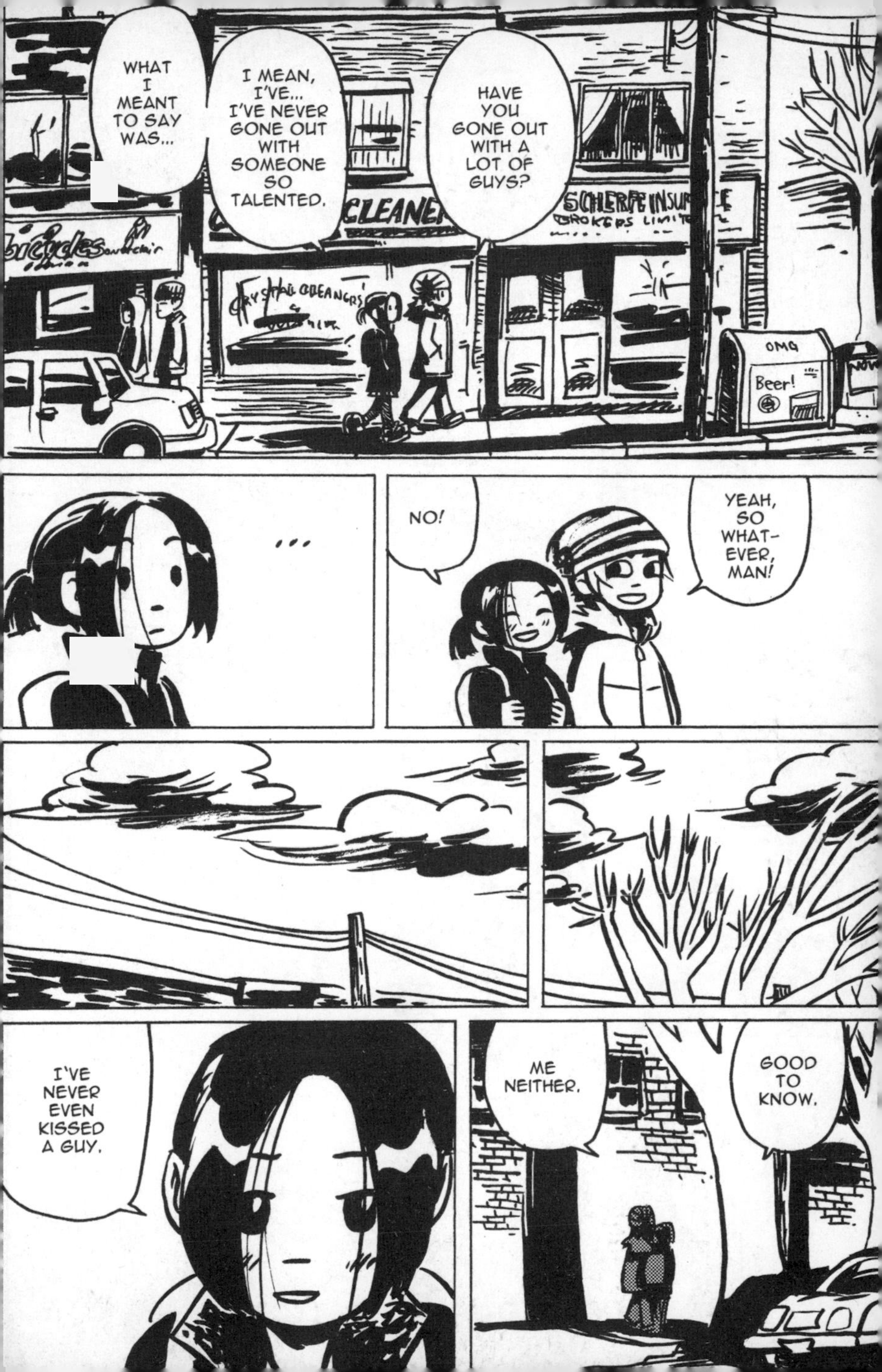
WHAT I MEANT TO SAY WAS...
I MEAN, I'VE... I'VE NEVER GONE OUT WITH SOMEONE SO TALENTED.
HAVE YOU GONE OUT WITH A LOT OF GUYS?
OMG
Beer!
...
NO!
YEAH, SO WHAT-EVER, MAN!
I'VE NEVER EVEN KISSED A GUY.
ME NEITHER.
GOOD TO KNOW.

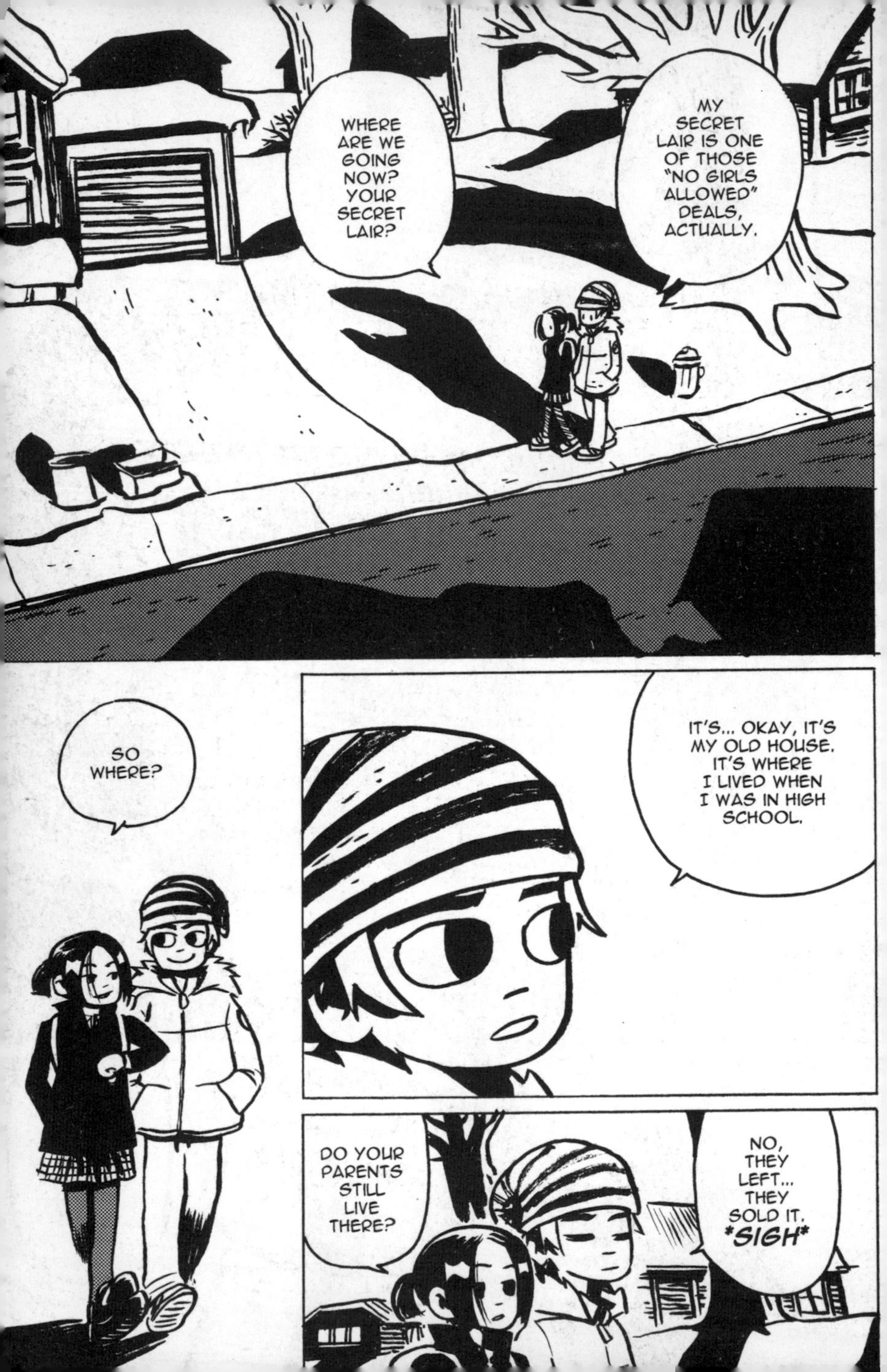
WHERE ARE WE GOING NOW? YOUR SECRET LAIR?
MY SECRET LAIR IS ONE OF THOSE "NO GIRLS ALLOWED" DEALS, ACTUALLY.
SO WHERE?
IT'S... OKAY, IT'S MY OLD HOUSE. IT'S WHERE I LIVED WHEN I WAS IN HIGH SCHOOL.
DO YOUR PARENTS STILL LIVE THERE?
NO, THEY LEFT... THEY SOLD IT.
SIGH

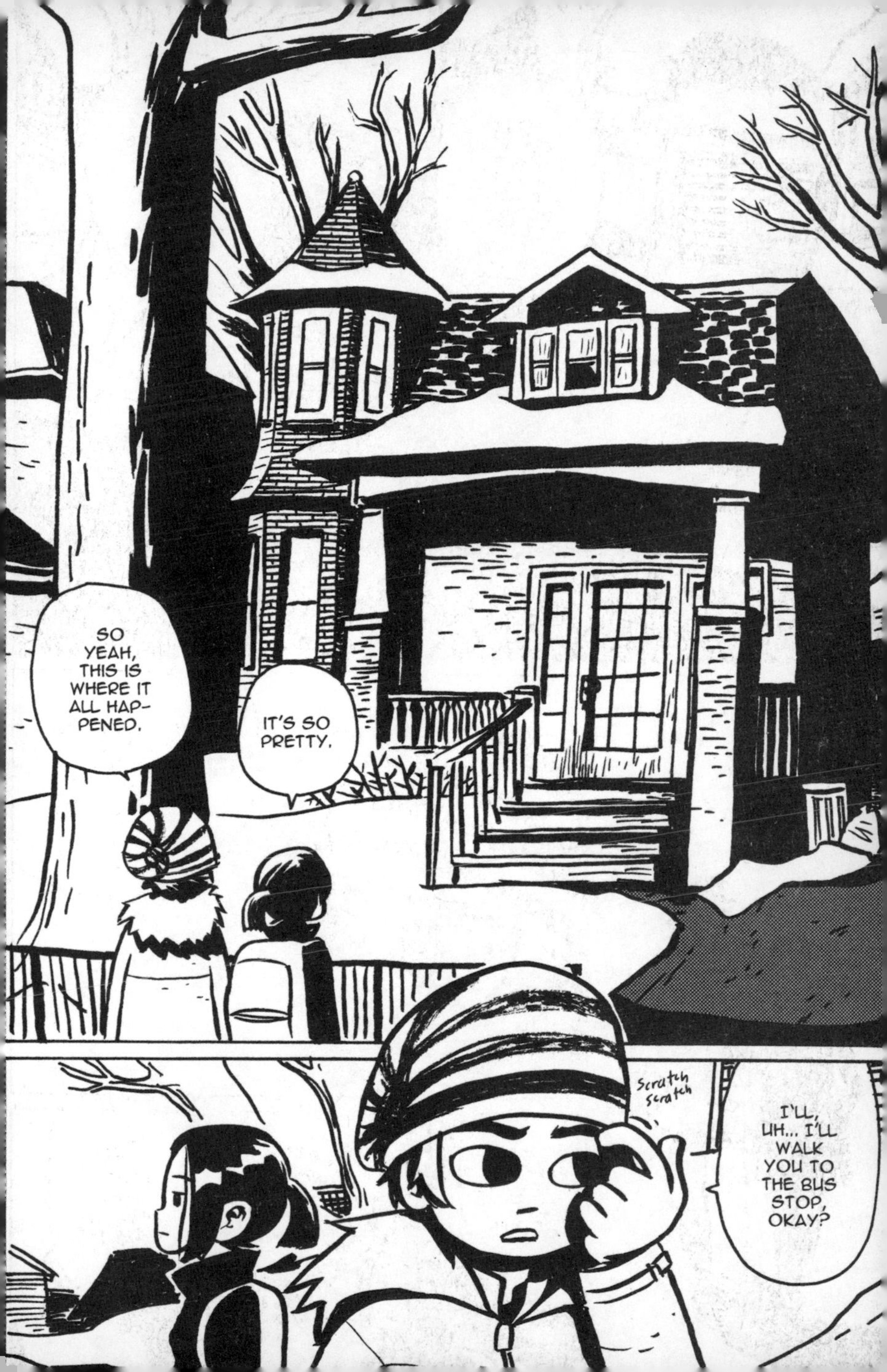
SO YEAH, THIS IS WHERE IT ALL HAP-PENED.
IT'S SO PRETTY.
Scratch scratch
I'LL, UH... I'LL WALK YOU TO THE BUS STOP, OKAY?

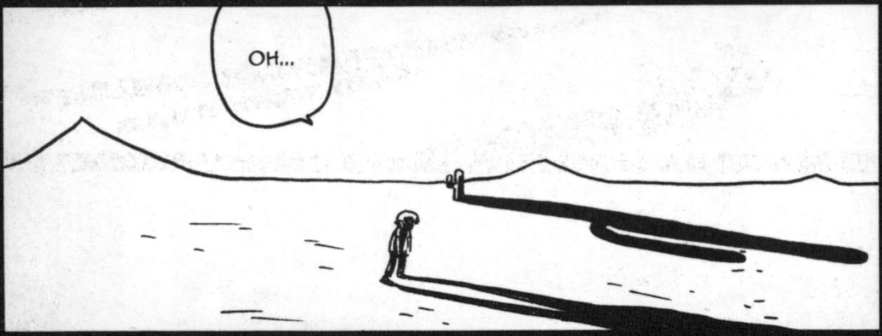
OH...

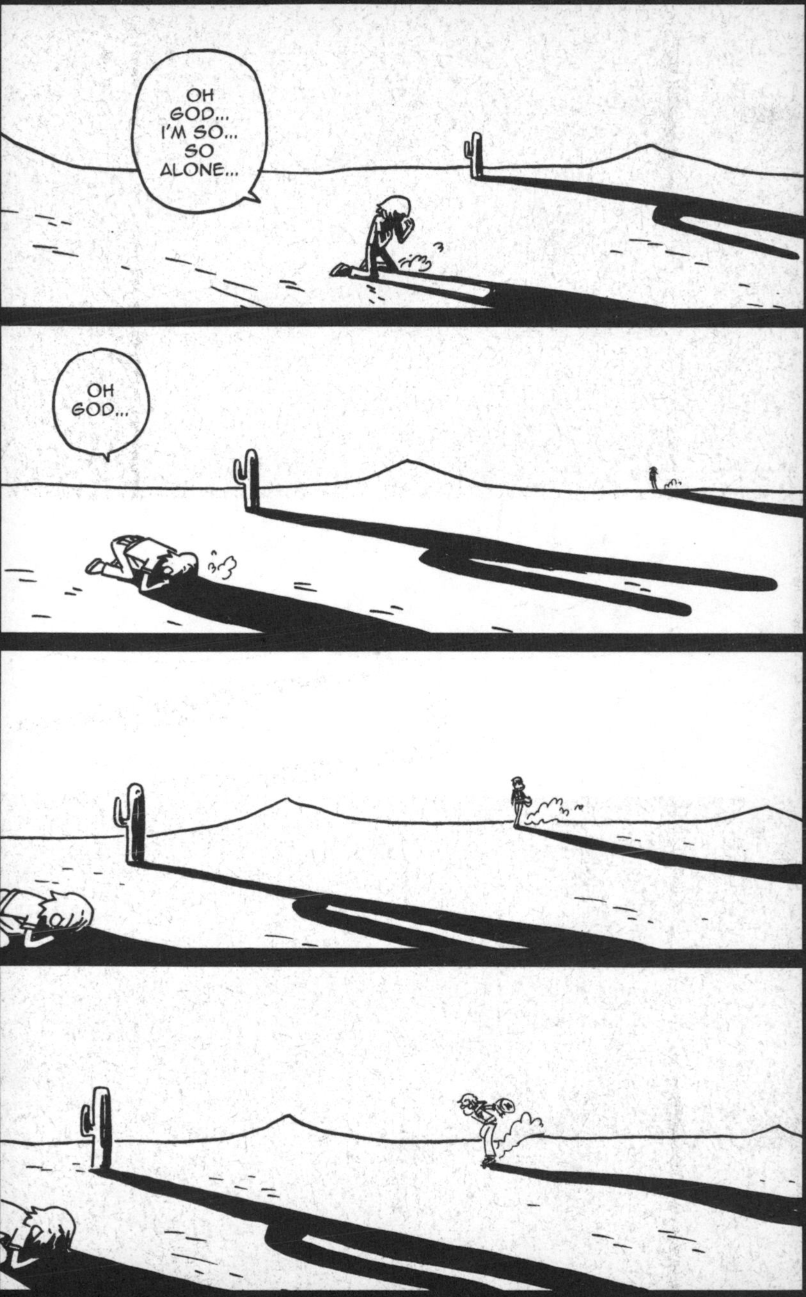
OH GOD... I'M SO... SO ALONE...
OH GOD...

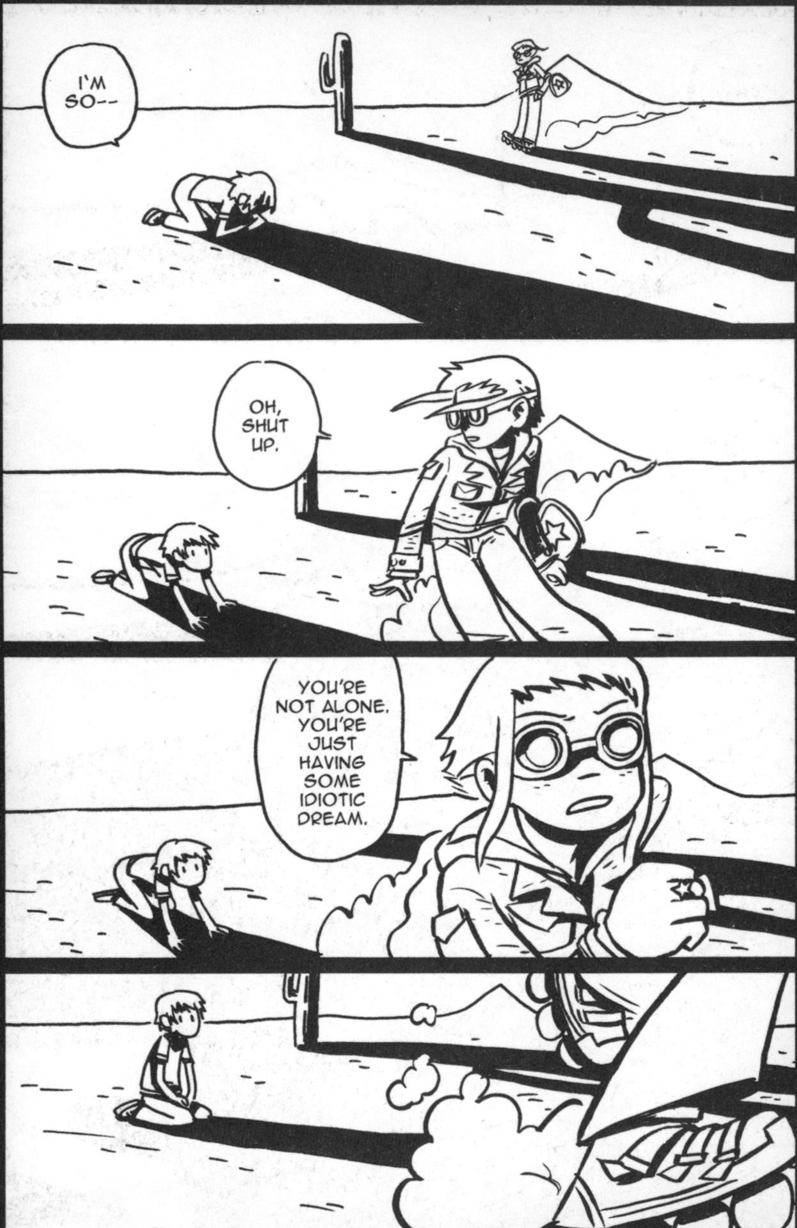
I'M SO--
OH, SHUT UP.
YOU'RE NOT ALONE. YOU'RE JUST HAVING SOME IDIOTIC DREAM.

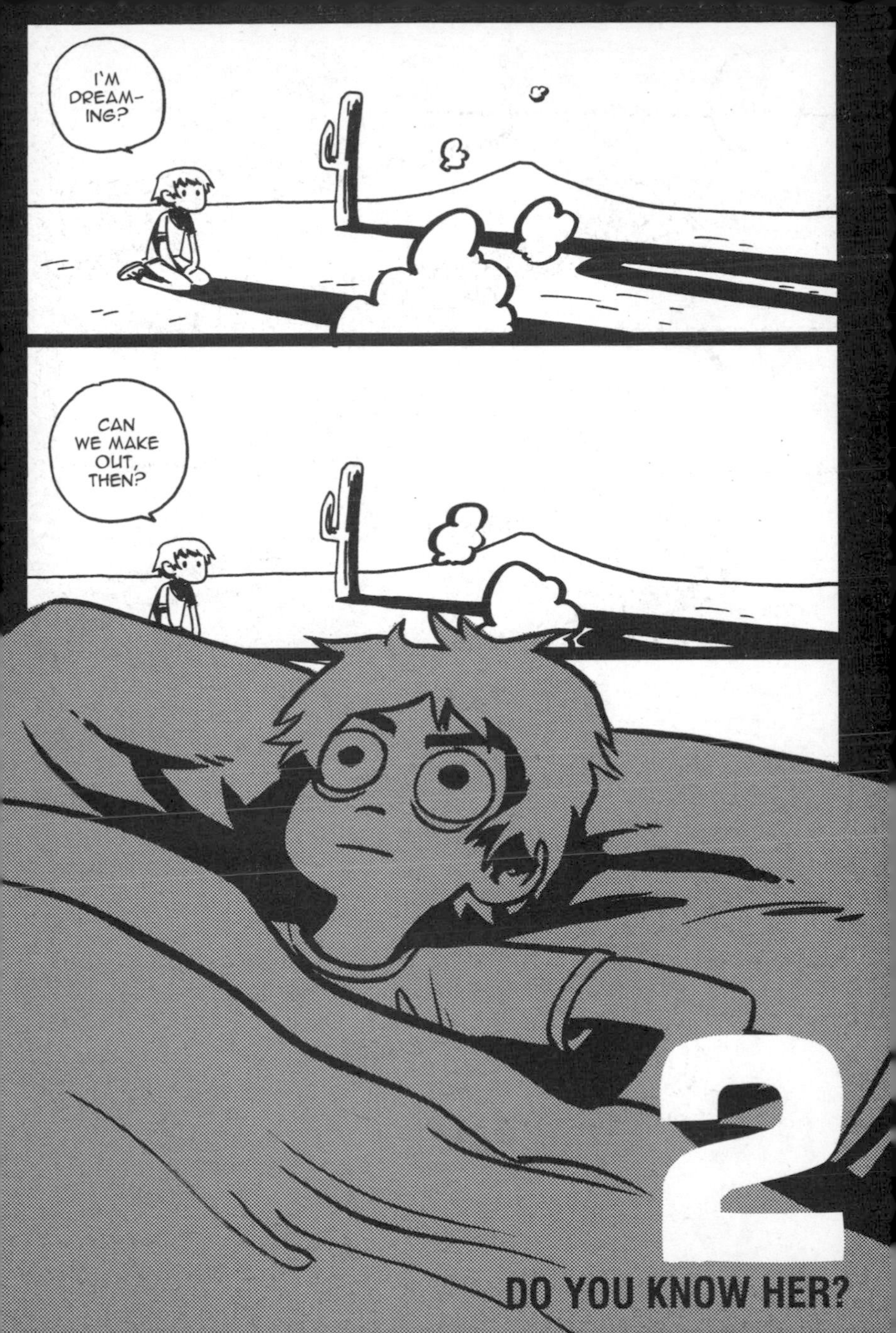

I'M DREAMING?
CAN WE MAKE OUT, THEN?
2
DO YOU KNOW HER?

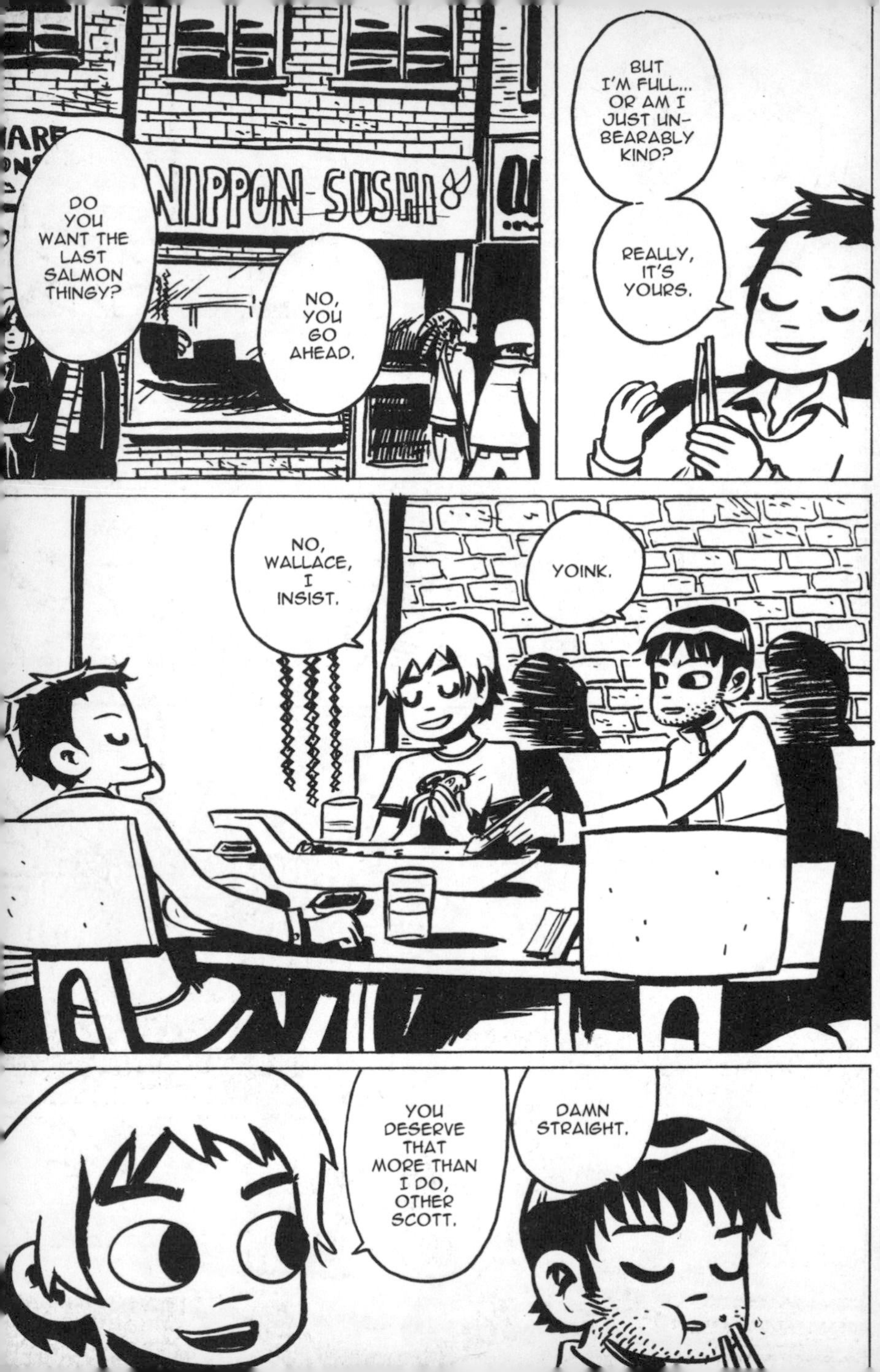
NIPPON SUSHI
DO YOU WANT THE LAST SALMON THINGY?
NO, YOU GO AHEAD.
BUT I'M FULL... OR AM I JUST UN-BEARABLY KIND?
REALLY, IT'S YOURS.
NO, WALLACE, I INSIST.
YOINK.
YOU DESERVE THAT MORE THAN I DO, OTHER SCOTT.
DAMN STRAIGHT.

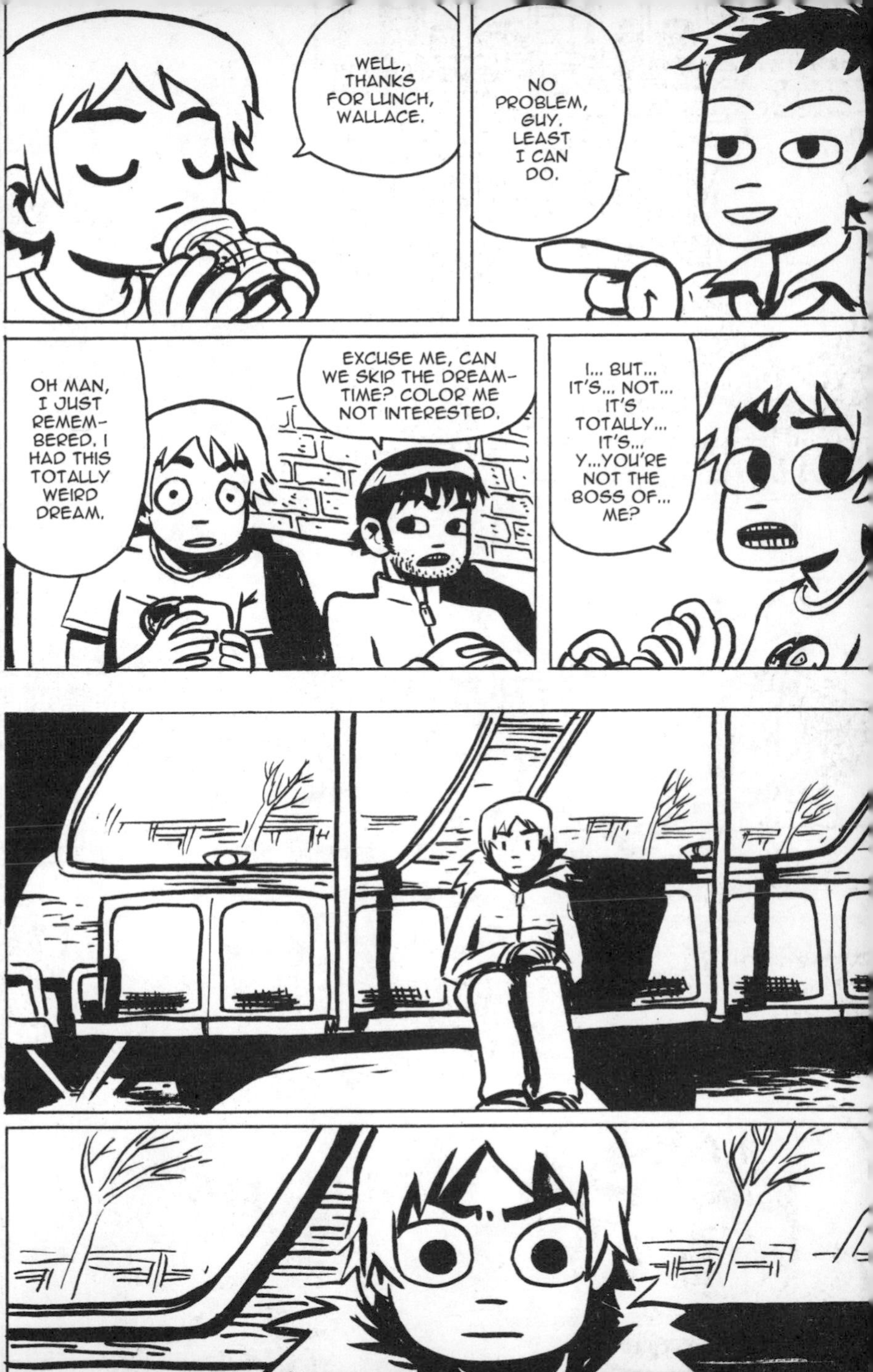
WELL, THANKS FOR LUNCH, WALLACE.
NO PROBLEM, GUY. LEAST I CAN DO.
OH MAN, I JUST REMEMBERED. I HAD THIS TOTALLY WEIRD DREAM.
EXCUSE ME, CAN WE SKIP THE DREAM-TIME? COLOR ME NOT INTERESTED.
I... BUT... IT'S... NOT... IT'S TOTALLY... IT'S... Y...YOU'RE NOT THE BOSS OF... ME?

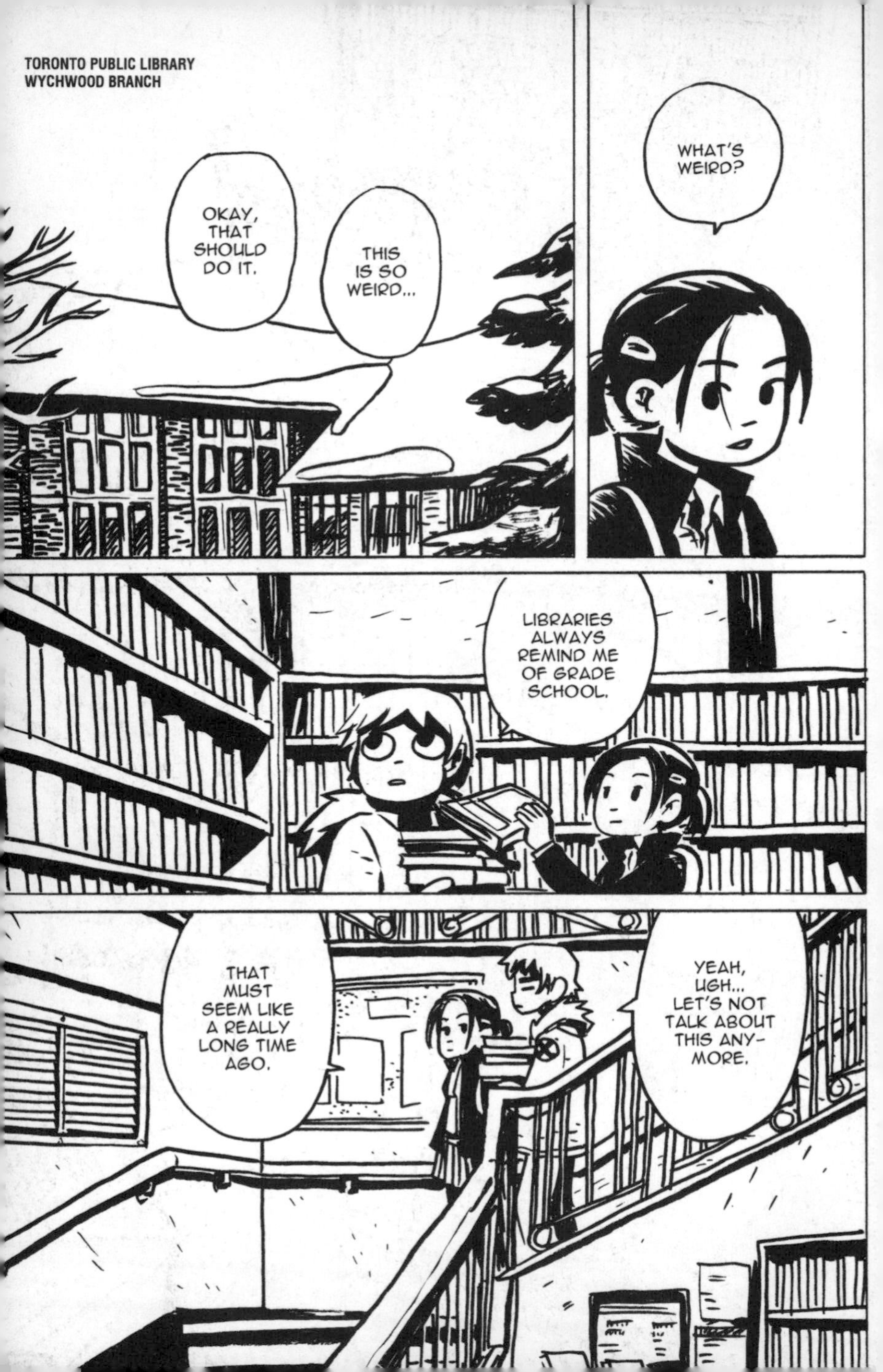

TORONTO PUBLIC LIBRARY
WYCHWOOD BRANCH
OKAY, THAT SHOULD DO IT.
THIS IS SO WEIRD...
WHAT'S WEIRD?
LIBRARIES ALWAYS REMIND ME OF GRADE SCHOOL.
THAT MUST SEEM LIKE A REALLY LONG TIME AGO.
YEAH, UGH... LET'S NOT TALK ABOUT THIS ANY-MORE.

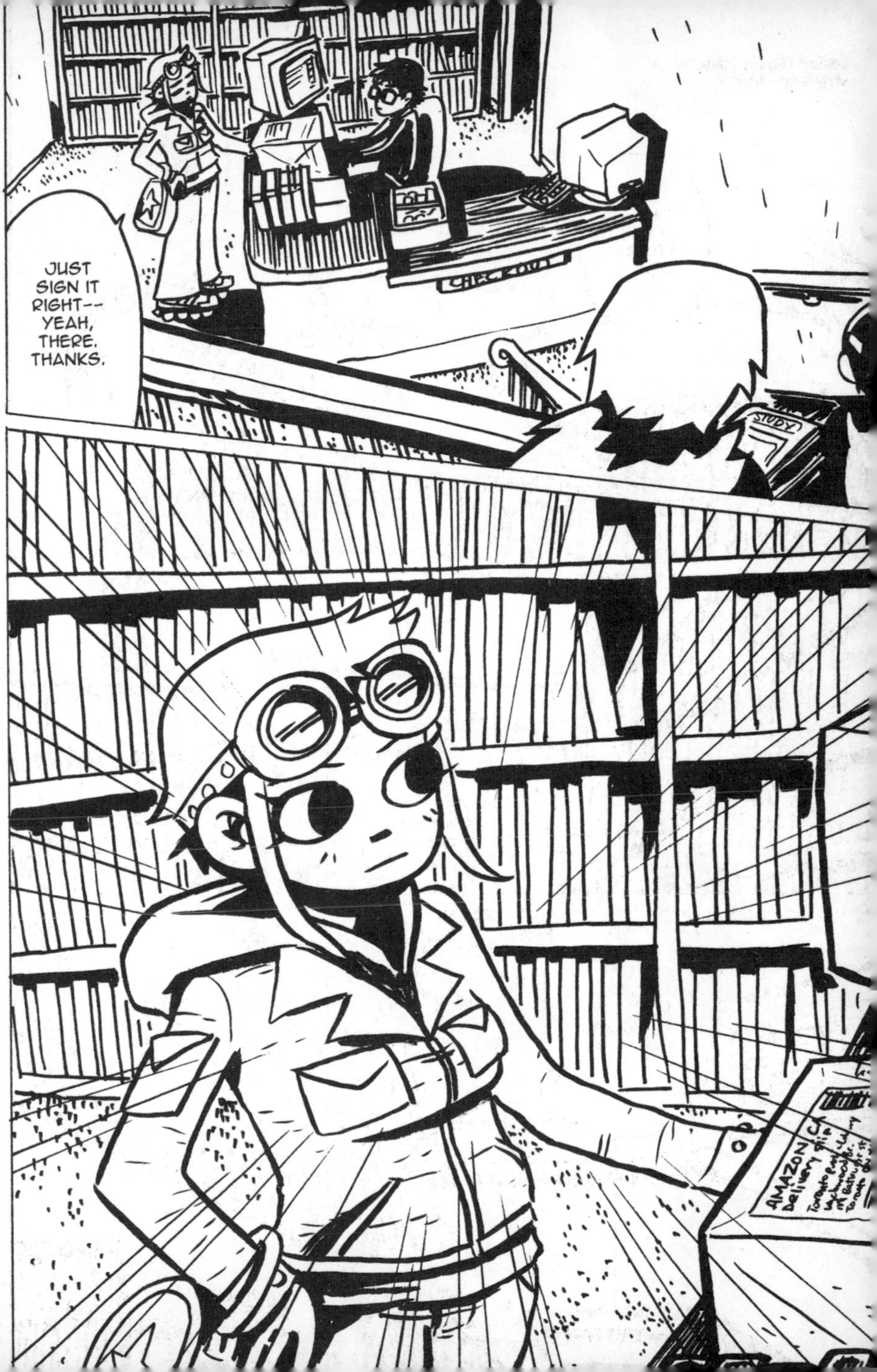
JUST SIGN IT RIGHT-- YEAH, THERE. THANKS.
STUDY
AMAZON

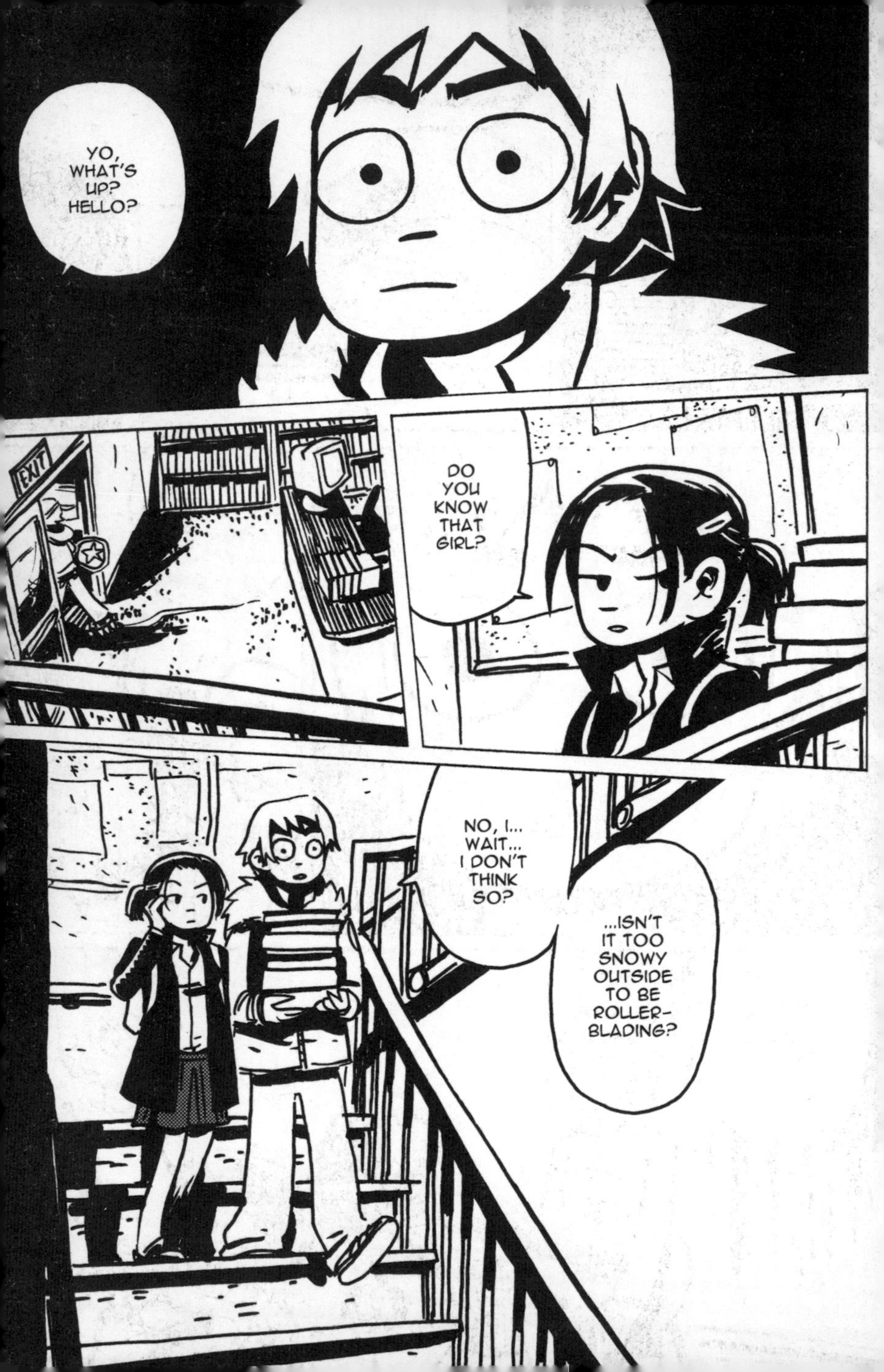
YO, WHAT'S UP? HELLO?
DO YOU KNOW THAT GIRL?
NO, I... WAIT... I DON'T THINK SO?
...ISN'T IT TOO SNOWY OUTSIDE TO BE ROLLER-BLADING?

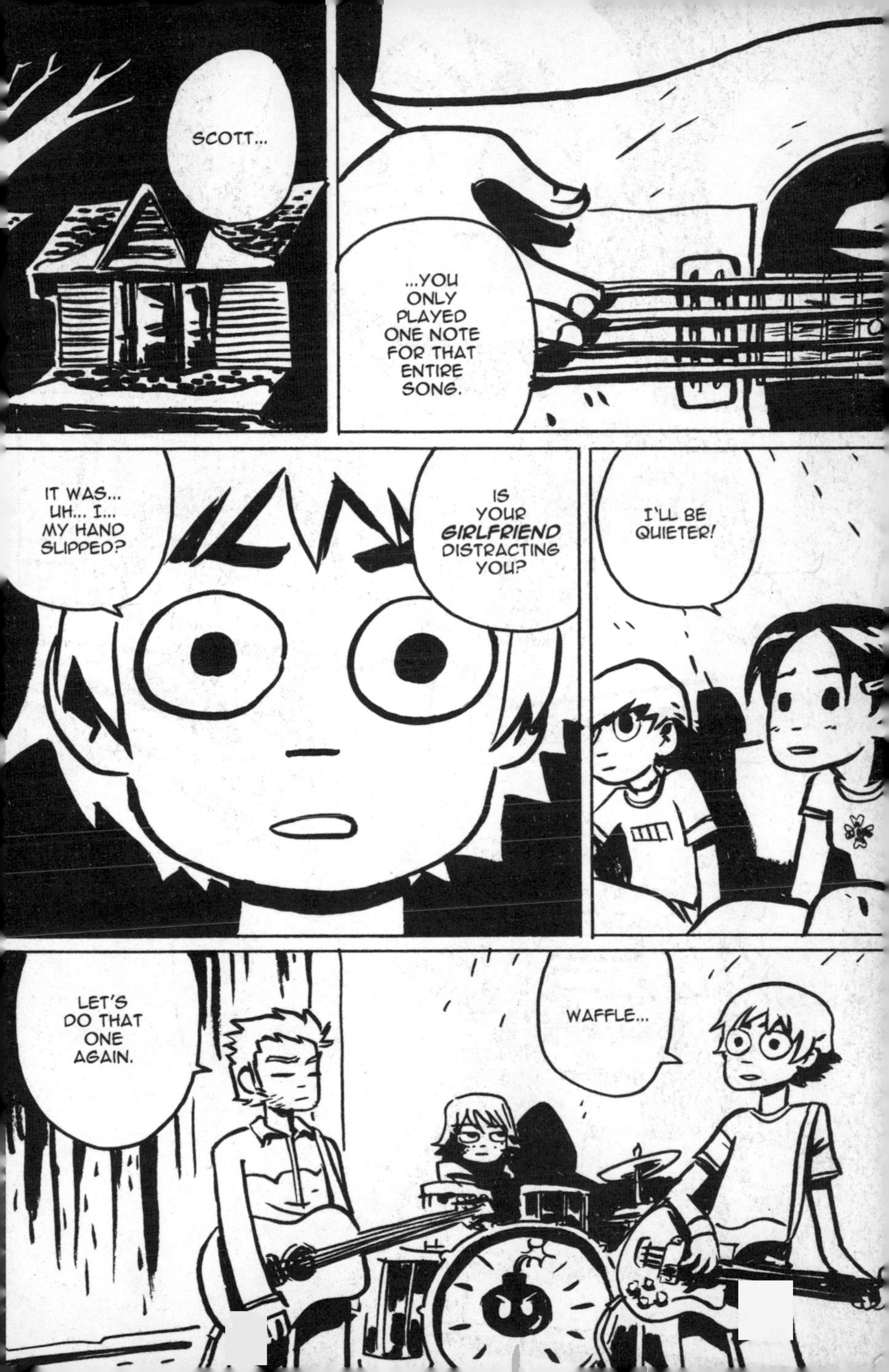
SCOTT...
...YOU ONLY PLAYED ONE NOTE FOR THAT ENTIRE SONG.
IT WAS... UH... I... MY HAND SLIPPED?
IS YOUR *GIRLFRIEND* DISTRACTING YOU?
I'LL BE QUIETER!
LET'S DO THAT ONE AGAIN.
WAFFLE...

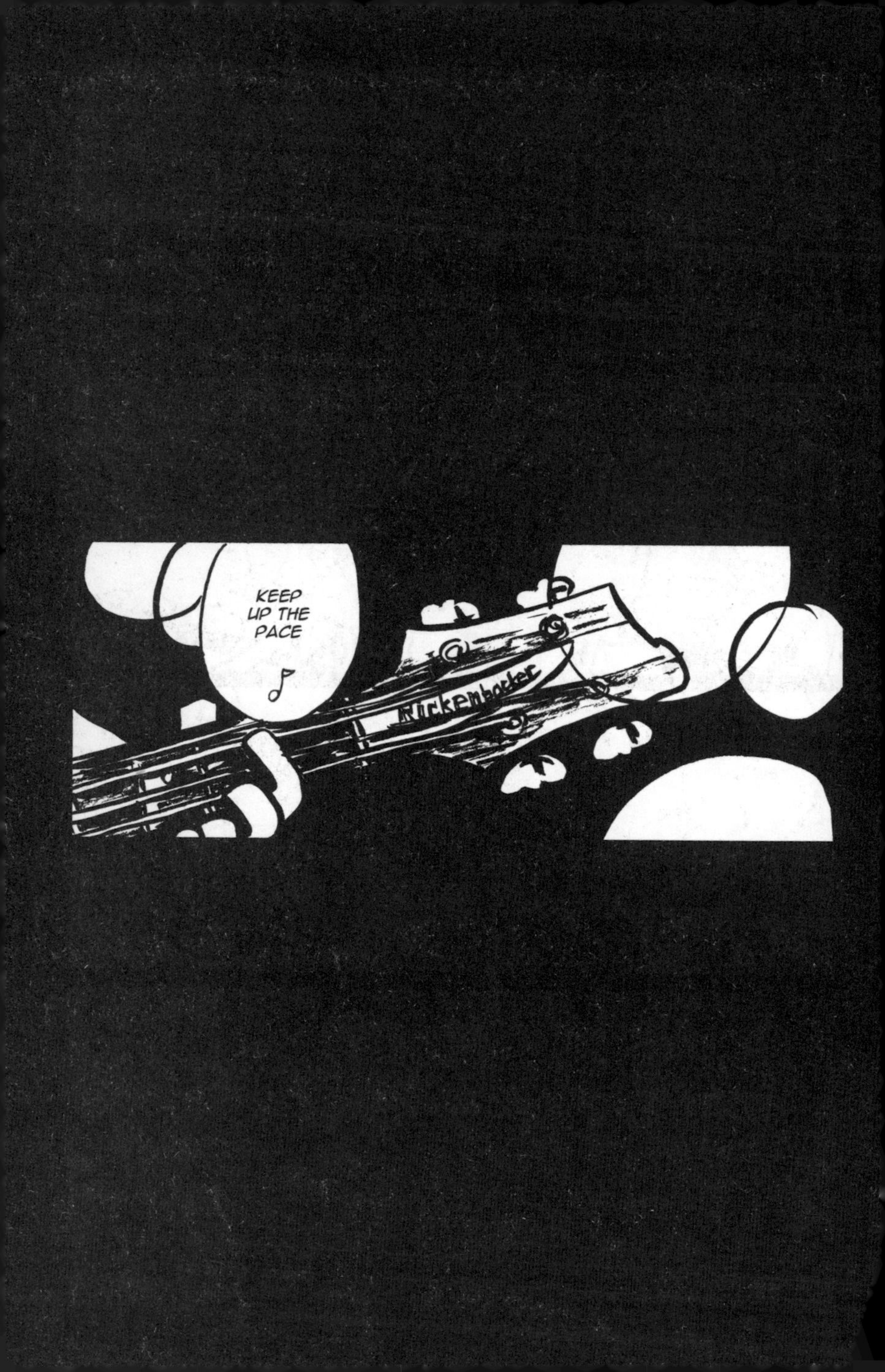
KEEP UP THE PACE

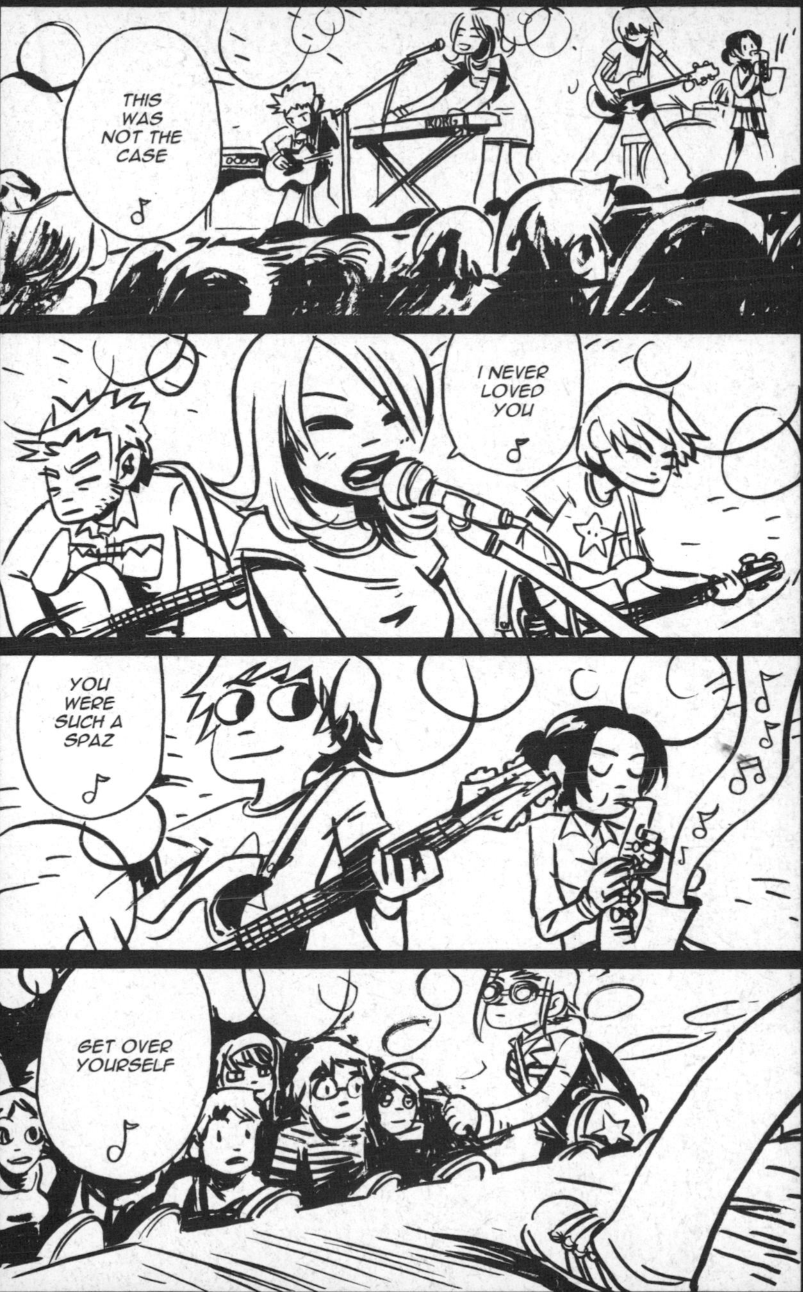
THIS WAS NOT THE CASE ♪
KORG
I NEVER LOVED YOU ♪
YOU WERE SUCH A SPAZ ♪
GET OVER YOURSELF ♪

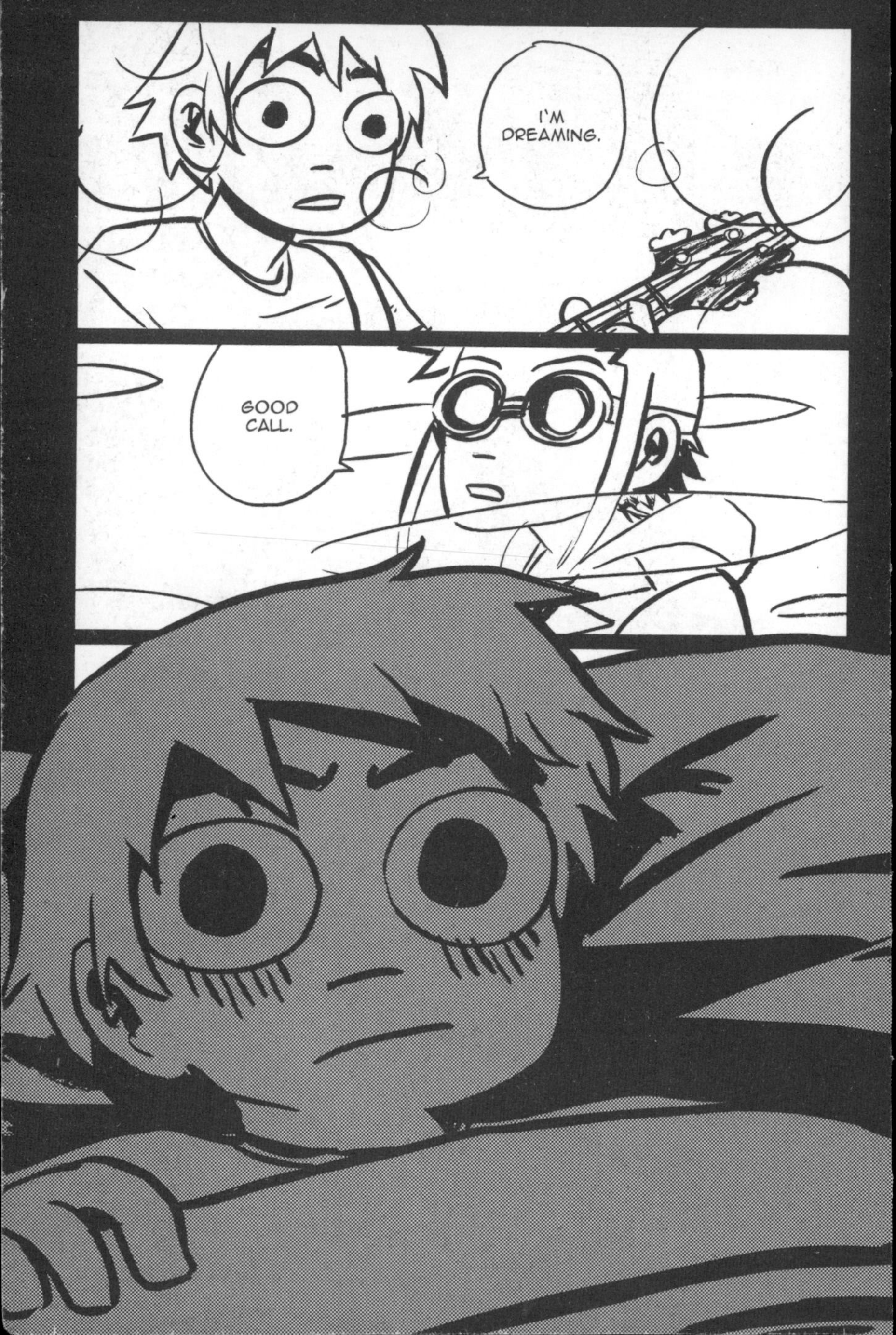
I'M DREAMING.
GOOD CALL.

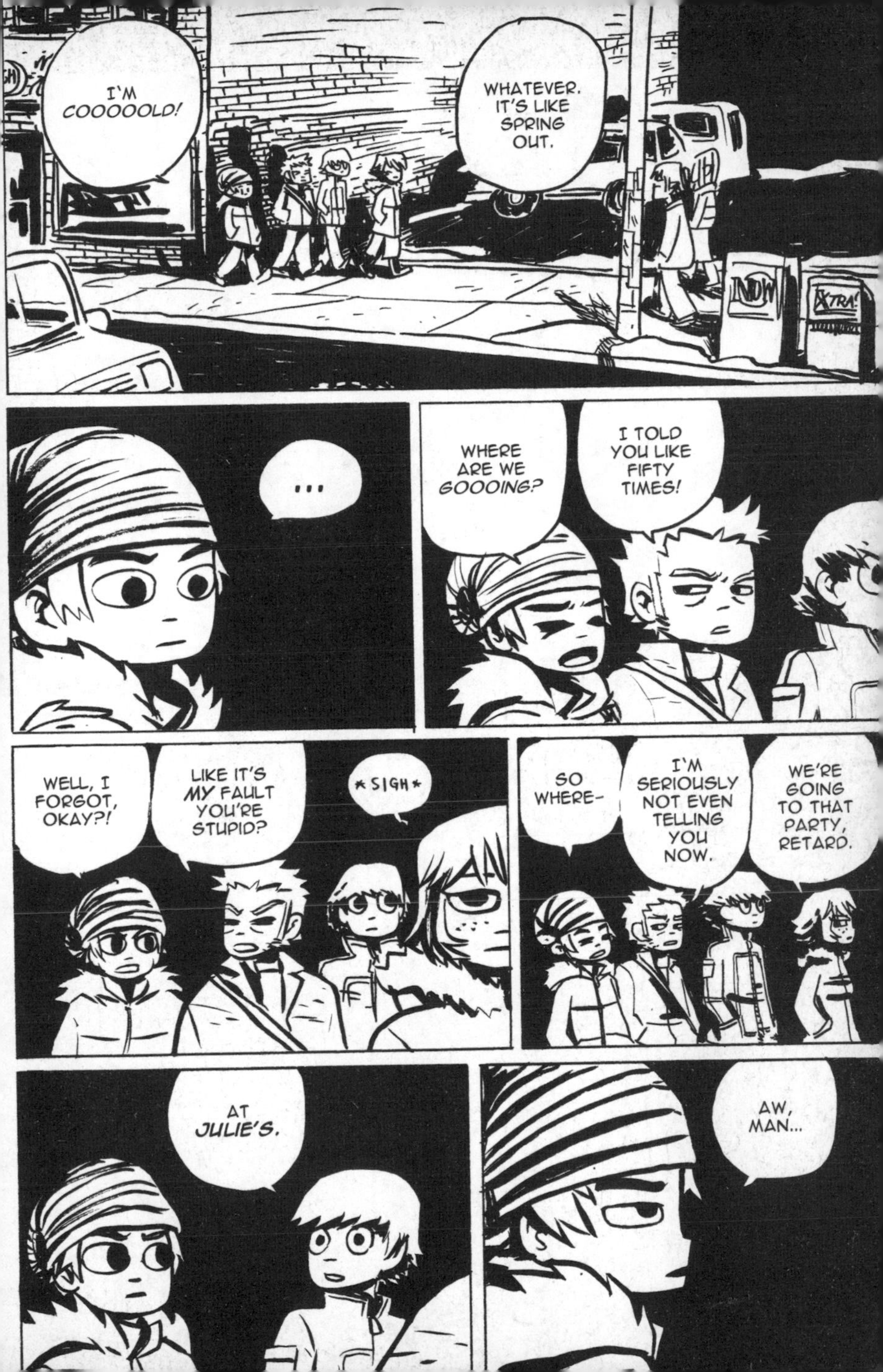
I'M COOOOOLD!
WHATEVER. IT'S LIKE SPRING OUT.
NOW
XTRA!
...
WHERE ARE WE GOOOING?
I TOLD YOU LIKE FIFTY TIMES!
WELL, I FORGOT, OKAY?!
LIKE IT'S MY FAULT YOU'RE STUPID?
SIGH
SO WHERE-
I'M SERIOUSLY NOT EVEN TELLING YOU NOW.
WE'RE GOING TO THAT PARTY, RETARD.
AT JULIE'S.
AW, MAN...

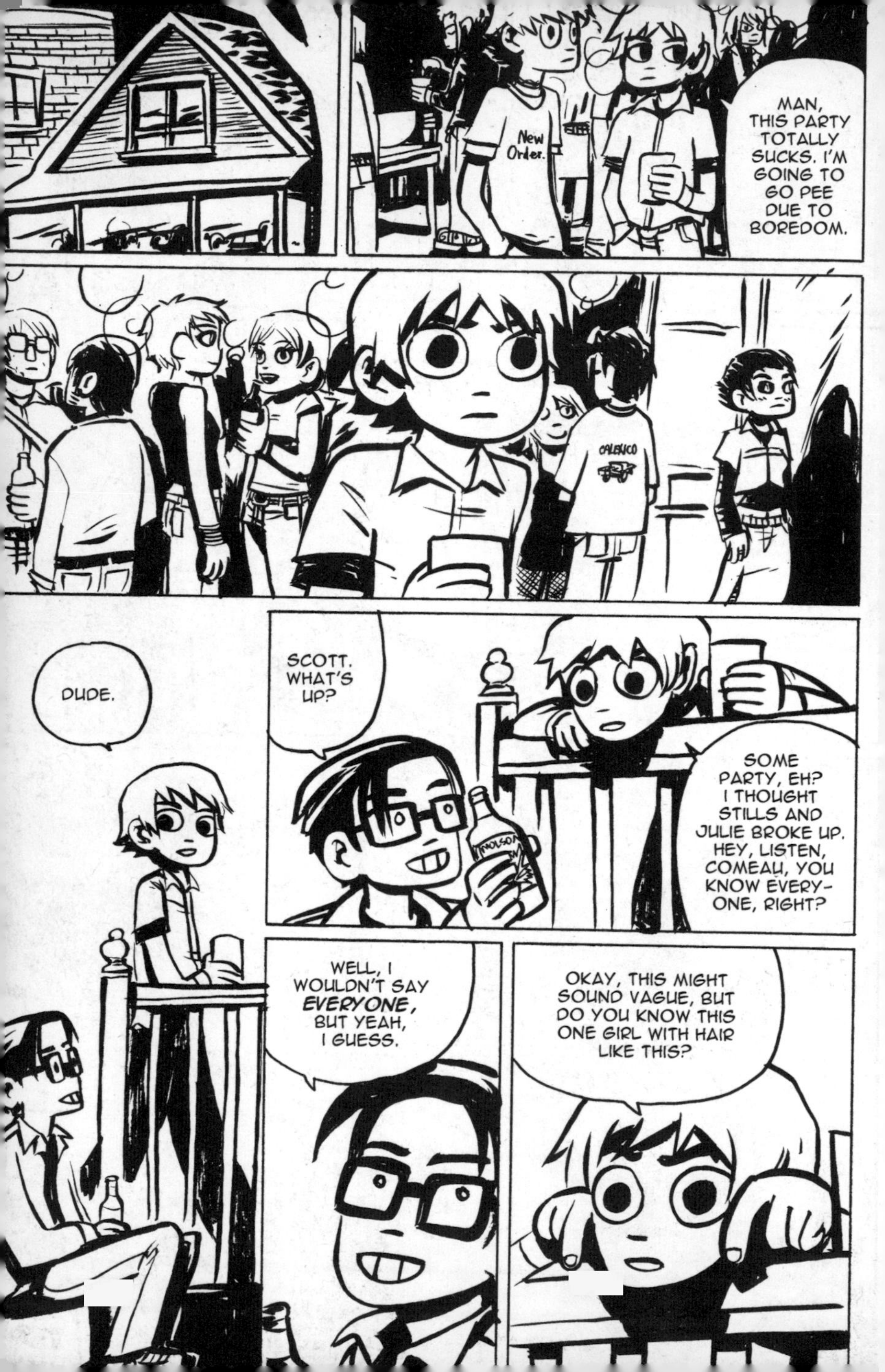
New Order.
MAN, THIS PARTY TOTALLY SUCKS. I'M GOING TO GO PEE DUE TO BOREDOM.
CALEXICO
DUDE.
SCOTT. WHAT'S UP?
SOME PARTY, EH? I THOUGHT STILLS AND JULIE BROKE UP. HEY, LISTEN, COMEAU, YOU KNOW EVERY-ONE, RIGHT?
WELL, I WOULDN'T SAY *EVERYONE*, BUT YEAH, I GUESS.
OKAY, THIS MIGHT SOUND VAGUE, BUT DO YOU KNOW THIS ONE GIRL WITH HAIR LIKE THIS?

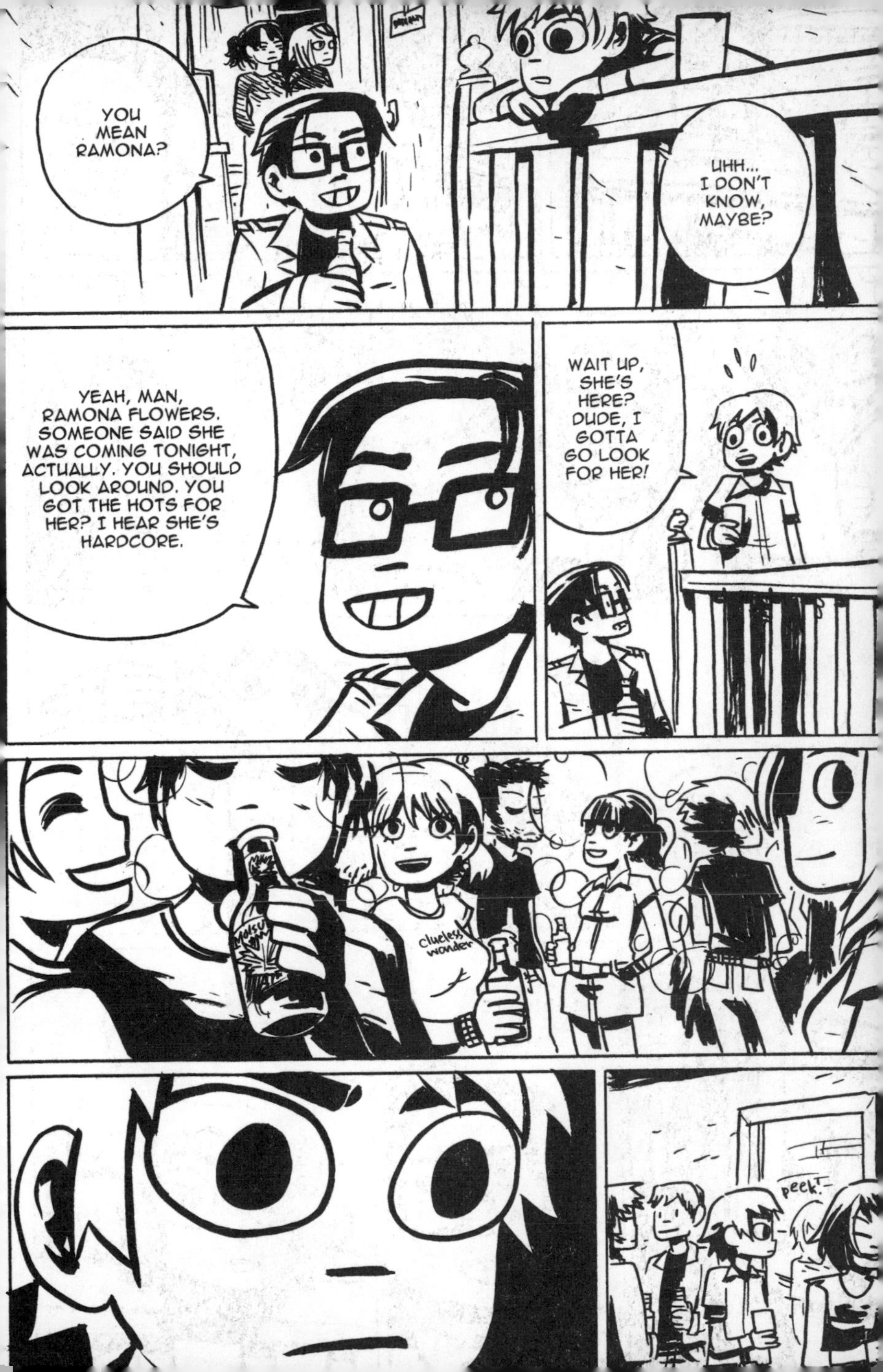
YOU MEAN RAMONA?
UHH... I DON'T KNOW, MAYBE?
YEAH, MAN, RAMONA FLOWERS. SOMEONE SAID SHE WAS COMING TONIGHT, ACTUALLY. YOU SHOULD LOOK AROUND. YOU GOT THE HOTS FOR HER? I HEAR SHE'S HARDCORE.
WAIT UP, SHE'S HERE? DUDE, I GOTTA GO LOOK FOR HER!
clueless wonder
peek!

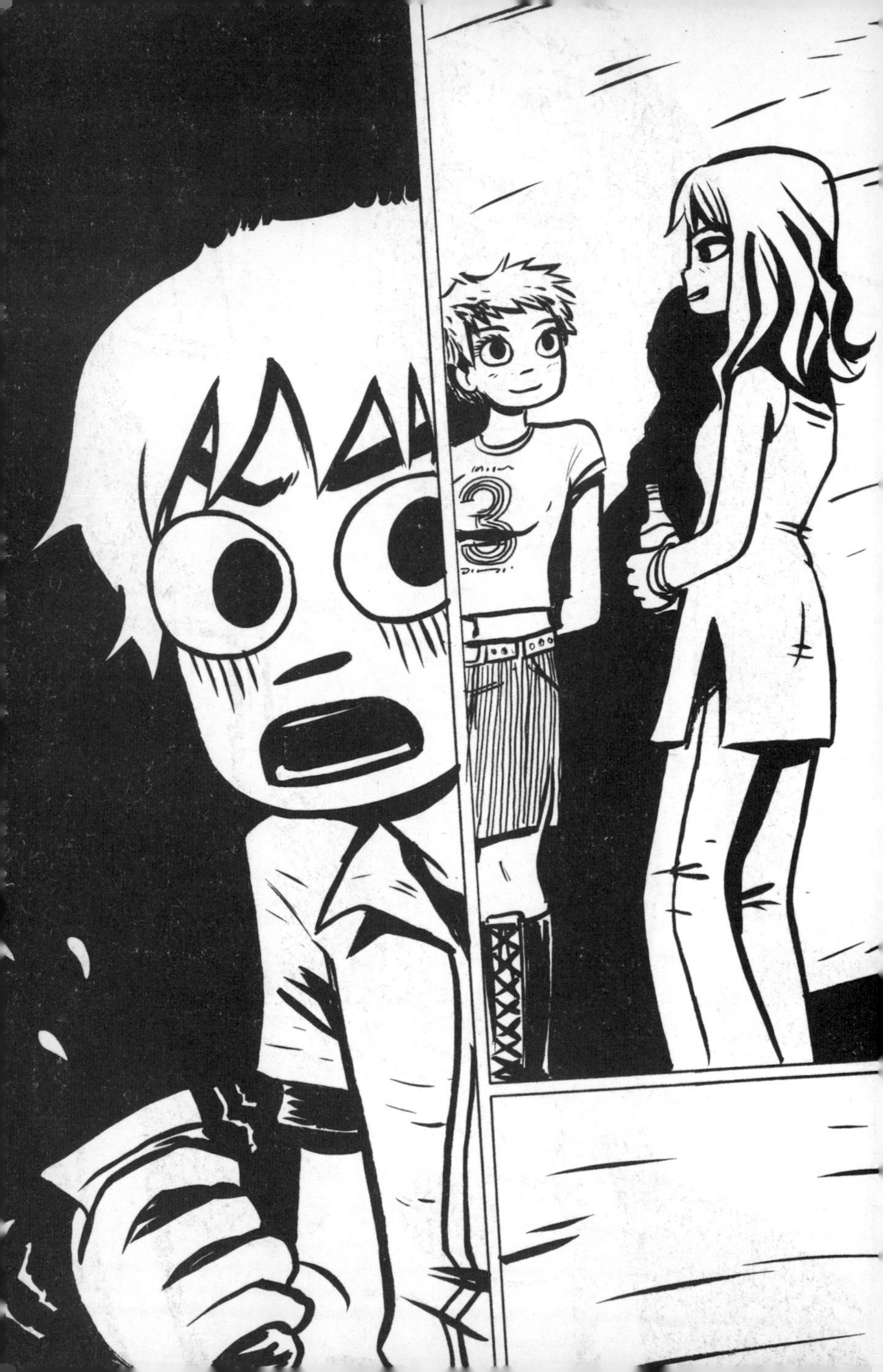

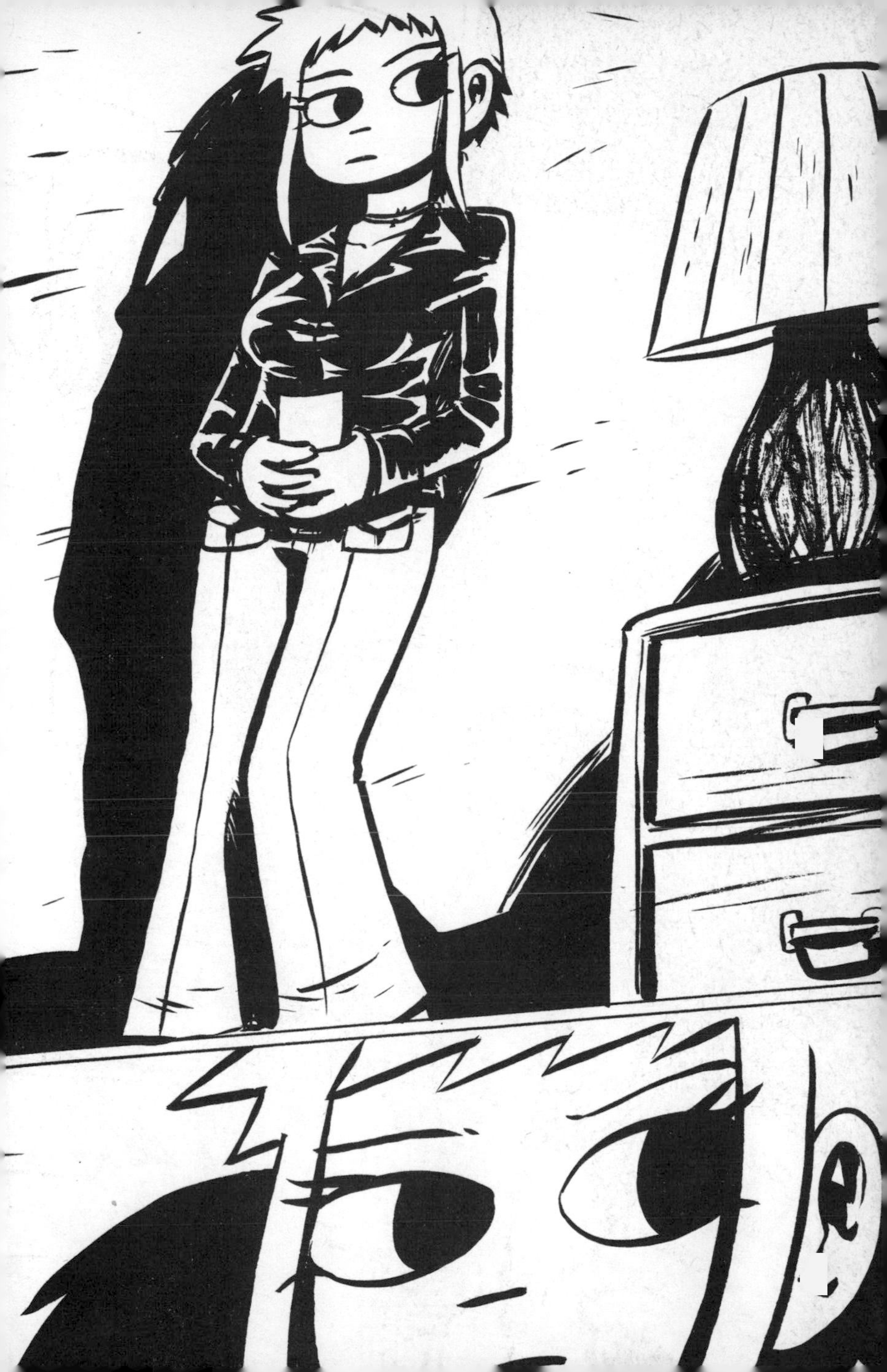

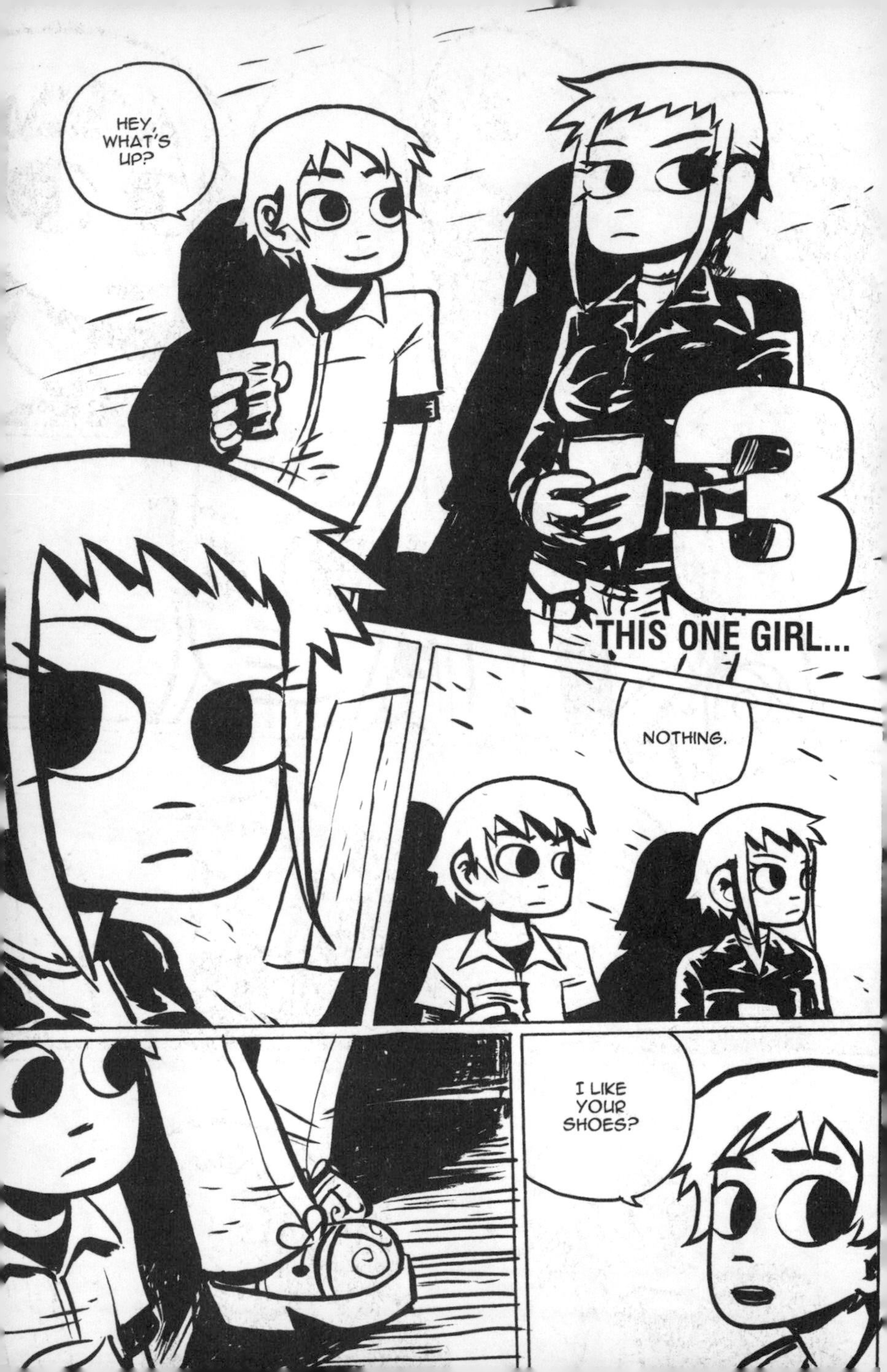

HEY, WHAT'S UP?
3
THIS ONE GIRL...
NOTHING.
I LIKE YOUR SHOES?

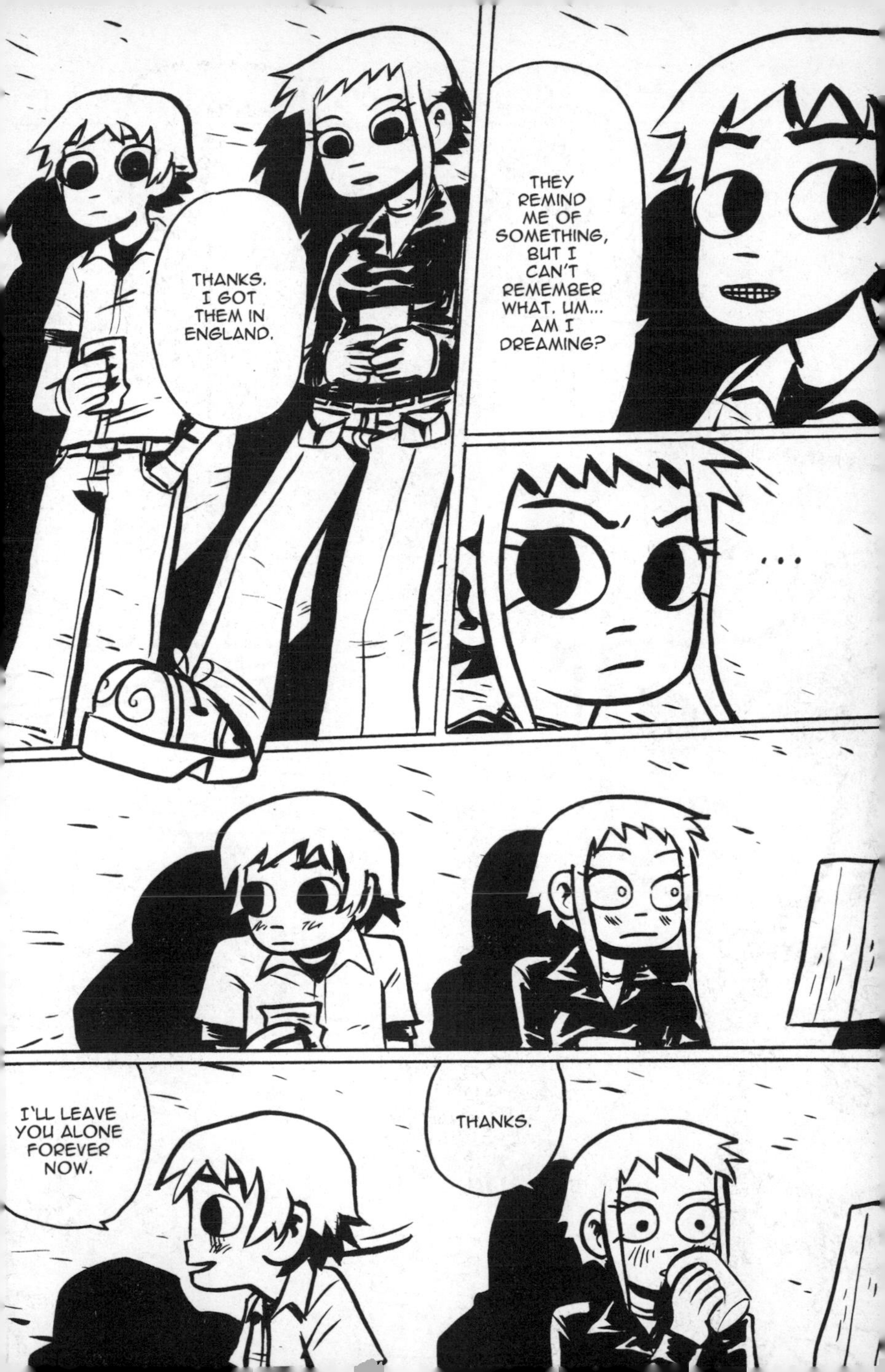
THANKS. I GOT THEM IN ENGLAND.
THEY REMIND ME OF SOMETHING, BUT I CAN'T REMEMBER WHAT. UM... AM I DREAMING?
...
I'LL LEAVE YOU ALONE FOREVER NOW.
THANKS.

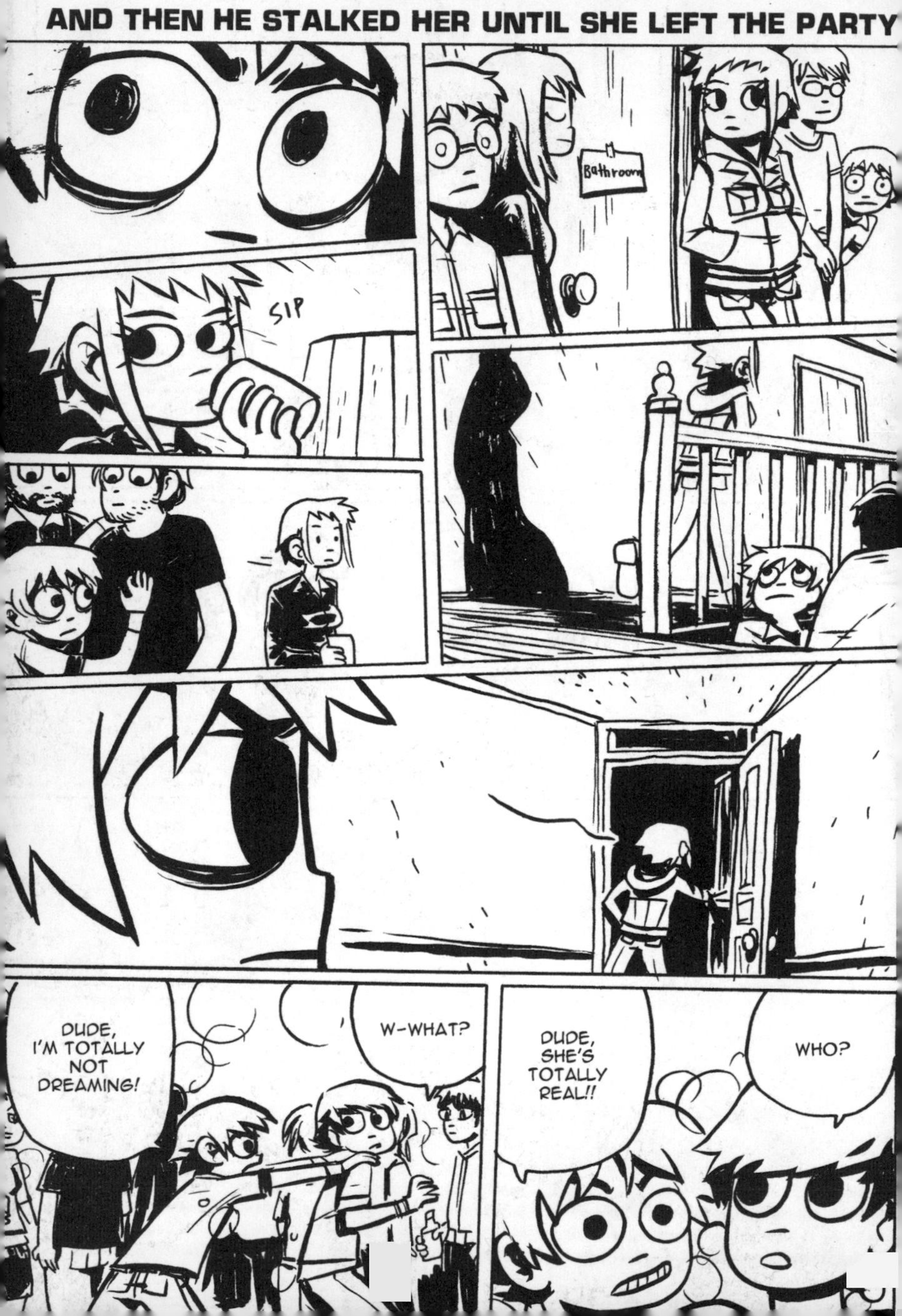
AND THEN HE STALKED HER UNTIL SHE LEFT THE PARTY
Bathroom
SIP
DUDE, I'M TOTALLY NOT DREAMING!
W-WHAT?
DUDE, SHE'S TOTALLY REAL!!
WHO?

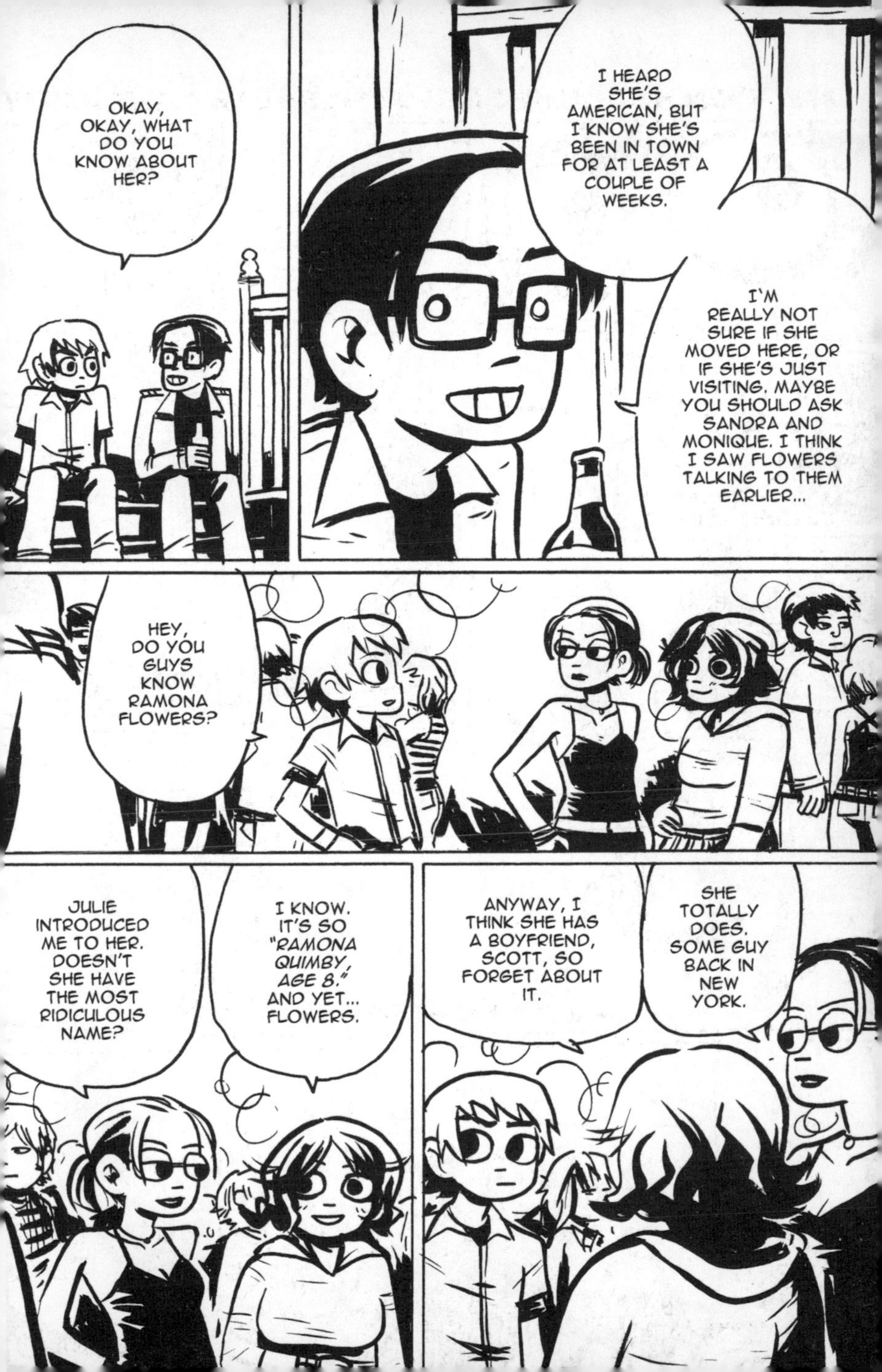
OKAY, OKAY, WHAT DO YOU KNOW ABOUT HER?
I HEARD SHE'S AMERICAN, BUT I KNOW SHE'S BEEN IN TOWN FOR AT LEAST A COUPLE OF WEEKS.
I'M REALLY NOT SURE IF SHE MOVED HERE, OR IF SHE'S JUST VISITING. MAYBE YOU SHOULD ASK SANDRA AND MONIQUE. I THINK I SAW FLOWERS TALKING TO THEM EARLIER...
HEY, DO YOU GUYS KNOW RAMONA FLOWERS?
JULIE INTRODUCED ME TO HER. DOESN'T SHE HAVE THE MOST RIDICULOUS NAME?
I KNOW. IT'S SO "RAMONA QUIMBY, AGE 8." AND YET... FLOWERS.
ANYWAY, I THINK SHE HAS A BOYFRIEND, SCOTT, SO FORGET ABOUT IT.
SHE TOTALLY DOES. SOME GUY BACK IN NEW YORK.

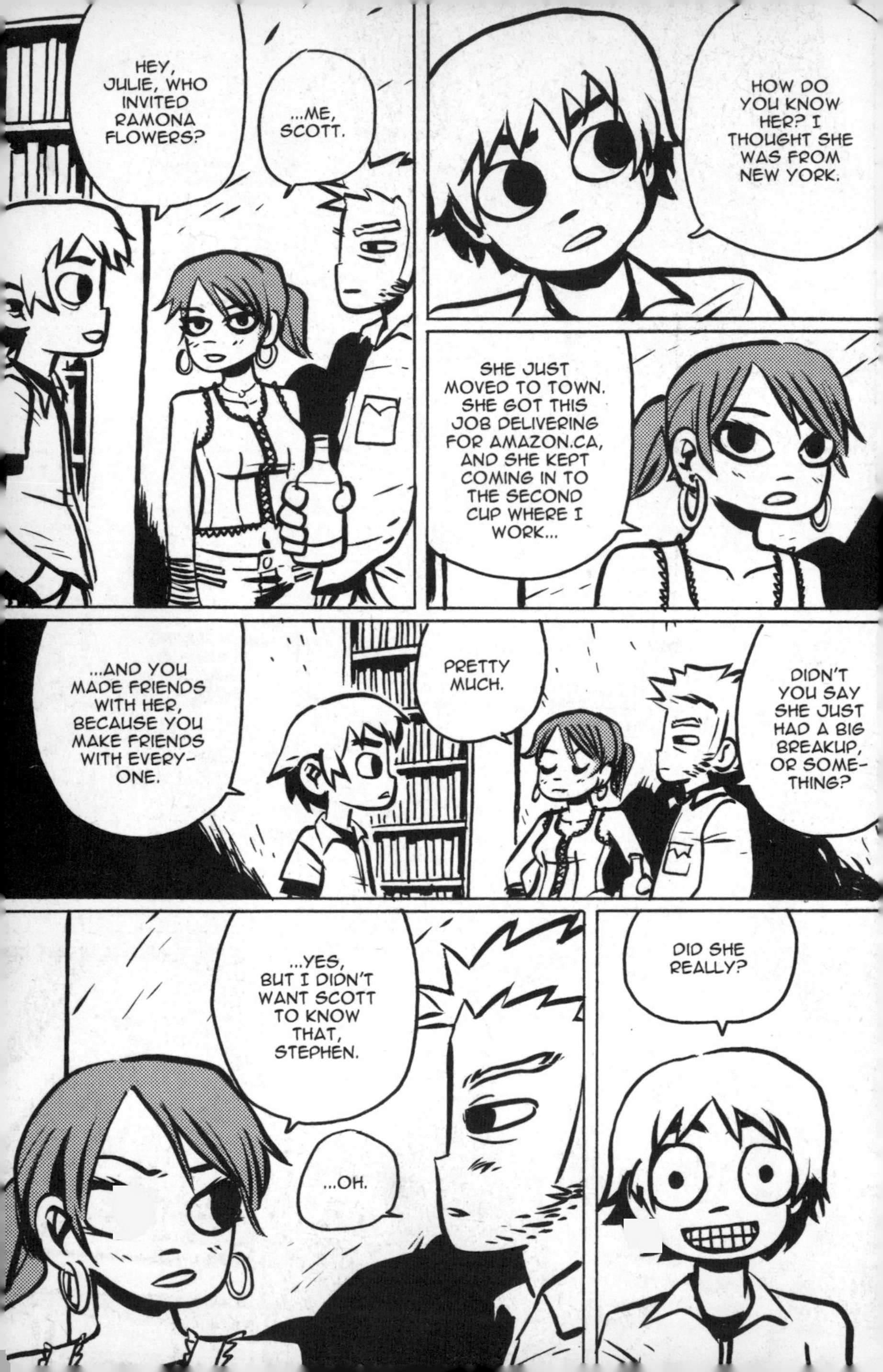

HEY, JULIE, WHO INVITED RAMONA FLOWERS?
...ME, SCOTT.
HOW DO YOU KNOW HER? I THOUGHT SHE WAS FROM NEW YORK.
SHE JUST MOVED TO TOWN. SHE GOT THIS JOB DELIVERING FOR AMAZON.CA, AND SHE KEPT COMING IN TO THE SECOND CUP WHERE I WORK...
...AND YOU MADE FRIENDS WITH HER, BECAUSE YOU MAKE FRIENDS WITH EVERY-ONE.
PRETTY MUCH.
DIDN'T YOU SAY SHE JUST HAD A BIG BREAKUP, OR SOME-THING?
...YES, BUT I DIDN'T WANT SCOTT TO KNOW THAT, STEPHEN.
...OH.
DID SHE REALLY?

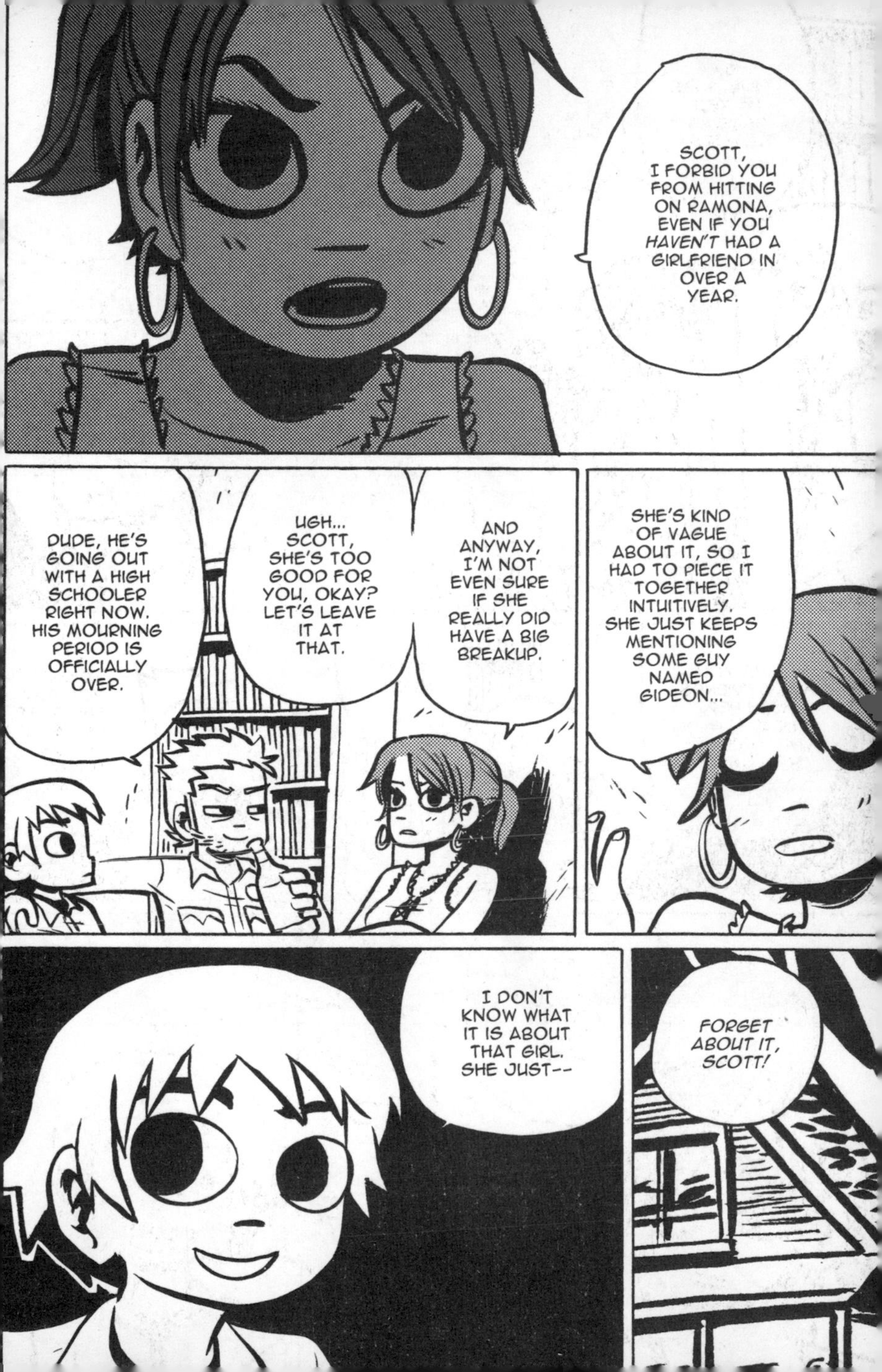
SCOTT, I FORBID YOU FROM HITTING ON RAMONA, EVEN IF YOU *HAVEN'T* HAD A GIRLFRIEND IN OVER A YEAR.
DUDE, HE'S GOING OUT WITH A HIGH SCHOOLER RIGHT NOW. HIS MOURNING PERIOD IS OFFICIALLY OVER.
UGH... SCOTT, SHE'S TOO GOOD FOR YOU, OKAY? LET'S LEAVE IT AT THAT.
AND ANYWAY, I'M NOT EVEN SURE IF SHE REALLY DID HAVE A BIG BREAKUP.
SHE'S KIND OF VAGUE ABOUT IT, SO I HAD TO PIECE IT TOGETHER INTUITIVELY. SHE JUST KEEPS MENTIONING SOME GUY NAMED GIDEON...
I DON'T KNOW WHAT IT IS ABOUT THAT GIRL. SHE JUST--
FORGET ABOUT IT, SCOTT!

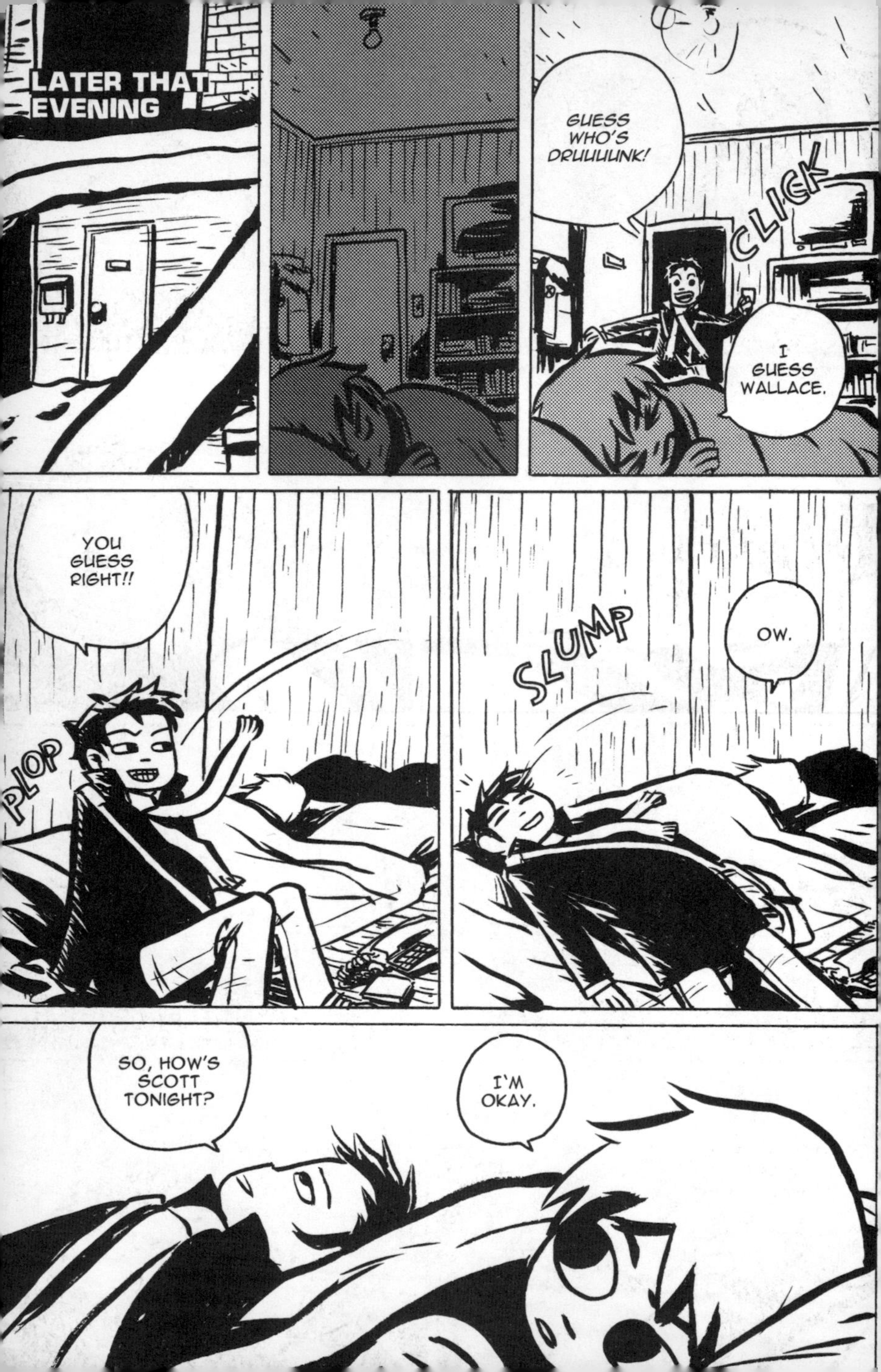
LATER THAT EVENING
GUESS WHO'S DRUUUUNK!
CLICK
I GUESS WALLACE.
YOU GUESS RIGHT!!
PLOP
SLUMP
OW.
SO, HOW'S SCOTT TONIGHT?
I'M OKAY.

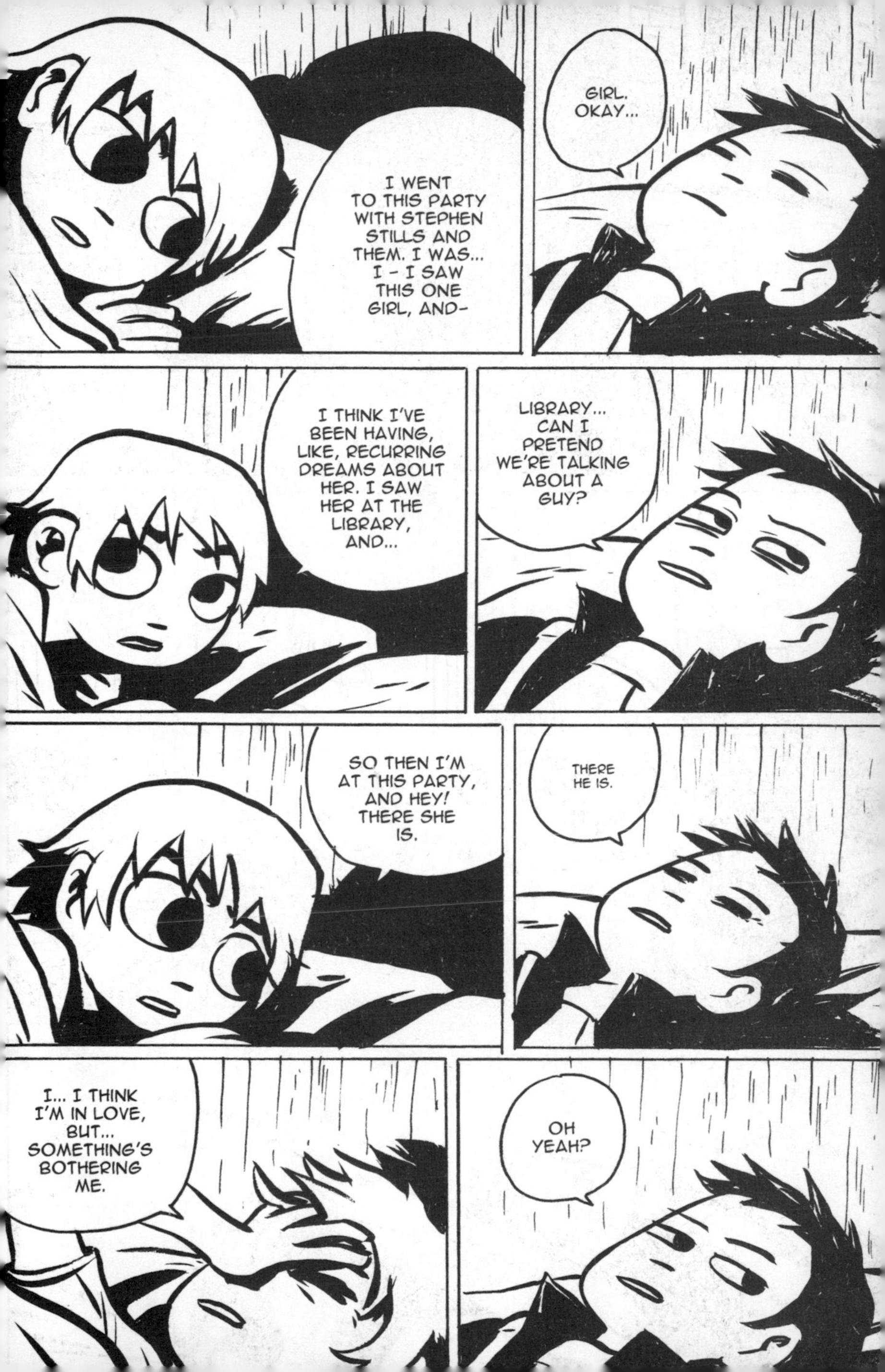
I WENT TO THIS PARTY WITH STEPHEN STILLS AND THEM. I WAS... I - I SAW THIS ONE GIRL, AND-
GIRL. OKAY...
I THINK I'VE BEEN HAVING, LIKE, RECURRING DREAMS ABOUT HER. I SAW HER AT THE LIBRARY, AND...
LIBRARY... CAN I PRETEND WE'RE TALKING ABOUT A GUY?
SO THEN I'M AT THIS PARTY, AND HEY! THERE SHE IS.
THERE HE IS.
I... I THINK I'M IN LOVE, BUT... SOMETHING'S BOTHERING ME.
OH YEAH?

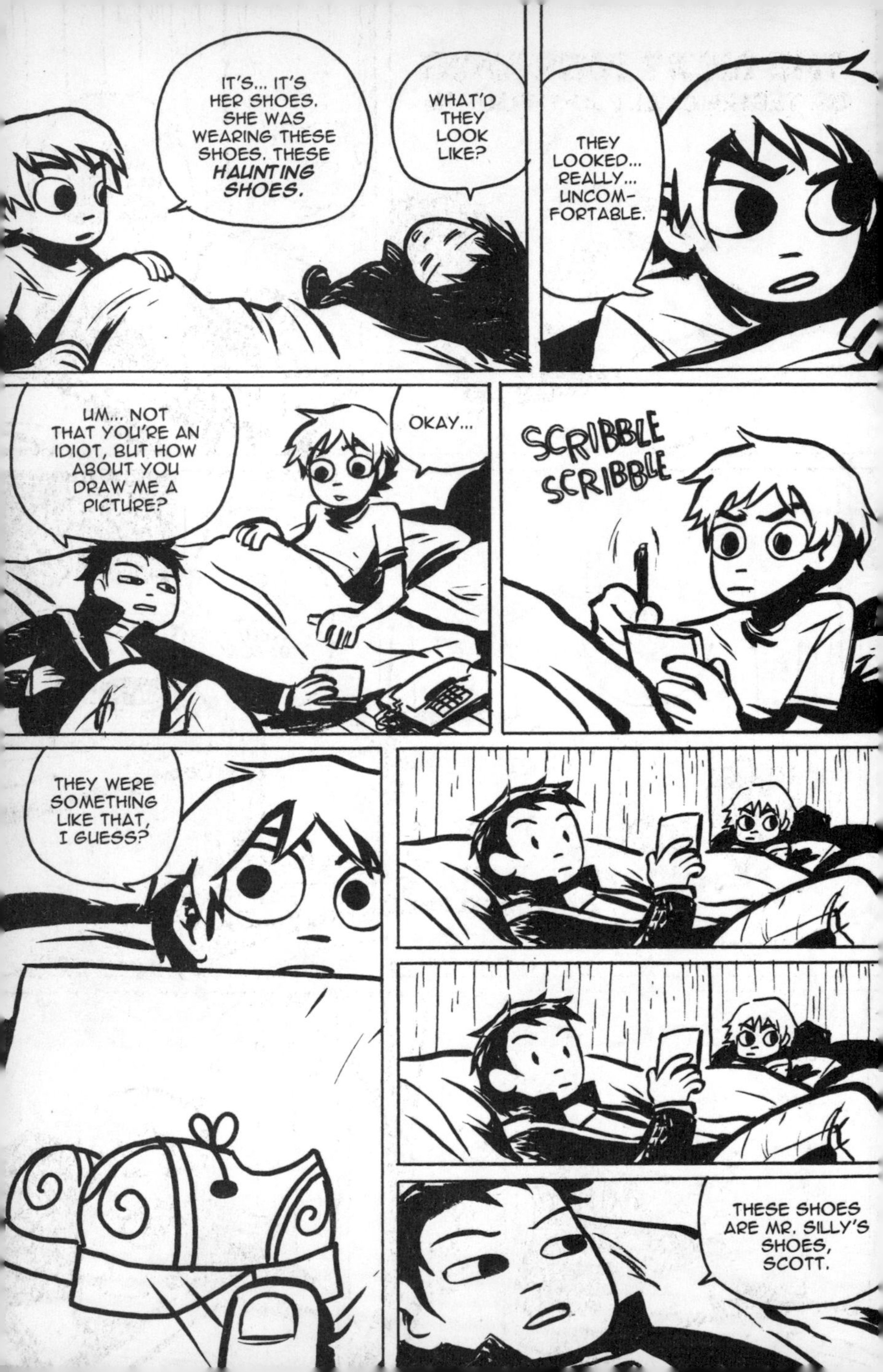
IT'S... IT'S HER SHOES. SHE WAS WEARING THESE SHOES. THESE ***HAUNTING SHOES.***
WHAT'D THEY LOOK LIKE?
THEY LOOKED... REALLY... UNCOM-FORTABLE.
UM... NOT THAT YOU'RE AN IDIOT, BUT HOW ABOUT YOU DRAW ME A PICTURE?
OKAY...
SCRIBBLE SCRIBBLE
THEY WERE SOMETHING LIKE THAT, I GUESS?
THESE SHOES ARE MR. SILLY'S SHOES, SCOTT.

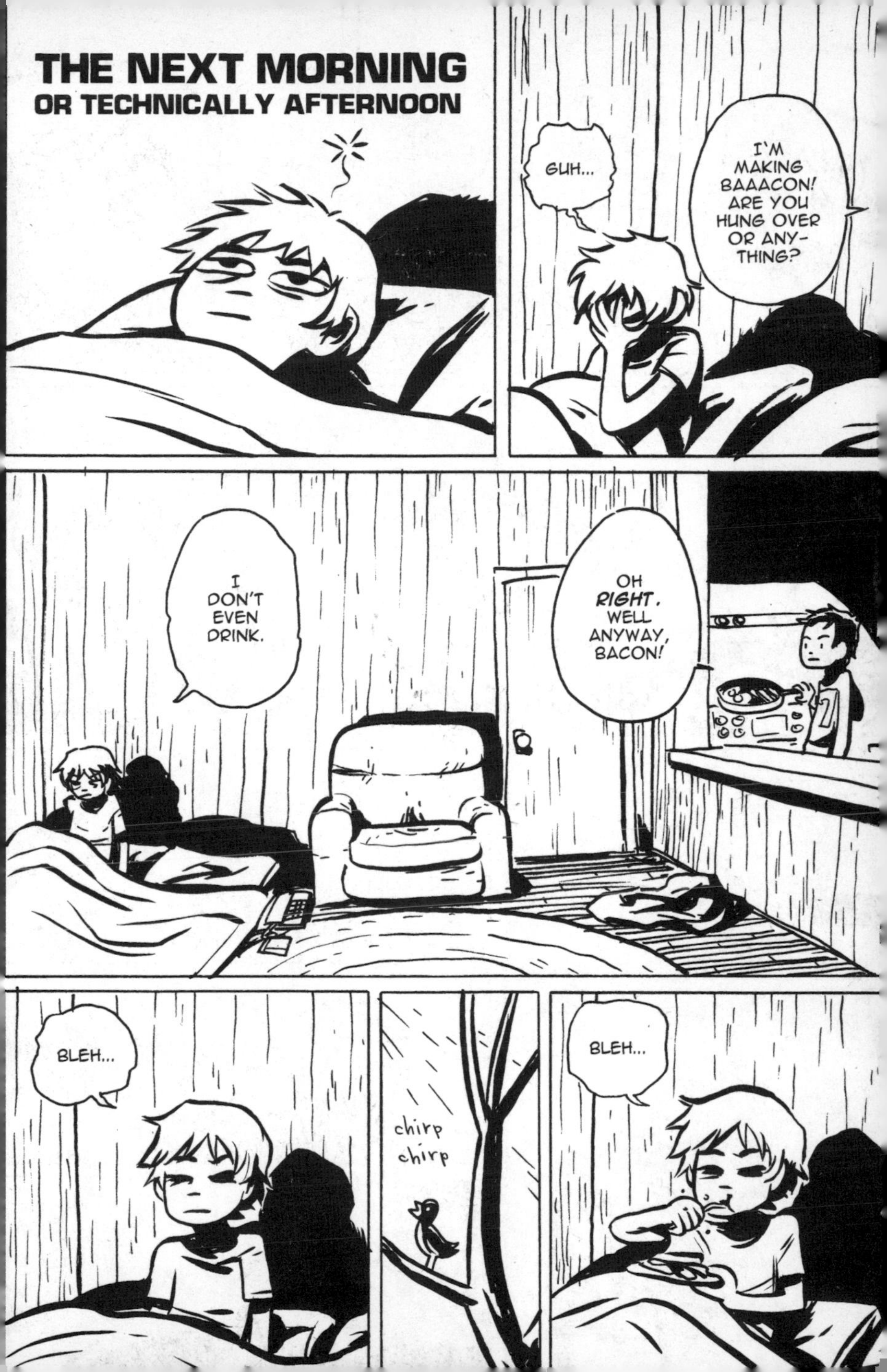
THE NEXT MORNING
OR TECHNICALLY AFTERNOON
GUH...
I'M MAKING BAAACON! ARE YOU HUNG OVER OR ANY-THING?
I DON'T EVEN DRINK.
OH RIGHT. WELL ANYWAY, BACON!
BLEH...
chirp chirp
BLEH...

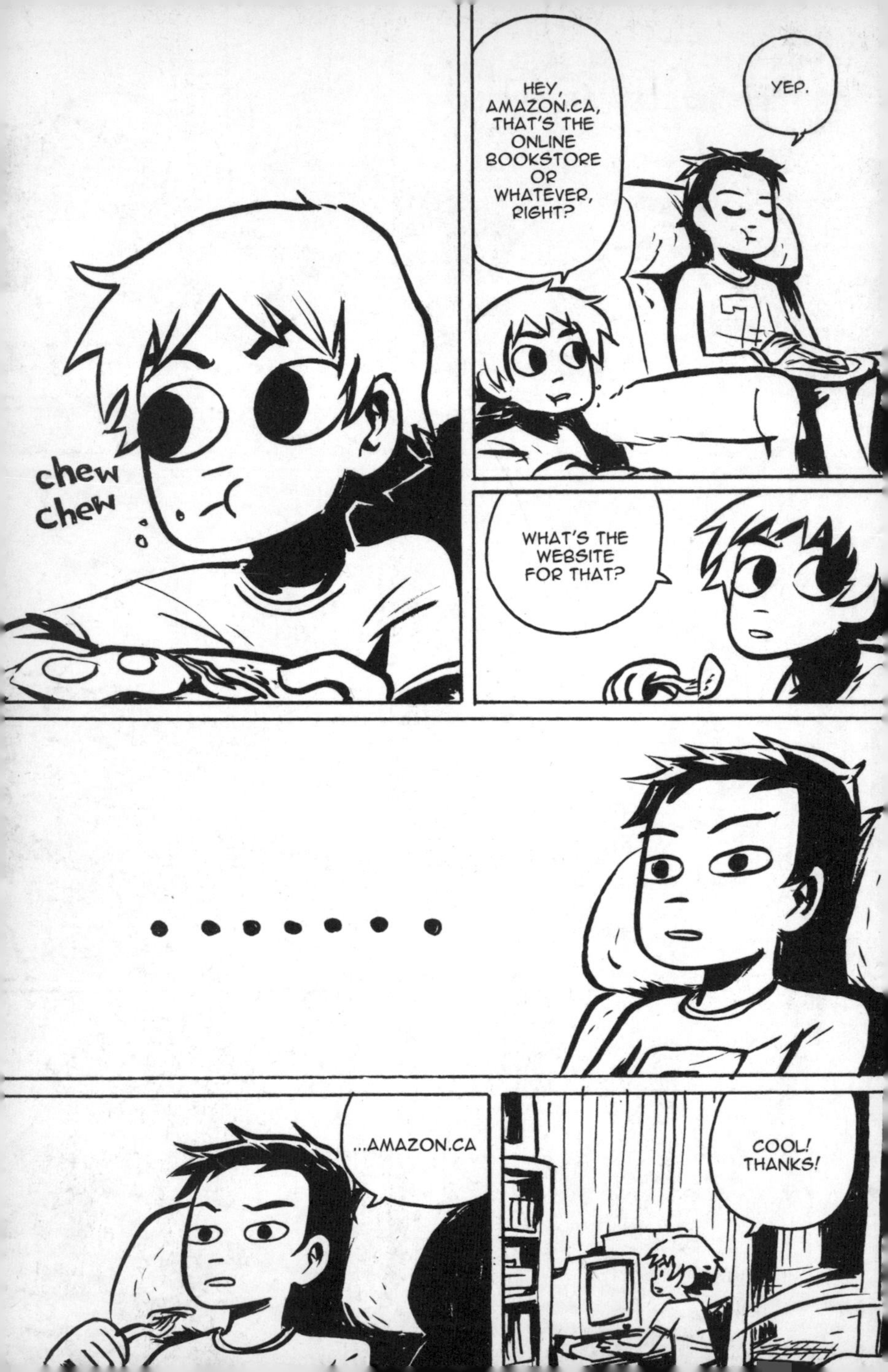
chew
chew
HEY, AMAZON.CA, THAT'S THE ONLINE BOOKSTORE OR WHATEVER, RIGHT?
YEP.
WHAT'S THE WEBSITE FOR THAT?
....
...AMAZON.CA
COOL! THANKS!

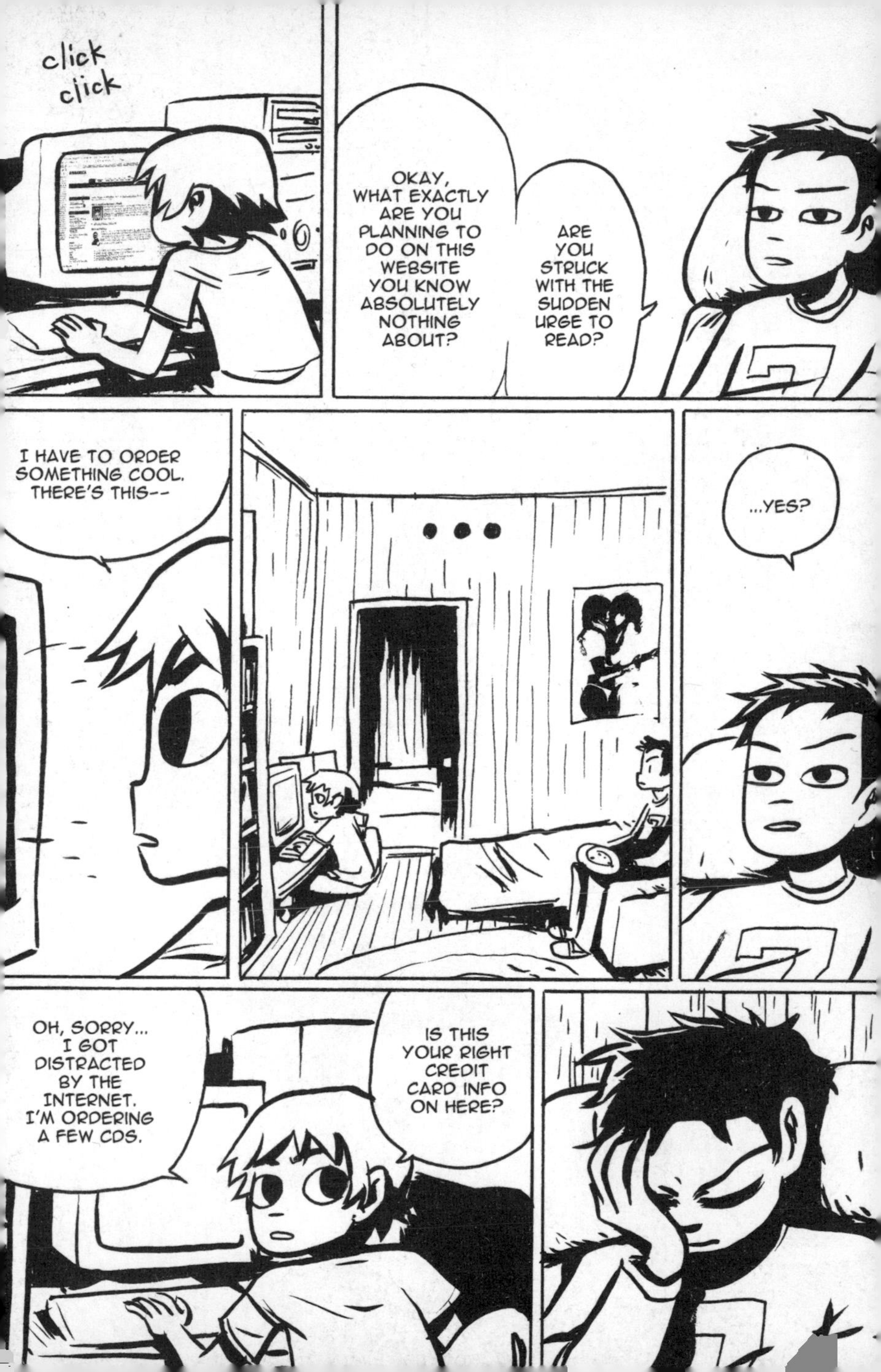
click click
OKAY, WHAT EXACTLY ARE YOU PLANNING TO DO ON THIS WEBSITE YOU KNOW ABSOLUTELY NOTHING ABOUT?
ARE YOU STRUCK WITH THE SUDDEN URGE TO READ?
I HAVE TO ORDER SOMETHING COOL. THERE'S THIS--
...YES?
OH, SORRY... I GOT DISTRACTED BY THE INTERNET. I'M ORDERING A FEW CDS.
IS THIS YOUR RIGHT CREDIT CARD INFO ON HERE?

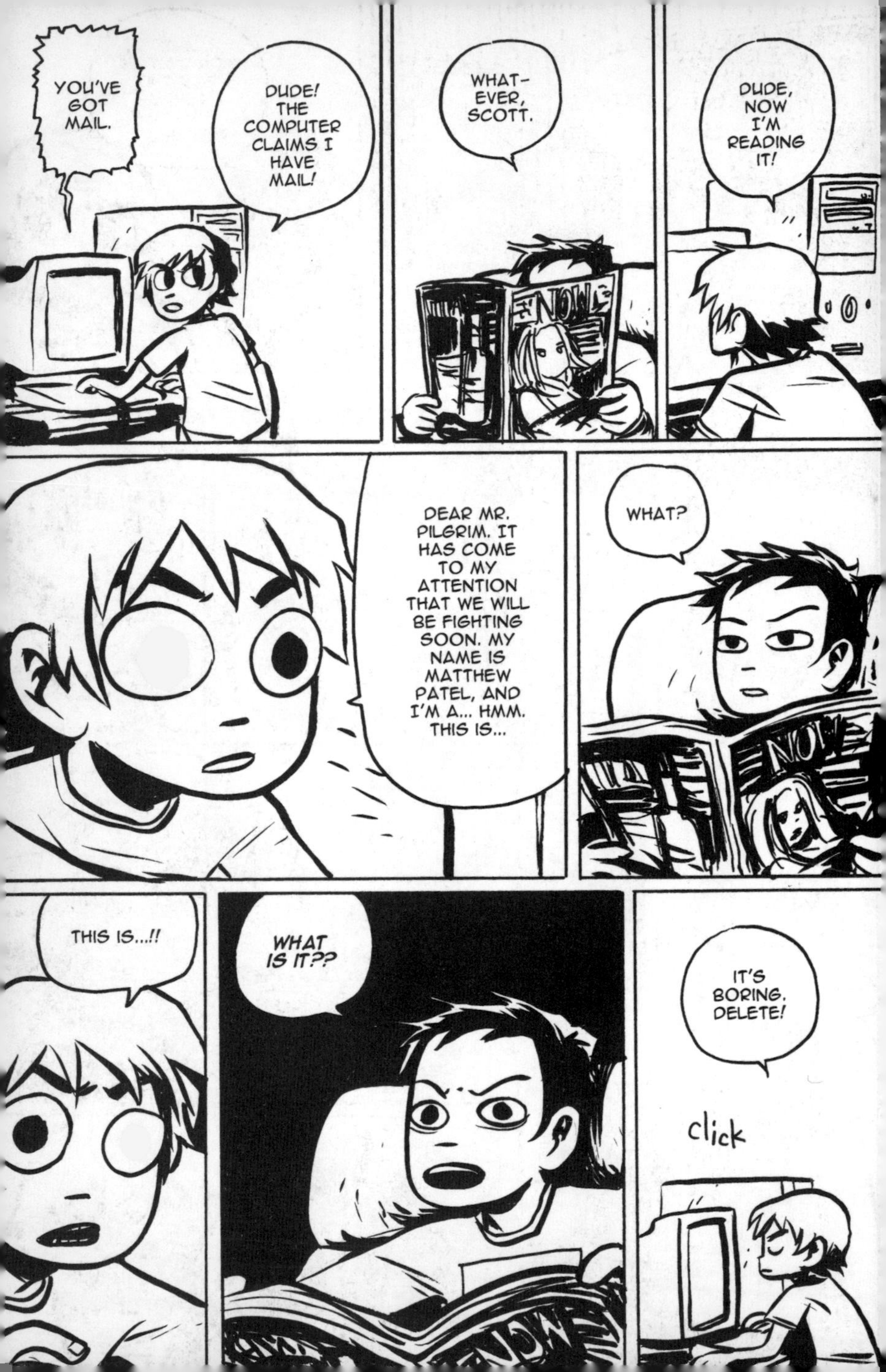
YOU'VE GOT MAIL.
DUDE! THE COMPUTER CLAIMS I HAVE MAIL!
WHAT-EVER, SCOTT.
DUDE, NOW I'M READING IT!
NOW
DEAR MR. PILGRIM. IT HAS COME TO MY ATTENTION THAT WE WILL BE FIGHTING SOON. MY NAME IS MATTHEW PATEL, AND I'M A... HMM. THIS IS...
WHAT?
NOW
THIS IS...!!
WHAT IS IT??
IT'S BORING. DELETE!
click

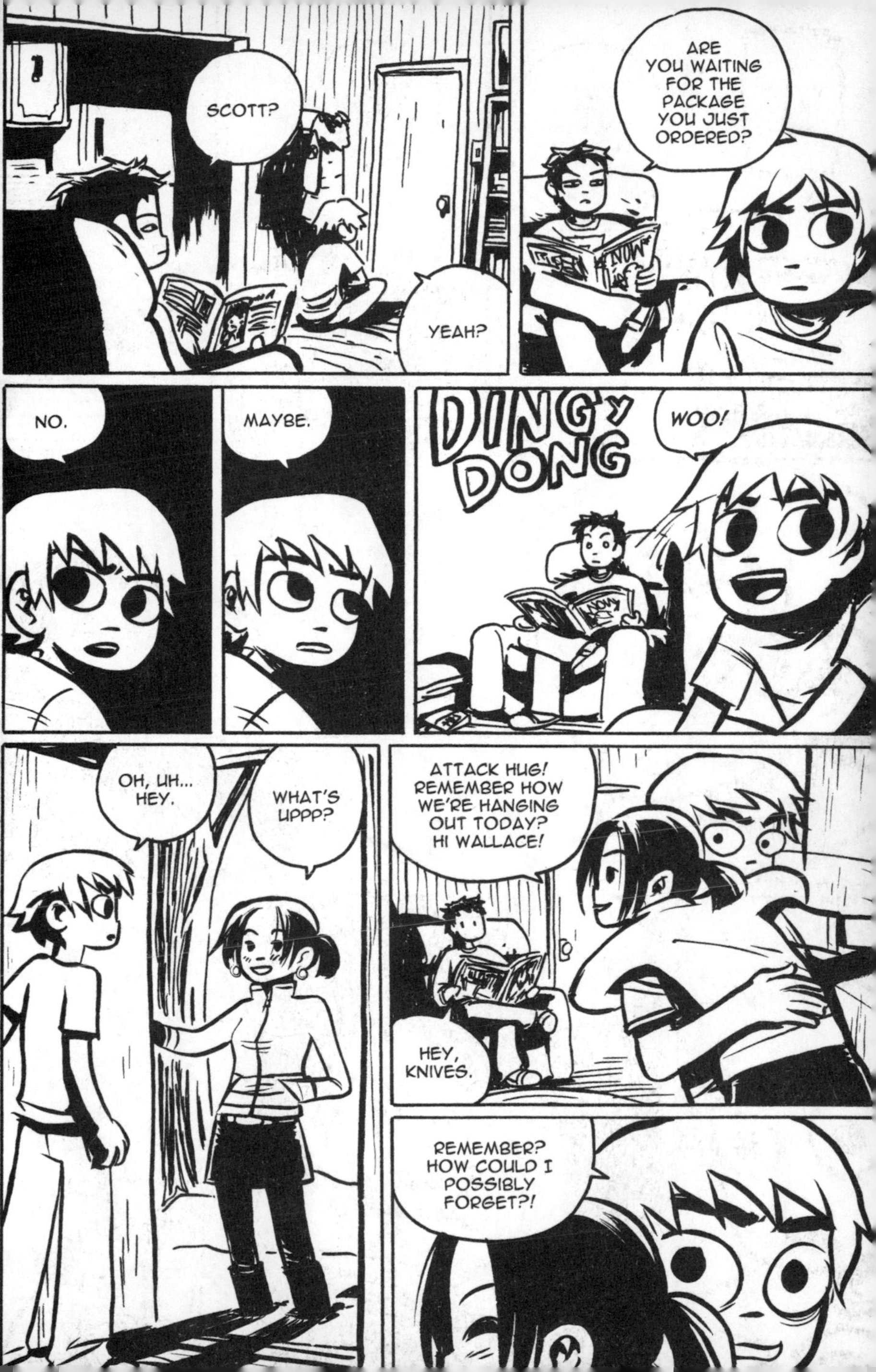
SCOTT?
YEAH?
ARE YOU WAITING FOR THE PACKAGE YOU JUST ORDERED?
NO.
MAYBE.
DING DONG
WOO!
OH, UH... HEY.
WHAT'S UPPP?
ATTACK HUG! REMEMBER HOW WE'RE HANGING OUT TODAY? HI WALLACE!
HEY, KNIVES.
REMEMBER? HOW COULD I POSSIBLY FORGET?!

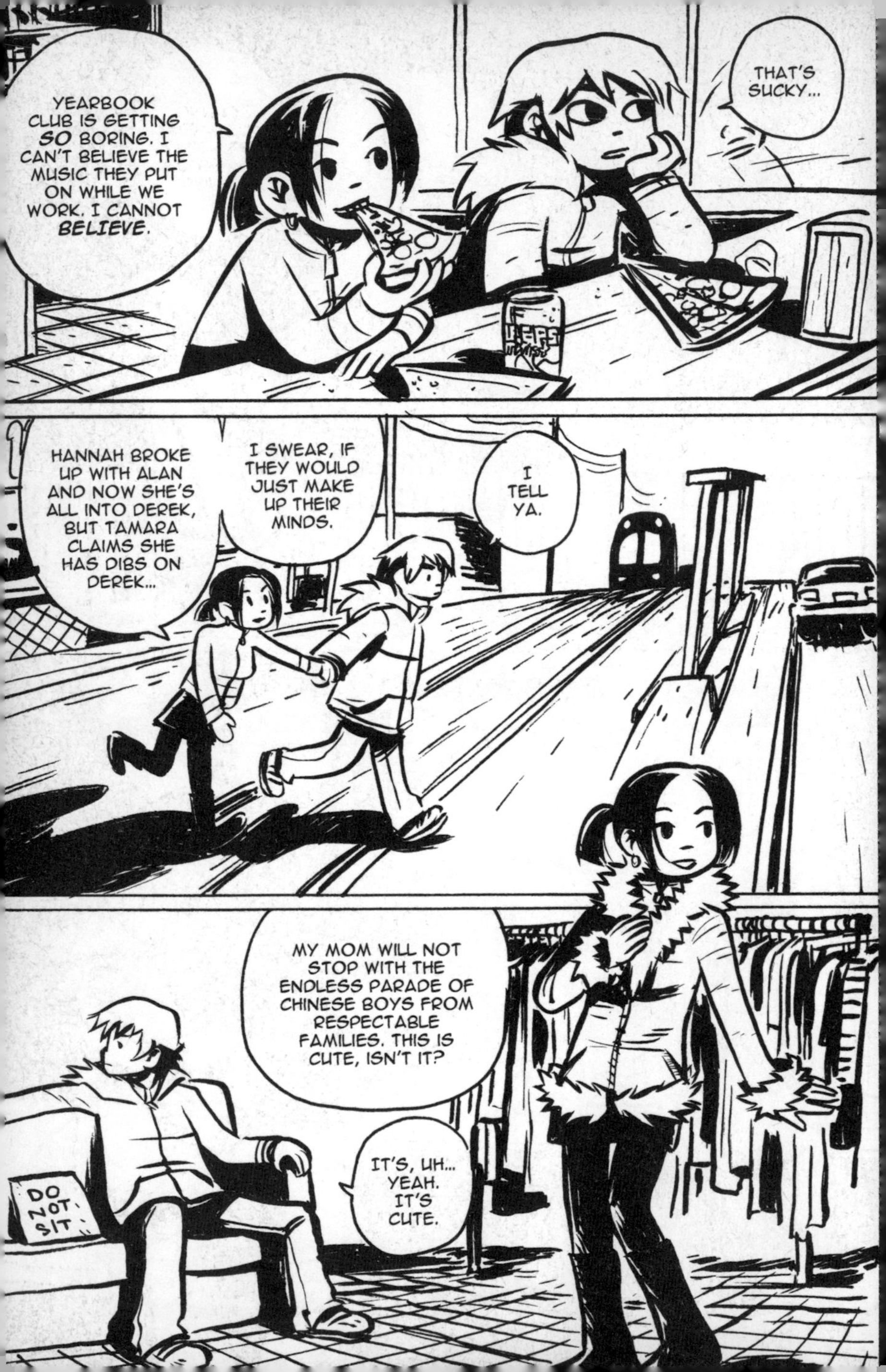
YEARBOOK CLUB IS GETTING SO BORING. I CAN'T BELIEVE THE MUSIC THEY PUT ON WHILE WE WORK. I CANNOT BELIEVE.
THAT'S SUCKY...
HANNAH BROKE UP WITH ALAN AND NOW SHE'S ALL INTO DEREK, BUT TAMARA CLAIMS SHE HAS DIBS ON DEREK...
I SWEAR, IF THEY WOULD JUST MAKE UP THEIR MINDS.
I TELL YA.
MY MOM WILL NOT STOP WITH THE ENDLESS PARADE OF CHINESE BOYS FROM RESPECTABLE FAMILIES. THIS IS CUTE, ISN'T IT?
DO NOT SIT
IT'S, UH... YEAH. IT'S CUTE.

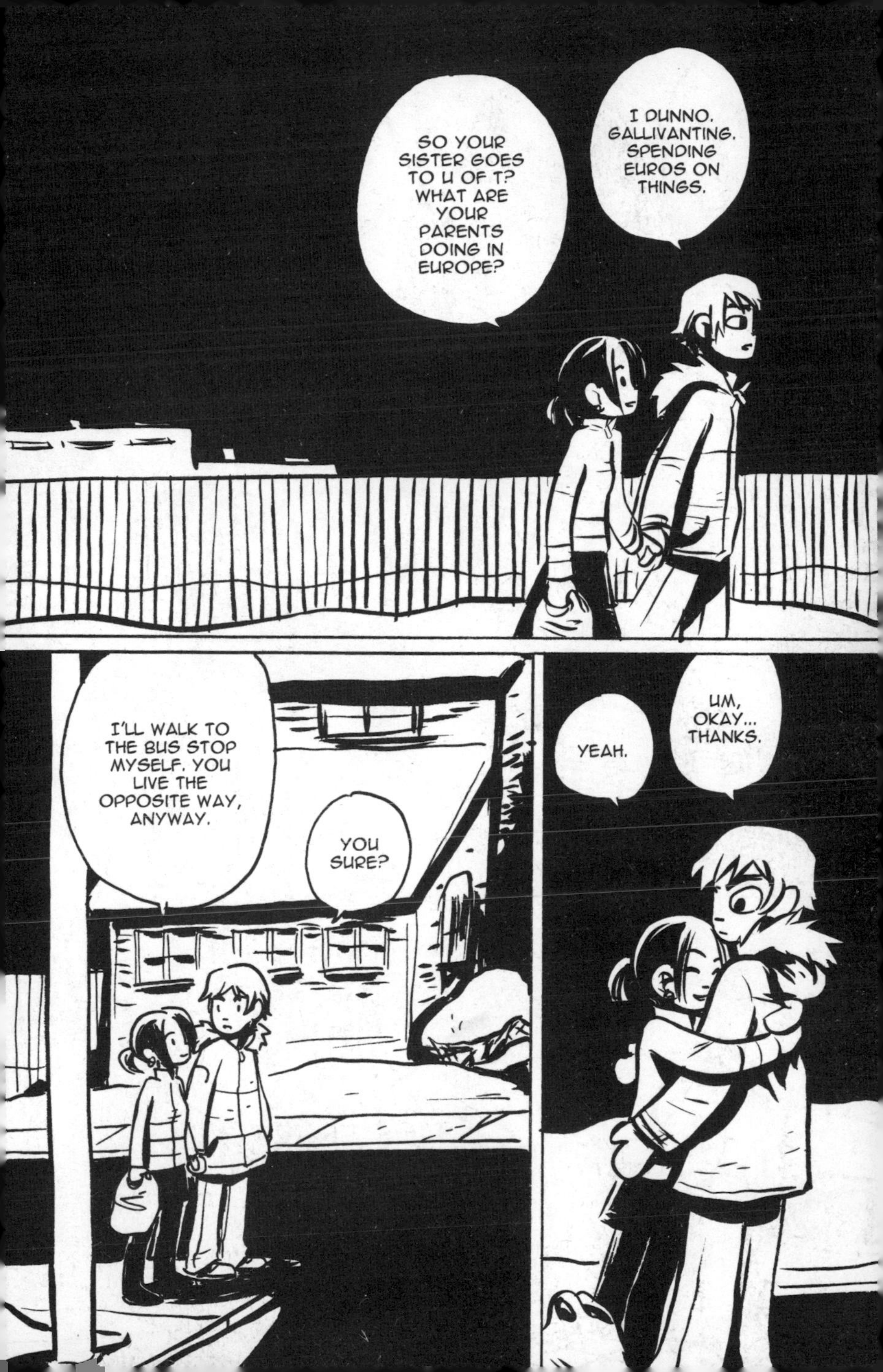
SO YOUR SISTER GOES TO U OF T? WHAT ARE YOUR PARENTS DOING IN EUROPE?
I DUNNO. GALLIVANTING. SPENDING EUROS ON THINGS.
I'LL WALK TO THE BUS STOP MYSELF. YOU LIVE THE OPPOSITE WAY, ANYWAY.
YOU SURE?
YEAH.
UM, OKAY... THANKS.

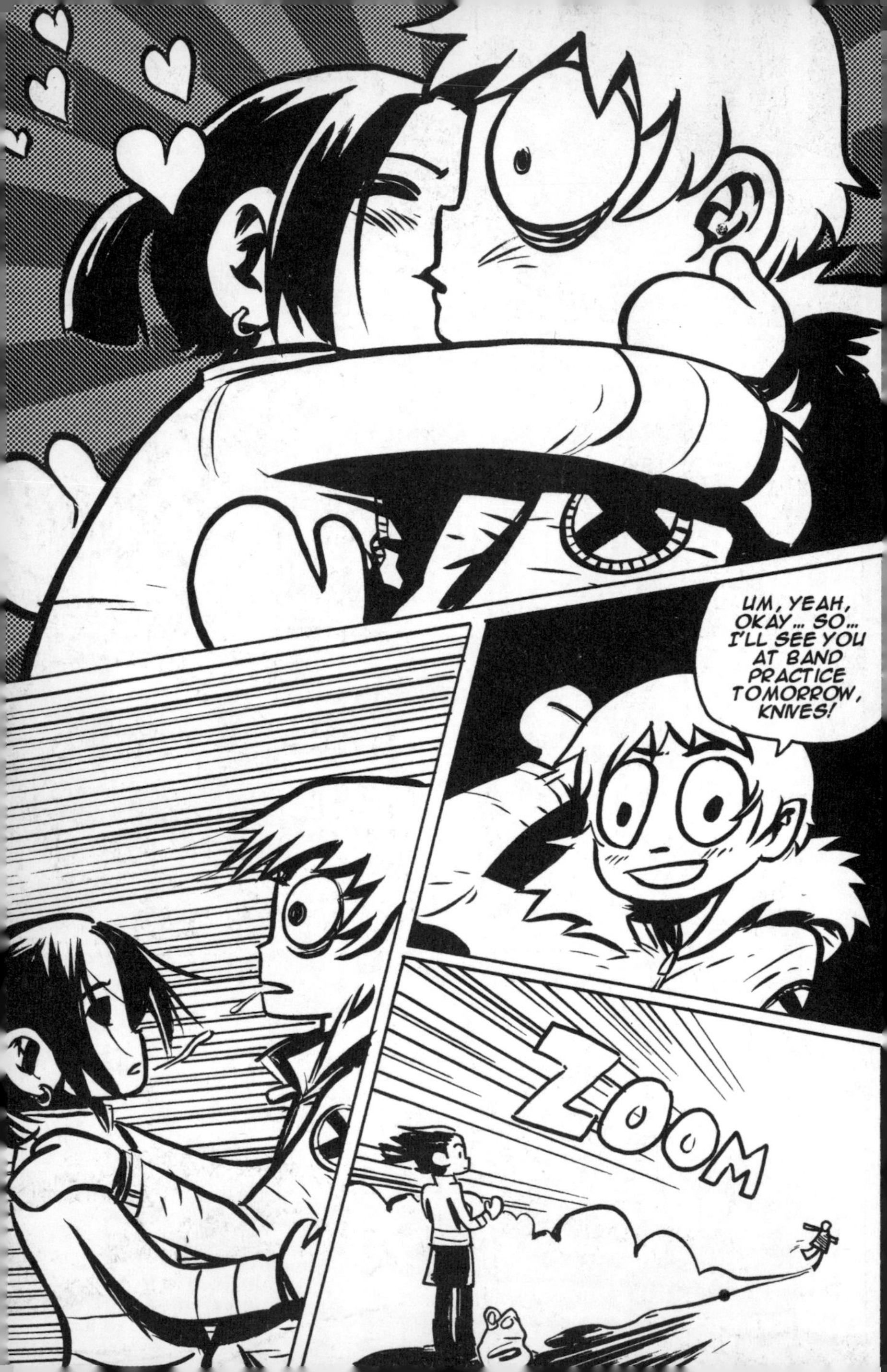
UM, YEAH, OKAY... SO... I'LL SEE YOU AT BAND PRACTICE TOMORROW, KNIVES!
ZOOM

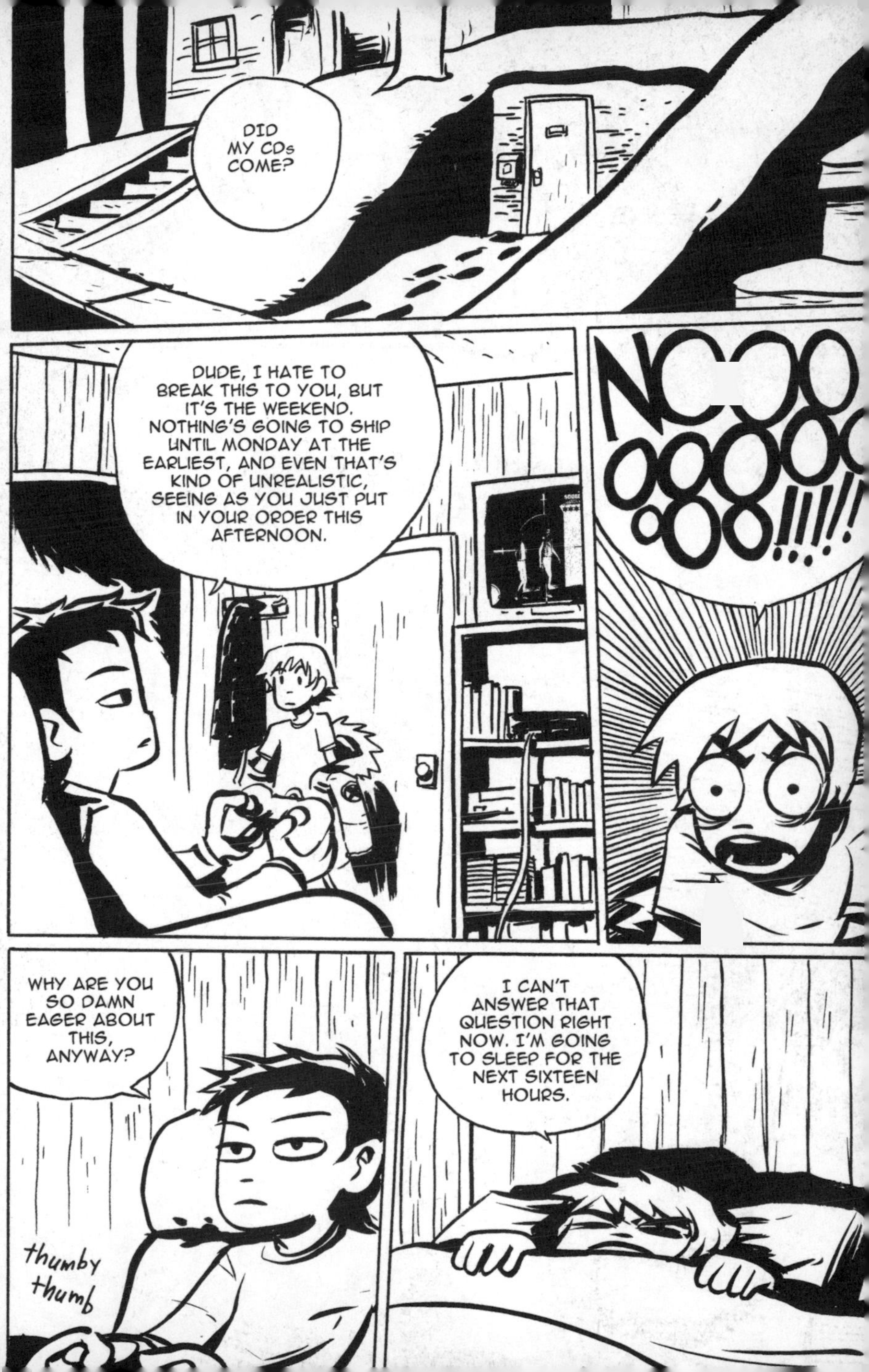
DID MY CDs COME?
DUDE, I HATE TO BREAK THIS TO YOU, BUT IT'S THE WEEKEND. NOTHING'S GOING TO SHIP UNTIL MONDAY AT THE EARLIEST, AND EVEN THAT'S KIND OF UNREALISTIC, SEEING AS YOU JUST PUT IN YOUR ORDER THIS AFTERNOON.
NOOOOOOOOOOOO!!!!!
WHY ARE YOU SO DAMN EAGER ABOUT THIS, ANYWAY?
thumby thumb
I CAN'T ANSWER THAT QUESTION RIGHT NOW. I'M GOING TO SLEEP FOR THE NEXT SIXTEEN HOURS.

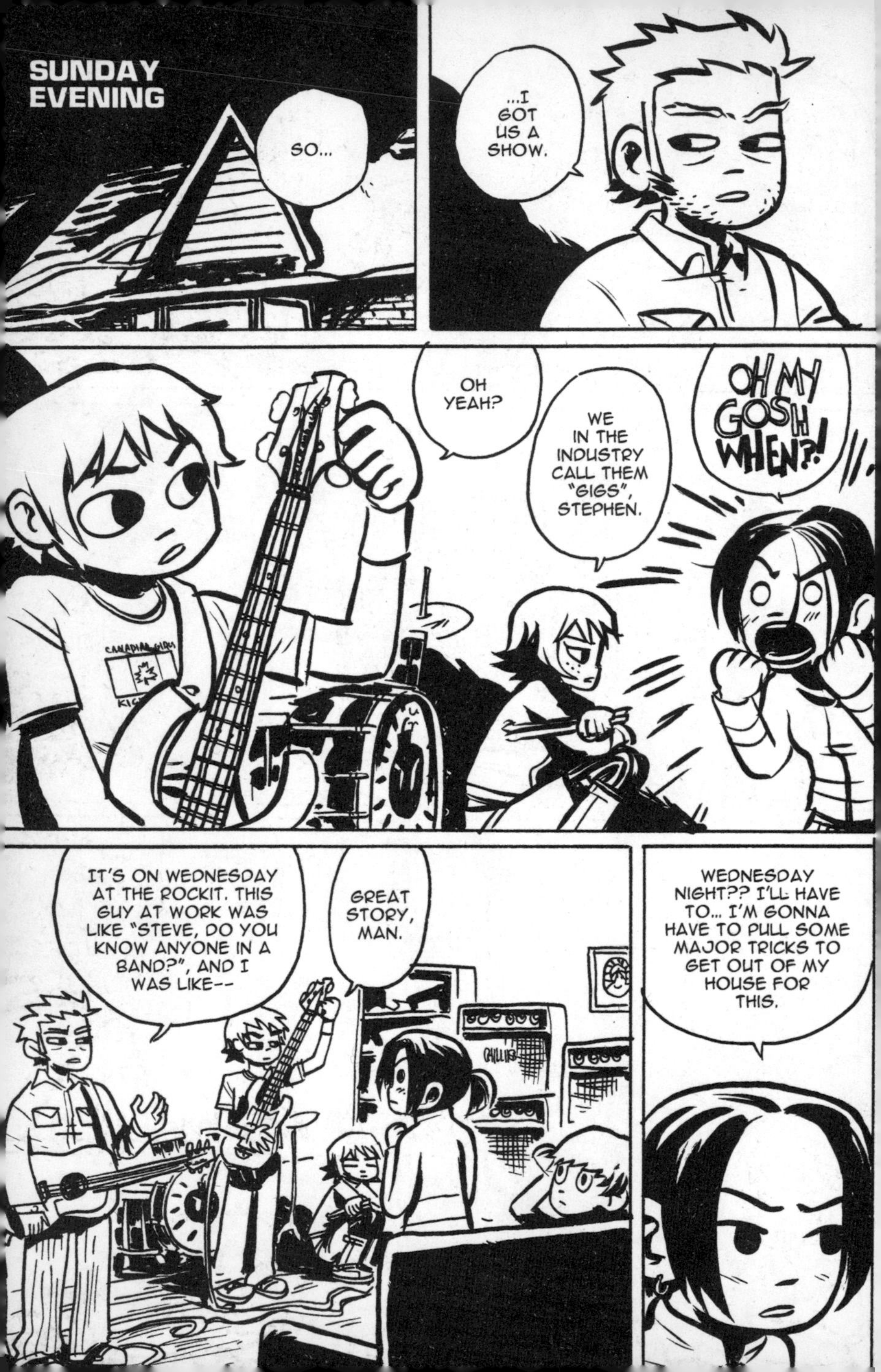
SUNDAY EVENING
SO...
...I GOT US A SHOW.
OH YEAH?
WE IN THE INDUSTRY CALL THEM "GIGS", STEPHEN.
OH MY GOSH WHEN?!
IT'S ON WEDNESDAY AT THE ROCKIT. THIS GUY AT WORK WAS LIKE "STEVE, DO YOU KNOW ANYONE IN A BAND?", AND I WAS LIKE--
GREAT STORY, MAN.
WEDNESDAY NIGHT?? I'LL HAVE TO... I'M GONNA HAVE TO PULL SOME MAJOR TRICKS TO GET OUT OF MY HOUSE FOR THIS.

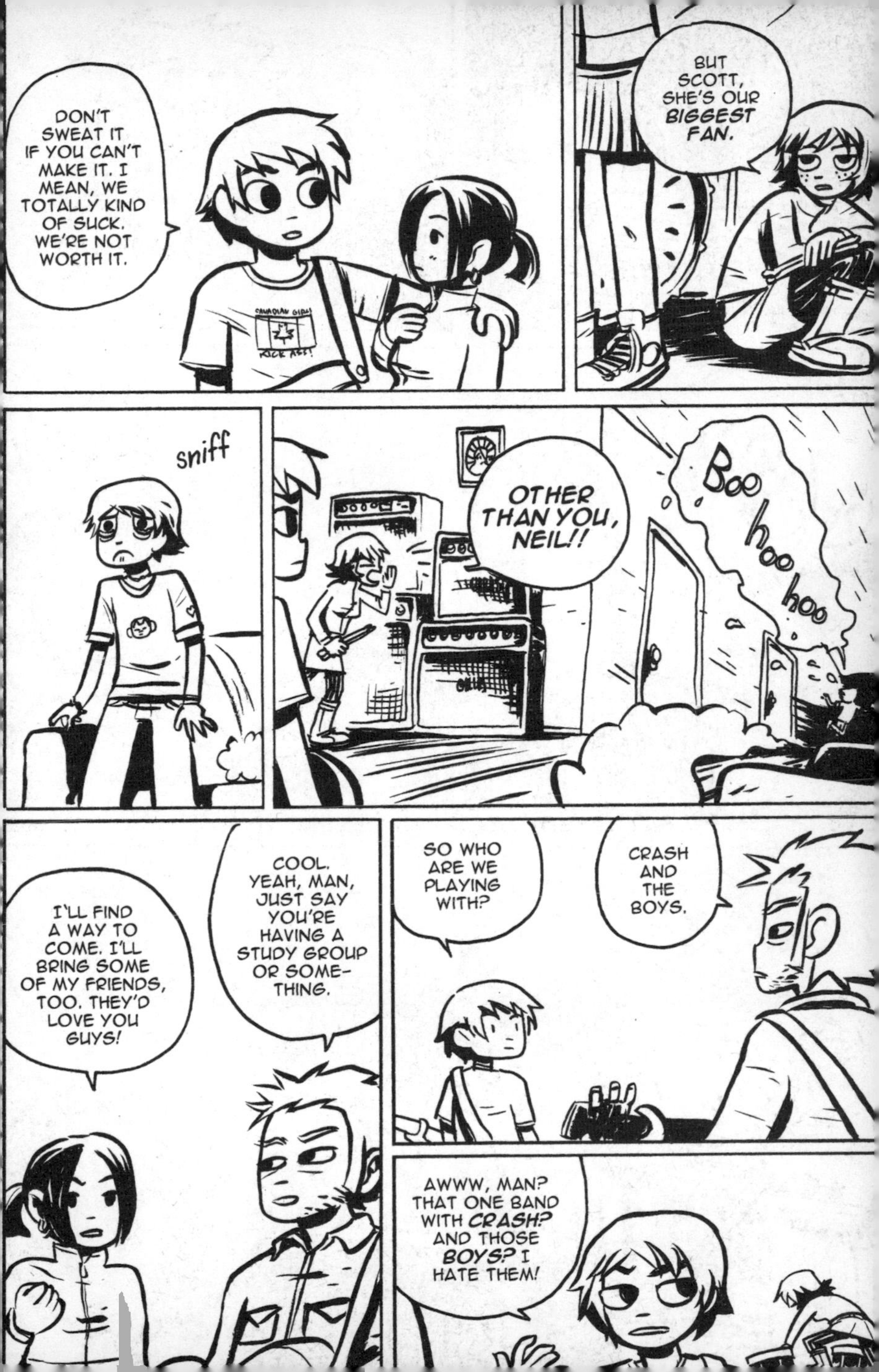
DON'T SWEAT IT IF YOU CAN'T MAKE IT. I MEAN, WE TOTALLY KIND OF SUCK. WE'RE NOT WORTH IT.
CANADIAN GIRLS KICK ASS!
BUT SCOTT, SHE'S OUR BIGGEST FAN.
sniff
OTHER THAN YOU, NEIL!!
Boo hoo hoo hoo
I'LL FIND A WAY TO COME. I'LL BRING SOME OF MY FRIENDS, TOO. THEY'D LOVE YOU GUYS!
COOL. YEAH, MAN, JUST SAY YOU'RE HAVING A STUDY GROUP OR SOME-THING.
SO WHO ARE WE PLAYING WITH?
CRASH AND THE BOYS.
AWWW, MAN? THAT ONE BAND WITH CRASH? AND THOSE BOYS? I HATE THEM!

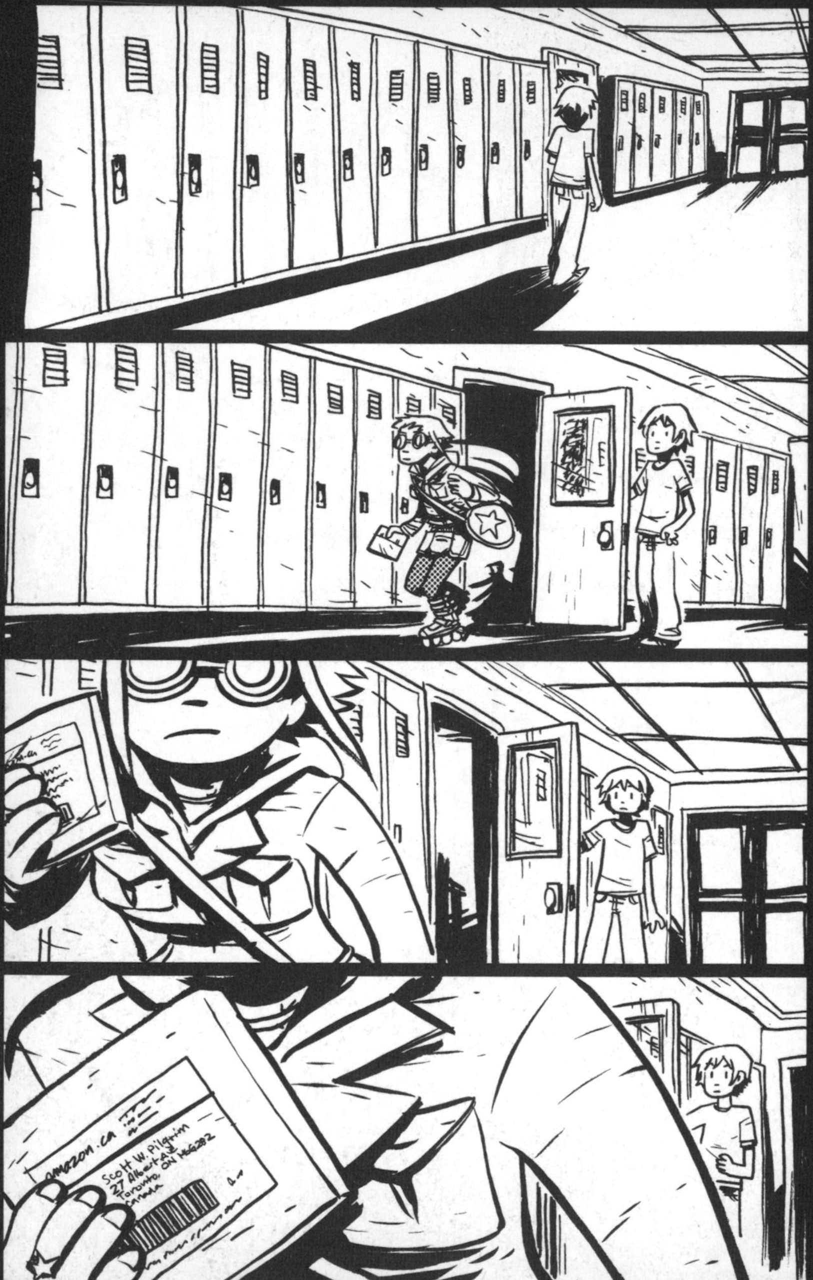
amazon.ca
Scott W. Pilgrim
27 Albert Ave
Toronto, ON M6G2B2
Canada

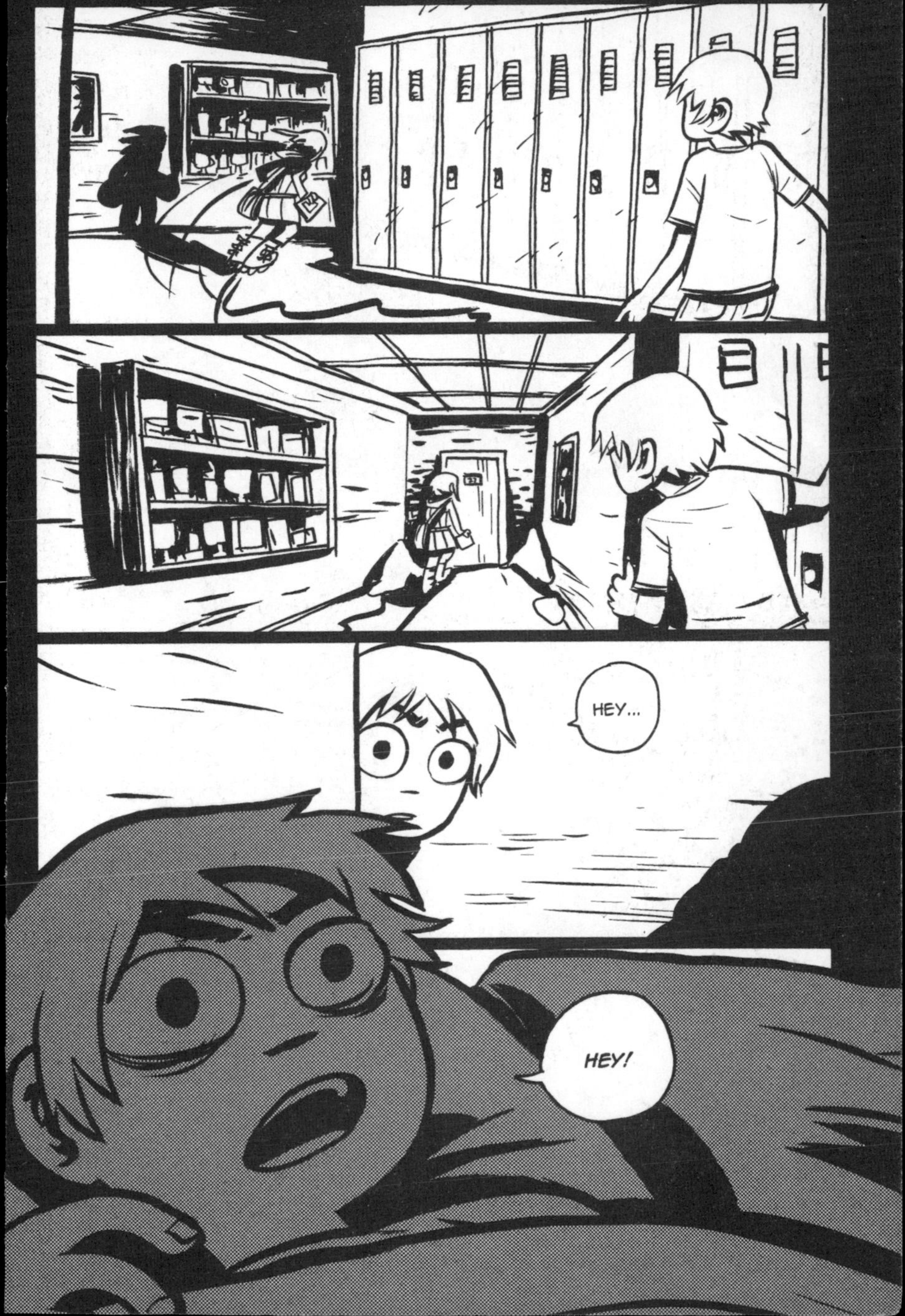
HEY...
HEY!

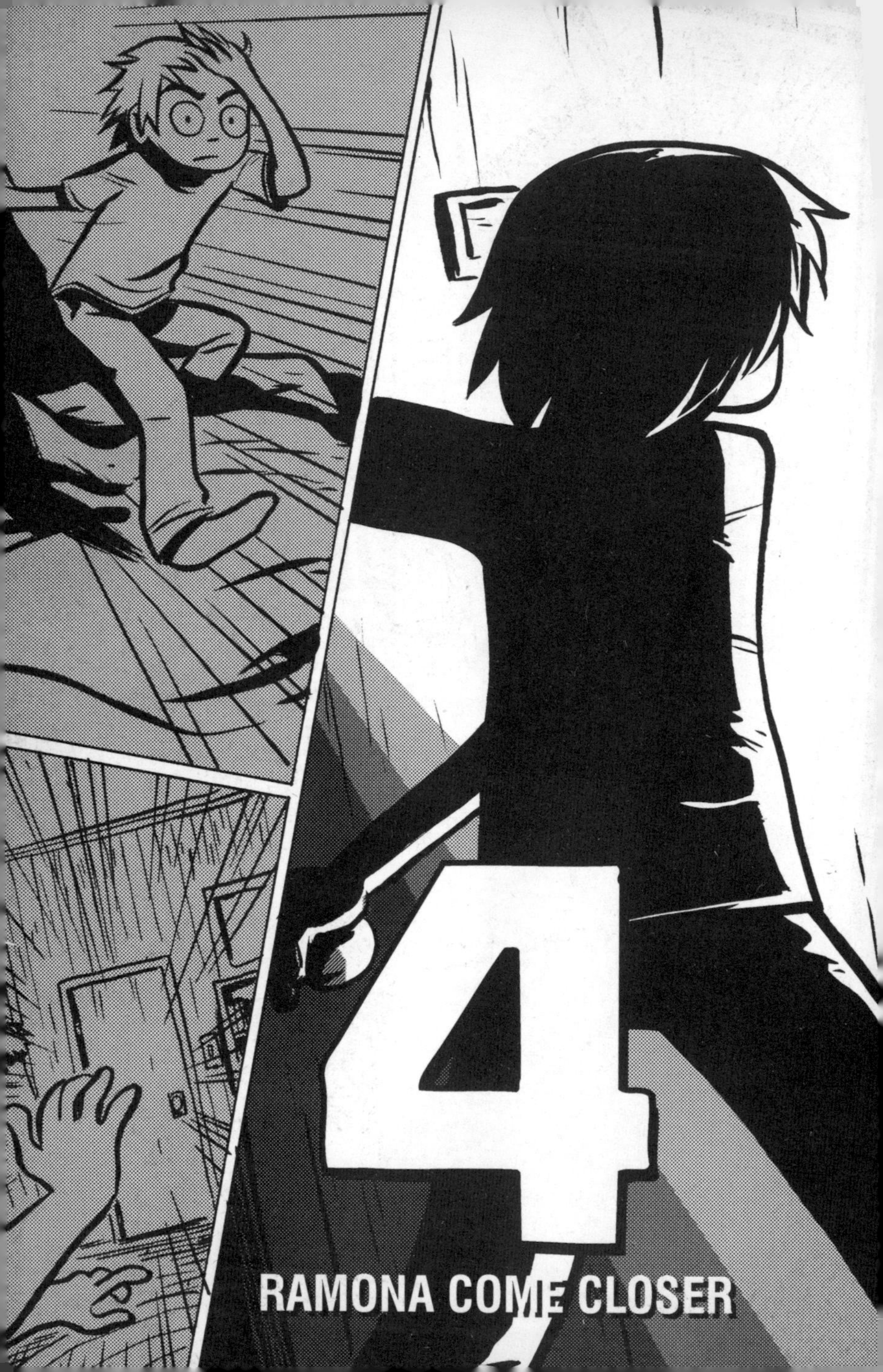
4
RAMONA COME CLOSER

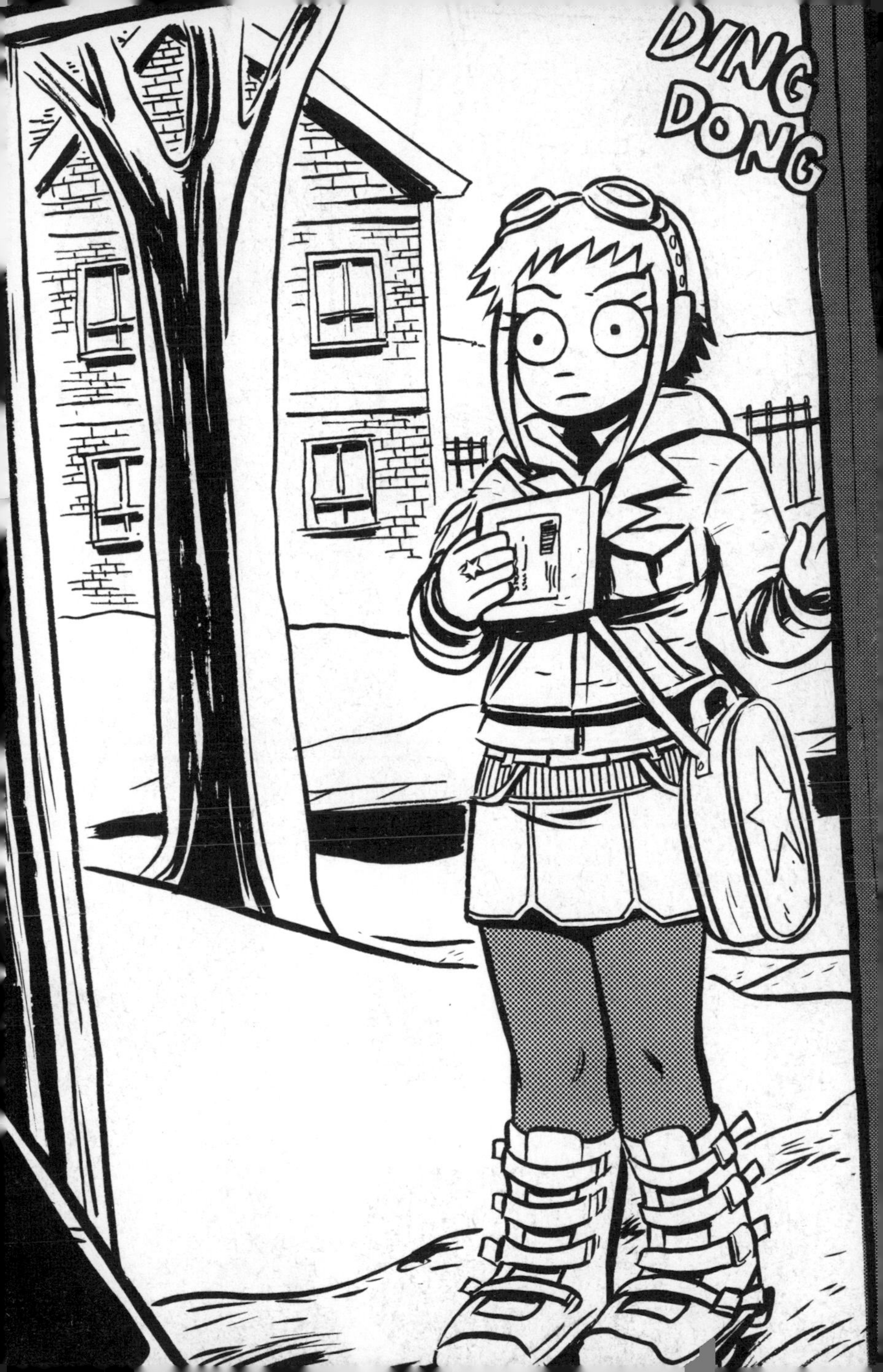
DING DONG

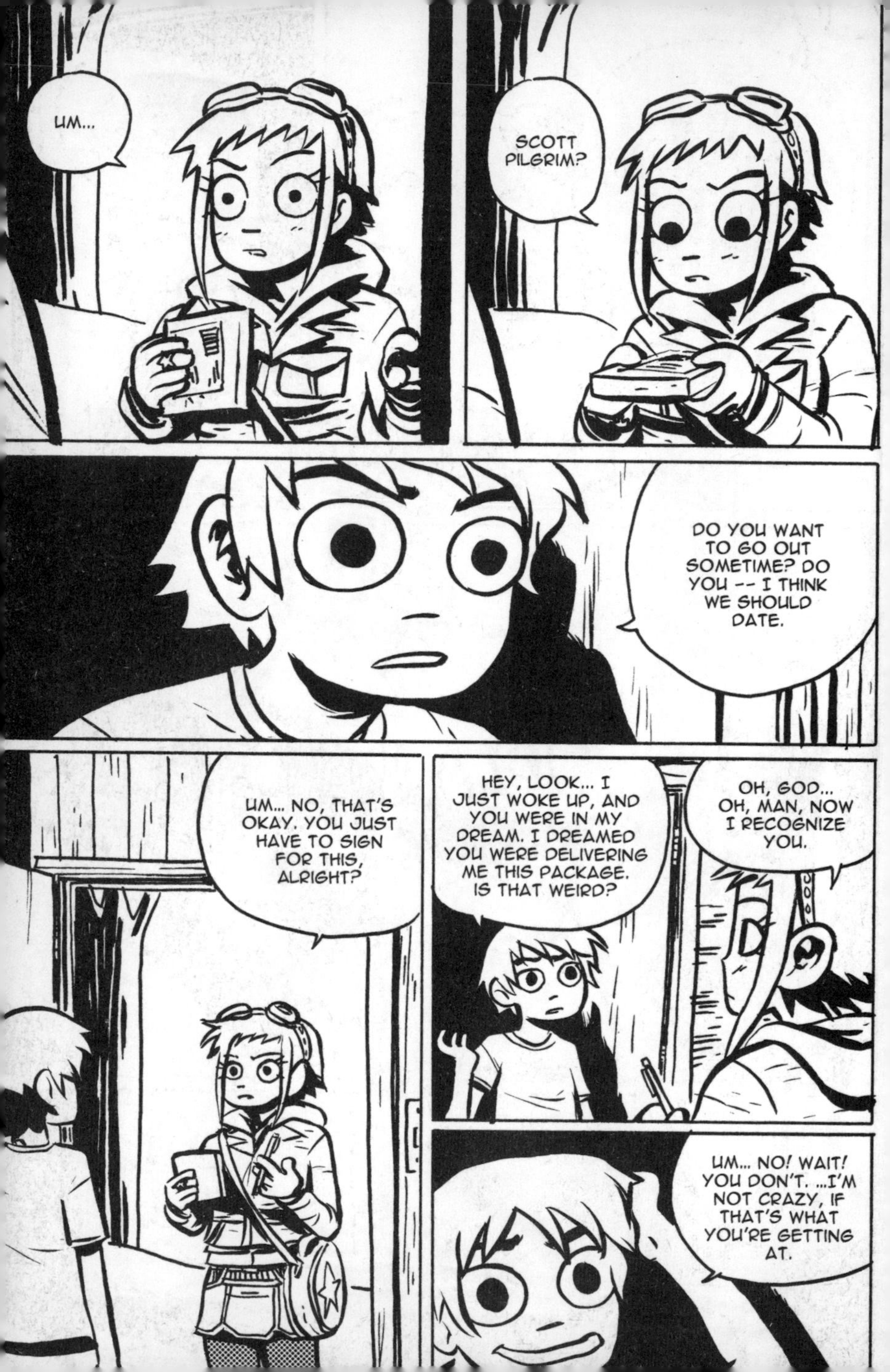
UM...
SCOTT PILGRIM?
DO YOU WANT TO GO OUT SOMETIME? DO YOU -- I THINK WE SHOULD DATE.
UM... NO, THAT'S OKAY. YOU JUST HAVE TO SIGN FOR THIS, ALRIGHT?
HEY, LOOK... I JUST WOKE UP, AND YOU WERE IN MY DREAM. I DREAMED YOU WERE DELIVERING ME THIS PACKAGE. IS THAT WEIRD?
OH, GOD... OH, MAN, NOW I RECOGNIZE YOU.
UM... NO! WAIT! YOU DON'T. ...I'M NOT CRAZY, IF THAT'S WHAT YOU'RE GETTING AT.

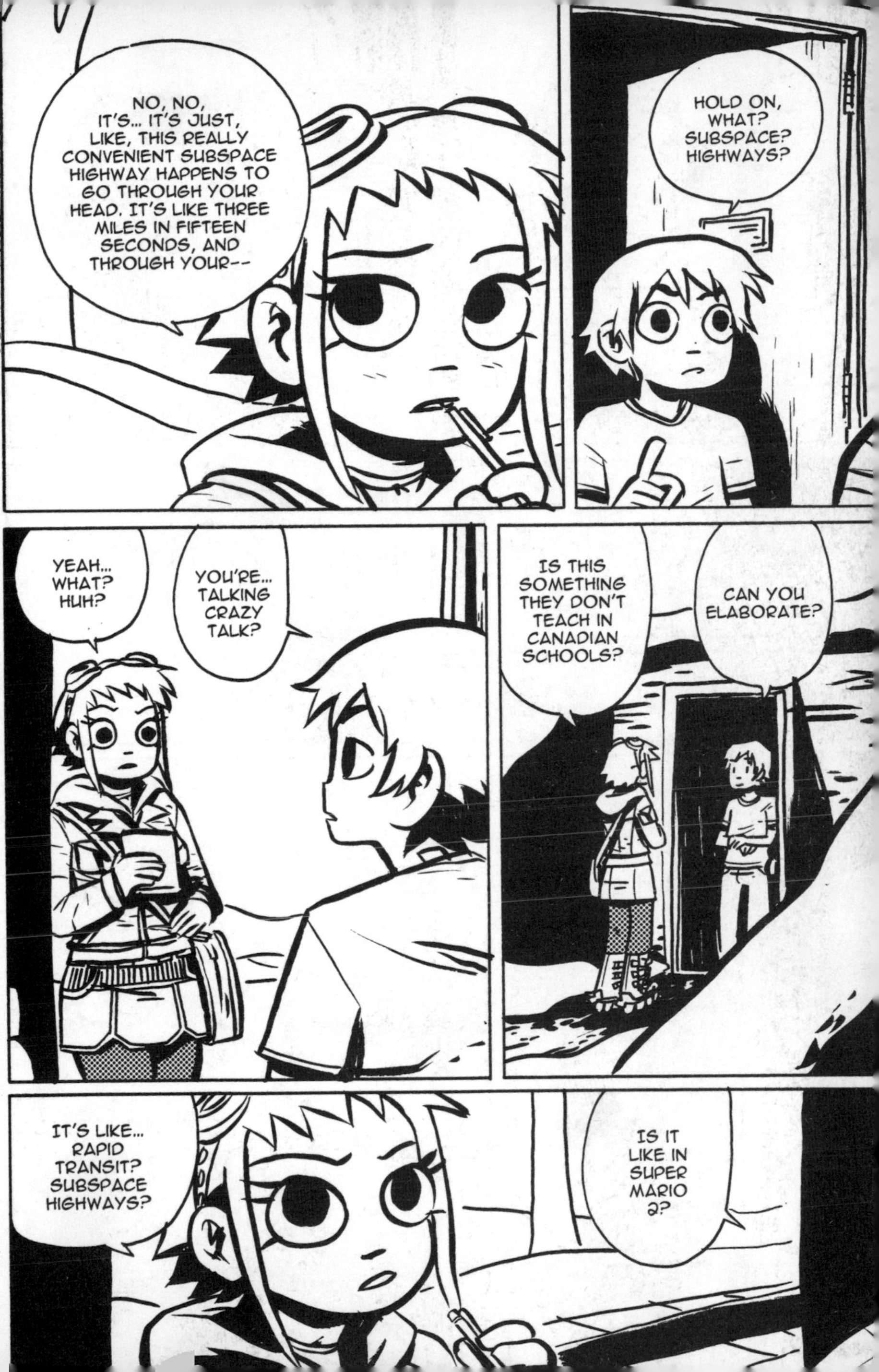
NO, NO, IT'S... IT'S JUST, LIKE, THIS REALLY CONVENIENT SUBSPACE HIGHWAY HAPPENS TO GO THROUGH YOUR HEAD. IT'S LIKE THREE MILES IN FIFTEEN SECONDS, AND THROUGH YOUR--
HOLD ON, WHAT? SUBSPACE? HIGHWAYS?
YEAH... WHAT? HUH?
YOU'RE... TALKING CRAZY TALK?
IS THIS SOMETHING THEY DON'T TEACH IN CANADIAN SCHOOLS?
CAN YOU ELABORATE?
IT'S LIKE... RAPID TRANSIT? SUBSPACE HIGHWAYS?
IS IT LIKE IN SUPER MARIO 2?

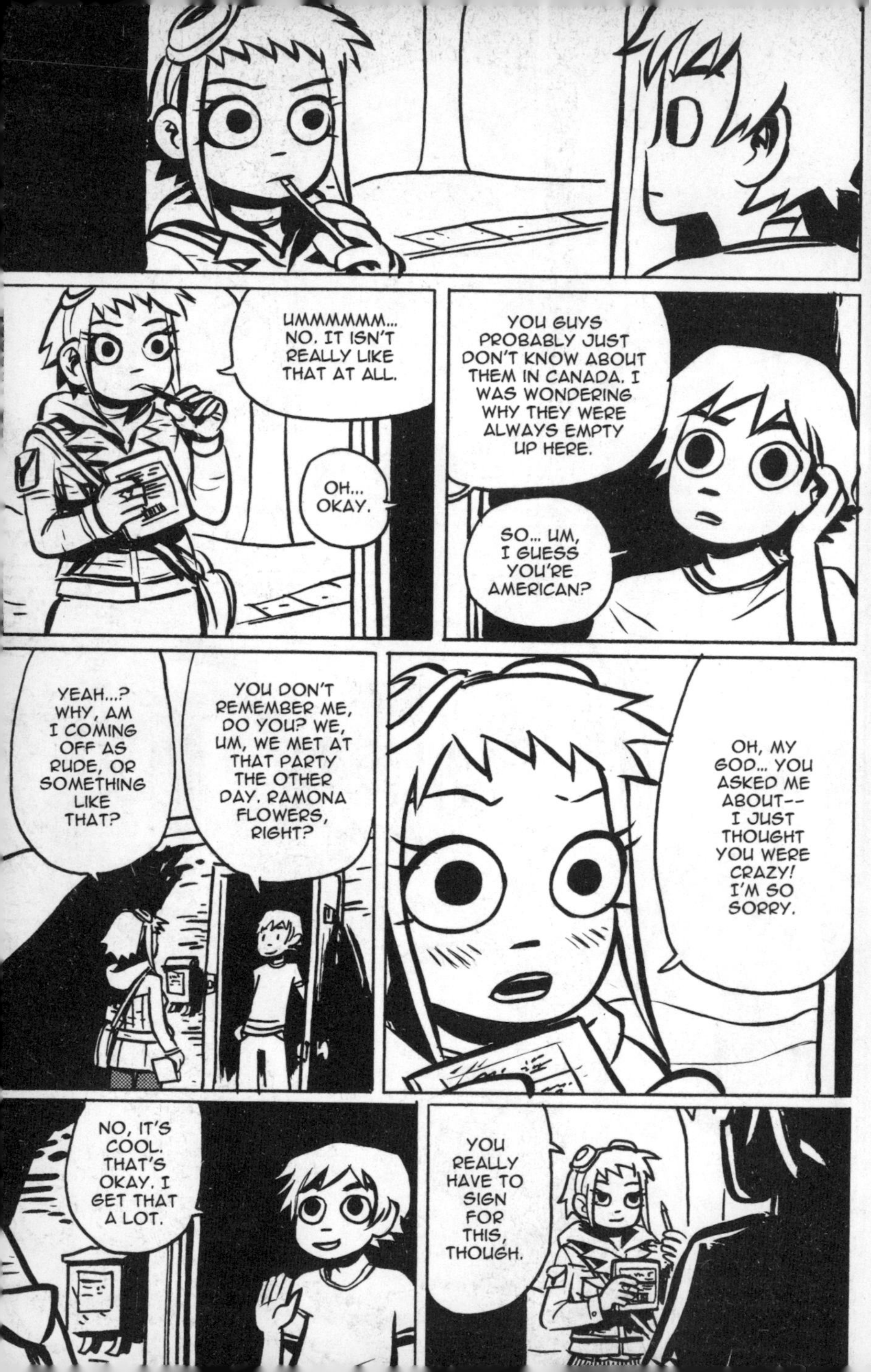
UMMMMMM... NO. IT ISN'T REALLY LIKE THAT AT ALL.
OH... OKAY.
YOU GUYS PROBABLY JUST DON'T KNOW ABOUT THEM IN CANADA. I WAS WONDERING WHY THEY WERE ALWAYS EMPTY UP HERE.
SO... UM, I GUESS YOU'RE AMERICAN?
YEAH...? WHY, AM I COMING OFF AS RUDE, OR SOMETHING LIKE THAT?
YOU DON'T REMEMBER ME, DO YOU? WE, UM, WE MET AT THAT PARTY THE OTHER DAY. RAMONA FLOWERS, RIGHT?
OH, MY GOD... YOU ASKED ME ABOUT-- I JUST THOUGHT YOU WERE CRAZY! I'M SO SORRY.
NO, IT'S COOL. THAT'S OKAY. I GET THAT A LOT.
YOU REALLY HAVE TO SIGN FOR THIS, THOUGH.

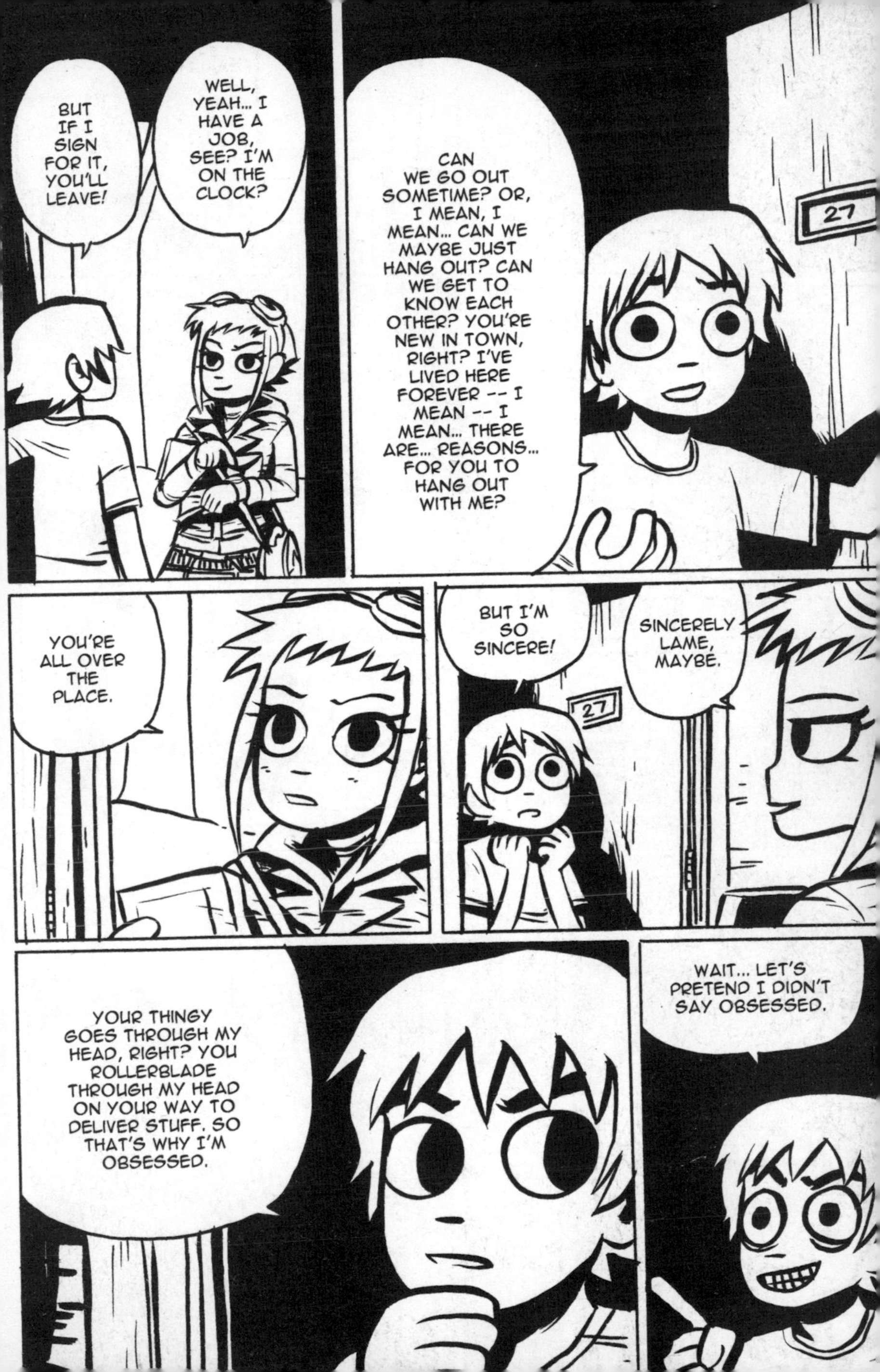
BUT IF I SIGN FOR IT, YOU'LL LEAVE!
WELL, YEAH... I HAVE A JOB, SEE? I'M ON THE CLOCK?
CAN WE GO OUT SOMETIME? OR, I MEAN, I MEAN... CAN WE MAYBE JUST HANG OUT? CAN WE GET TO KNOW EACH OTHER? YOU'RE NEW IN TOWN, RIGHT? I'VE LIVED HERE FOREVER -- I MEAN -- I MEAN... THERE ARE... REASONS... FOR YOU TO HANG OUT WITH ME?
27
YOU'RE ALL OVER THE PLACE.
BUT I'M SO SINCERE!
27
SINCERELY LAME, MAYBE.
YOUR THINGY GOES THROUGH MY HEAD, RIGHT? YOU ROLLERBLADE THROUGH MY HEAD ON YOUR WAY TO DELIVER STUFF. SO THAT'S WHY I'M OBSESSED.
WAIT... LET'S PRETEND I DIDN'T SAY OBSESSED.

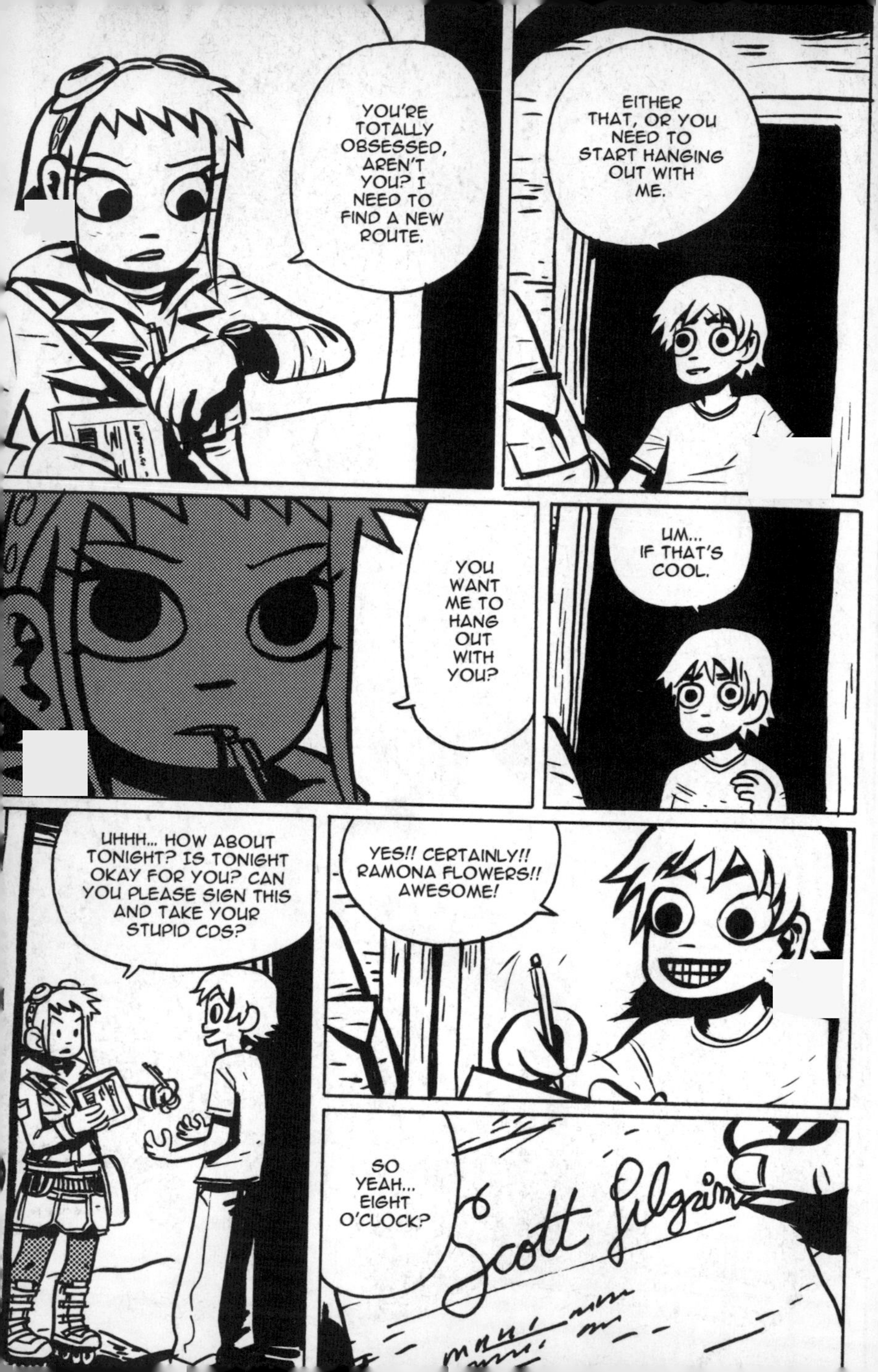
YOU'RE TOTALLY OBSESSED, AREN'T YOU? I NEED TO FIND A NEW ROUTE.
EITHER THAT, OR YOU NEED TO START HANGING OUT WITH ME.
YOU WANT ME TO HANG OUT WITH YOU?
UM... IF THAT'S COOL.
UHHH... HOW ABOUT TONIGHT? IS TONIGHT OKAY FOR YOU? CAN YOU PLEASE SIGN THIS AND TAKE YOUR STUPID CDS?
YES!! CERTAINLY!! RAMONA FLOWERS!! AWESOME!
SO YEAH... EIGHT O'CLOCK?
Scott Pilgrim

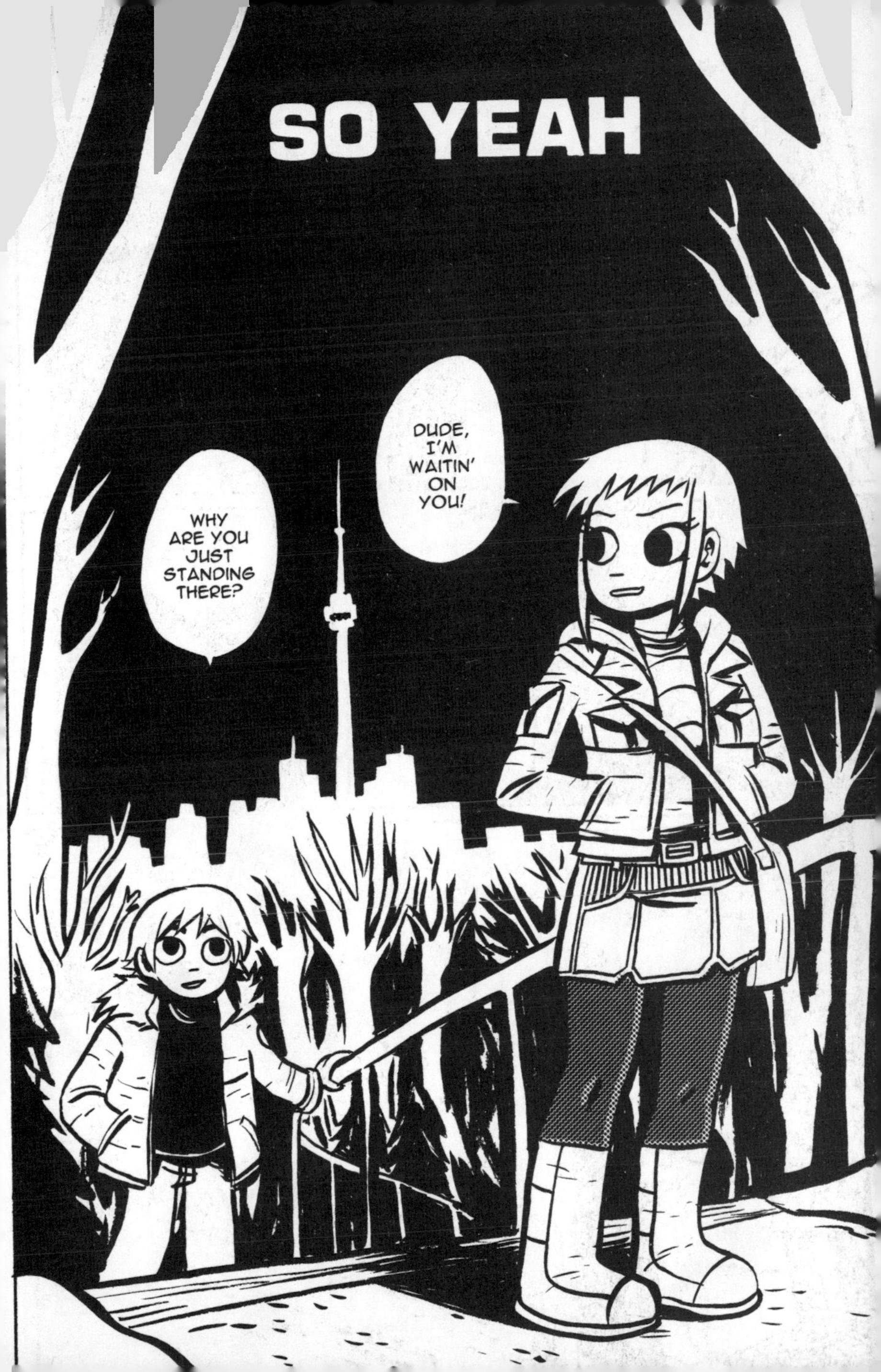
SO YEAH
WHY ARE YOU JUST STANDING THERE?
DUDE, I'M WAITIN' ON YOU!

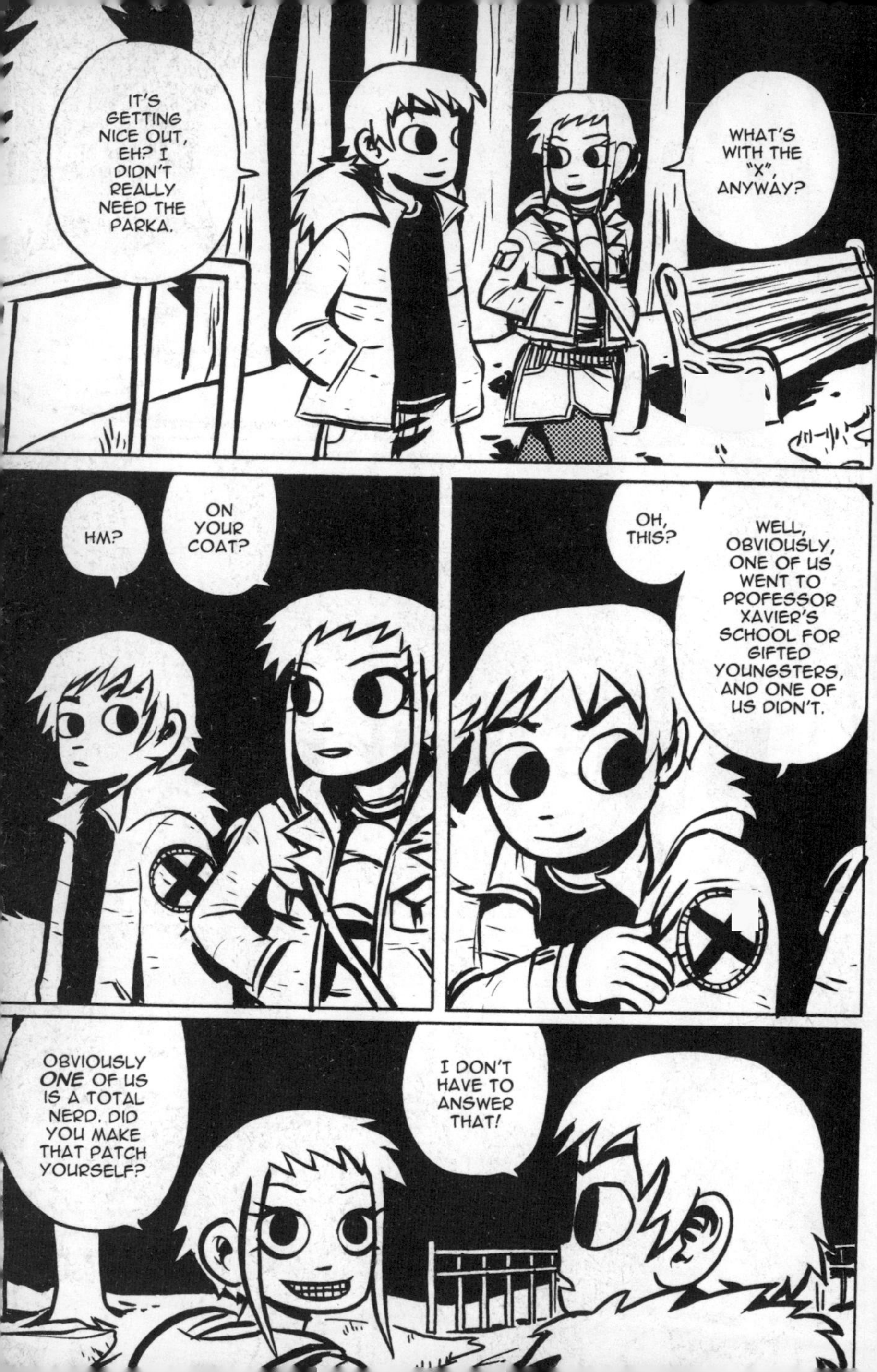
IT'S GETTING NICE OUT, EH? I DIDN'T REALLY NEED THE PARKA.
WHAT'S WITH THE "X", ANYWAY?
HM?
ON YOUR COAT?
OH, THIS?
WELL, OBVIOUSLY, ONE OF US WENT TO PROFESSOR XAVIER'S SCHOOL FOR GIFTED YOUNGSTERS, AND ONE OF US DIDN'T.
OBVIOUSLY *ONE* OF US IS A TOTAL NERD. DID YOU MAKE THAT PATCH YOURSELF?
I DON'T HAVE TO ANSWER THAT!

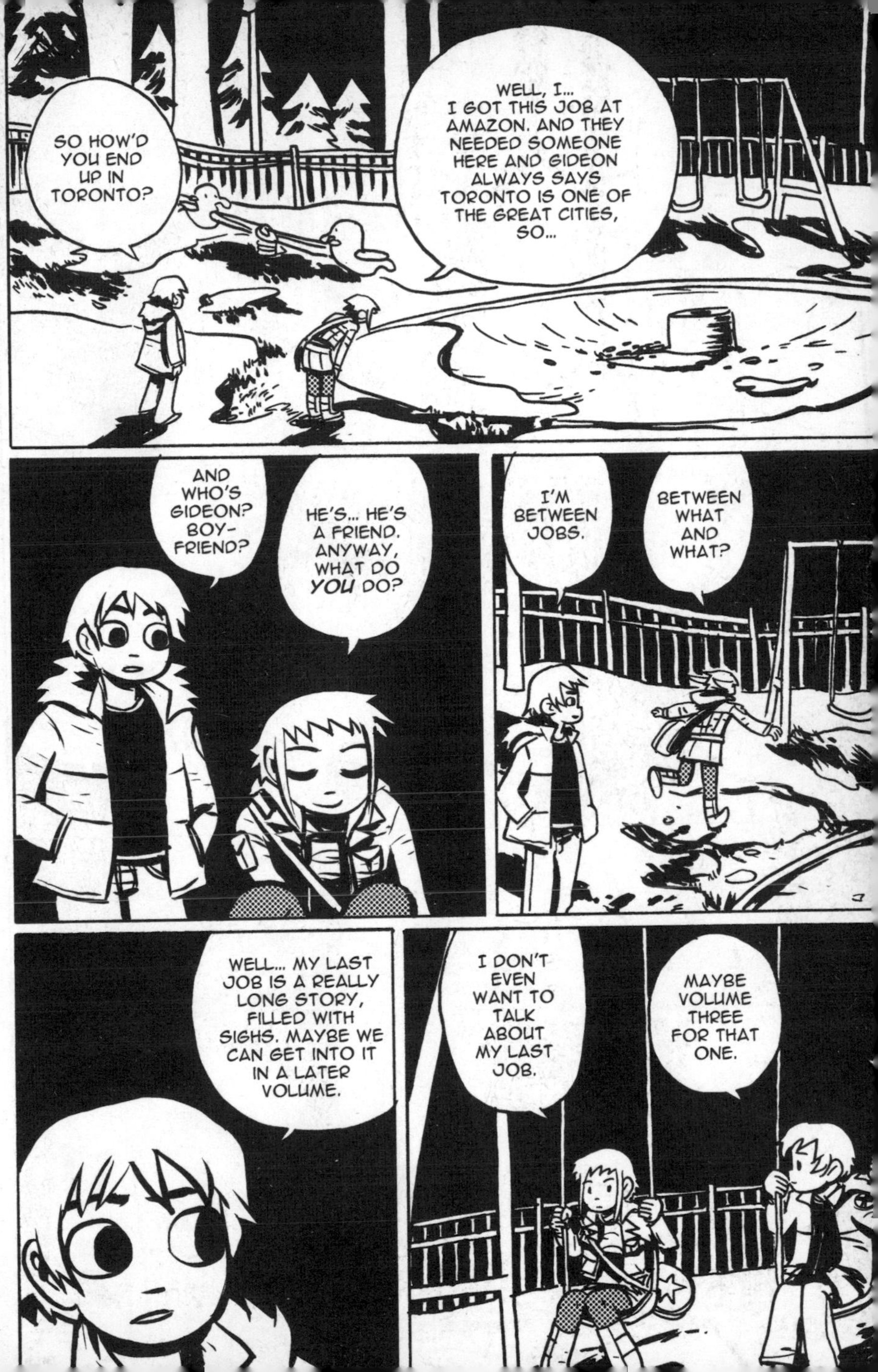
SO HOW'D YOU END UP IN TORONTO?
WELL, I... I GOT THIS JOB AT AMAZON. AND THEY NEEDED SOMEONE HERE AND GIDEON ALWAYS SAYS TORONTO IS ONE OF THE GREAT CITIES, SO...
AND WHO'S GIDEON? BOY-FRIEND?
HE'S... HE'S A FRIEND. ANYWAY, WHAT DO *YOU* DO?
I'M BETWEEN JOBS.
BETWEEN WHAT AND WHAT?
WELL... MY LAST JOB IS A REALLY LONG STORY, FILLED WITH SIGHS. MAYBE WE CAN GET INTO IT IN A LATER VOLUME.
I DON'T EVEN WANT TO TALK ABOUT MY LAST JOB.
MAYBE VOLUME THREE FOR THAT ONE.

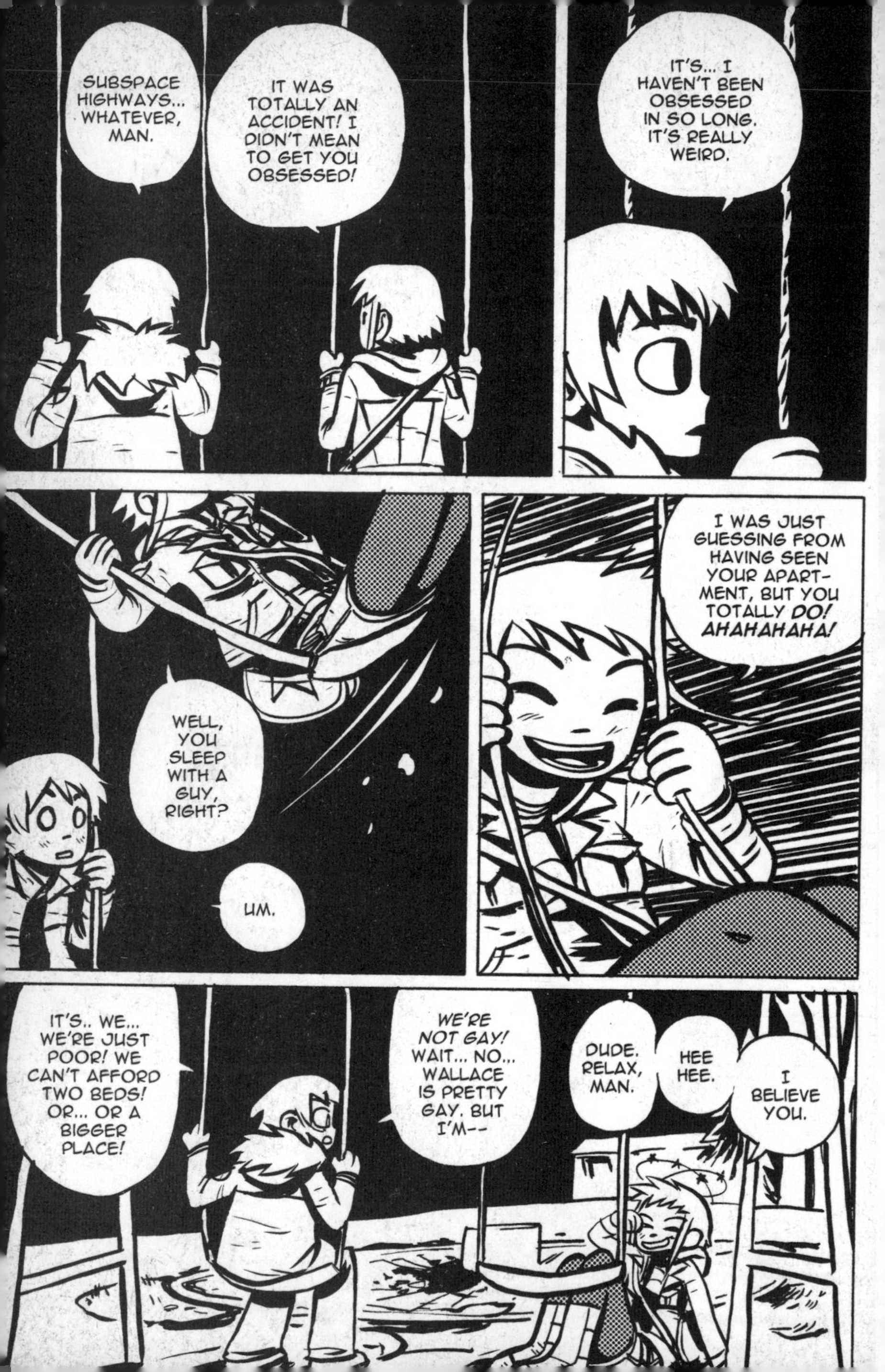
SUBSPACE HIGHWAYS... WHATEVER, MAN.
IT WAS TOTALLY AN ACCIDENT! I DIDN'T MEAN TO GET YOU OBSESSED!
IT'S... I HAVEN'T BEEN OBSESSED IN SO LONG. IT'S REALLY WEIRD.
WELL, YOU SLEEP WITH A GUY, RIGHT?
UM.
I WAS JUST GUESSING FROM HAVING SEEN YOUR APARTMENT, BUT YOU TOTALLY DO! AHAHAHAHA!
IT'S.. WE... WE'RE JUST POOR! WE CAN'T AFFORD TWO BEDS! OR... OR A BIGGER PLACE!
WE'RE NOT GAY! WAIT... NO... WALLACE IS PRETTY GAY. BUT I'M--
DUDE. RELAX, MAN.
HEE HEE.
I BELIEVE YOU.

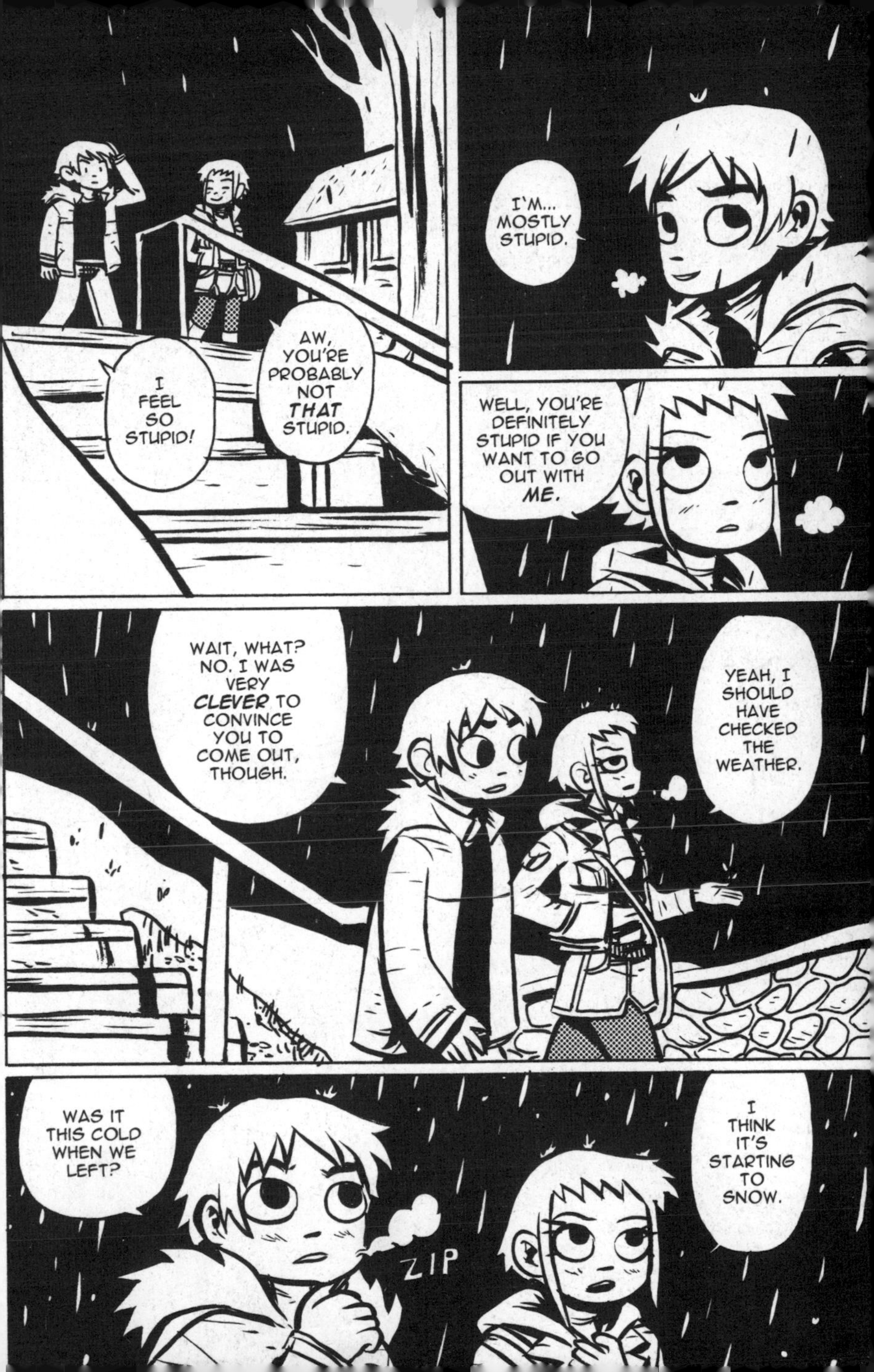
I FEEL SO STUPID!
AW, YOU'RE PROBABLY NOT *THAT* STUPID.
I'M... MOSTLY STUPID.
WELL, YOU'RE DEFINITELY STUPID IF YOU WANT TO GO OUT WITH *ME.*
WAIT, WHAT? NO. I WAS VERY *CLEVER* TO CONVINCE YOU TO COME OUT, THOUGH.
YEAH, I SHOULD HAVE CHECKED THE WEATHER.
WAS IT THIS COLD WHEN WE LEFT?
ZIP
I THINK IT'S STARTING TO SNOW.

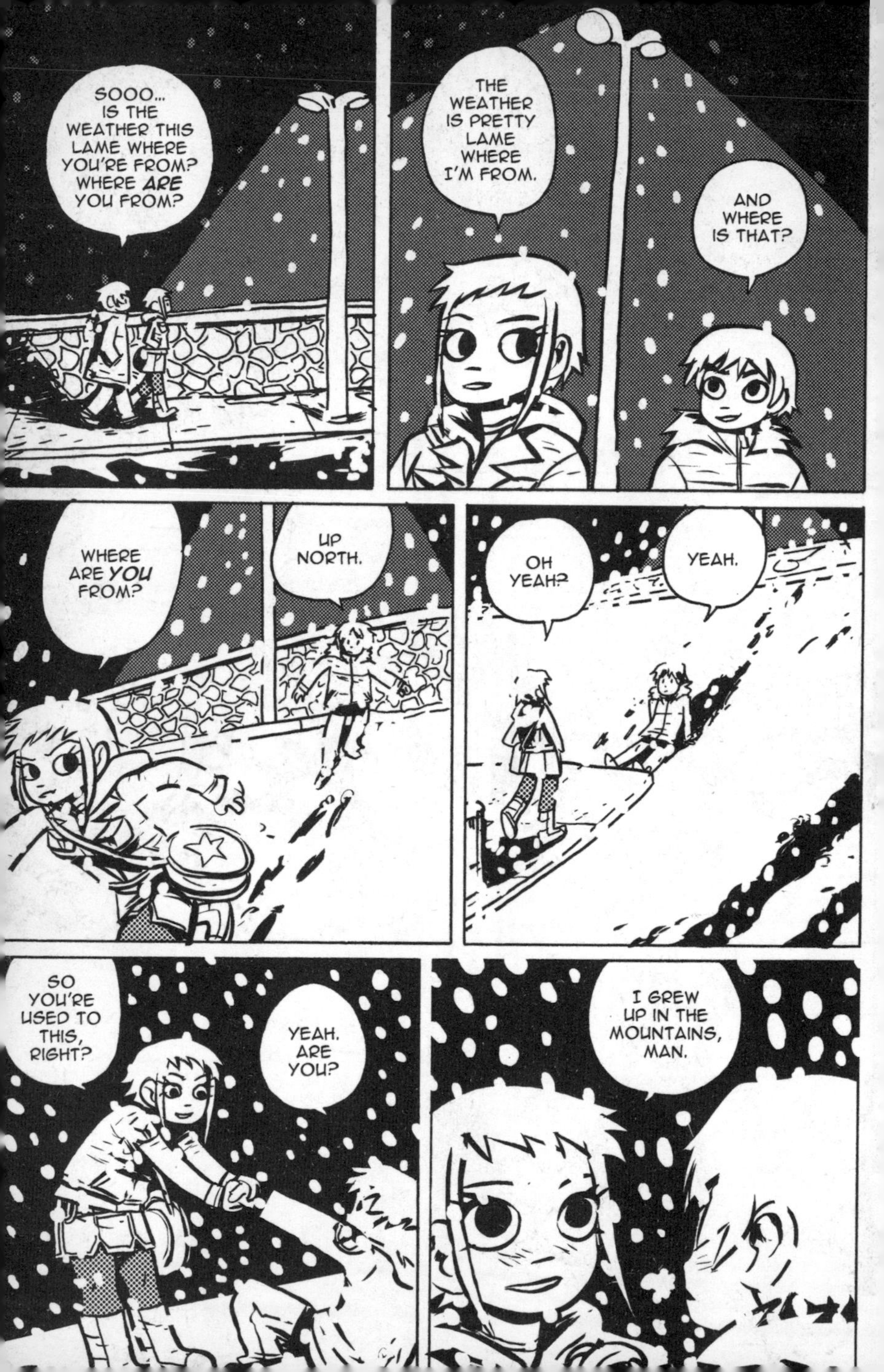
SOOO... IS THE WEATHER THIS LAME WHERE YOU'RE FROM? WHERE *ARE* YOU FROM?
THE WEATHER IS PRETTY LAME WHERE I'M FROM.
AND WHERE IS THAT?
WHERE ARE *YOU* FROM?
UP NORTH.
OH YEAH?
YEAH.
SO YOU'RE USED TO THIS, RIGHT?
YEAH. ARE YOU?
I GREW UP IN THE MOUNTAINS, MAN.

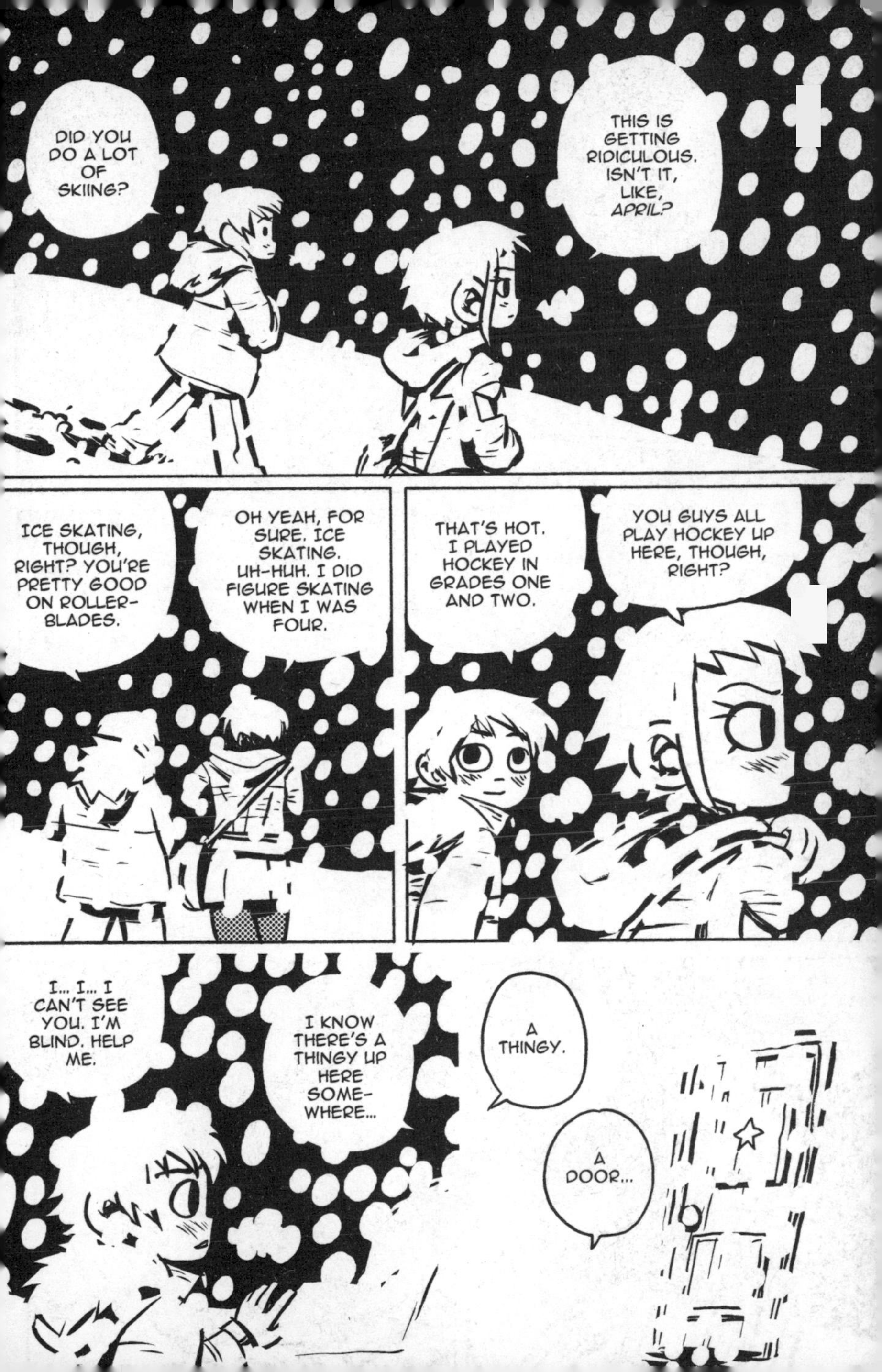
DID YOU DO A LOT OF SKIING?
THIS IS GETTING RIDICULOUS. ISN'T IT, LIKE, APRIL?
ICE SKATING, THOUGH, RIGHT? YOU'RE PRETTY GOOD ON ROLLER-BLADES.
OH YEAH, FOR SURE. ICE SKATING. UH-HUH. I DID FIGURE SKATING WHEN I WAS FOUR.
THAT'S HOT. I PLAYED HOCKEY IN GRADES ONE AND TWO.
YOU GUYS ALL PLAY HOCKEY UP HERE, THOUGH, RIGHT?
I... I... I CAN'T SEE YOU. I'M BLIND. HELP ME.
I KNOW THERE'S A THINGY UP HERE SOME-WHERE...
A THINGY.
A DOOR...

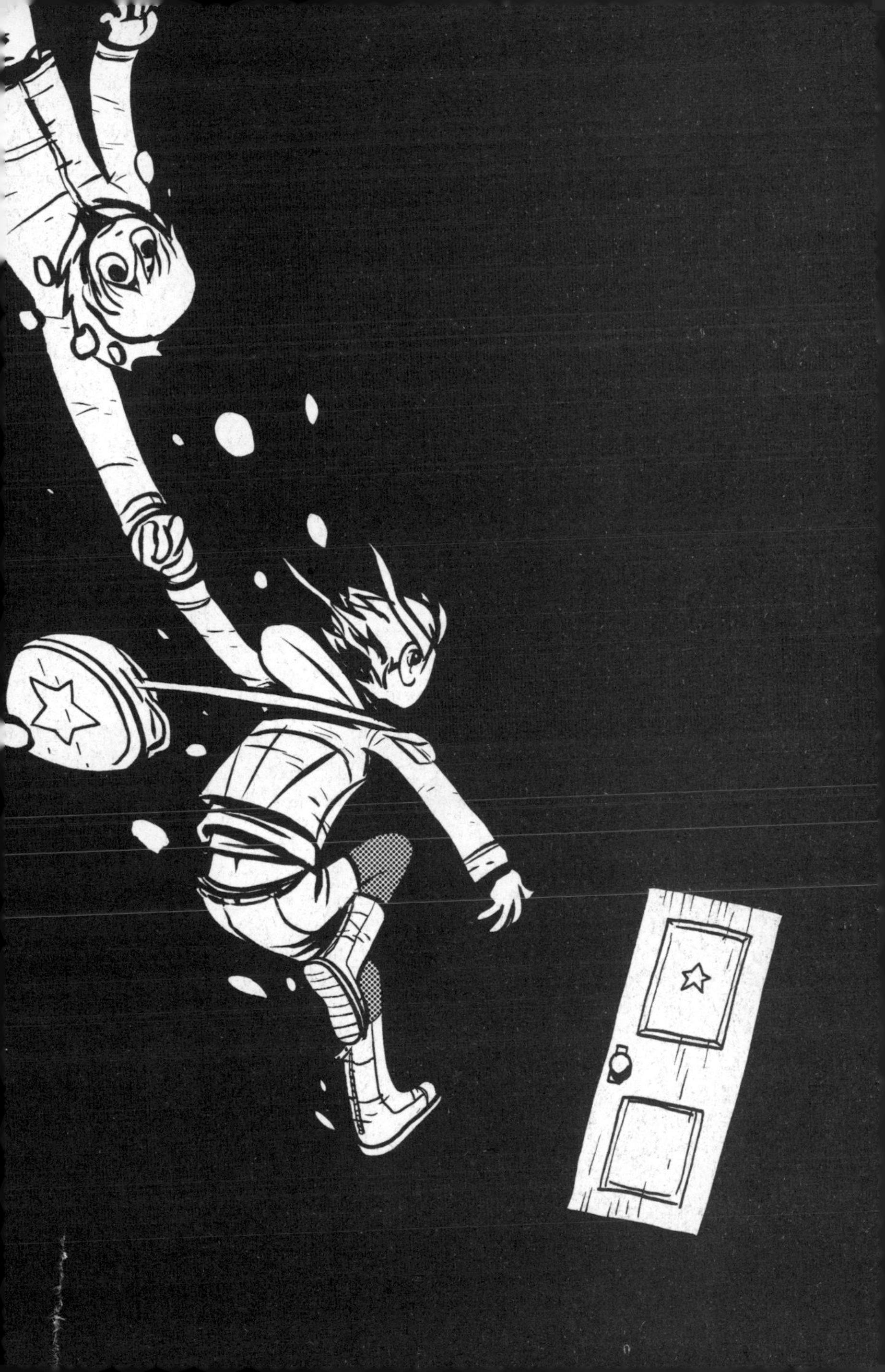

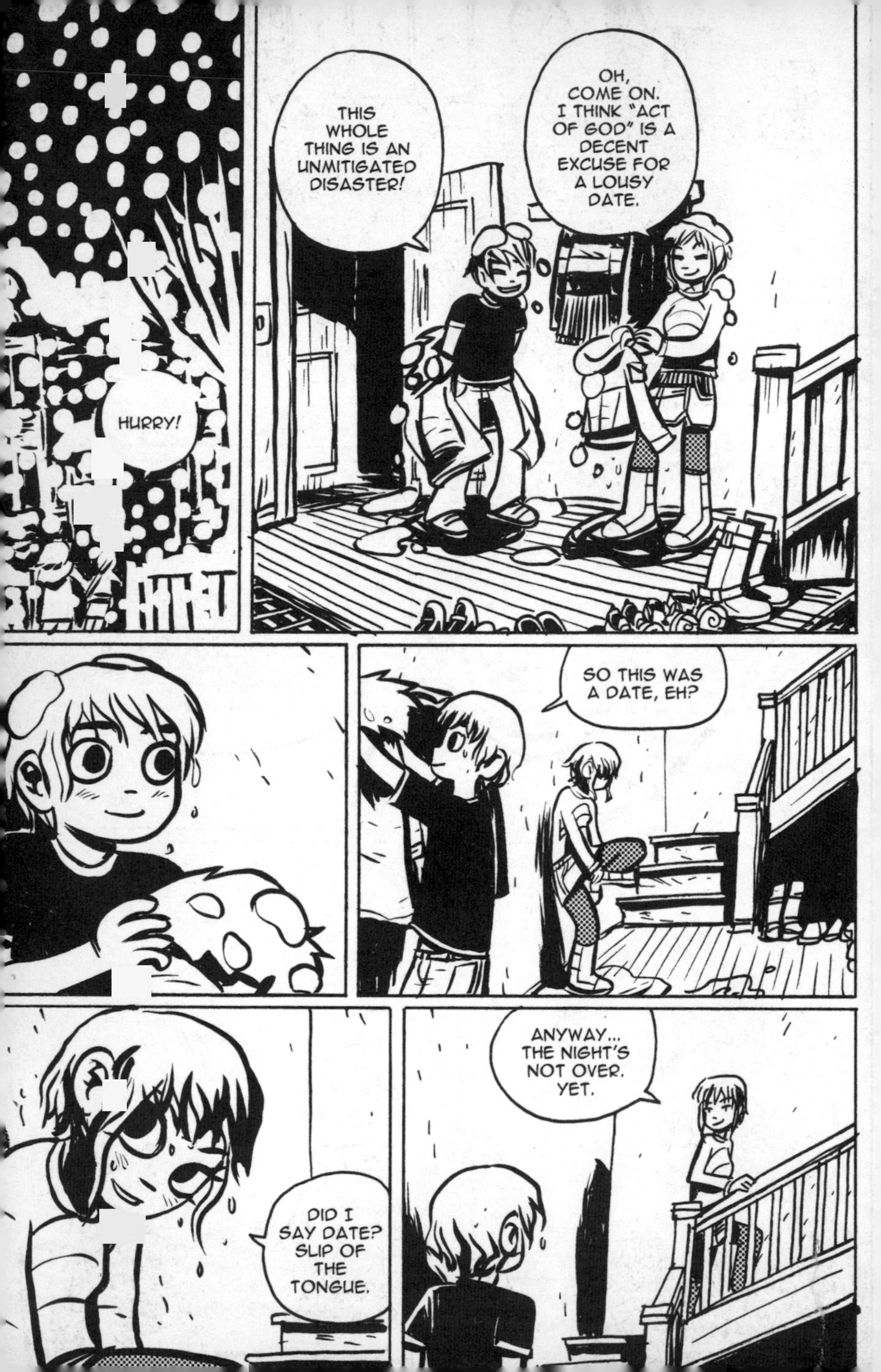
HURRY!
THIS WHOLE THING IS AN UNMITIGATED DISASTER!
OH, COME ON. I THINK "ACT OF GOD" IS A DECENT EXCUSE FOR A LOUSY DATE.
SO THIS WAS A DATE, EH?
DID I SAY DATE? SLIP OF THE TONGUE.
ANYWAY... THE NIGHT'S NOT OVER. YET.

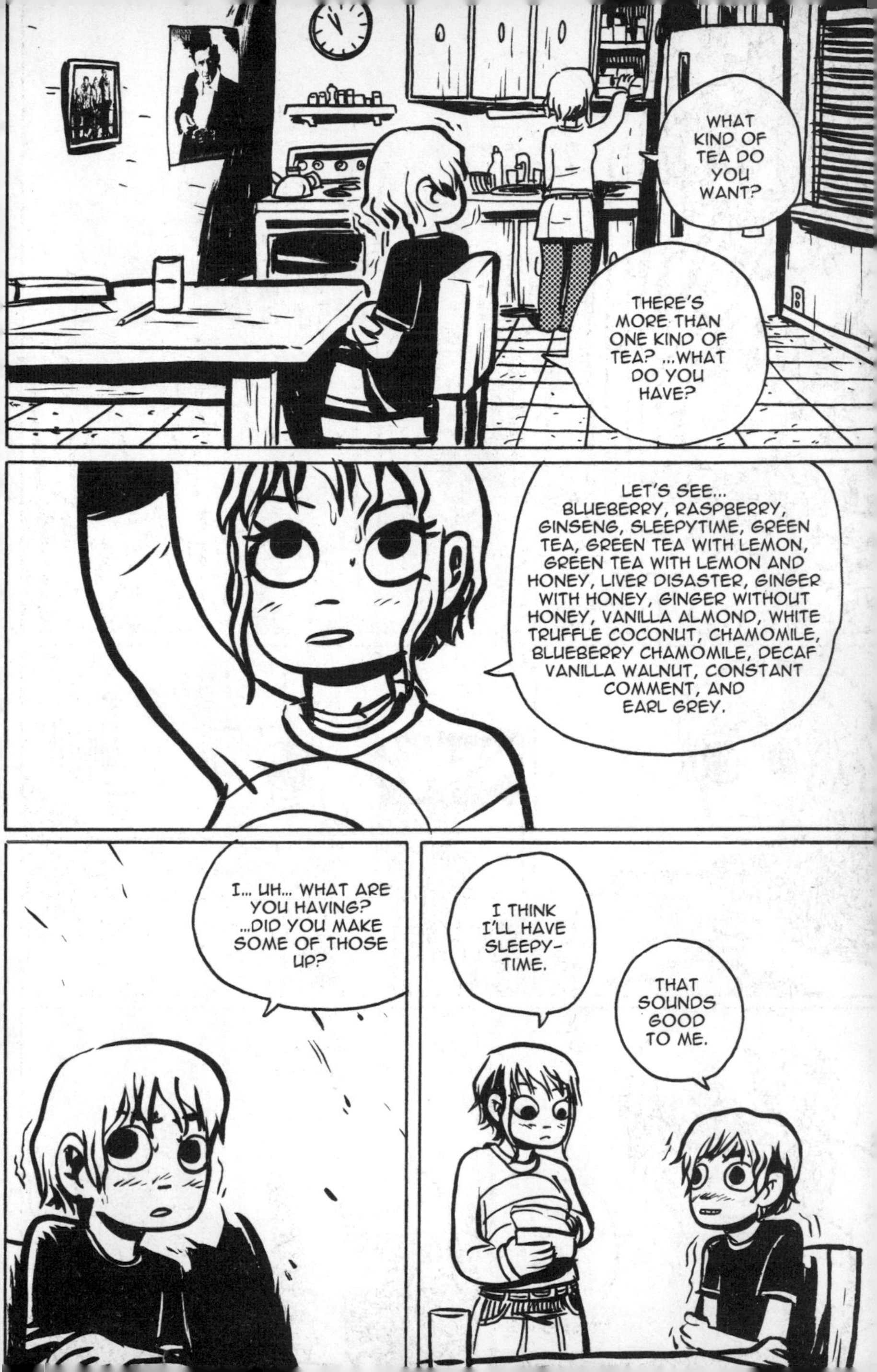
WHAT KIND OF TEA DO YOU WANT?
THERE'S MORE THAN ONE KIND OF TEA? ...WHAT DO YOU HAVE?
LET'S SEE... BLUEBERRY, RASPBERRY, GINSENG, SLEEPYTIME, GREEN TEA, GREEN TEA WITH LEMON, GREEN TEA WITH LEMON AND HONEY, LIVER DISASTER, GINGER WITH HONEY, GINGER WITHOUT HONEY, VANILLA ALMOND, WHITE TRUFFLE COCONUT, CHAMOMILE, BLUEBERRY CHAMOMILE, DECAF VANILLA WALNUT, CONSTANT COMMENT, AND EARL GREY.
I... UH... WHAT ARE YOU HAVING? ...DID YOU MAKE SOME OF THOSE UP?
I THINK I'LL HAVE SLEEPY-TIME.
THAT SOUNDS GOOD TO ME.

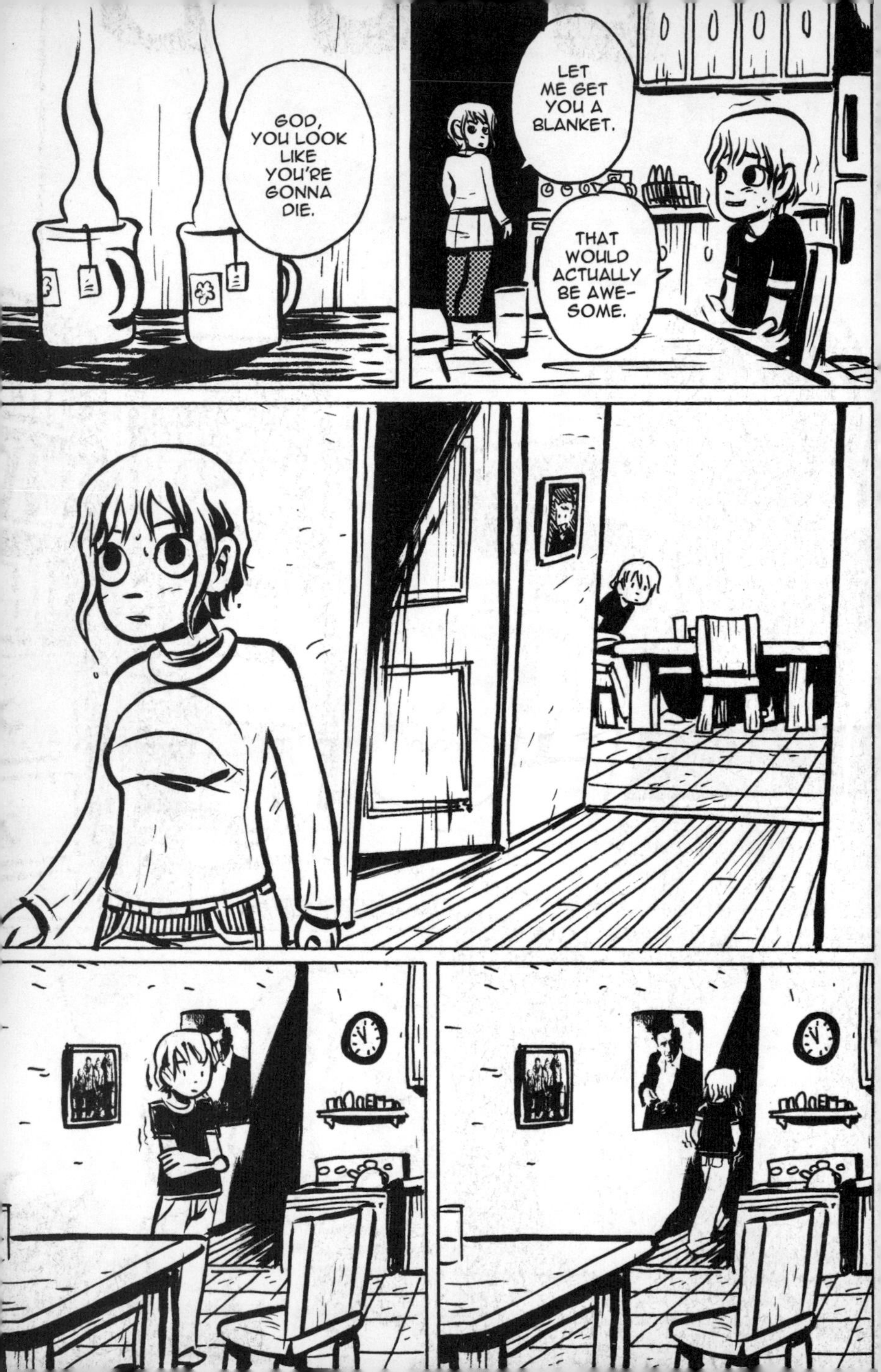
GOD, YOU LOOK LIKE YOU'RE GONNA DIE.
LET ME GET YOU A BLANKET.
THAT WOULD ACTUALLY BE AWE-SOME.

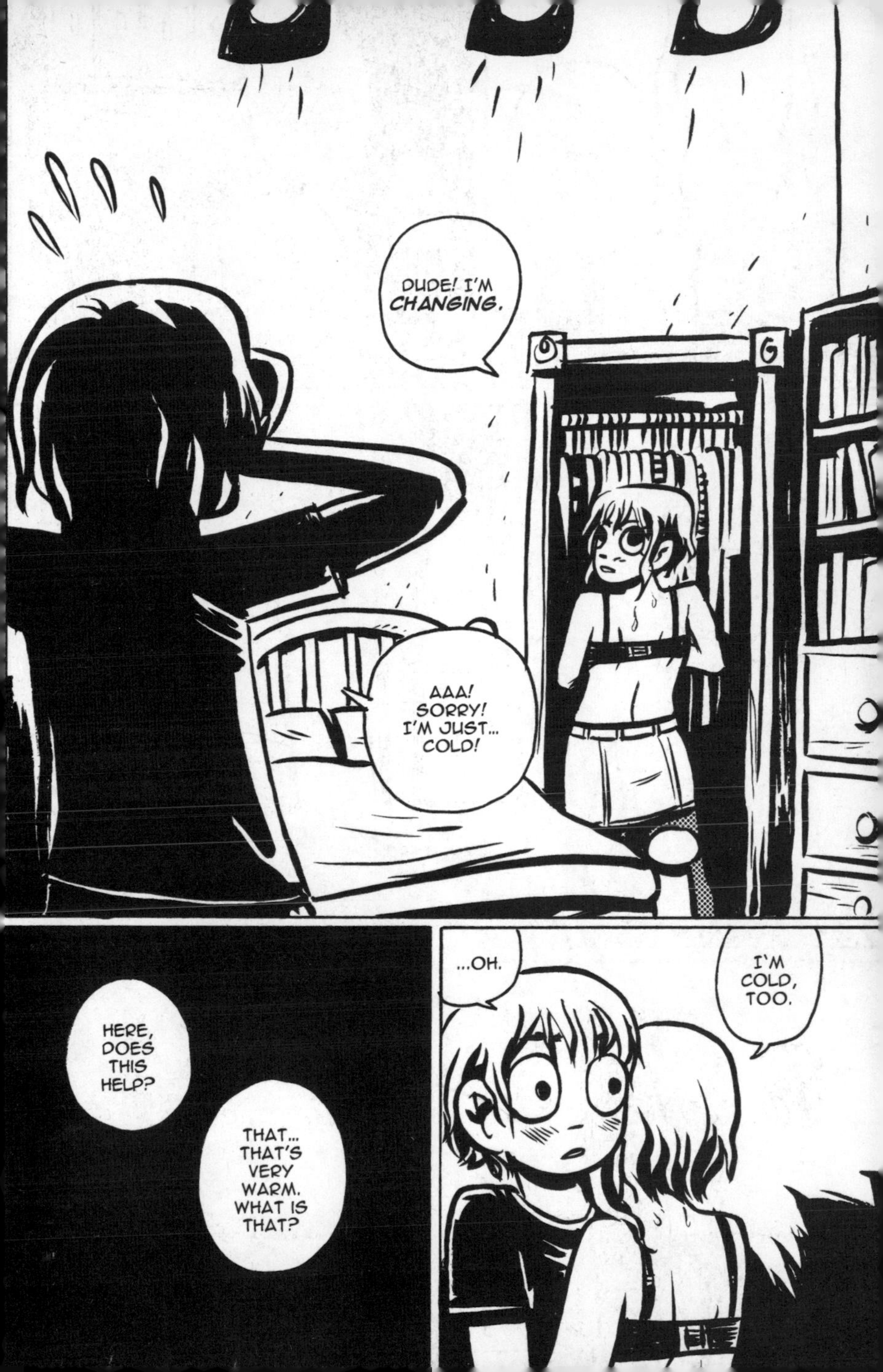
DUDE! I'M CHANGING.
AAA! SORRY! I'M JUST... COLD!
HERE, DOES THIS HELP?
THAT... THAT'S VERY WARM. WHAT IS THAT?
...OH.
I'M COLD, TOO.

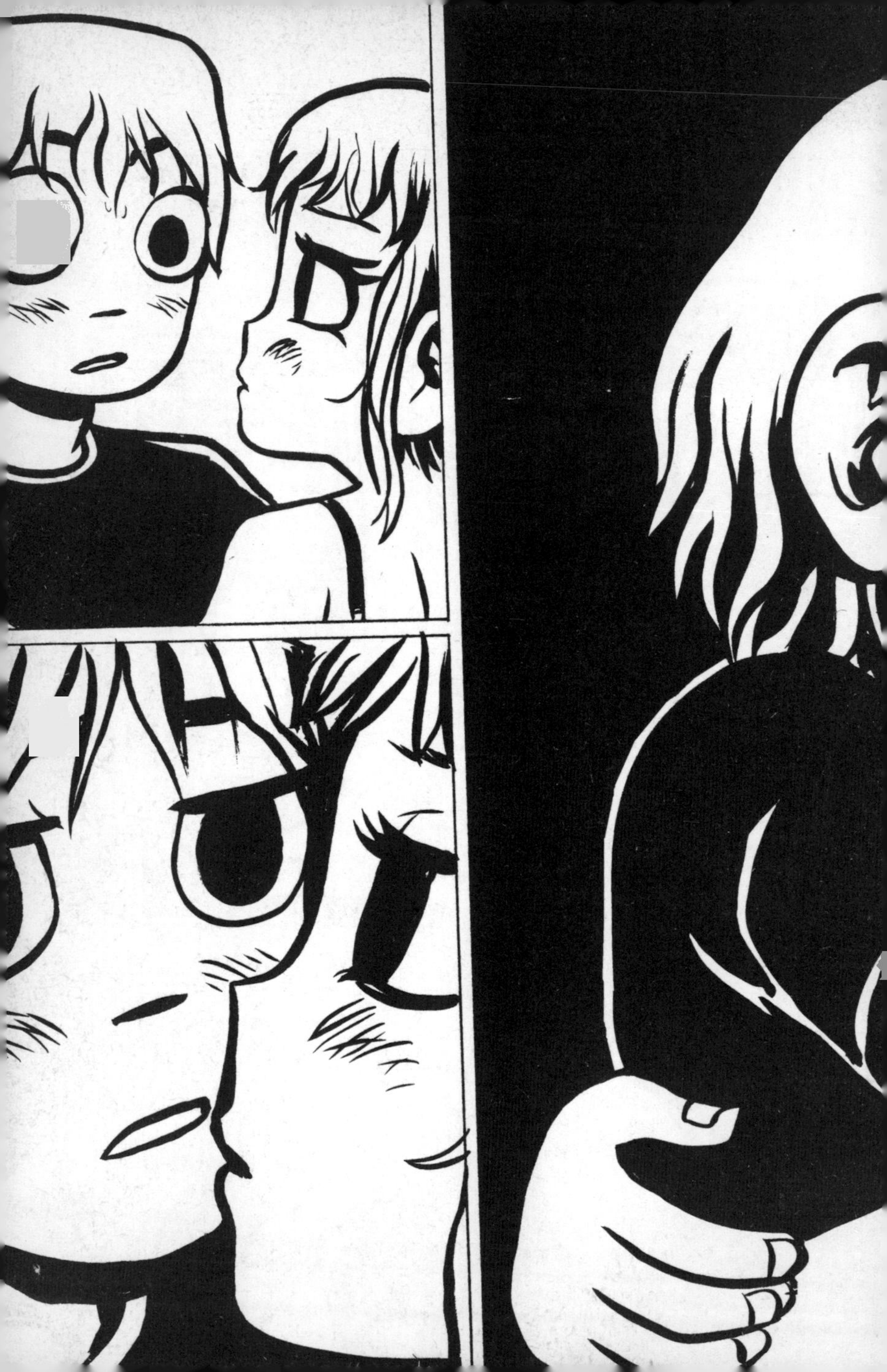

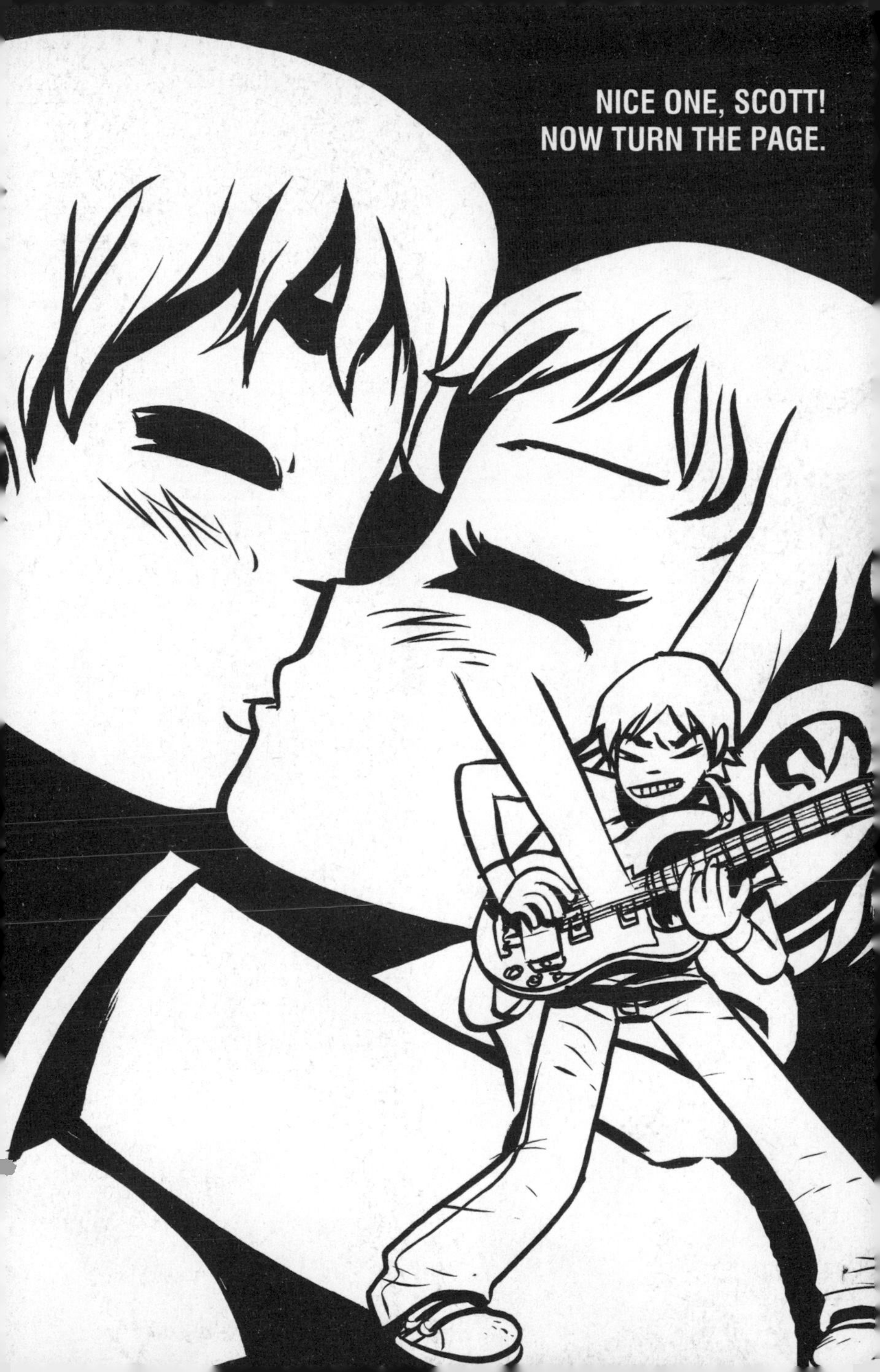
NICE ONE, SCOTT!
NOW TURN THE PAGE.

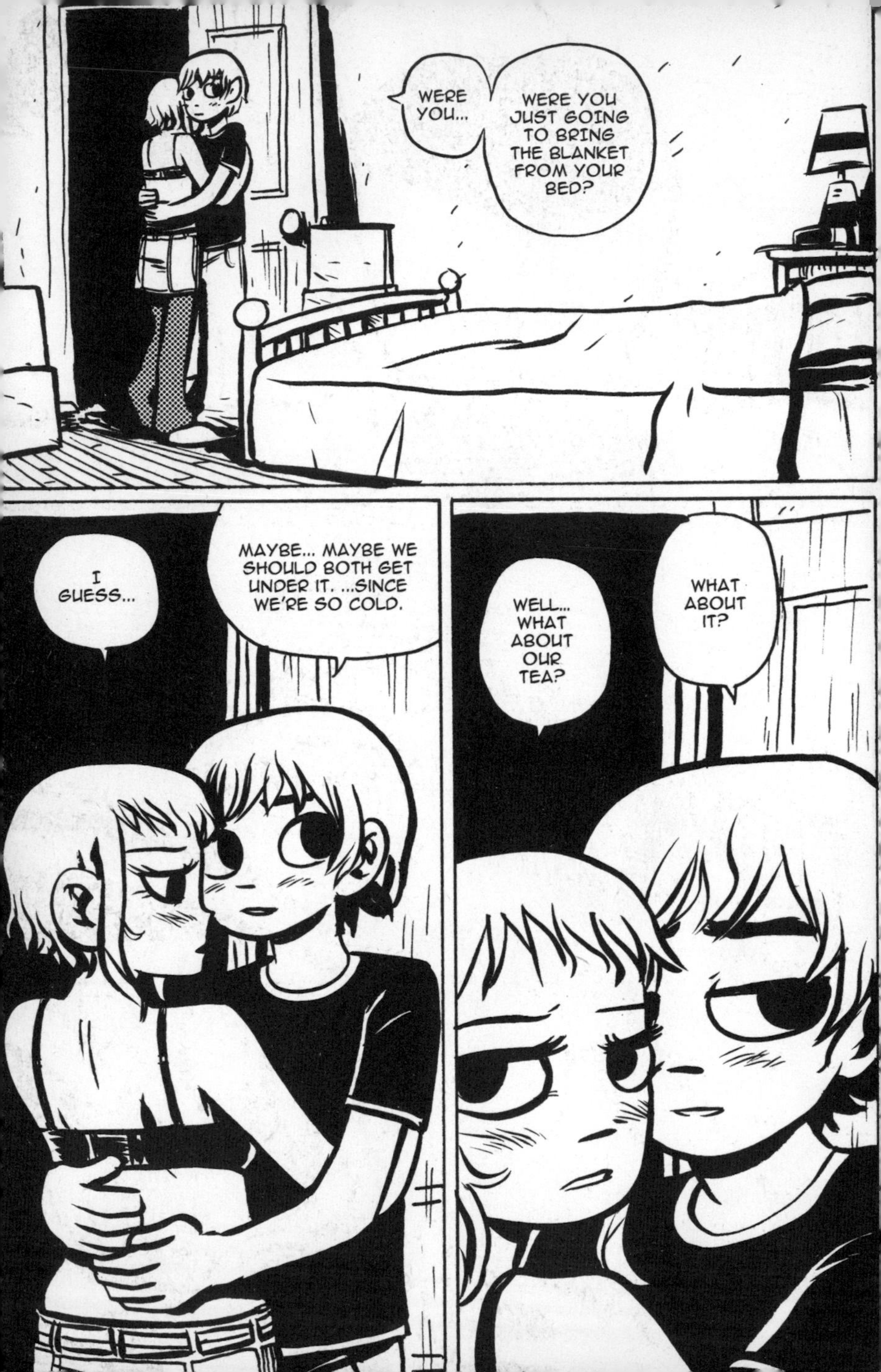
WERE YOU...
WERE YOU JUST GOING TO BRING THE BLANKET FROM YOUR BED?
I GUESS...
MAYBE... MAYBE WE SHOULD BOTH GET UNDER IT. ...SINCE WE'RE SO COLD.
WHAT ABOUT IT?
WELL... WHAT ABOUT OUR TEA?

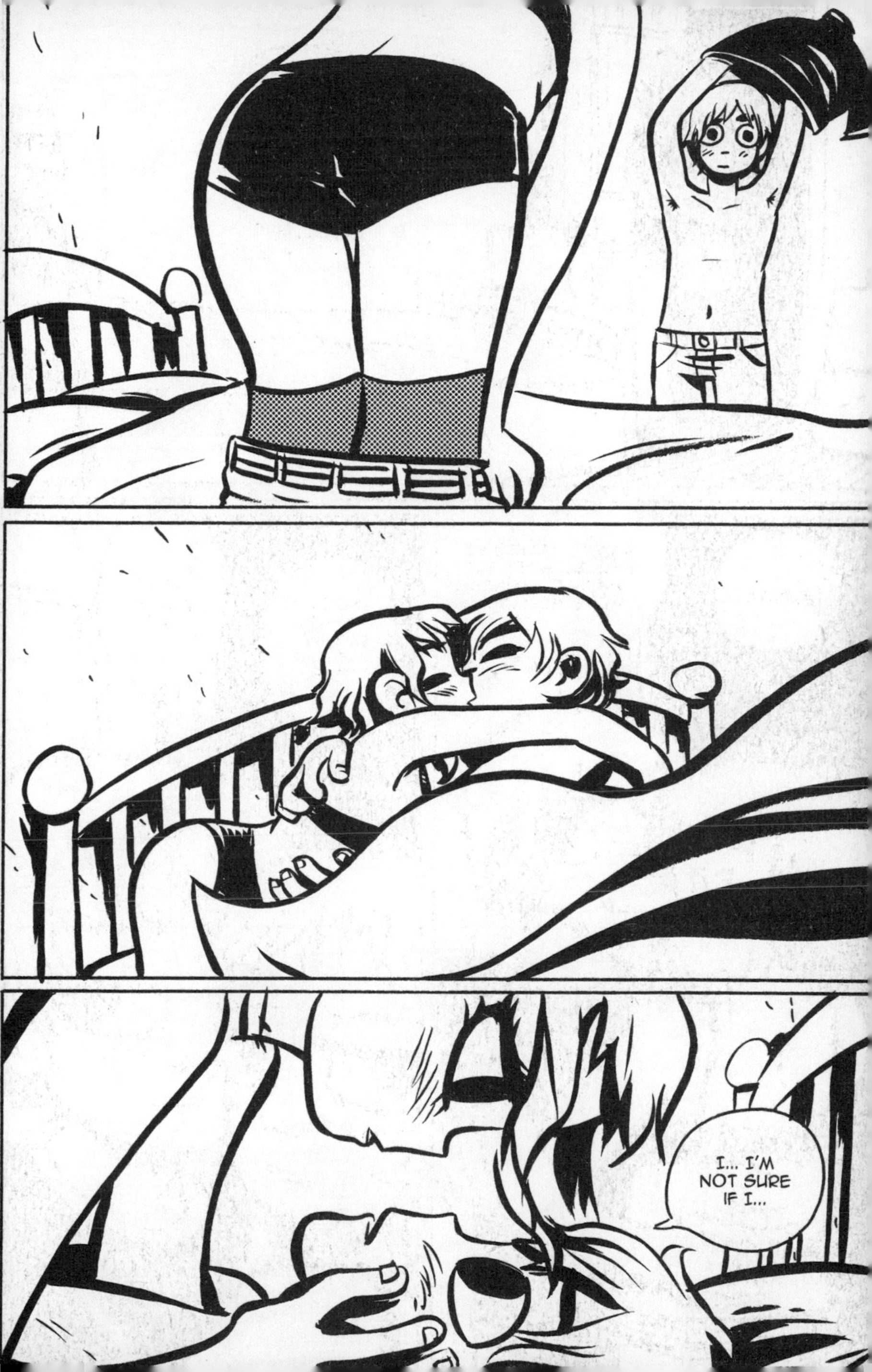
I... I'M NOT SURE IF I...

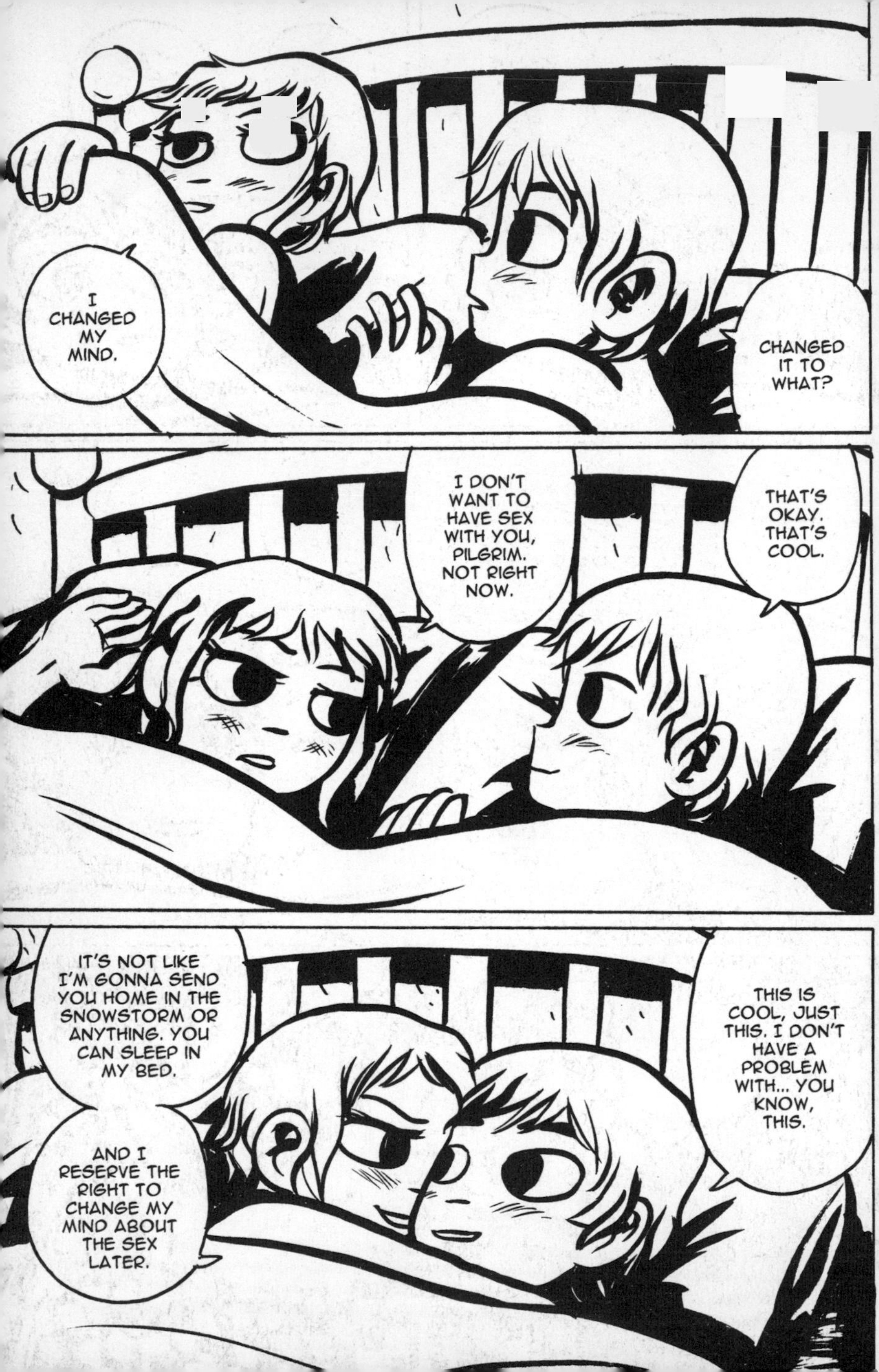
I CHANGED MY MIND.
CHANGED IT TO WHAT?
I DON'T WANT TO HAVE SEX WITH YOU, PILGRIM. NOT RIGHT NOW.
THAT'S OKAY. THAT'S COOL.
IT'S NOT LIKE I'M GONNA SEND YOU HOME IN THE SNOWSTORM OR ANYTHING. YOU CAN SLEEP IN MY BED.
AND I RESERVE THE RIGHT TO CHANGE MY MIND ABOUT THE SEX LATER.
THIS IS COOL, JUST THIS. I DON'T HAVE A PROBLEM WITH... YOU KNOW, THIS.

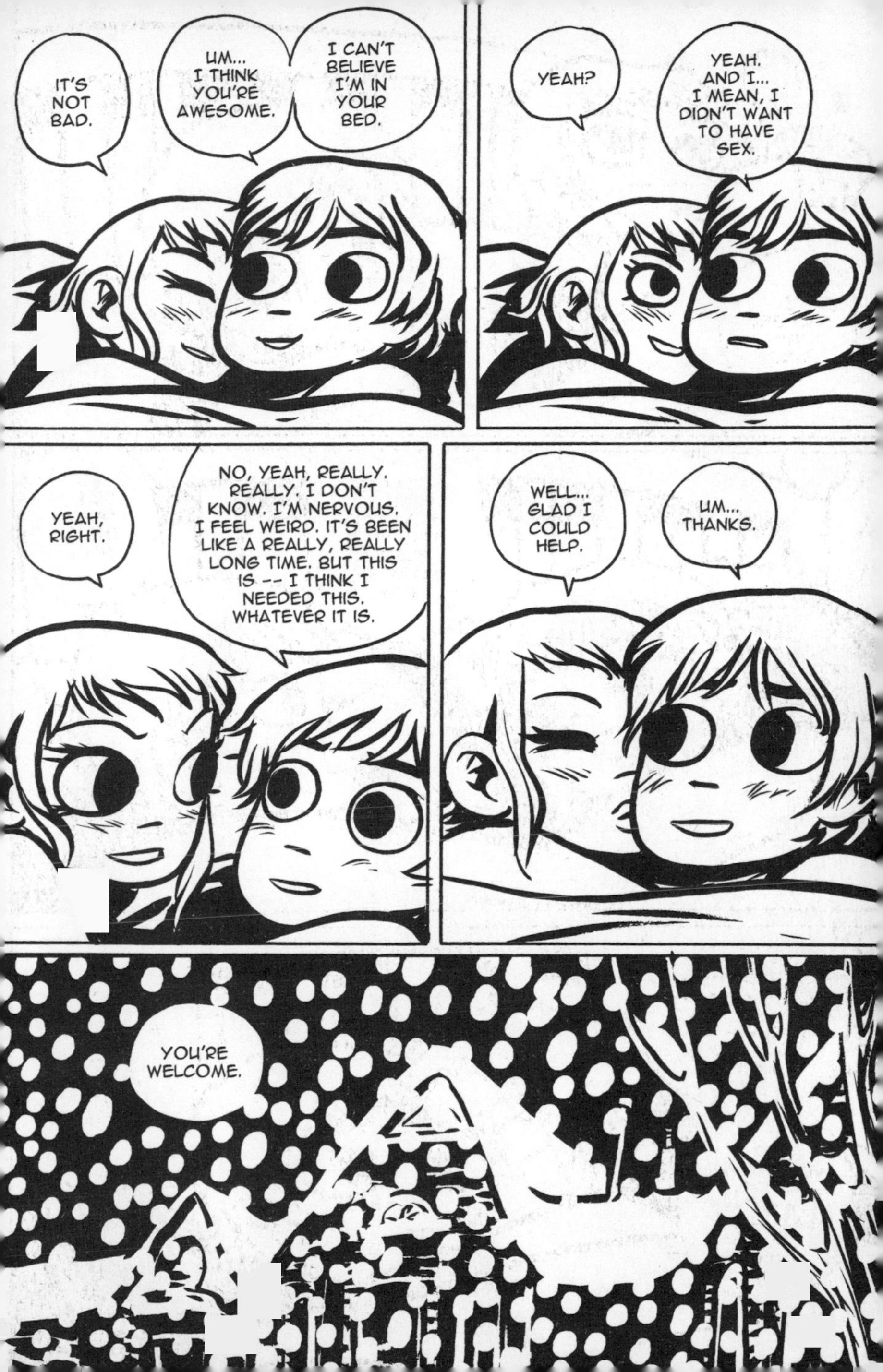
IT'S NOT BAD.
UM... I THINK YOU'RE AWESOME.
I CAN'T BELIEVE I'M IN YOUR BED.
YEAH?
YEAH. AND I... I MEAN, I DIDN'T WANT TO HAVE SEX.
YEAH, RIGHT.
NO, YEAH, REALLY. REALLY. I DON'T KNOW. I'M NERVOUS. I FEEL WEIRD. IT'S BEEN LIKE A REALLY, REALLY LONG TIME. BUT THIS IS -- I THINK I NEEDED THIS. WHATEVER IT IS.
WELL... GLAD I COULD HELP.
UM... THANKS.
YOU'RE WELCOME.

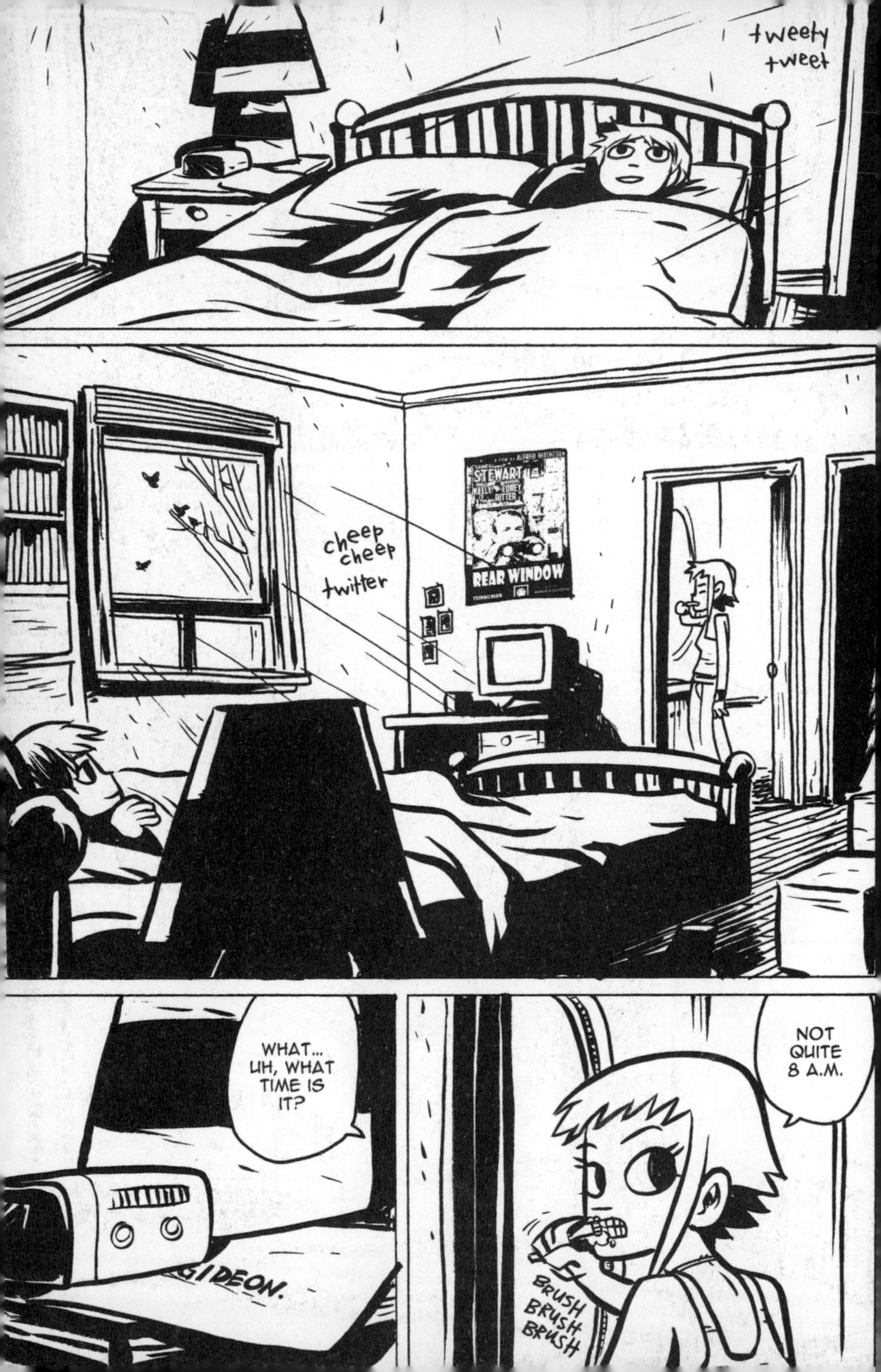
tweety tweet
STEWART
KELLY
COREY
RITTER
REAR WINDOW
cheep cheep
twitter
WHAT... UH, WHAT TIME IS IT?
GIDEON.
NOT QUITE 8 A.M.
BRUSH BRUSH BRUSH

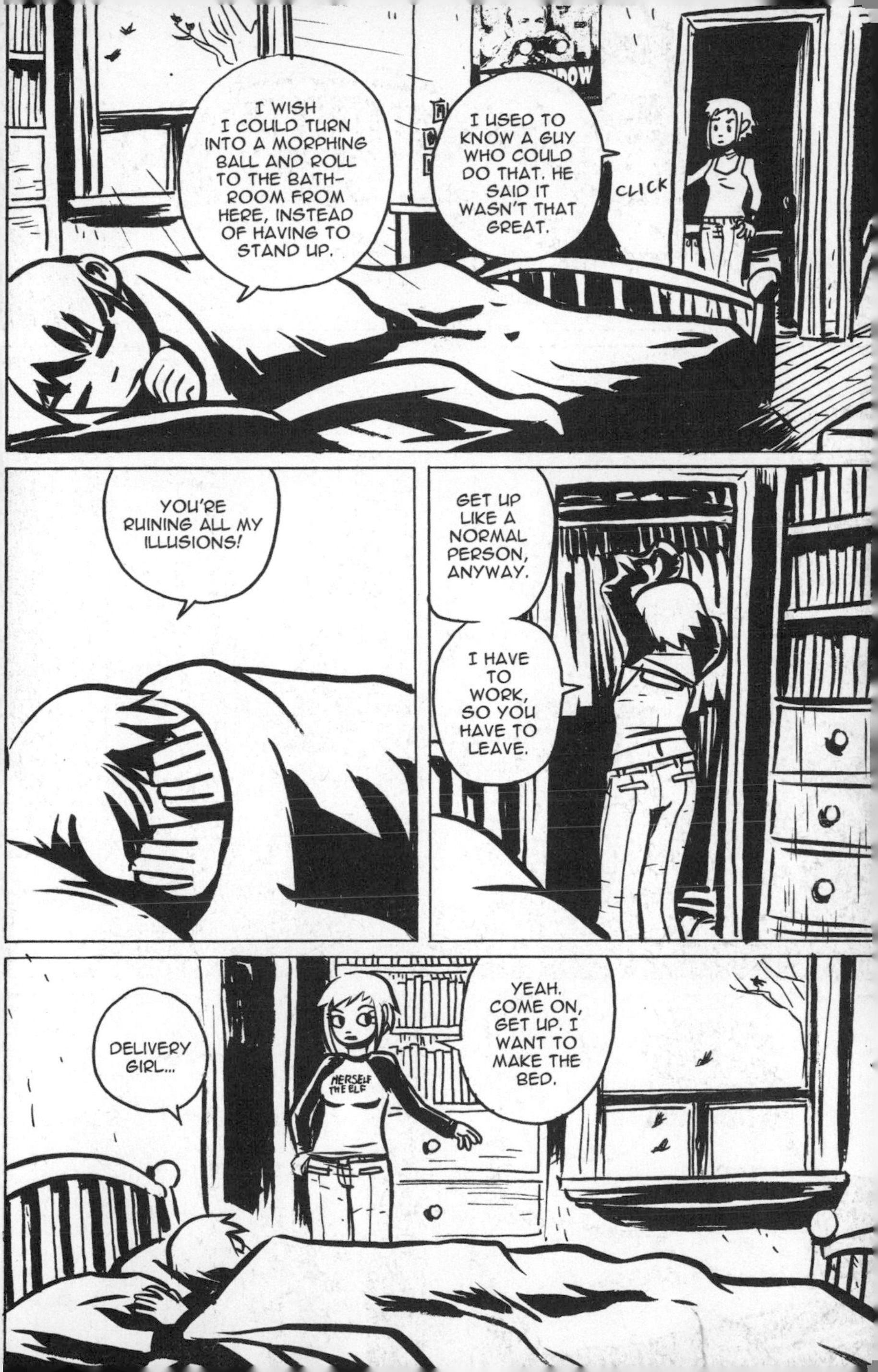
I WISH I COULD TURN INTO A MORPHING BALL AND ROLL TO THE BATH-ROOM FROM HERE, INSTEAD OF HAVING TO STAND UP.
I USED TO KNOW A GUY WHO COULD DO THAT. HE SAID IT WASN'T THAT GREAT.
CLICK
YOU'RE RUINING ALL MY ILLUSIONS!
GET UP LIKE A NORMAL PERSON, ANYWAY.
I HAVE TO WORK, SO YOU HAVE TO LEAVE.
DELIVERY GIRL...
YEAH. COME ON, GET UP. I WANT TO MAKE THE BED.
HERSELF THE ELF

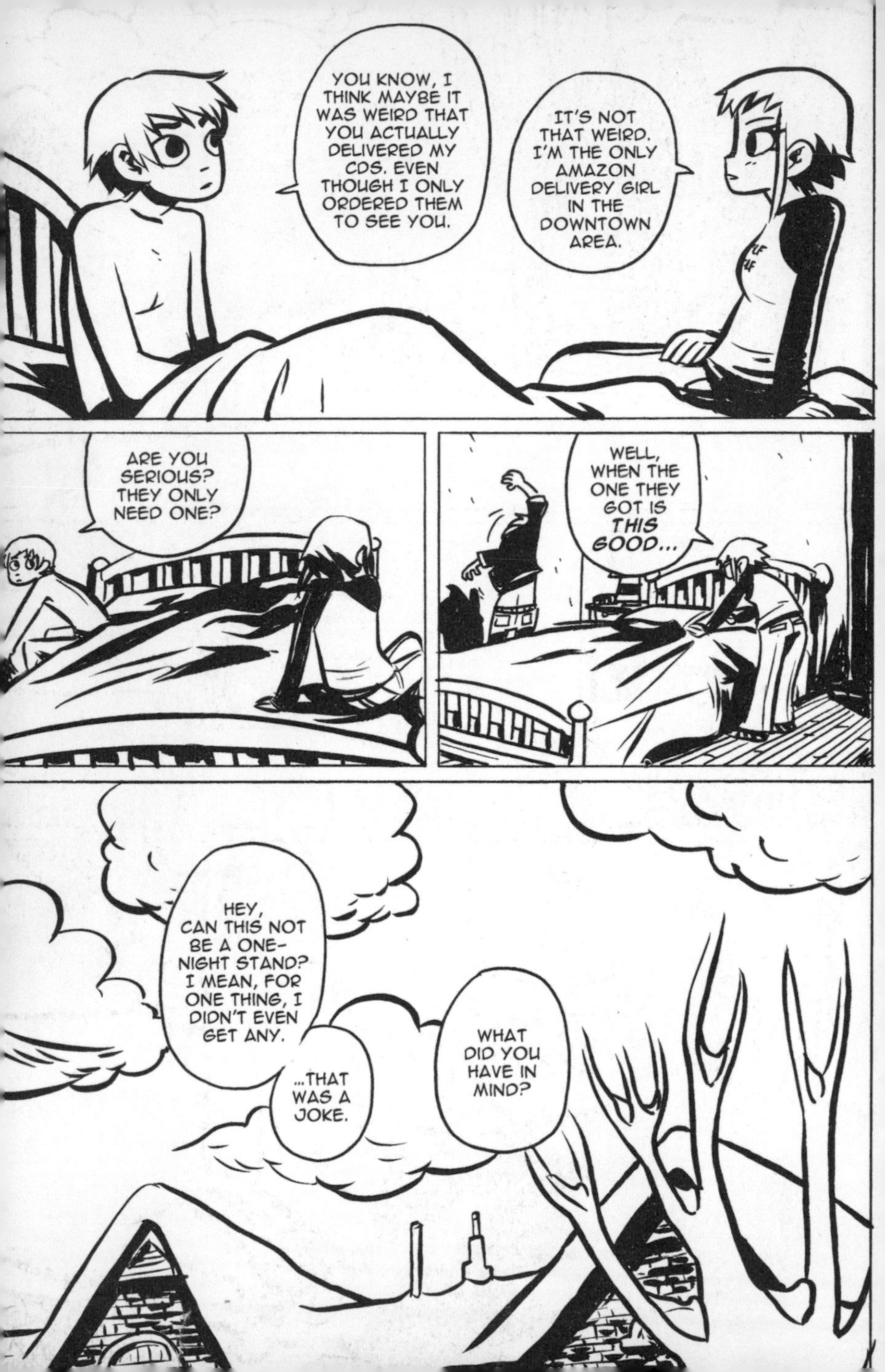

YOU KNOW, I THINK MAYBE IT WAS WEIRD THAT YOU ACTUALLY DELIVERED MY CDS. EVEN THOUGH I ONLY ORDERED THEM TO SEE YOU.
IT'S NOT THAT WEIRD. I'M THE ONLY AMAZON DELIVERY GIRL IN THE DOWNTOWN AREA.
ARE YOU SERIOUS? THEY ONLY NEED ONE?
WELL, WHEN THE ONE THEY GOT IS THIS GOOD...
HEY, CAN THIS NOT BE A ONE-NIGHT STAND? I MEAN, FOR ONE THING, I DIDN'T EVEN GET ANY.
...THAT WAS A JOKE.
WHAT DID YOU HAVE IN MIND?

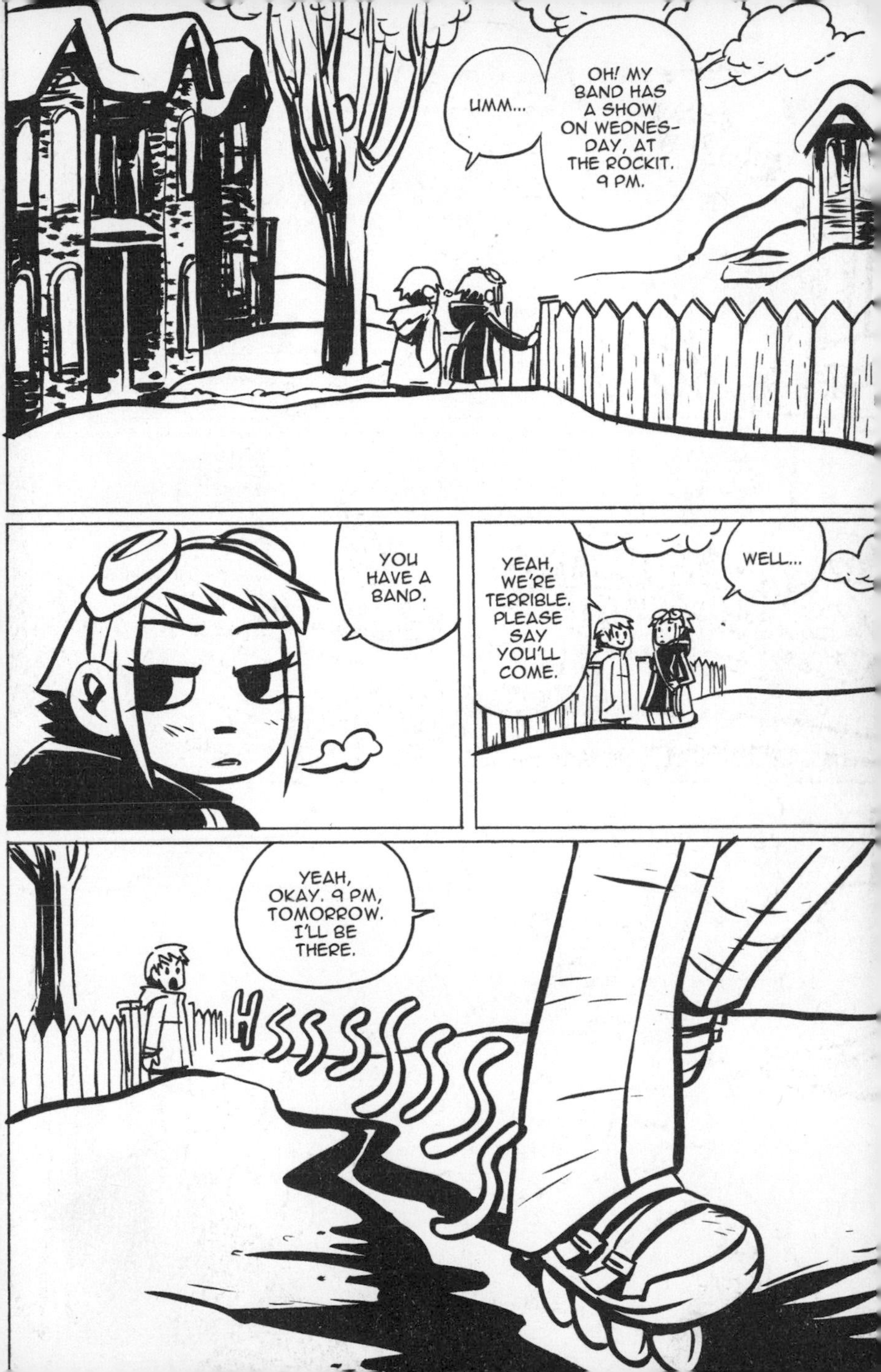
UMM...
OH! MY BAND HAS A SHOW ON WEDNES-DAY, AT THE ROCKIT. 9 PM.
YOU HAVE A BAND.
YEAH, WE'RE TERRIBLE. PLEASE SAY YOU'LL COME.
WELL...
YEAH, OKAY. 9 PM, TOMORROW. I'LL BE THERE.
HSSSSSSS

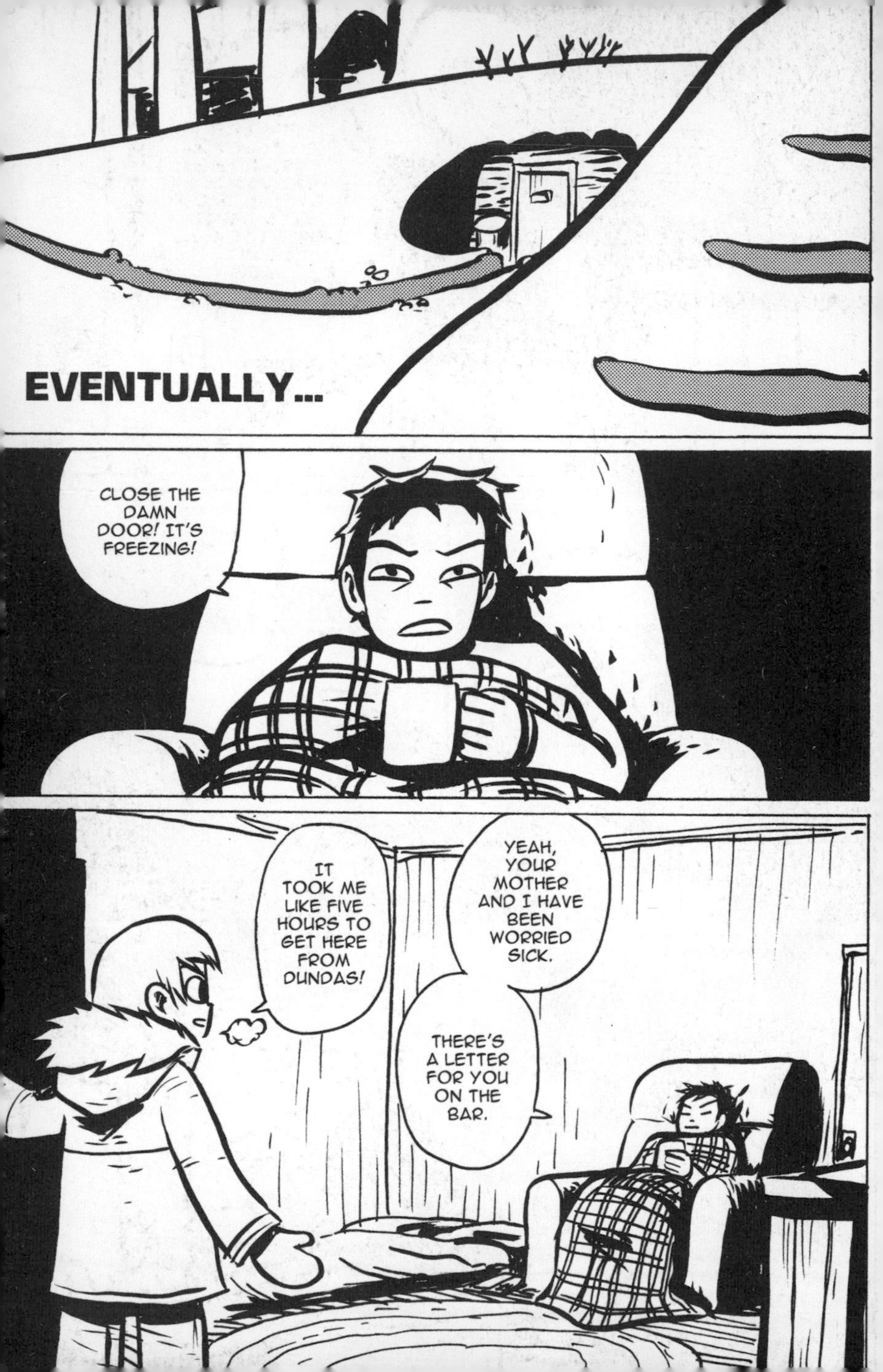
EVENTUALLY...
CLOSE THE DAMN DOOR! IT'S FREEZING!
IT TOOK ME LIKE FIVE HOURS TO GET HERE FROM DUNDAS!
YEAH, YOUR MOTHER AND I HAVE BEEN WORRIED SICK.
THERE'S A LETTER FOR YOU ON THE BAR.

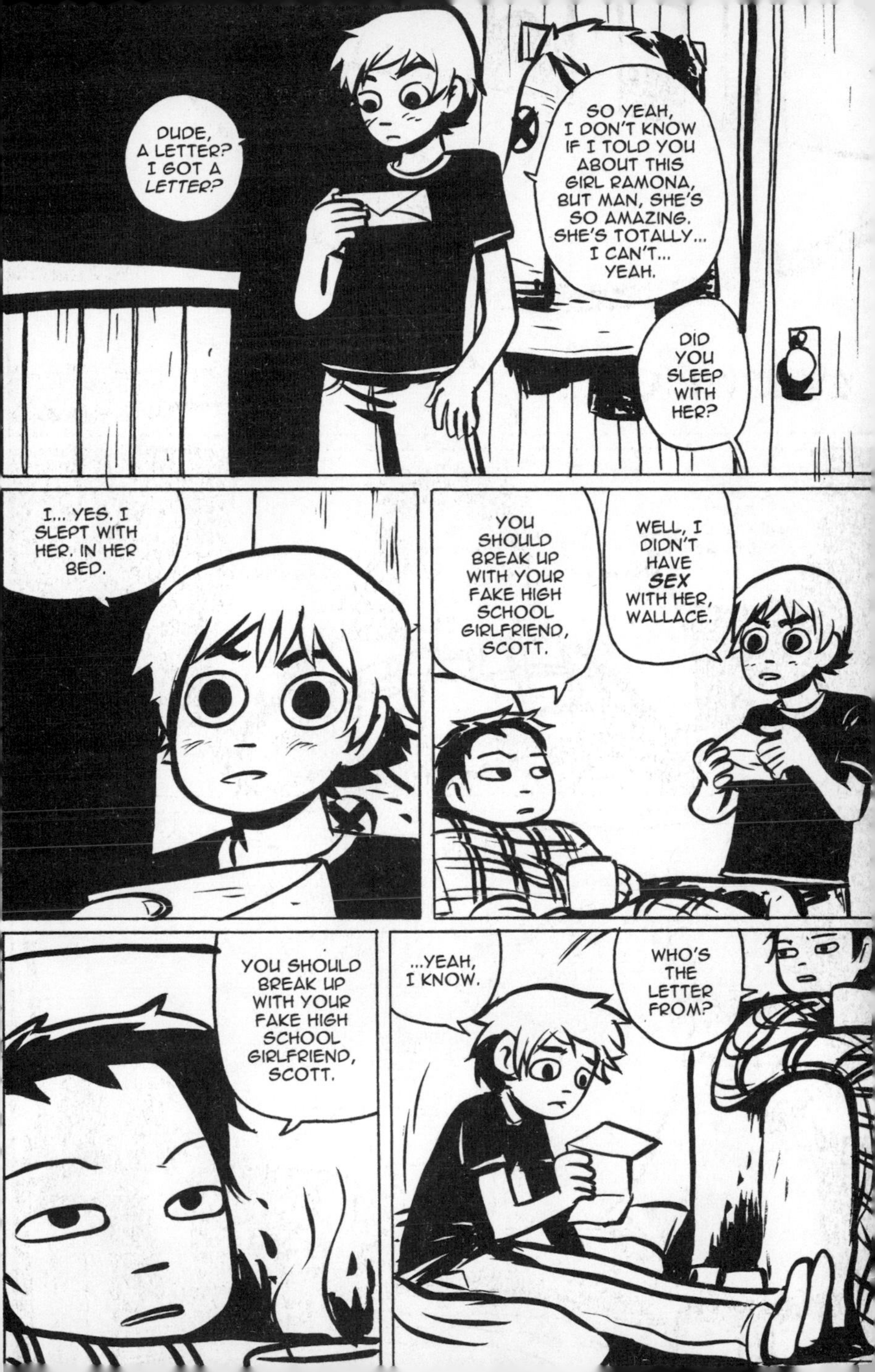
DUDE, A LETTER? I GOT A LETTER?
SO YEAH, I DON'T KNOW IF I TOLD YOU ABOUT THIS GIRL RAMONA, BUT MAN, SHE'S SO AMAZING. SHE'S TOTALLY... I CAN'T... YEAH.
DID YOU SLEEP WITH HER?
I... YES. I SLEPT WITH HER. IN HER BED.
YOU SHOULD BREAK UP WITH YOUR FAKE HIGH SCHOOL GIRLFRIEND, SCOTT.
WELL, I DIDN'T HAVE SEX WITH HER, WALLACE.
YOU SHOULD BREAK UP WITH YOUR FAKE HIGH SCHOOL GIRLFRIEND, SCOTT.
...YEAH, I KNOW.
WHO'S THE LETTER FROM?

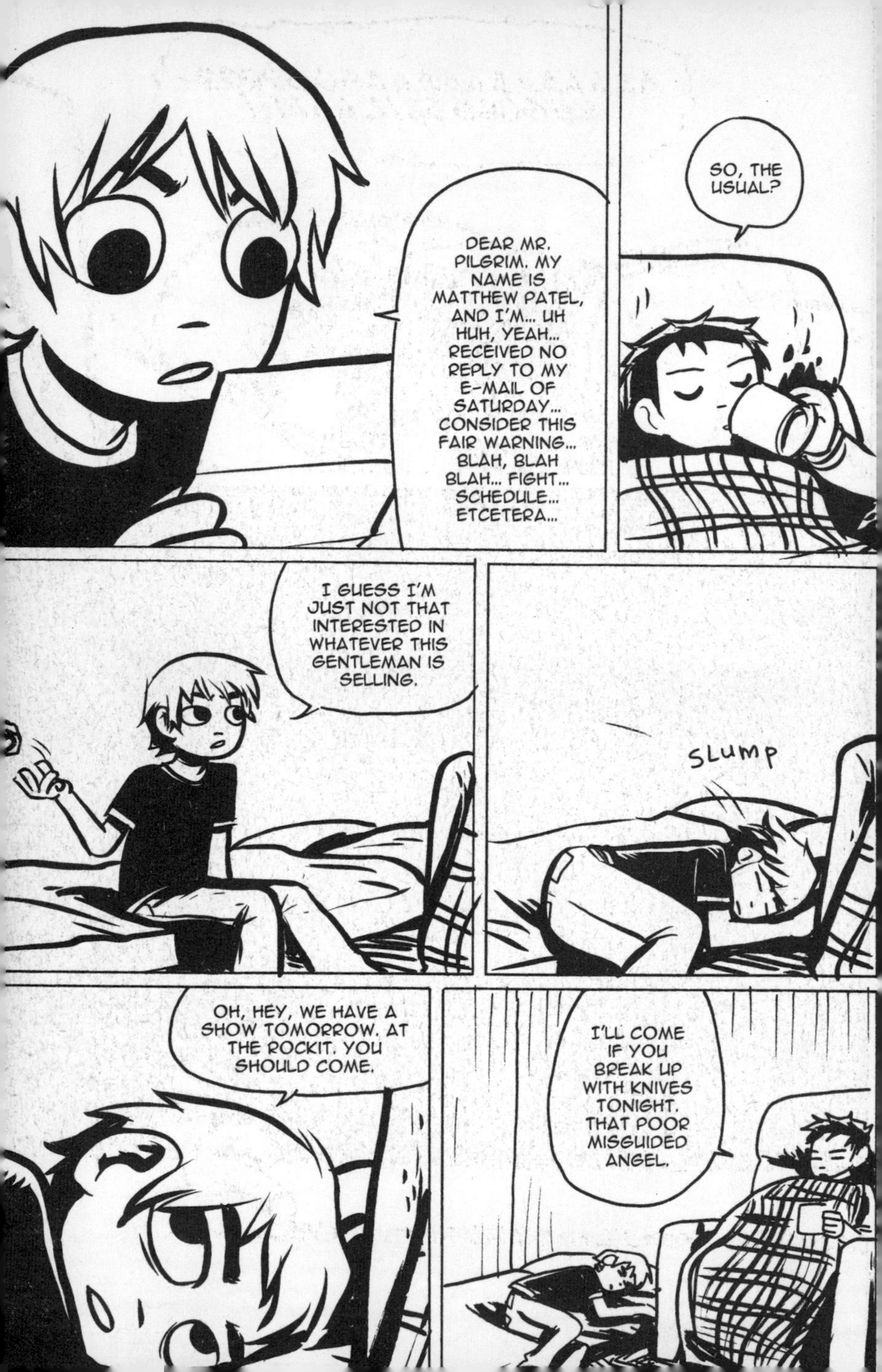
DEAR MR. PILGRIM. MY NAME IS MATTHEW PATEL, AND I'M... UH HUH, YEAH... RECEIVED NO REPLY TO MY E-MAIL OF SATURDAY... CONSIDER THIS FAIR WARNING... BLAH, BLAH BLAH... FIGHT... SCHEDULE... ETCETERA...
SO, THE USUAL?
I GUESS I'M JUST NOT THAT INTERESTED IN WHATEVER THIS GENTLEMAN IS SELLING.
SLUMP
OH, HEY, WE HAVE A SHOW TOMORROW. AT THE ROCKIT. YOU SHOULD COME.
I'LL COME IF YOU BREAK UP WITH KNIVES TONIGHT. THAT POOR MISGUIDED ANGEL.

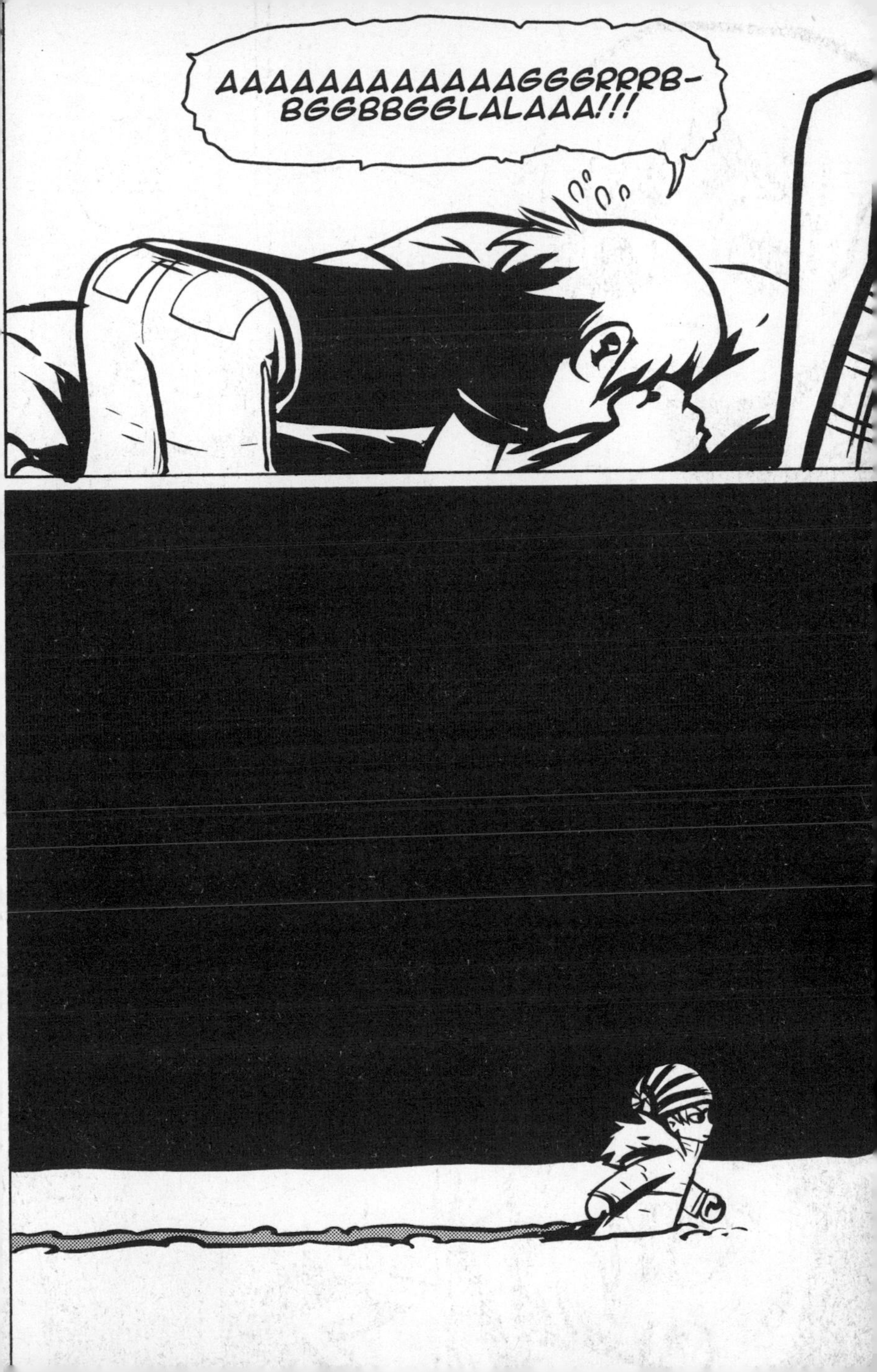
AAAAAAAAAAAAAGGGRRRB-BGGBBGGLALAAA!!!

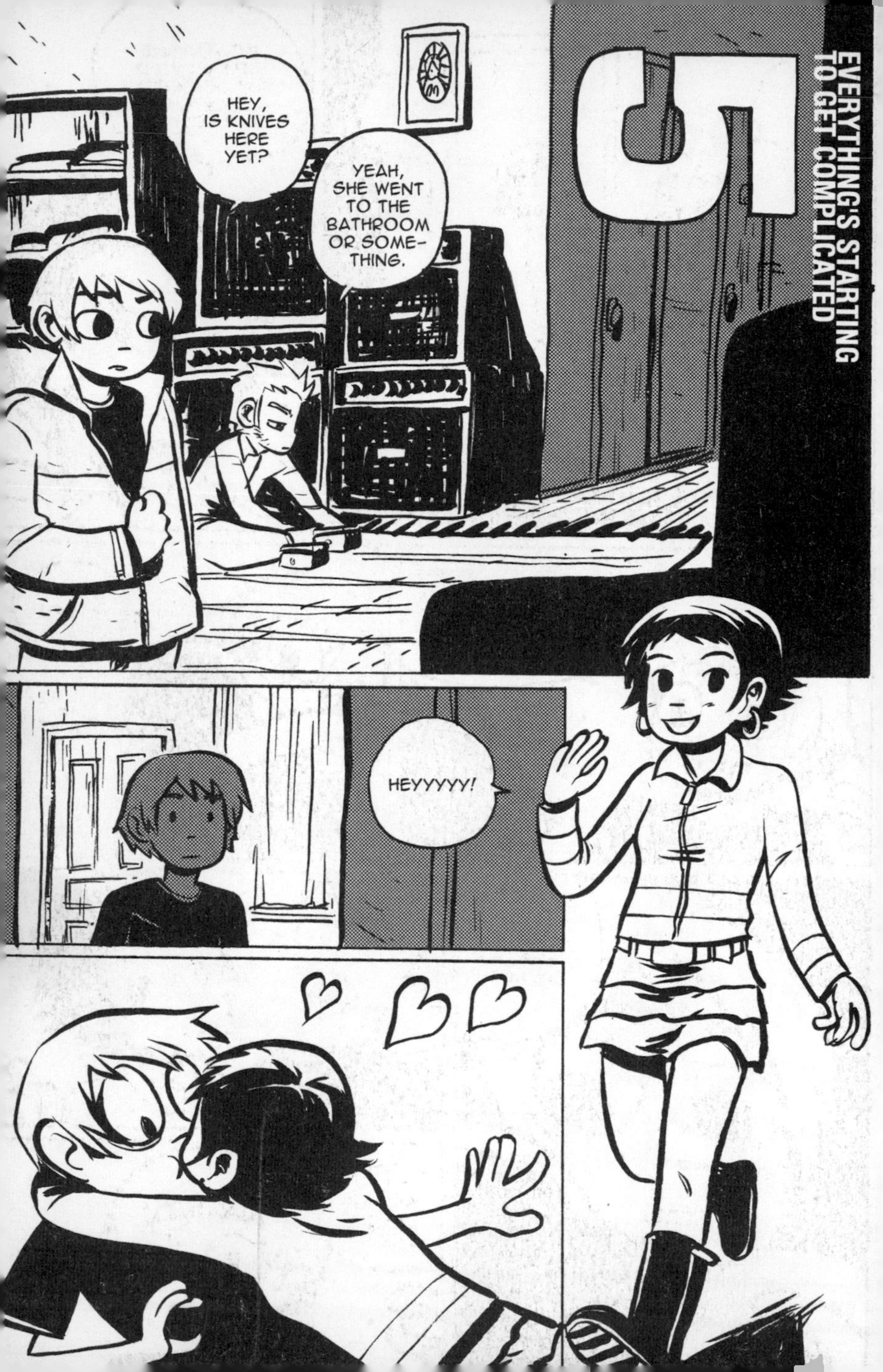
5
EVERYTHING'S STARTING TO GET COMPLICATED
HEY, IS KNIVES HERE YET?
YEAH, SHE WENT TO THE BATHROOM OR SOME-THING.
HEYYYYY!

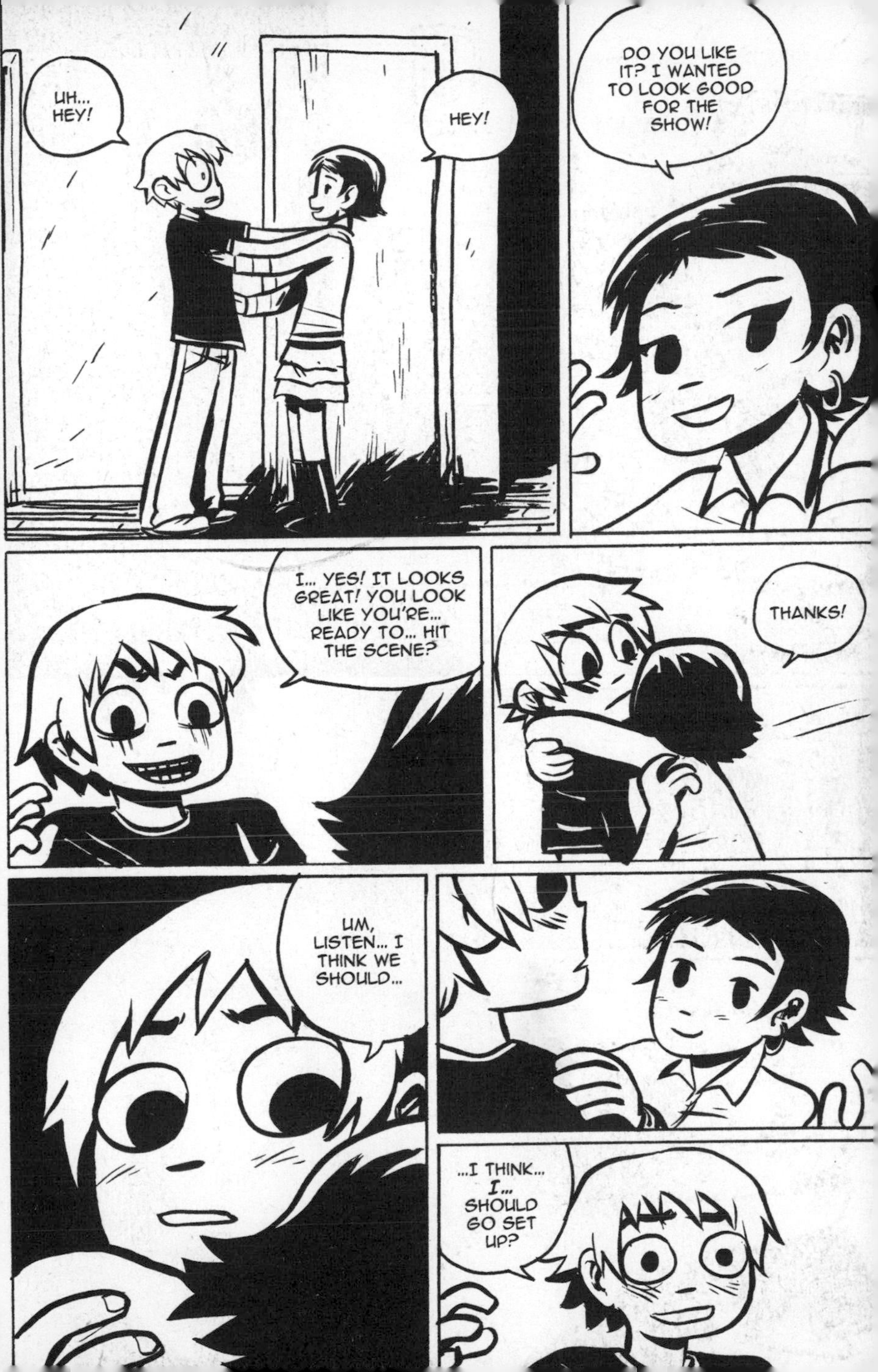
UH... HEY!
HEY!
DO YOU LIKE IT? I WANTED TO LOOK GOOD FOR THE SHOW!
I... YES! IT LOOKS GREAT! YOU LOOK LIKE YOU'RE... READY TO... HIT THE SCENE?
THANKS!
UM, LISTEN... I THINK WE SHOULD...
...I THINK... I... SHOULD GO SET UP?

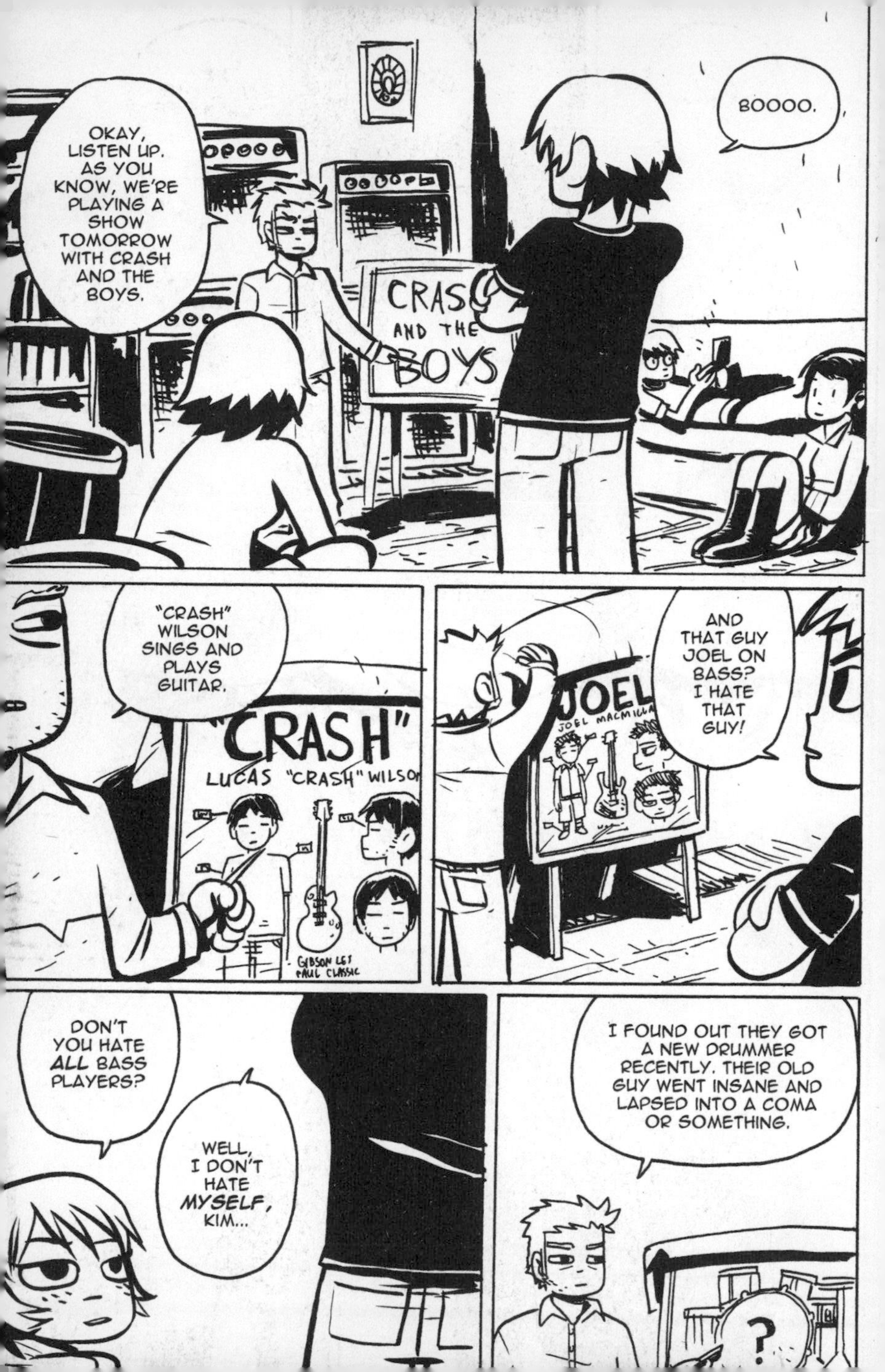
OKAY, LISTEN UP. AS YOU KNOW, WE'RE PLAYING A SHOW TOMORROW WITH CRASH AND THE BOYS.
CRASH AND THE BOYS
BOOOO.
"CRASH" WILSON SINGS AND PLAYS GUITAR.
"CRASH"
LUCAS "CRASH" WILSON
GIBSON LES PAUL CLASSIC
AND THAT GUY JOEL ON BASS? I HATE THAT GUY!
JOEL
DON'T YOU HATE ALL BASS PLAYERS?
WELL, I DON'T HATE MYSELF, KIM...
I FOUND OUT THEY GOT A NEW DRUMMER RECENTLY. THEIR OLD GUY WENT INSANE AND LAPSED INTO A COMA OR SOMETHING.
?

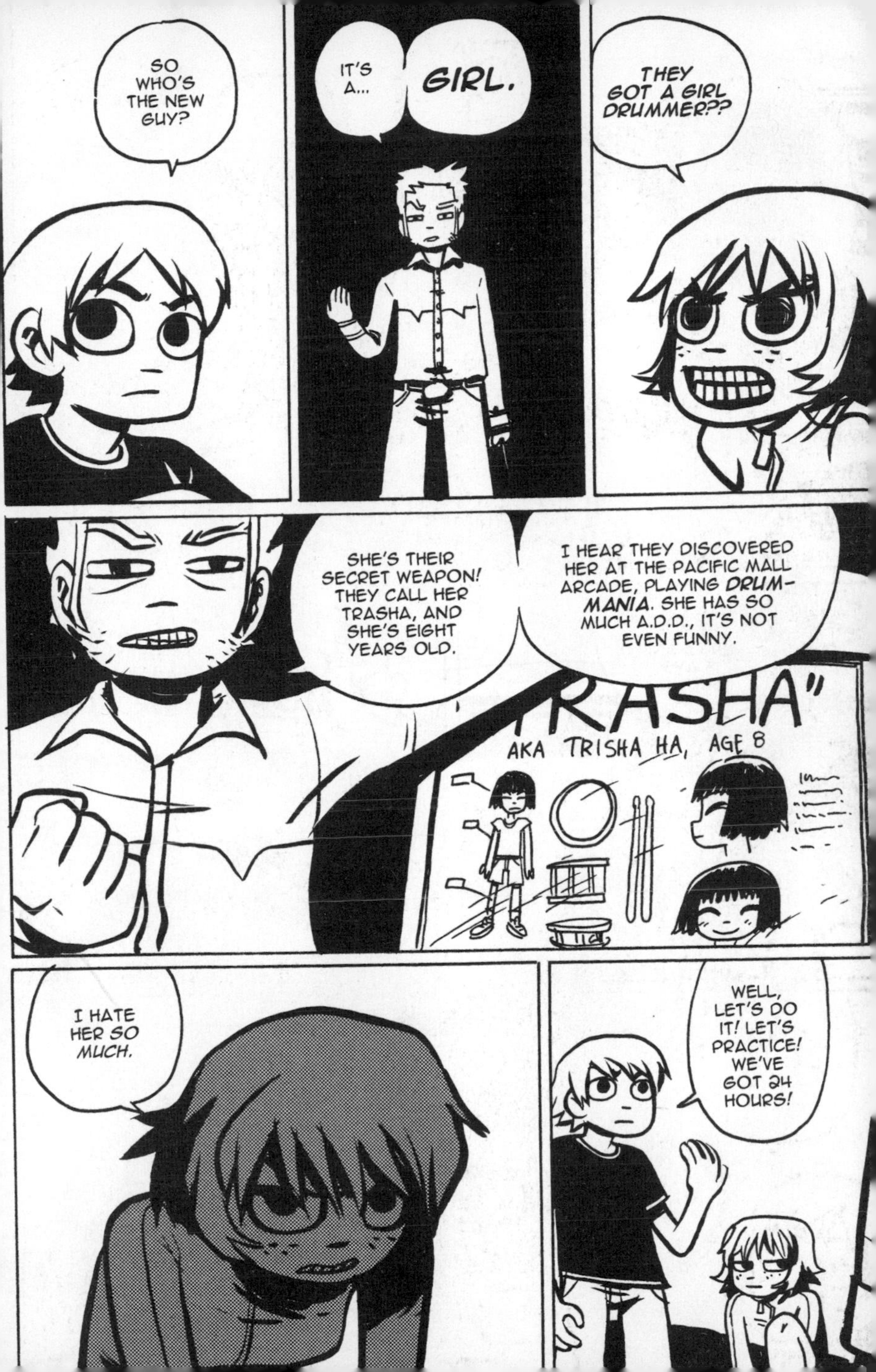
SO WHO'S THE NEW GUY?
IT'S A...
GIRL.
THEY GOT A GIRL DRUMMER??
SHE'S THEIR SECRET WEAPON! THEY CALL HER TRASHA, AND SHE'S EIGHT YEARS OLD.
I HEAR THEY DISCOVERED HER AT THE PACIFIC MALL ARCADE, PLAYING DRUM-MANIA. SHE HAS SO MUCH A.D.D., IT'S NOT EVEN FUNNY.
"TRASHA"
AKA TRISHA HA, AGE 8
I HATE HER SO MUCH.
WELL, LET'S DO IT! LET'S PRACTICE! WE'VE GOT 24 HOURS!

24 HRS

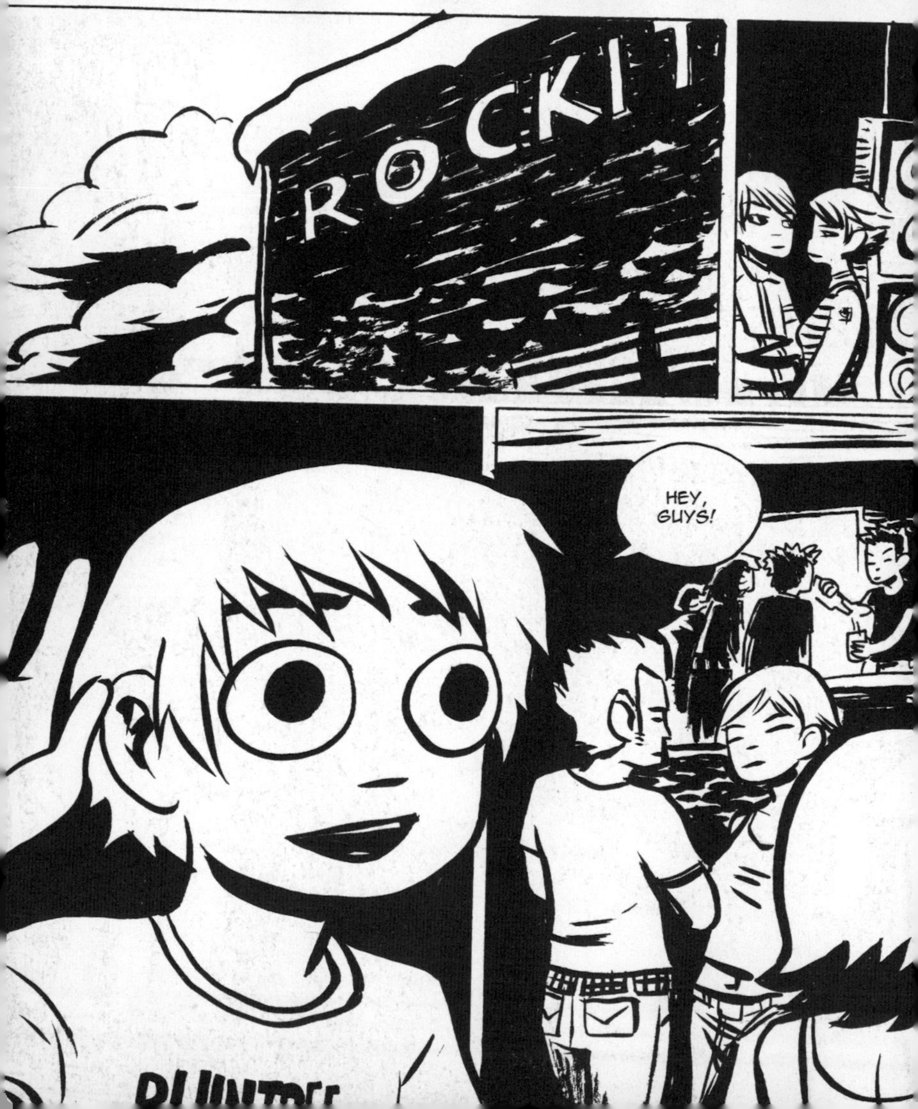
ROCKIT
HEY, GUYS!

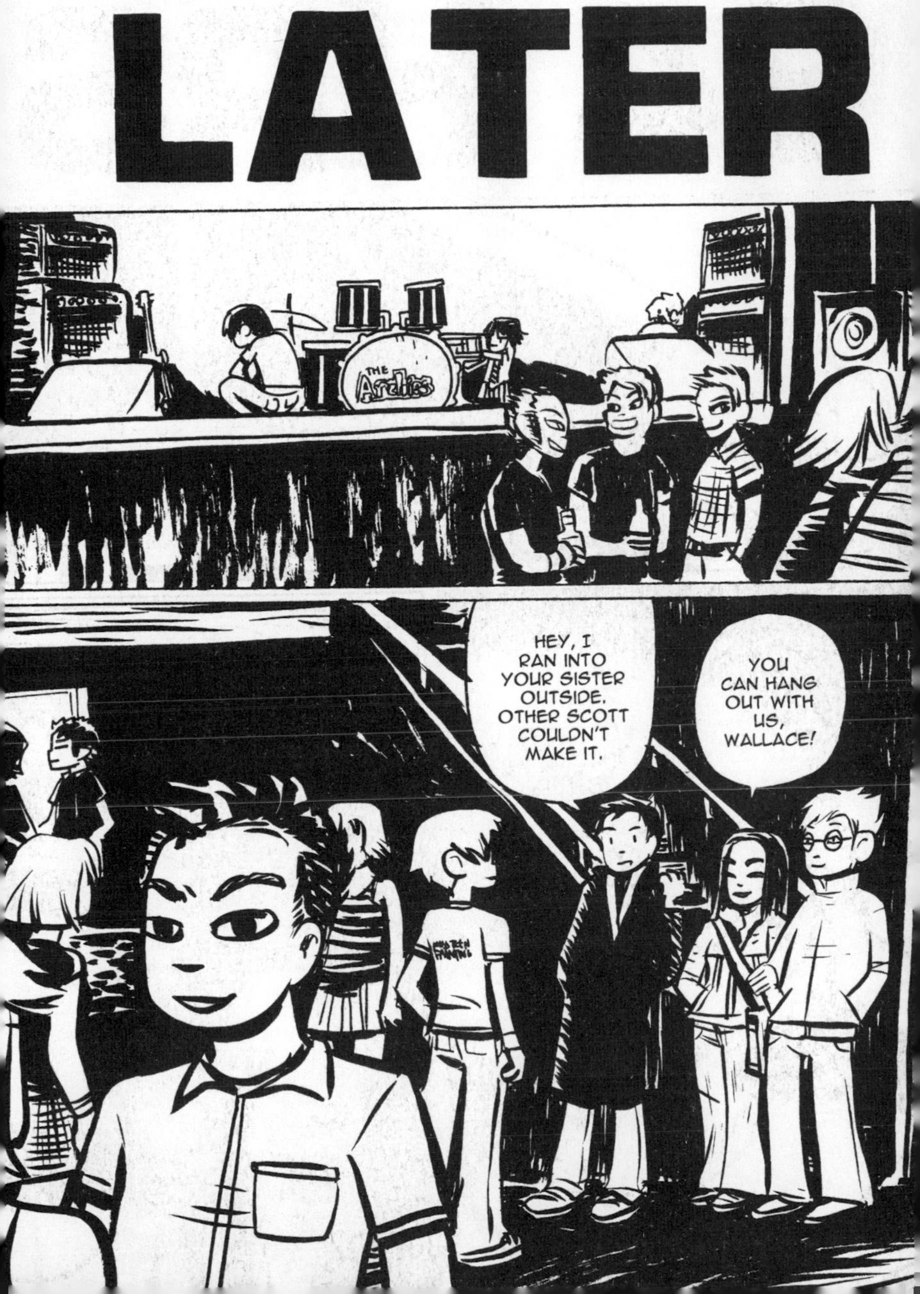
LATER
HEY, I RAN INTO YOUR SISTER OUTSIDE. OTHER SCOTT COULDN'T MAKE IT.
YOU CAN HANG OUT WITH US, WALLACE!

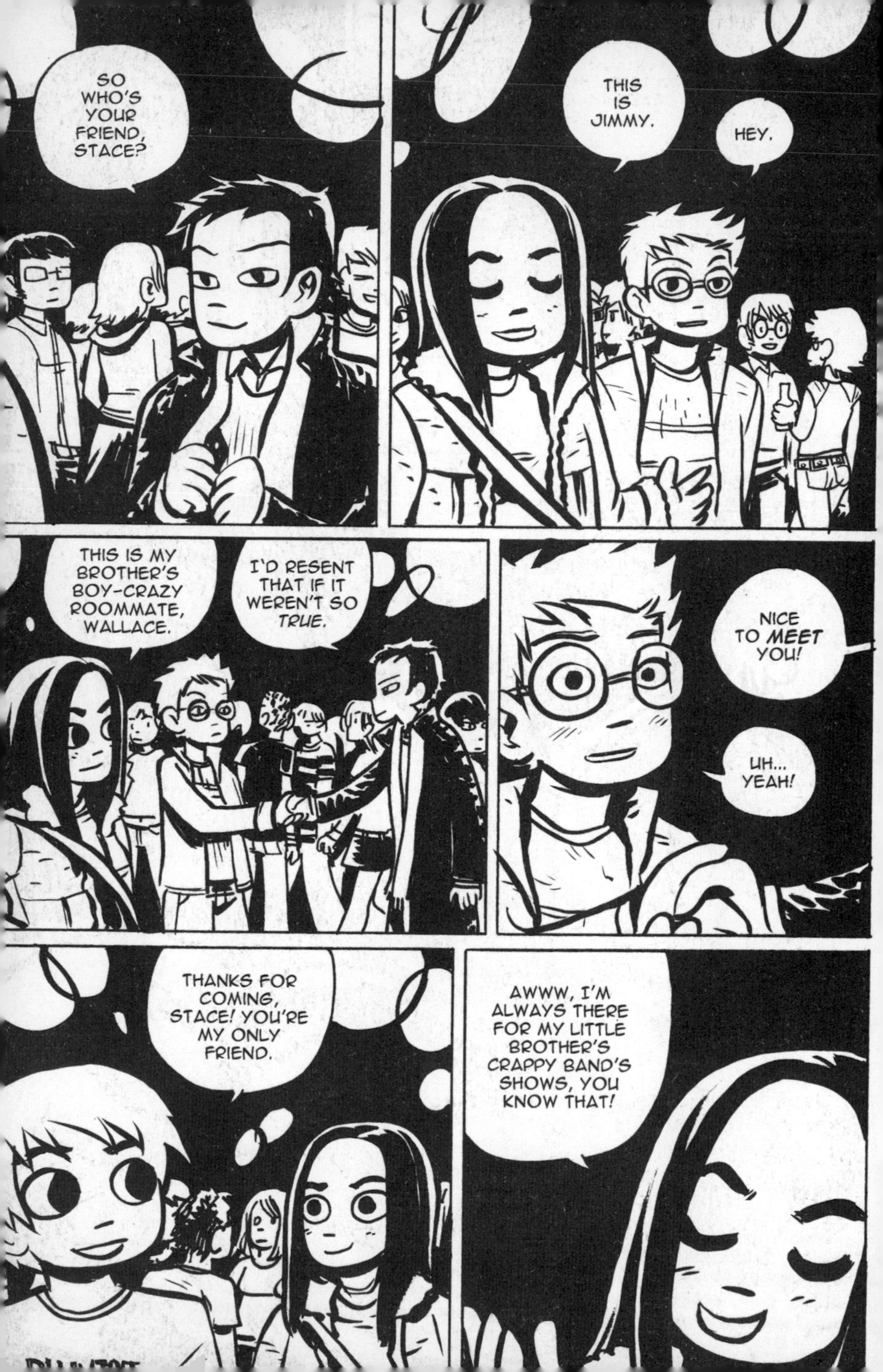
SO WHO'S YOUR FRIEND, STACE?
THIS IS JIMMY.
HEY.
THIS IS MY BROTHER'S BOY-CRAZY ROOMMATE, WALLACE.
I'D RESENT THAT IF IT WEREN'T SO TRUE.
NICE TO MEET YOU!
UH... YEAH!
THANKS FOR COMING, STACE! YOU'RE MY ONLY FRIEND.
AWWW, I'M ALWAYS THERE FOR MY LITTLE BROTHER'S CRAPPY BAND'S SHOWS, YOU KNOW THAT!

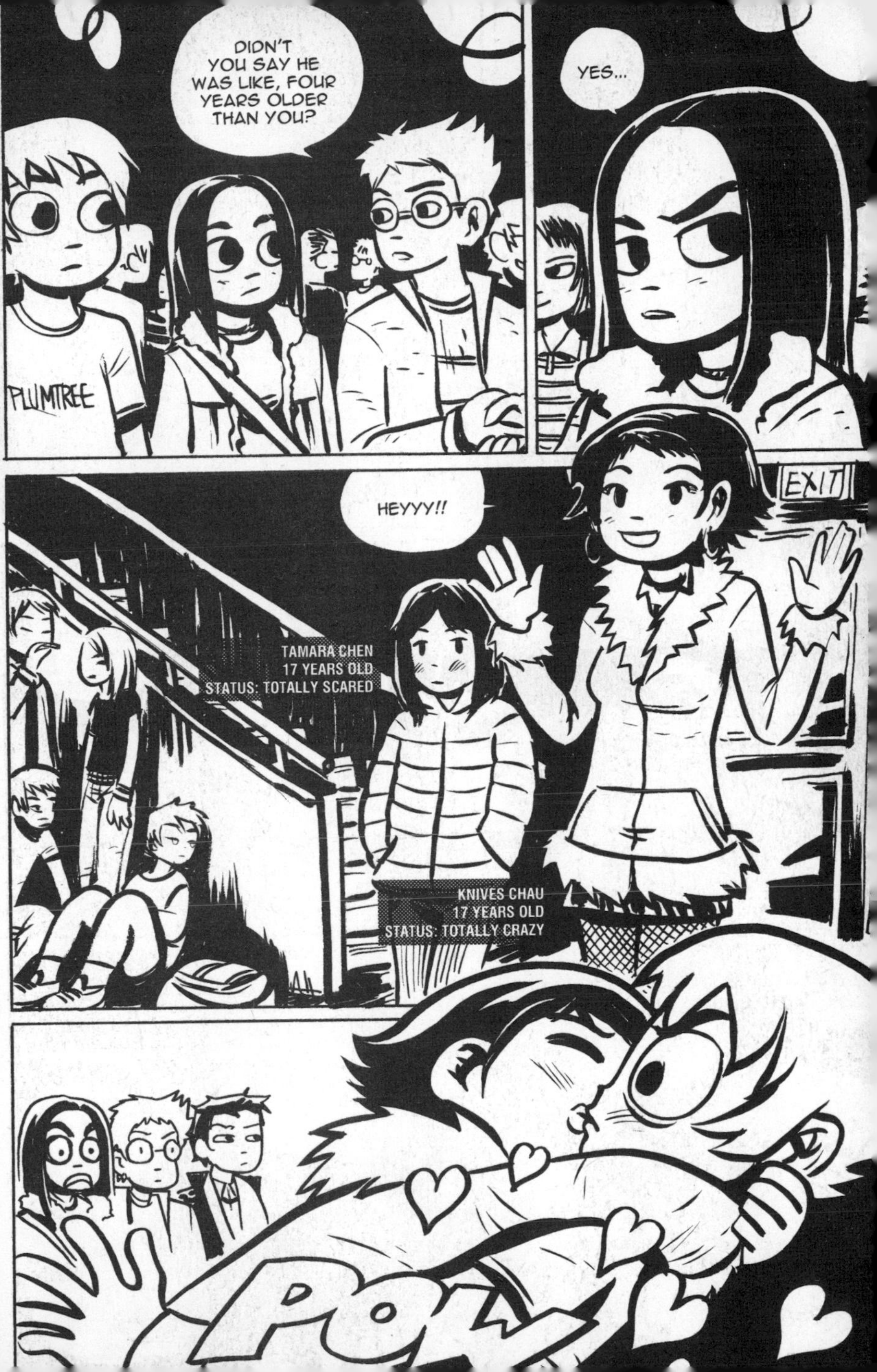

DIDN'T YOU SAY HE WAS LIKE, FOUR YEARS OLDER THAN YOU?
PLUMTREE
YES...
HEYYY!!
EXIT
TAMARA CHEN
17 YEARS OLD
STATUS: TOTALLY SCARED
KNIVES CHAU
17 YEARS OLD
STATUS: TOTALLY CRAZY

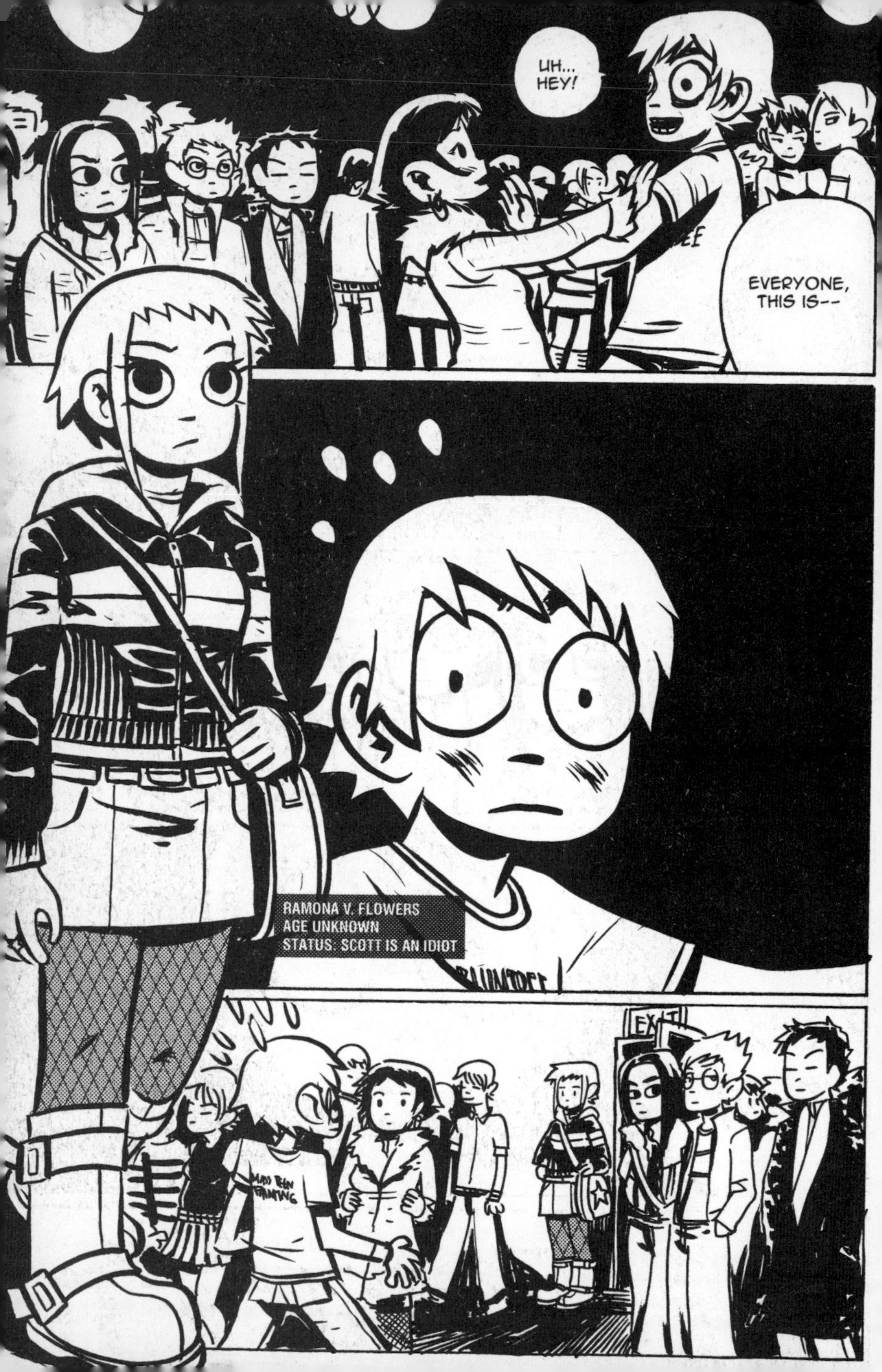
UH... HEY!
EVERYONE, THIS IS--
RAMONA V. FLOWERS
AGE UNKNOWN
STATUS: SCOTT IS AN IDIOT

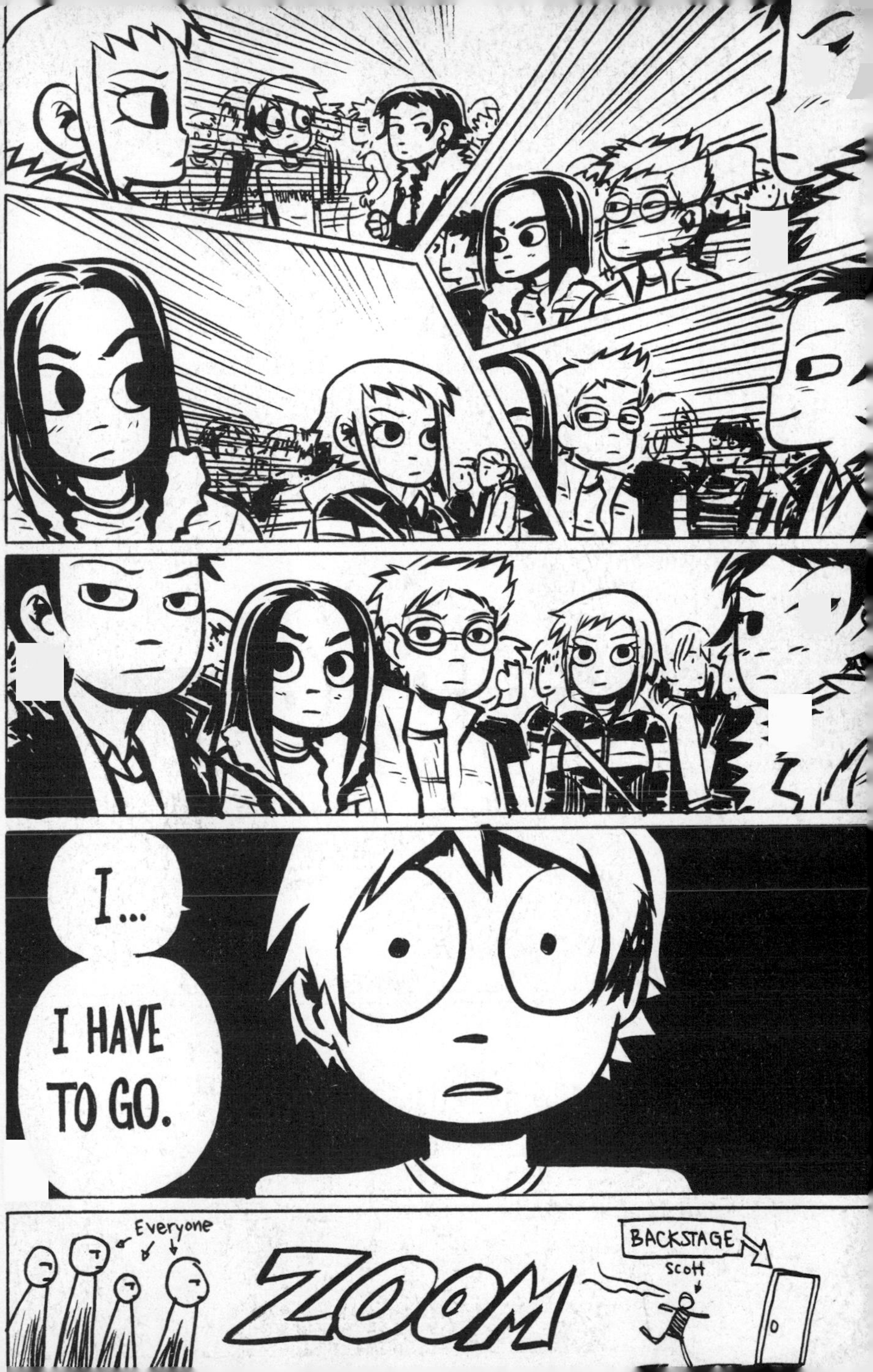
I...
I HAVE TO GO.
Everyone
ZOOM
BACKSTAGE
Scott

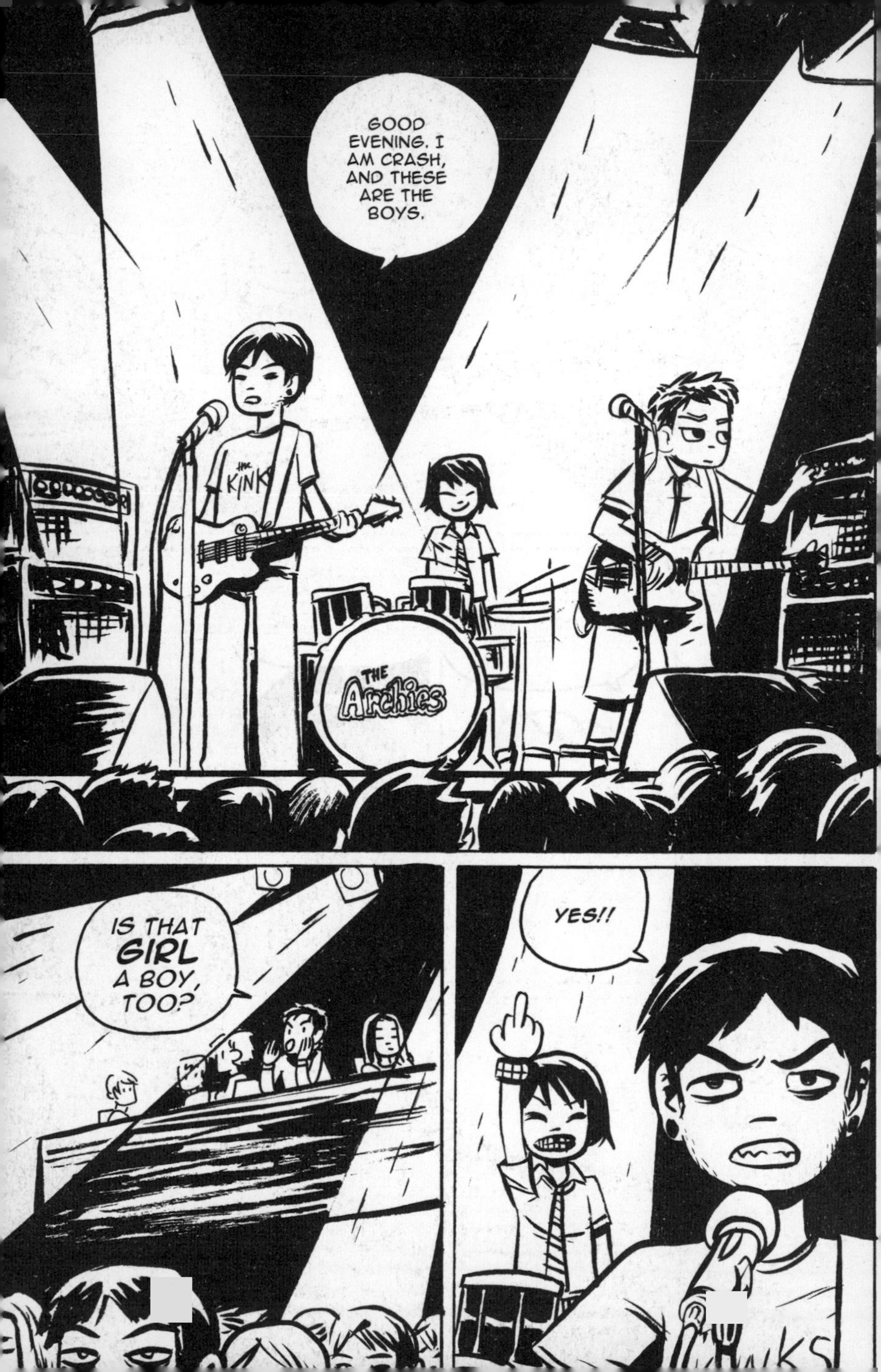
GOOD EVENING. I AM CRASH, AND THESE ARE THE BOYS.
THE Archies
IS THAT GIRL A BOY, TOO?
YES!!

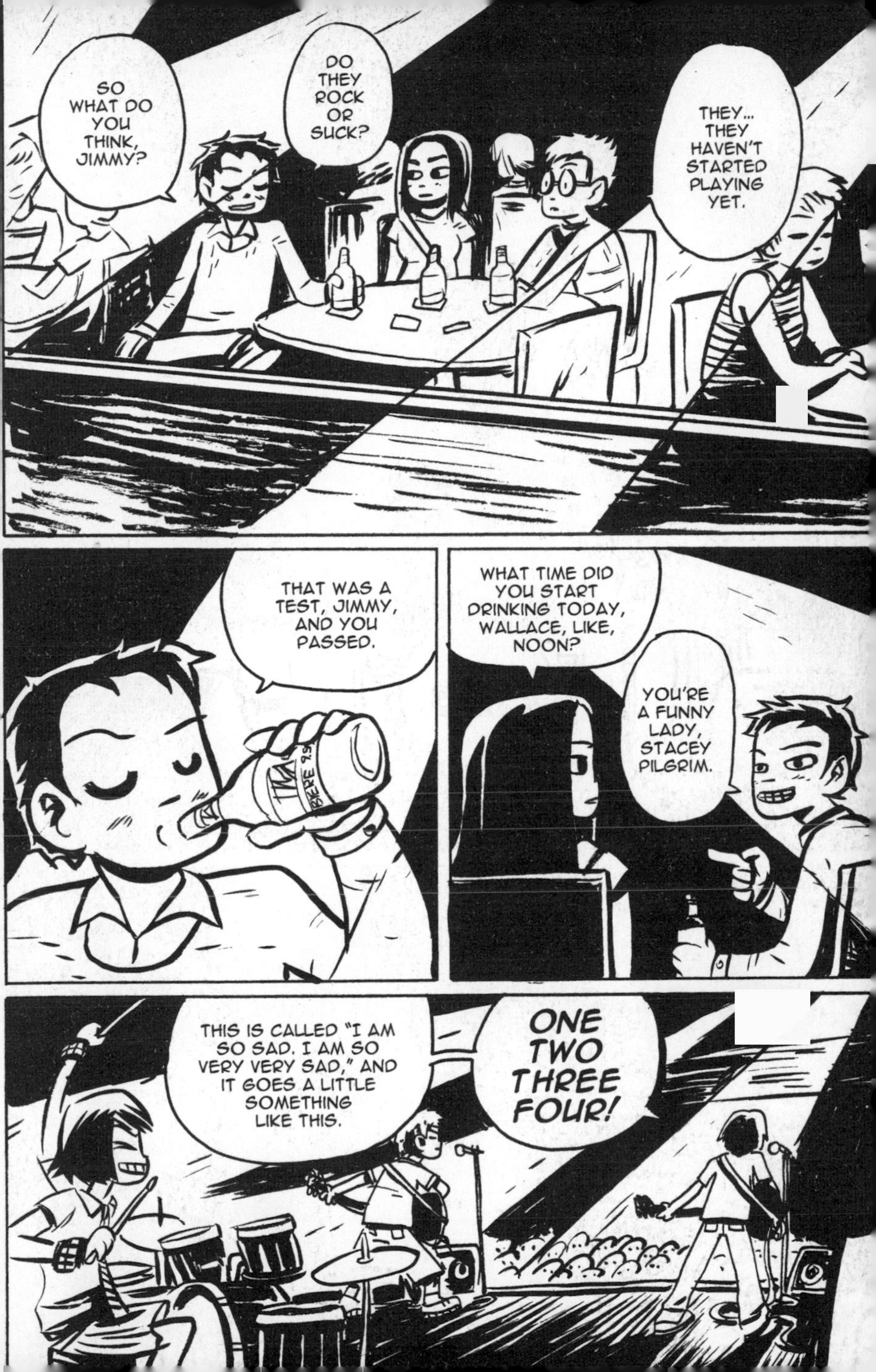

SO WHAT DO YOU THINK, JIMMY?
DO THEY ROCK OR SUCK?
THEY... THEY HAVEN'T STARTED PLAYING YET.
THAT WAS A TEST, JIMMY, AND YOU PASSED.
WHAT TIME DID YOU START DRINKING TODAY, WALLACE, LIKE, NOON?
YOU'RE A FUNNY LADY, STACEY PILGRIM.
THIS IS CALLED "I AM SO SAD. I AM SO VERY VERY SAD," AND IT GOES A LITTLE SOMETHING LIKE THIS.
ONE TWO THREE FOUR!

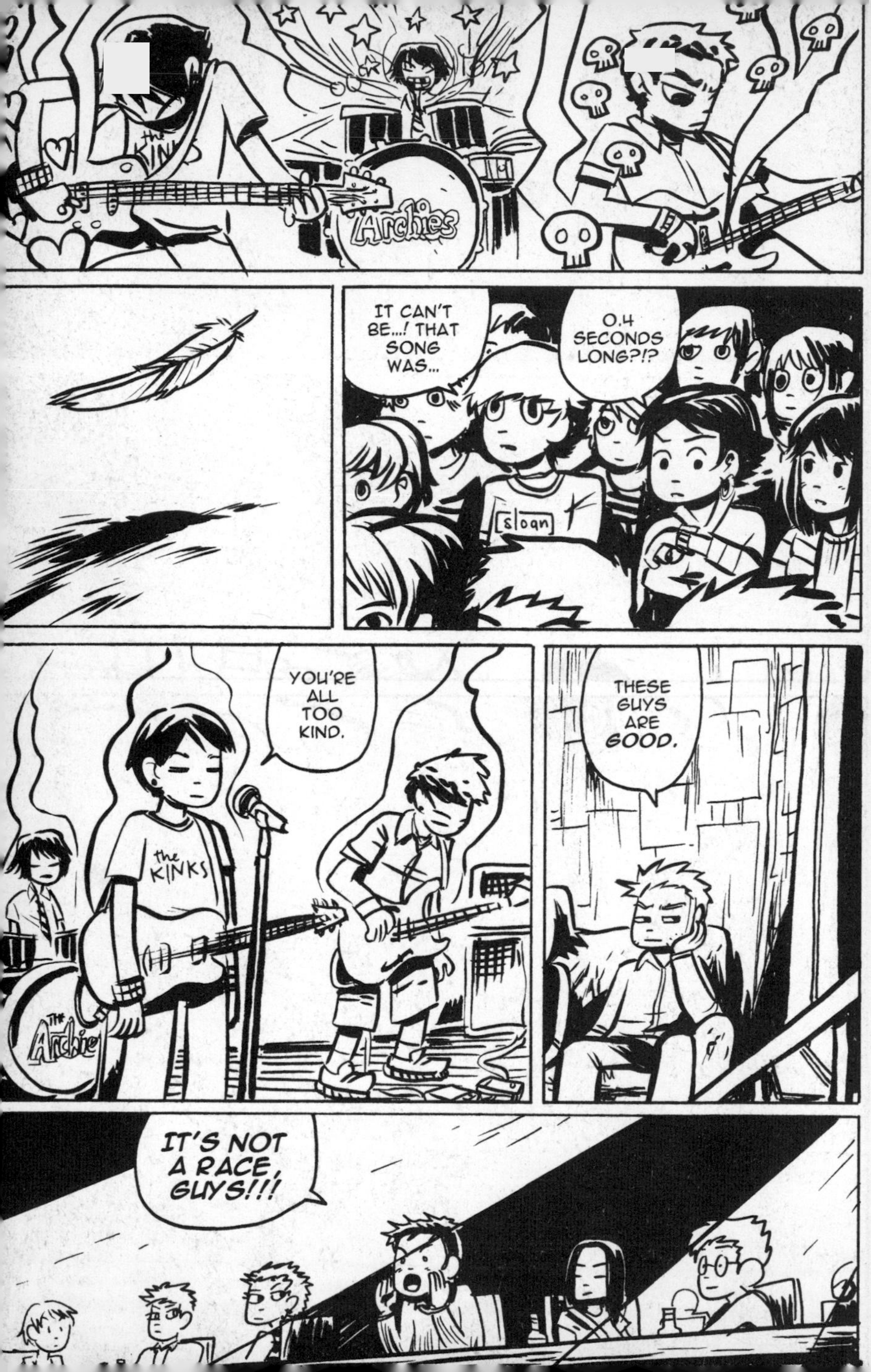
IT CAN'T BE...! THAT SONG WAS...
0.4 SECONDS LONG?!?
YOU'RE ALL TOO KIND.
THESE GUYS ARE GOOD.
IT'S NOT A RACE, GUYS!!!

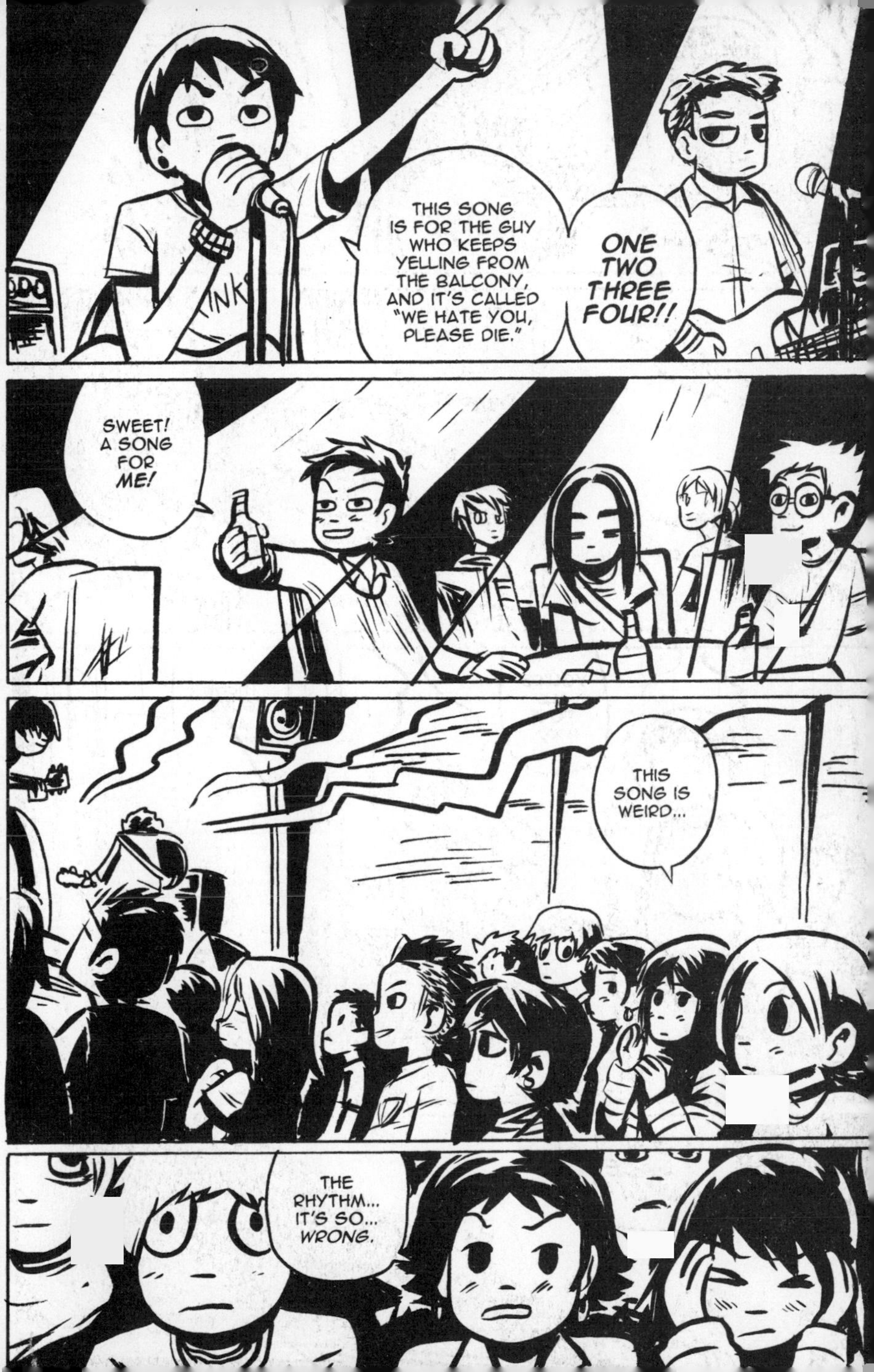
THIS SONG IS FOR THE GUY WHO KEEPS YELLING FROM THE BALCONY, AND IT'S CALLED "WE HATE YOU, PLEASE DIE."
ONE TWO THREE FOUR!!
SWEET! A SONG FOR *ME!*
THIS SONG IS WEIRD...
THE RHYTHM... IT'S SO... *WRONG.*

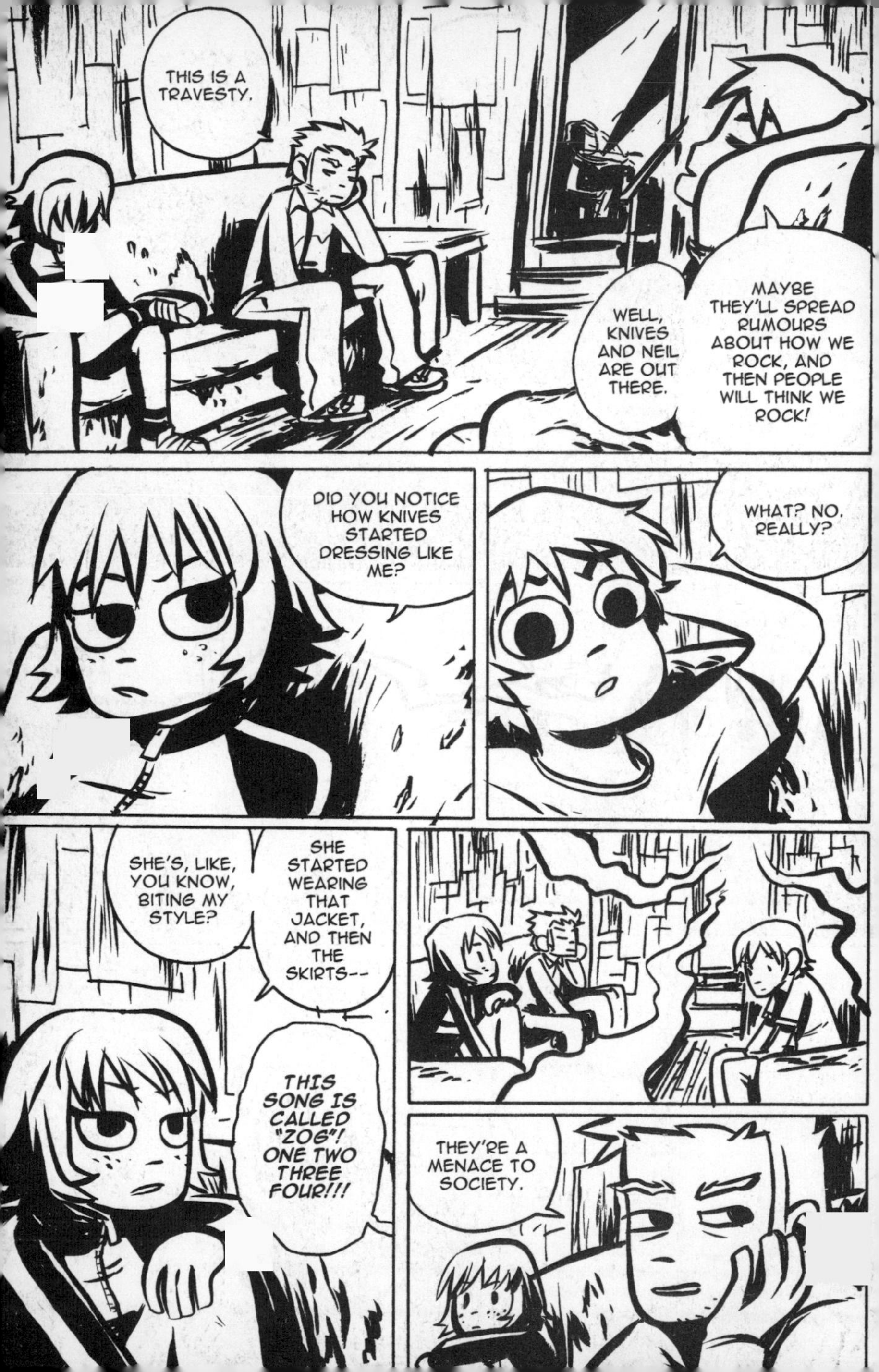
THIS IS A TRAVESTY.
WELL, KNIVES AND NEIL ARE OUT THERE.
MAYBE THEY'LL SPREAD RUMOURS ABOUT HOW WE ROCK, AND THEN PEOPLE WILL THINK WE ROCK!
DID YOU NOTICE HOW KNIVES STARTED DRESSING LIKE ME?
WHAT? NO. REALLY?
SHE'S, LIKE, YOU KNOW, BITING MY STYLE?
SHE STARTED WEARING THAT JACKET, AND THEN THE SKIRTS--
THIS SONG IS CALLED "ZOG"! ONE TWO THREE FOUR!!!
THEY'RE A MENACE TO SOCIETY.

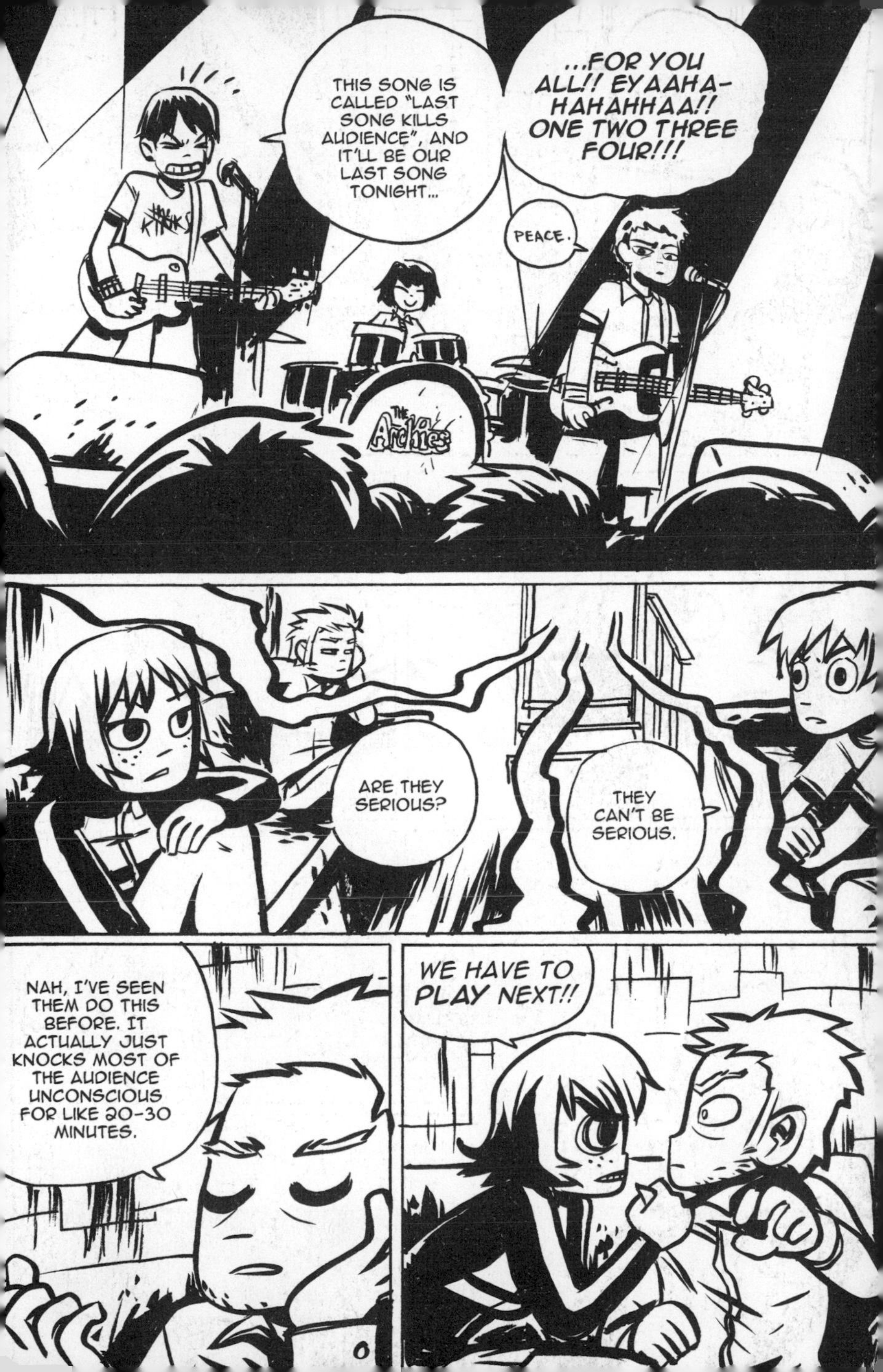
THIS SONG IS CALLED "LAST SONG KILLS AUDIENCE", AND IT'LL BE OUR LAST SONG TONIGHT...
...FOR YOU ALL!! EYAAHA-HAHAHHAA!! ONE TWO THREE FOUR!!!
PEACE.
THE Archies
ARE THEY SERIOUS?
THEY CAN'T BE SERIOUS.
NAH, I'VE SEEN THEM DO THIS BEFORE. IT ACTUALLY JUST KNOCKS MOST OF THE AUDIENCE UNCONSCIOUS FOR LIKE 20-30 MINUTES.
WE HAVE TO PLAY NEXT!!

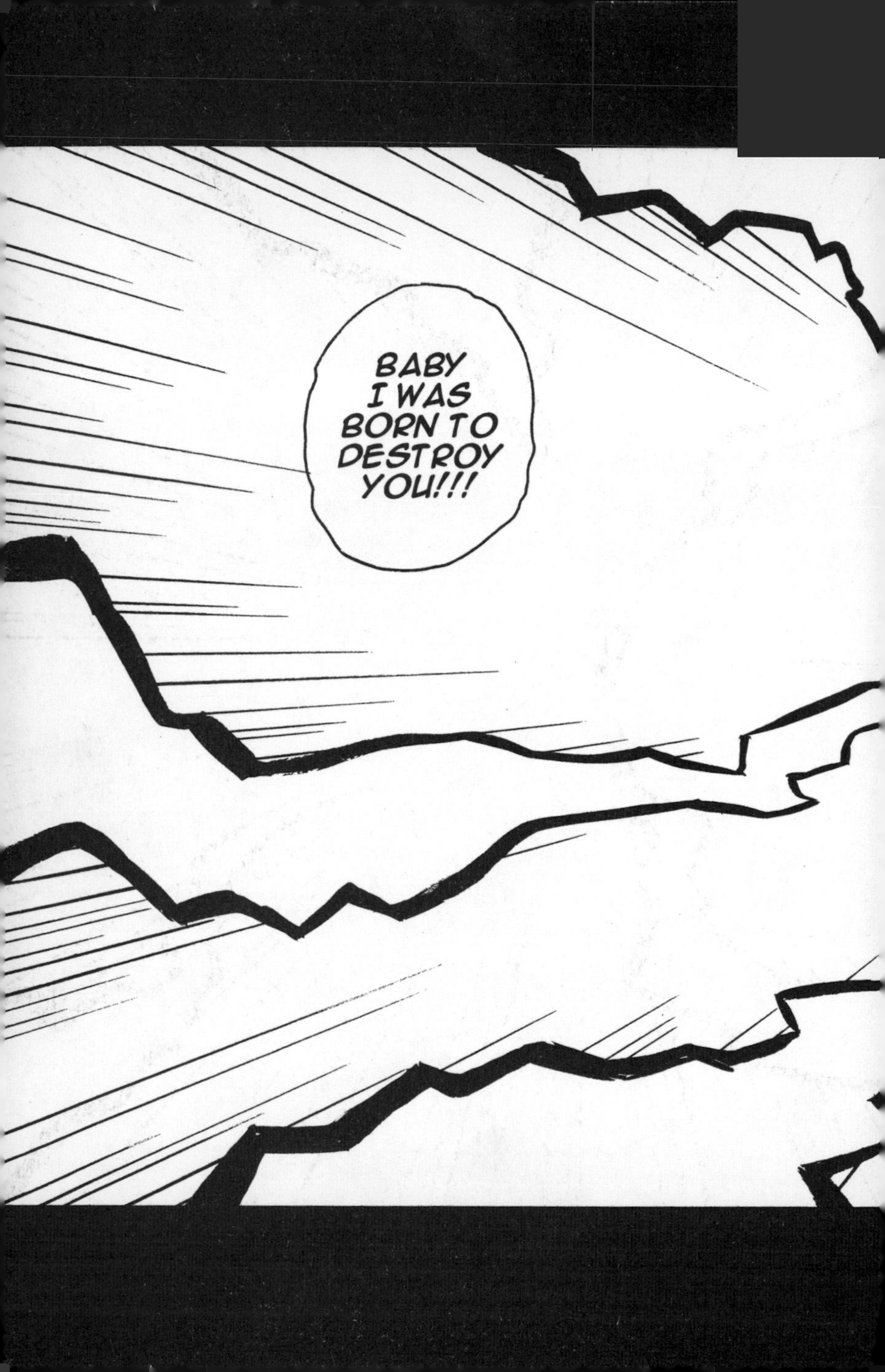
BABY I WAS BORN TO DESTROY YOU!!!

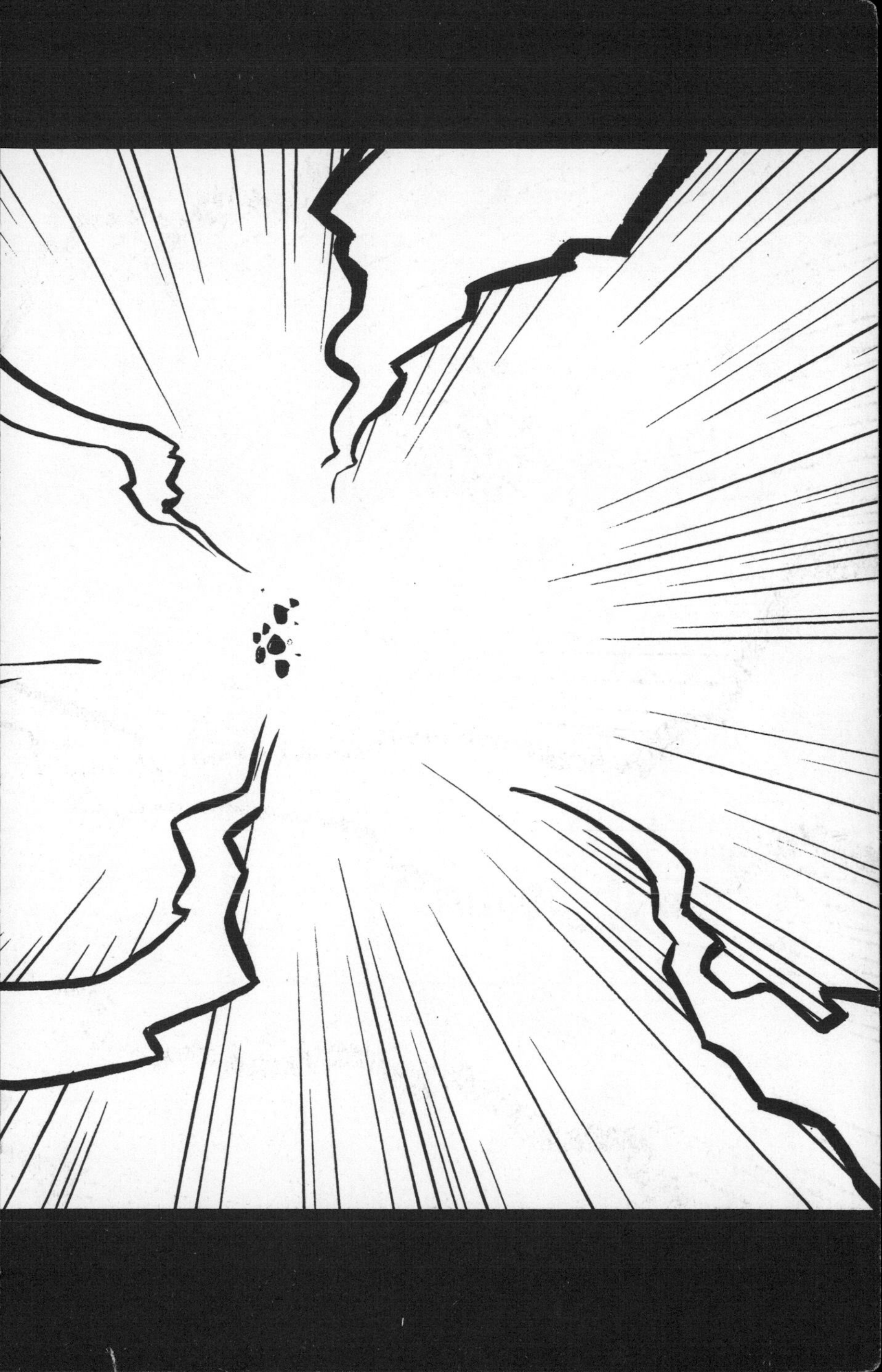

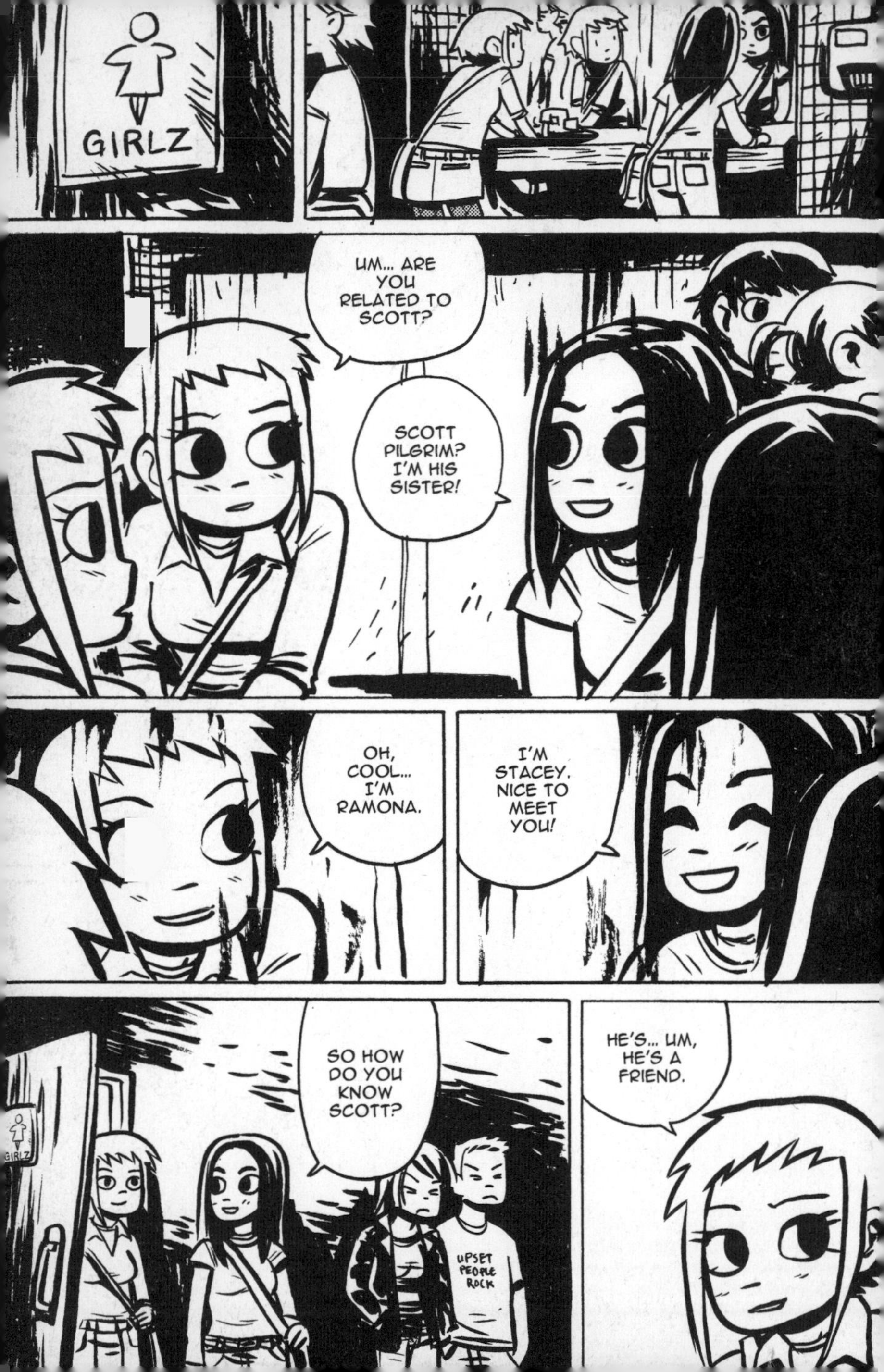
GIRLZ
UM... ARE YOU RELATED TO SCOTT?
SCOTT PILGRIM? I'M HIS SISTER!
OH, COOL... I'M RAMONA.
I'M STACEY. NICE TO MEET YOU!
SO HOW DO YOU KNOW SCOTT?
UPSET PEOPLE ROCK
HE'S... UM, HE'S A FRIEND.

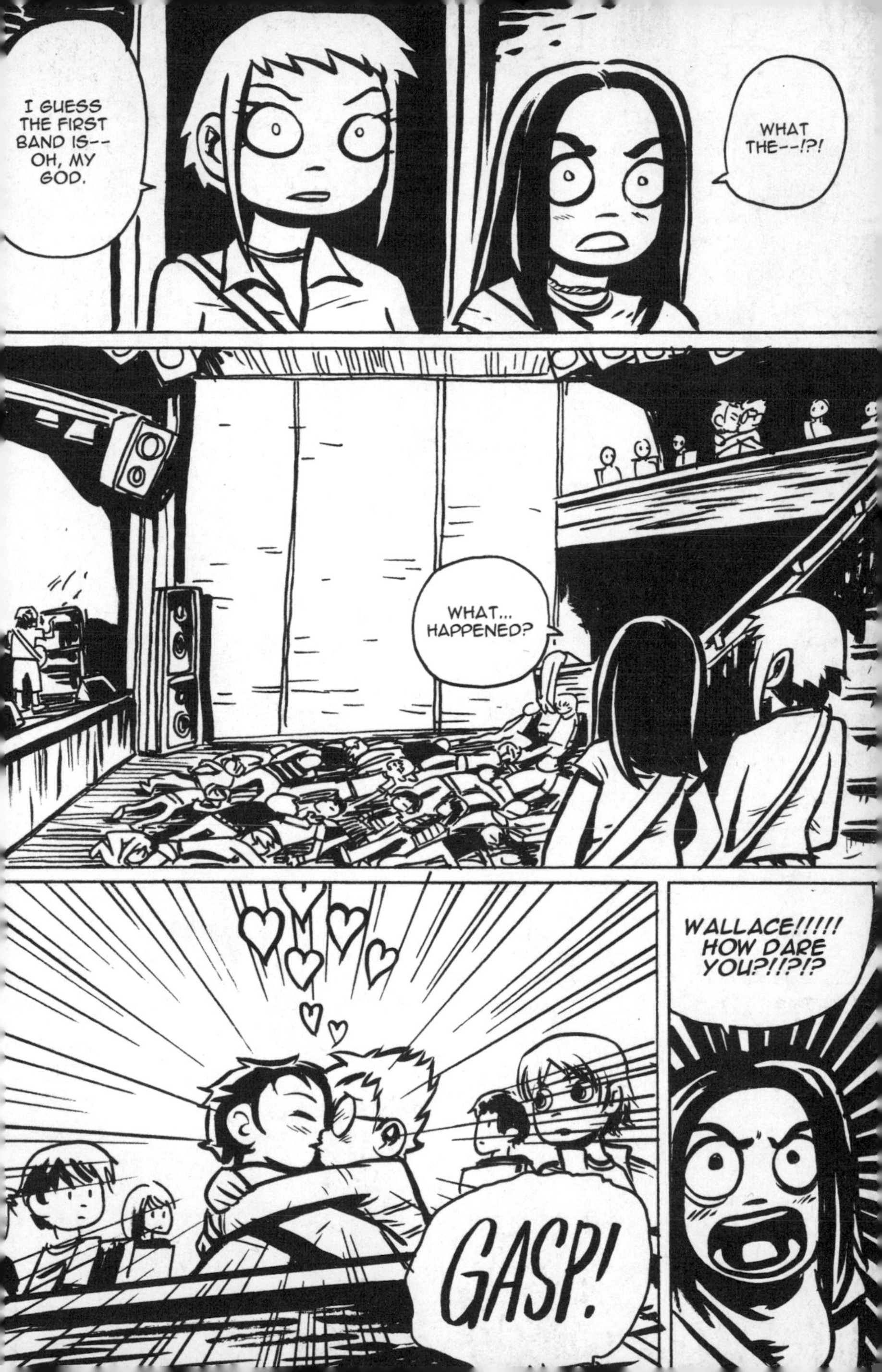
I GUESS THE FIRST BAND IS-- OH, MY GOD.
WHAT THE--!?!
WHAT... HAPPENED?
WALLACE!!!!! HOW DARE YOU?!!?!?
GASP!

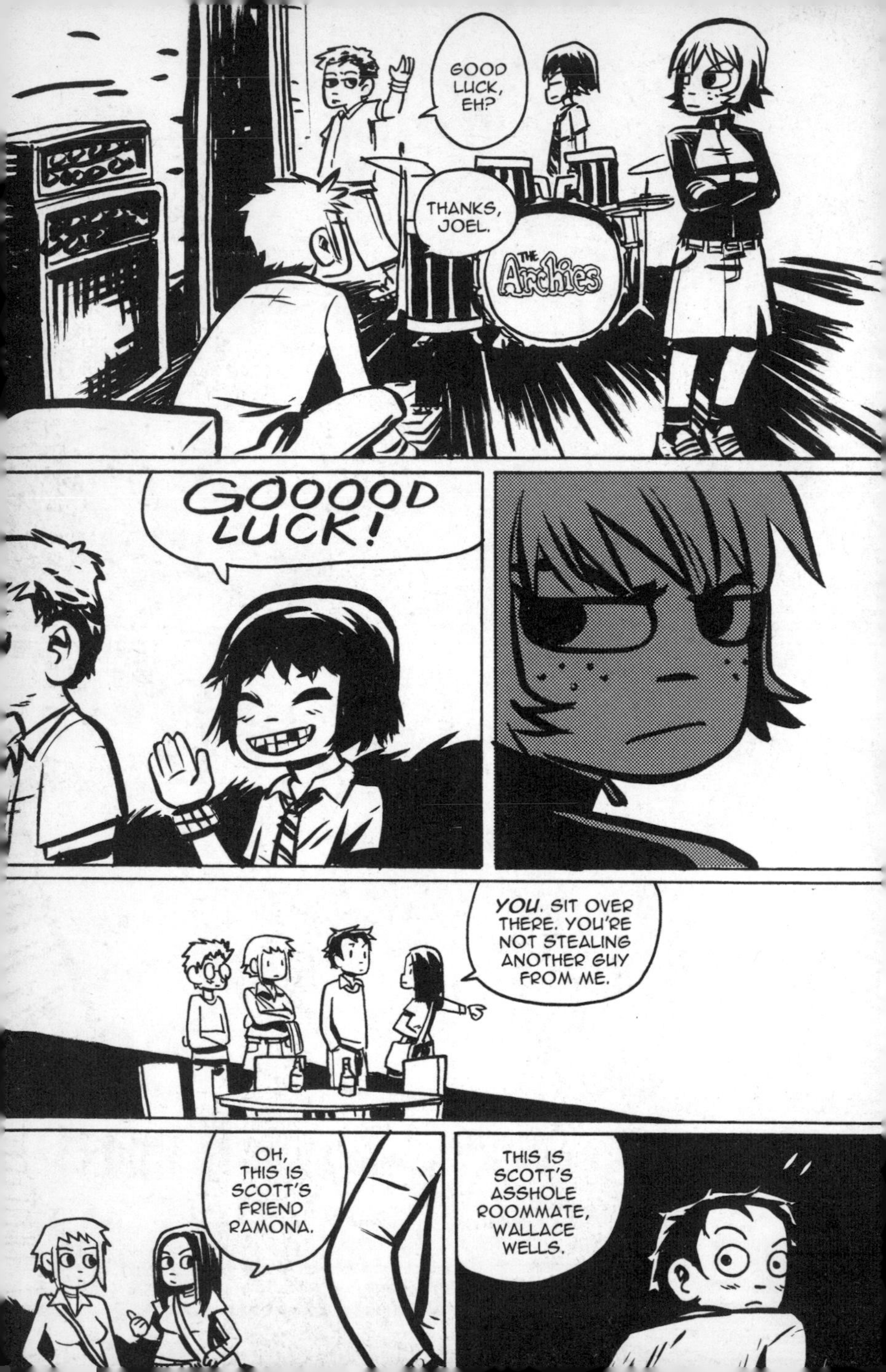
GOOD LUCK, EH?
THANKS, JOEL.
THE Archies
GOOOOD LUCK!
YOU. SIT OVER THERE. YOU'RE NOT STEALING ANOTHER GUY FROM ME.
OH, THIS IS SCOTT'S FRIEND RAMONA.
THIS IS SCOTT'S ASSHOLE ROOMMATE, WALLACE WELLS.

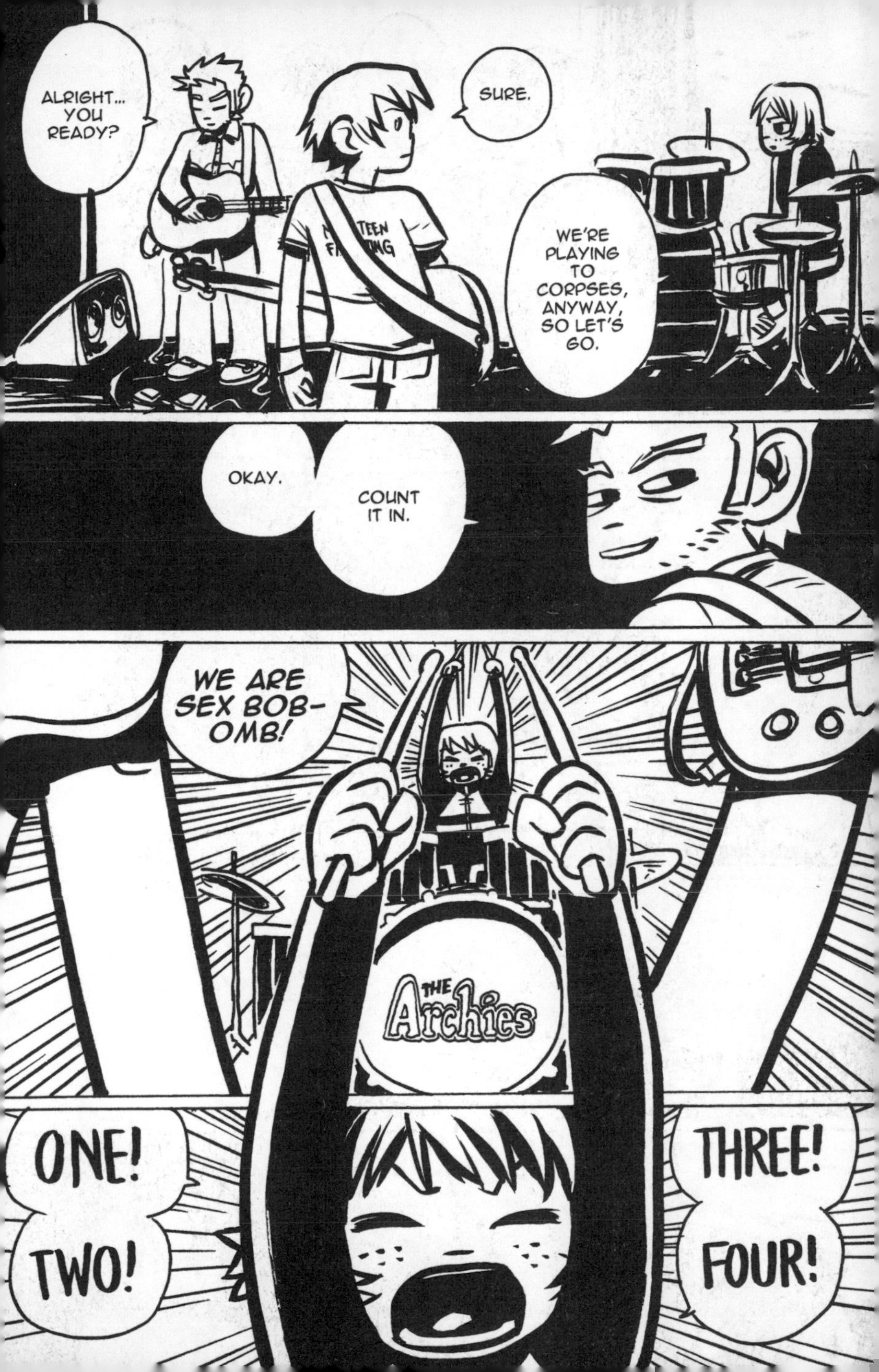
ALRIGHT... YOU READY?
SURE.
WE'RE PLAYING TO CORPSES, ANYWAY, SO LET'S GO.
OKAY.
COUNT IT IN.
WE ARE SEX BOB-OMB!
THE Archies
ONE!
TWO!
THREE!
FOUR!

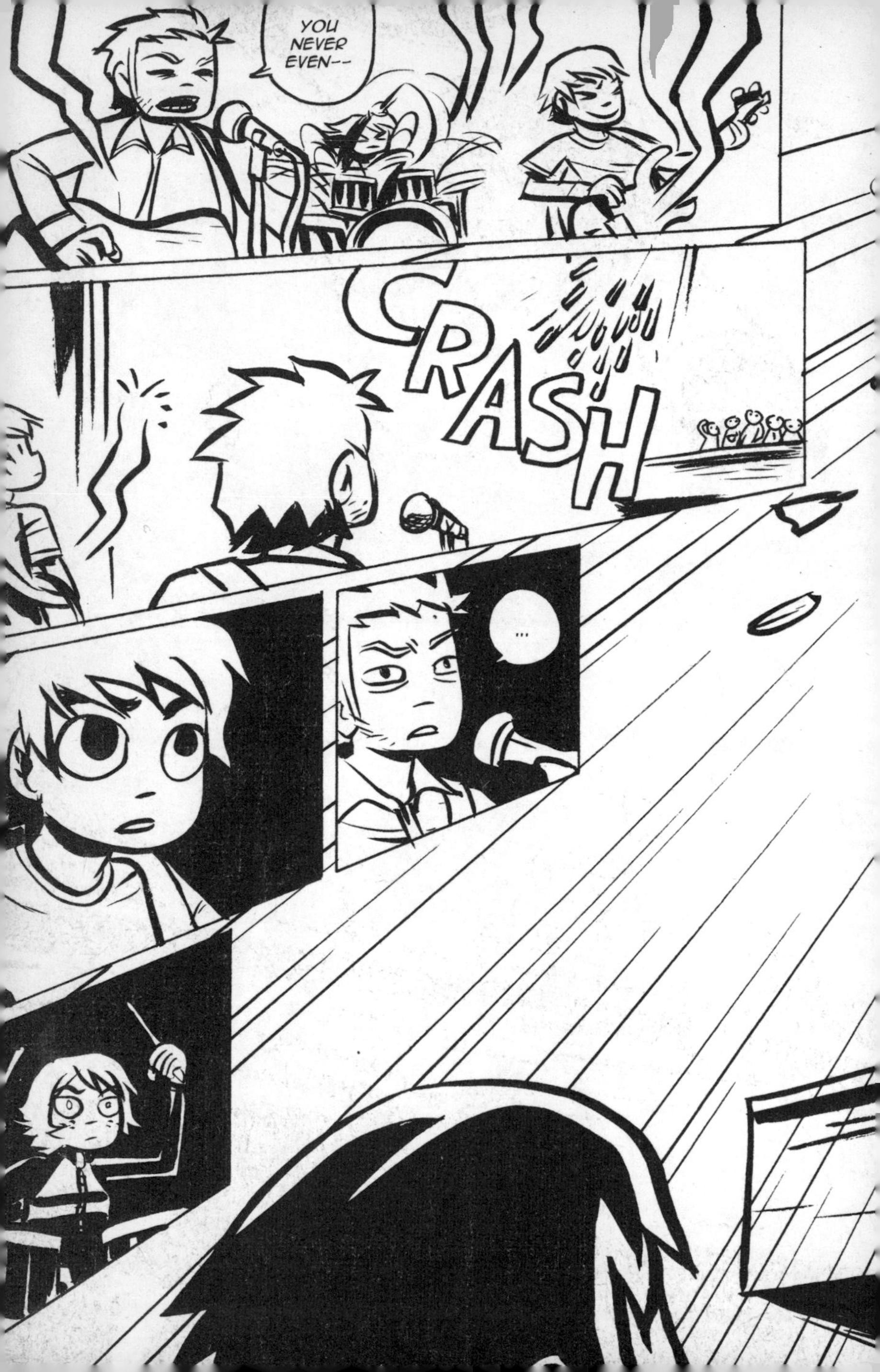
YOU NEVER EVEN--
CRASH
...

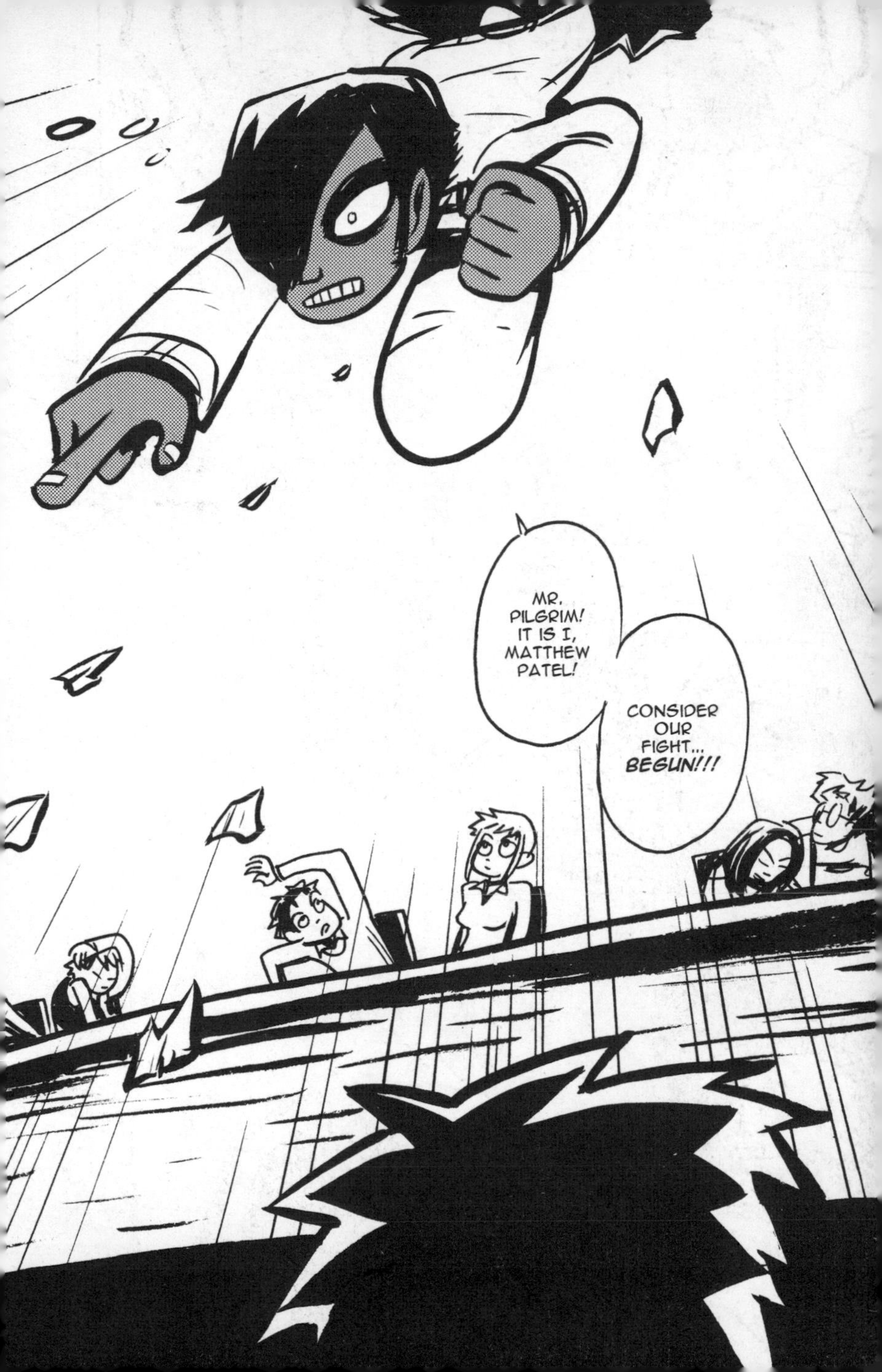
MR. PILGRIM! IT IS I, MATTHEW PATEL!
CONSIDER OUR FIGHT... BEGUN!!!

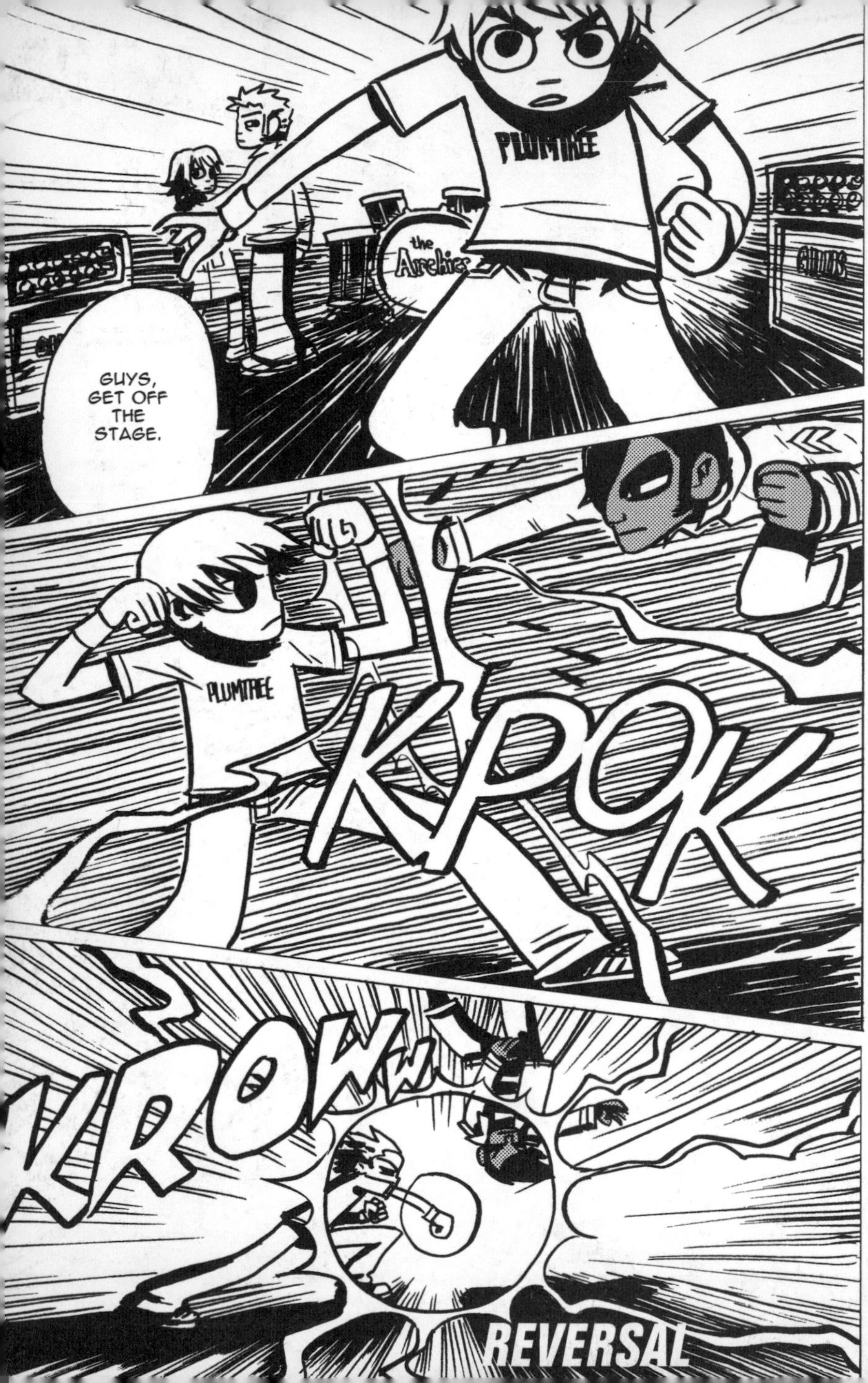

PLUMTREE
the Archies
GUYS, GET OFF THE STAGE.
PLUMTREE
KPOK
VROOM
REVERSAL

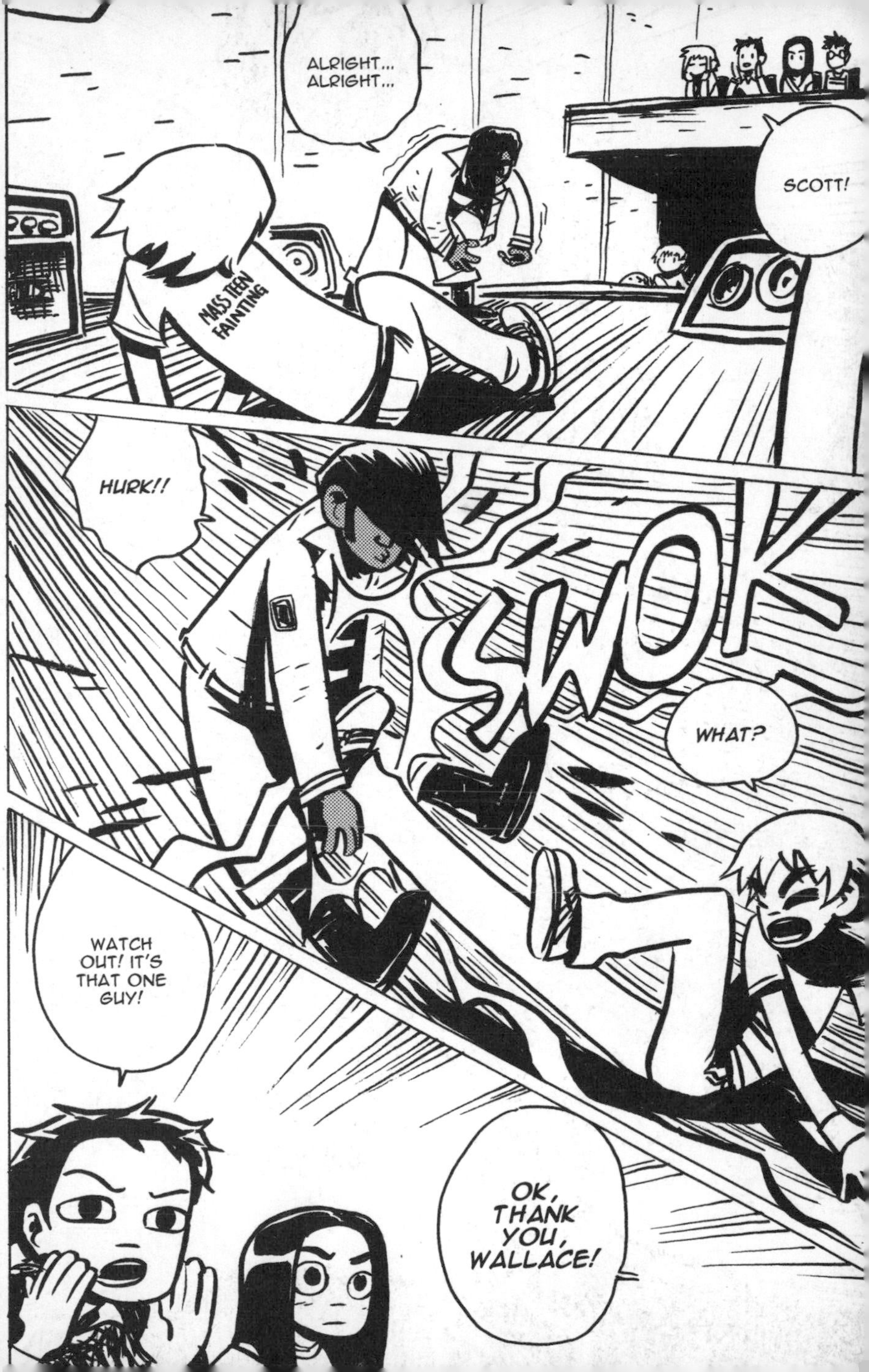
ALRIGHT... ALRIGHT...
SCOTT!
MASS TEEN FAINTING
HURK!!
SWOK
WHAT?
WATCH OUT! IT'S THAT ONE GUY!
OK, THANK YOU, WALLACE!

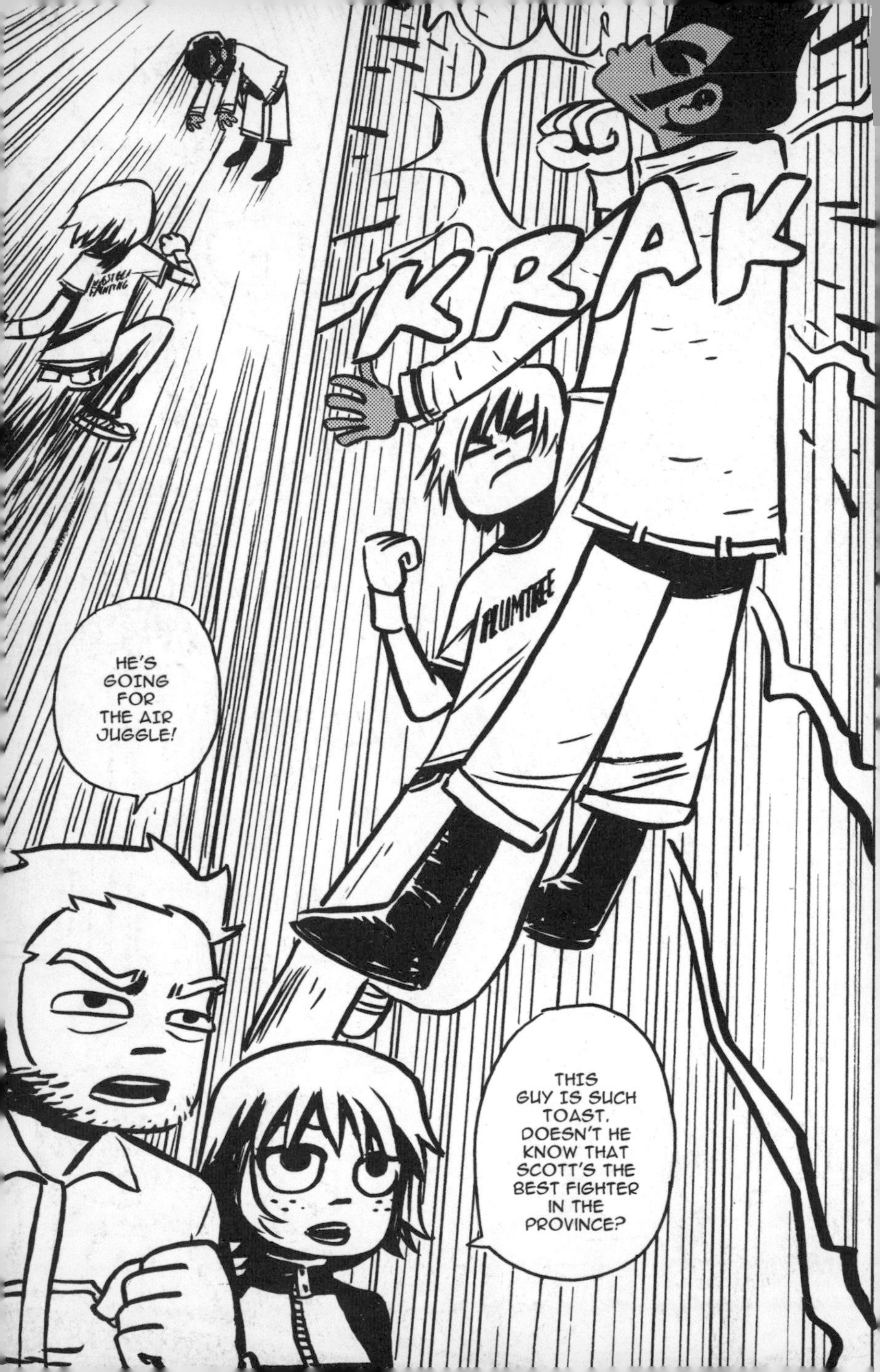
KRAK
HE'S GOING FOR THE AIR JUGGLE!
THIS GUY IS SUCH TOAST. DOESN'T HE KNOW THAT SCOTT'S THE BEST FIGHTER IN THE PROVINCE?
PLUMTREE

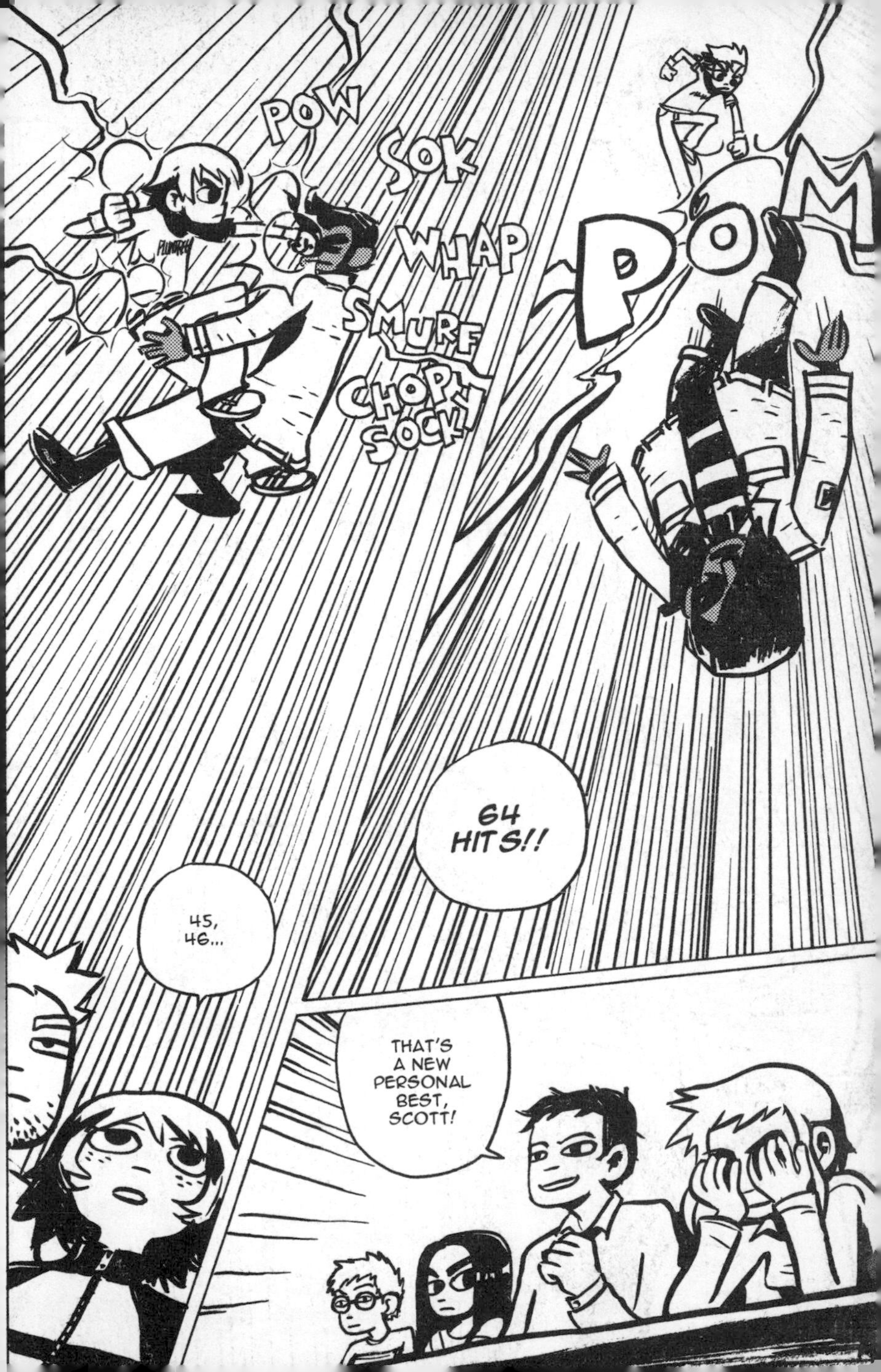
POW
SOK
WHAP
SMURF
CHOP
SOCK
POM
64 HITS!!
45, 46...
THAT'S A NEW PERSONAL BEST, SCOTT!

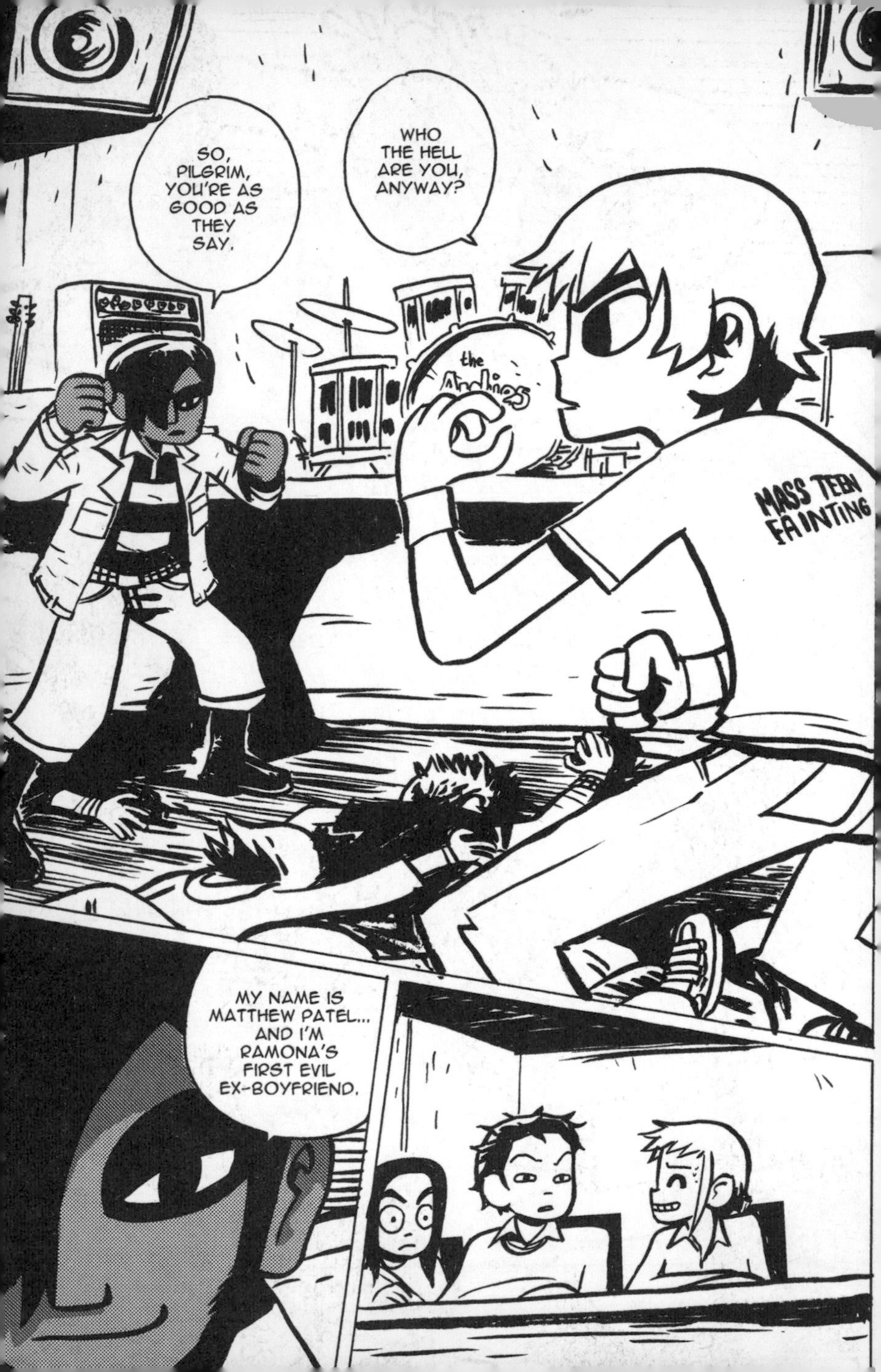
SO, PILGRIM, YOU'RE AS GOOD AS THEY SAY.
WHO THE HELL ARE YOU, ANYWAY?
MASS TEEN FAINTING
MY NAME IS MATTHEW PATEL... AND I'M RAMONA'S FIRST EVIL EX-BOYFRIEND.

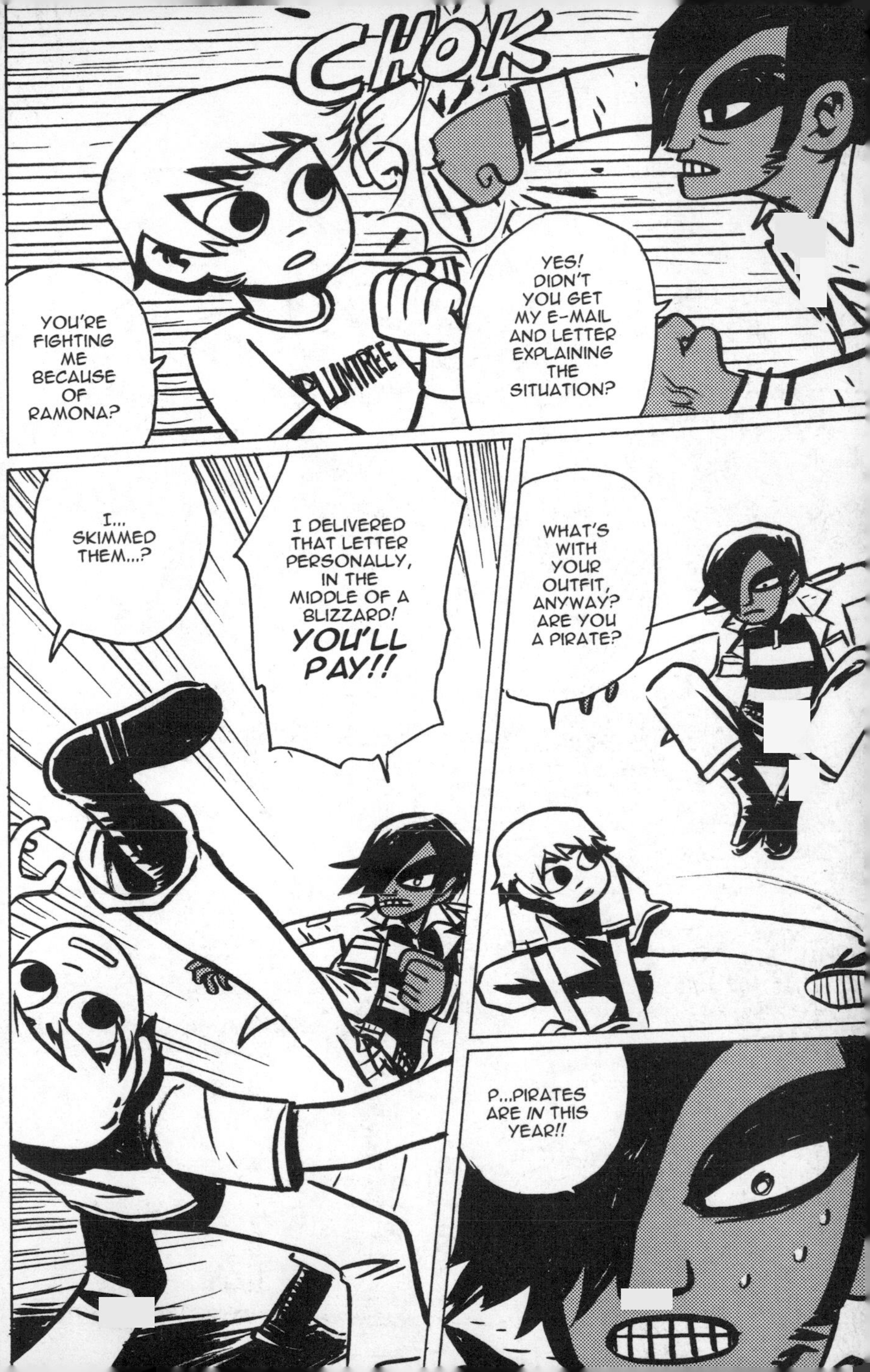
CHOK
YOU'RE FIGHTING ME BECAUSE OF RAMONA?
PLUMTREE
YES! DIDN'T YOU GET MY E-MAIL AND LETTER EXPLAINING THE SITUATION?
I... SKIMMED THEM...?
I DELIVERED THAT LETTER PERSONALLY, IN THE MIDDLE OF A BLIZZARD! *YOU'LL PAY!!*
WHAT'S WITH YOUR OUTFIT, ANYWAY? ARE YOU A PIRATE?
P...PIRATES ARE *IN* THIS YEAR!!

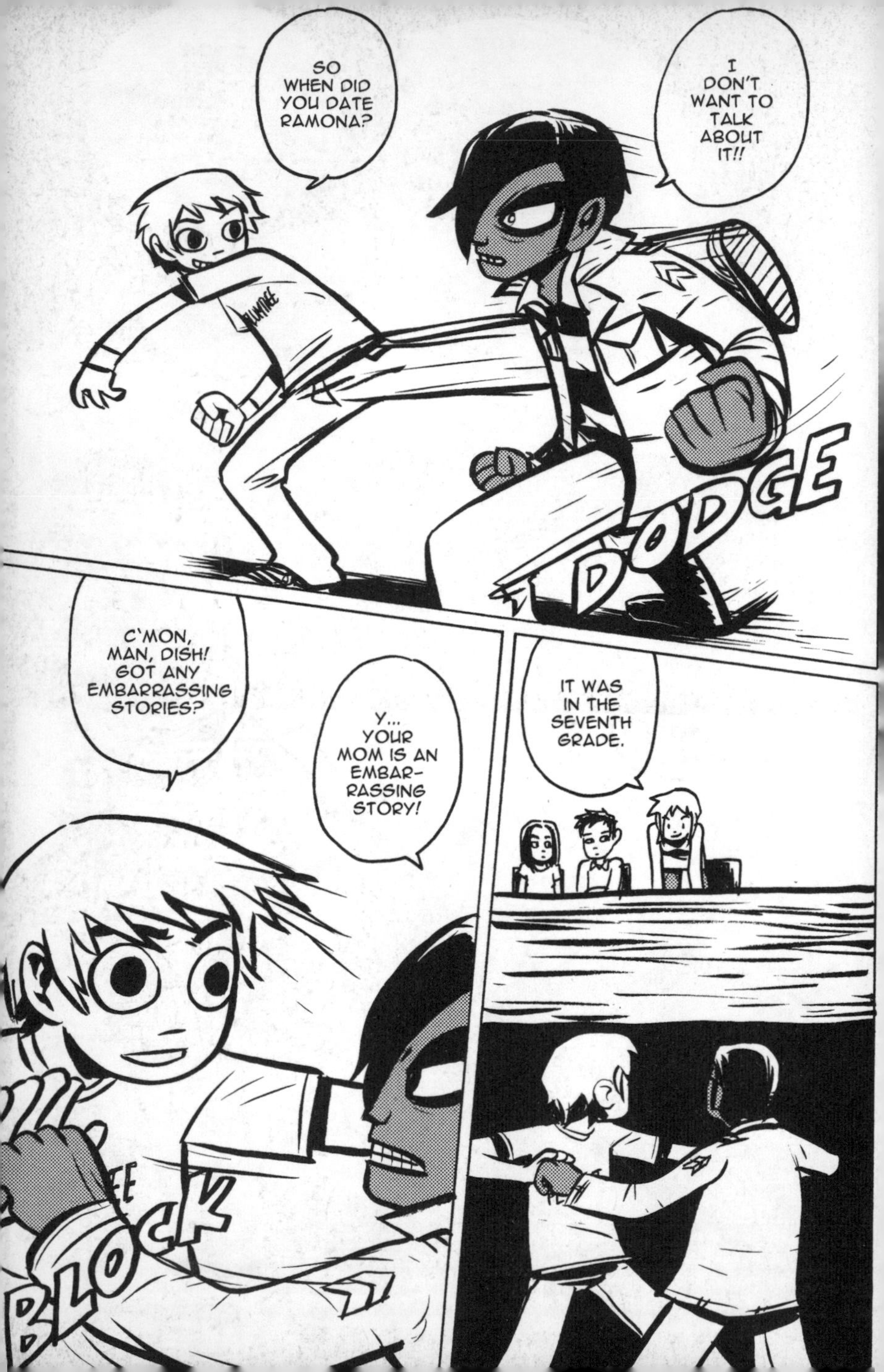
SO WHEN DID YOU DATE RAMONA?
I DON'T WANT TO TALK ABOUT IT!!
DODGE
C'MON, MAN, DISH! GOT ANY EMBARRASSING STORIES?
Y... YOUR MOM IS AN EMBAR-RASSING STORY!
BLOCK
IT WAS IN THE SEVENTH GRADE.

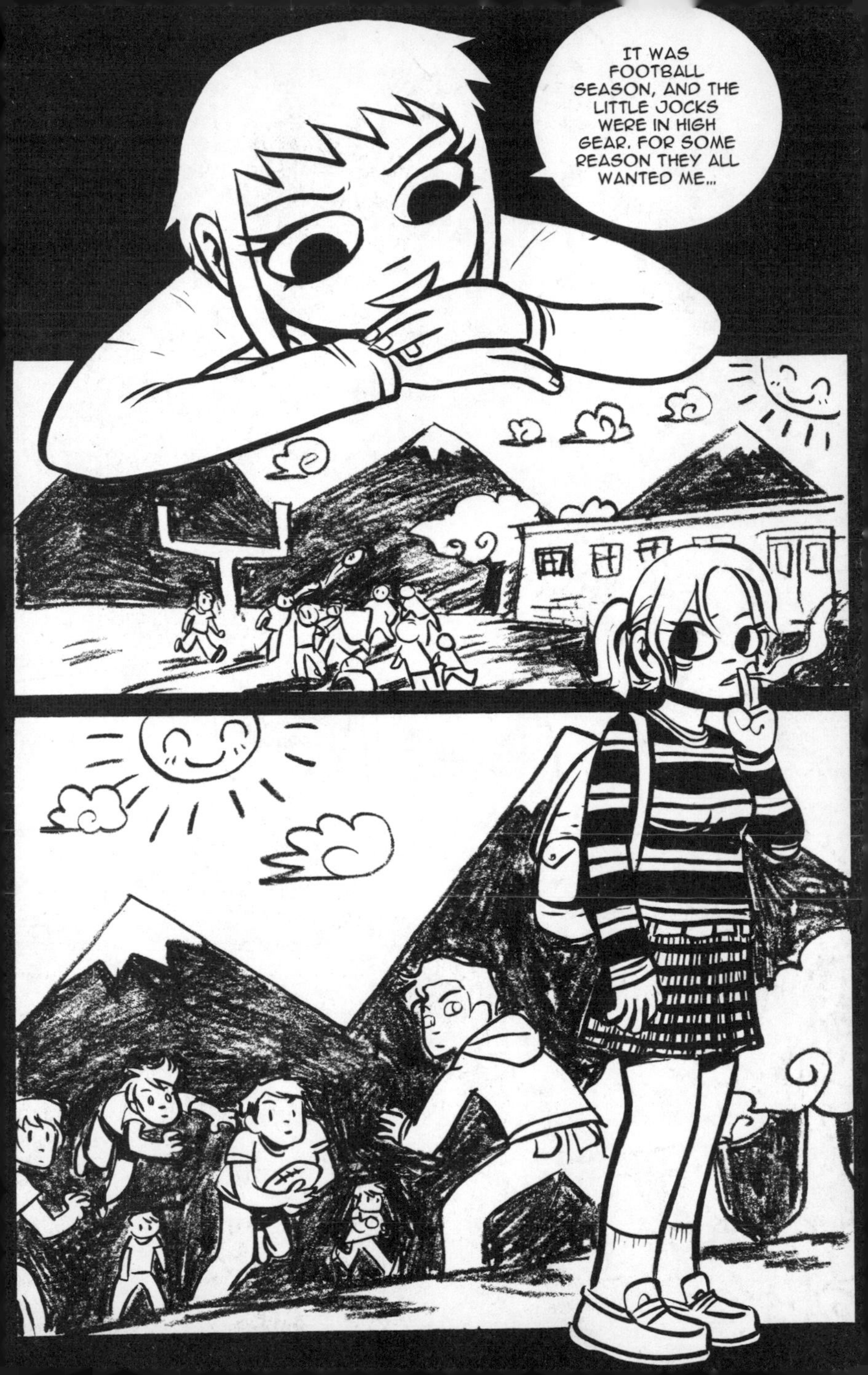
IT WAS FOOTBALL SEASON, AND THE LITTLE JOCKS WERE IN HIGH GEAR. FOR SOME REASON THEY ALL WANTED ME...

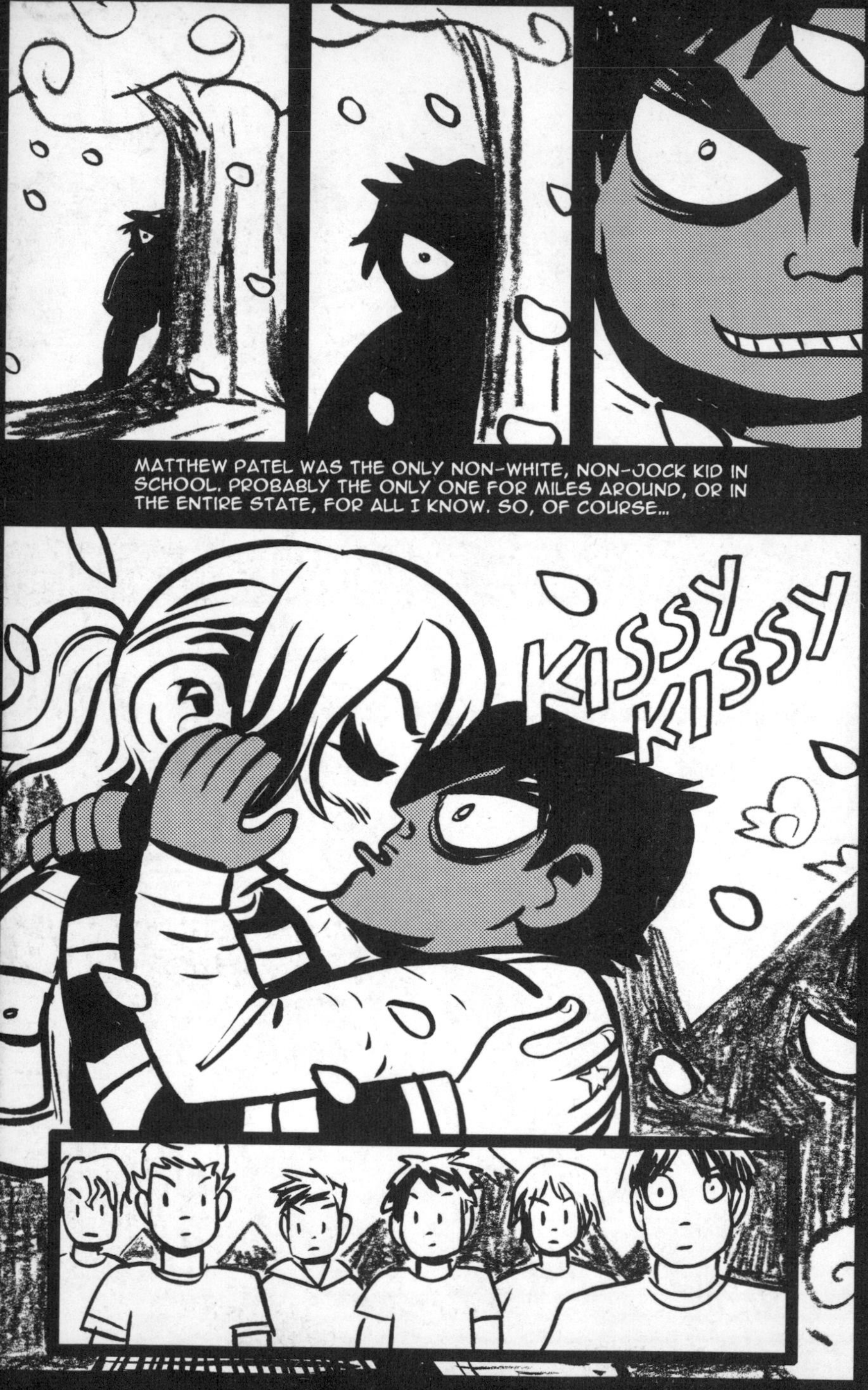
MATTHEW PATEL WAS THE ONLY NON-WHITE, NON-JOCK KID IN SCHOOL. PROBABLY THE ONLY ONE FOR MILES AROUND, OR IN THE ENTIRE STATE, FOR ALL I KNOW. SO, OF COURSE...
KISSY KISSY

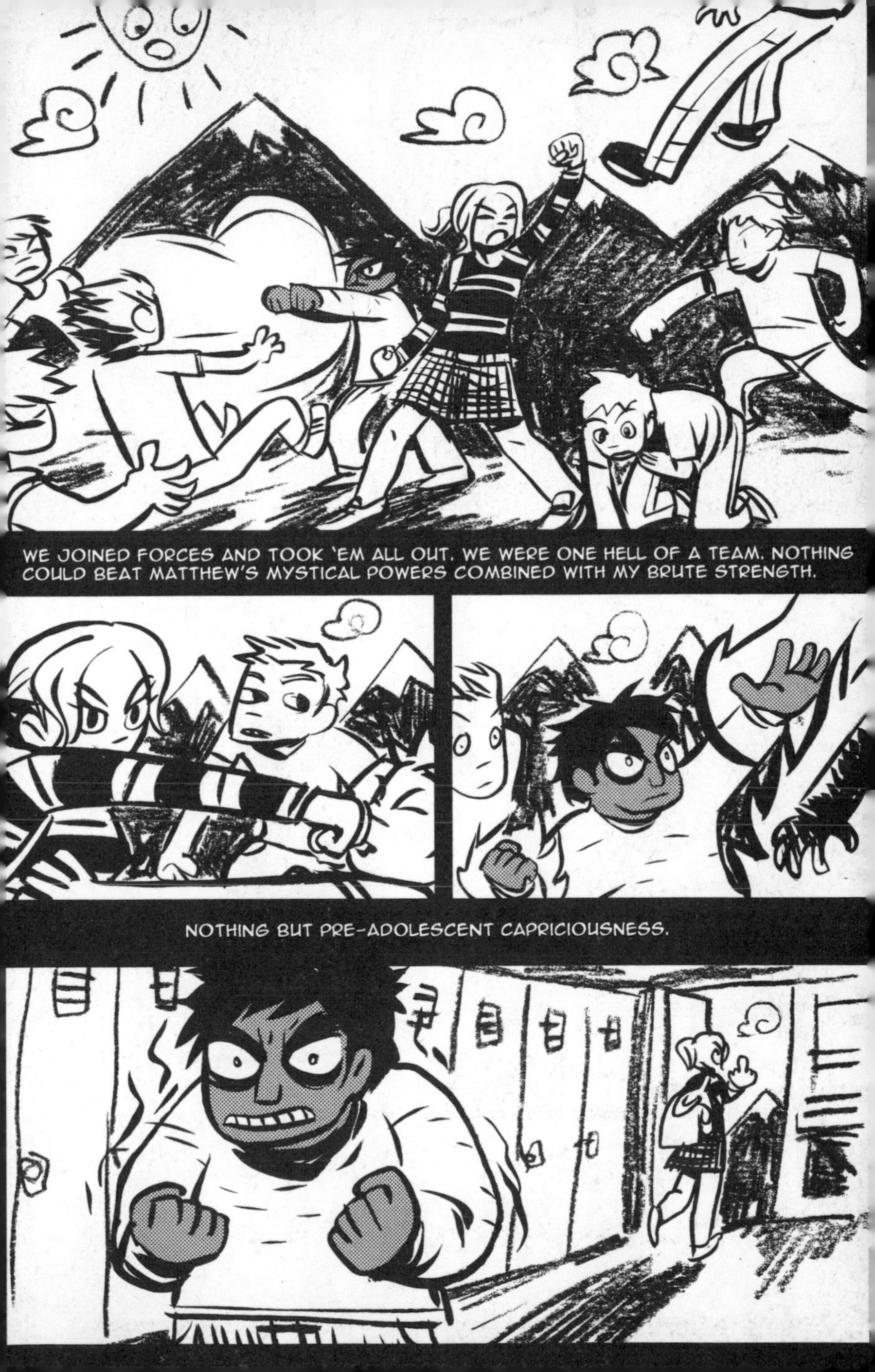
WE JOINED FORCES AND TOOK 'EM ALL OUT. WE WERE ONE HELL OF A TEAM. NOTHING COULD BEAT MATTHEW'S MYSTICAL POWERS COMBINED WITH MY BRUTE STRENGTH.
NOTHING BUT PRE-ADOLESCENT CAPRICIOUSNESS.

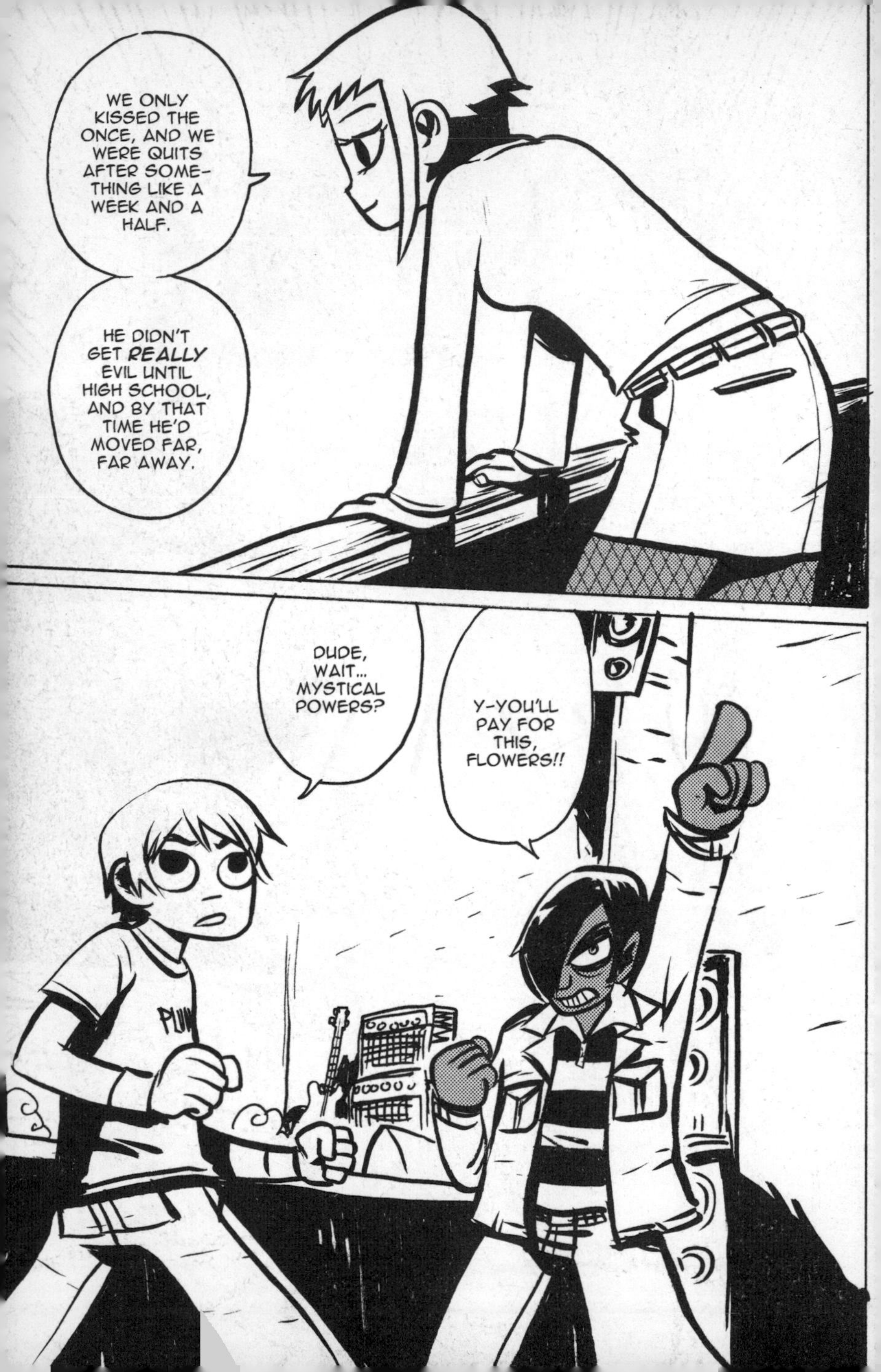
WE ONLY KISSED THE ONCE, AND WE WERE QUITS AFTER SOME-THING LIKE A WEEK AND A HALF.
HE DIDN'T GET *REALLY* EVIL UNTIL HIGH SCHOOL, AND BY THAT TIME HE'D MOVED FAR, FAR AWAY.
DUDE, WAIT... MYSTICAL POWERS?
Y-YOU'LL PAY FOR THIS, FLOWERS!!
PLUM

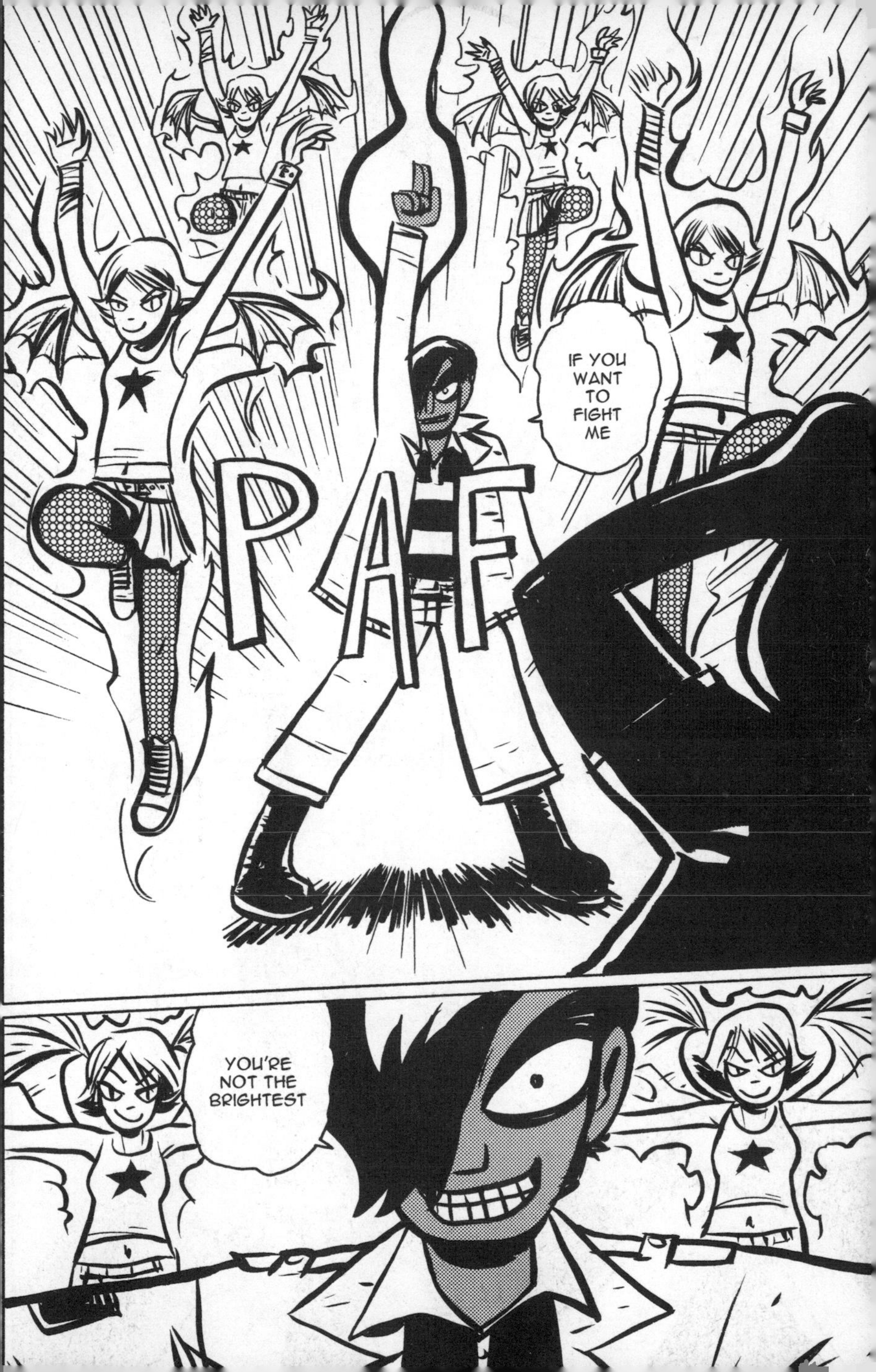
PAF
IF YOU WANT TO FIGHT ME
YOU'RE NOT THE BRIGHTEST

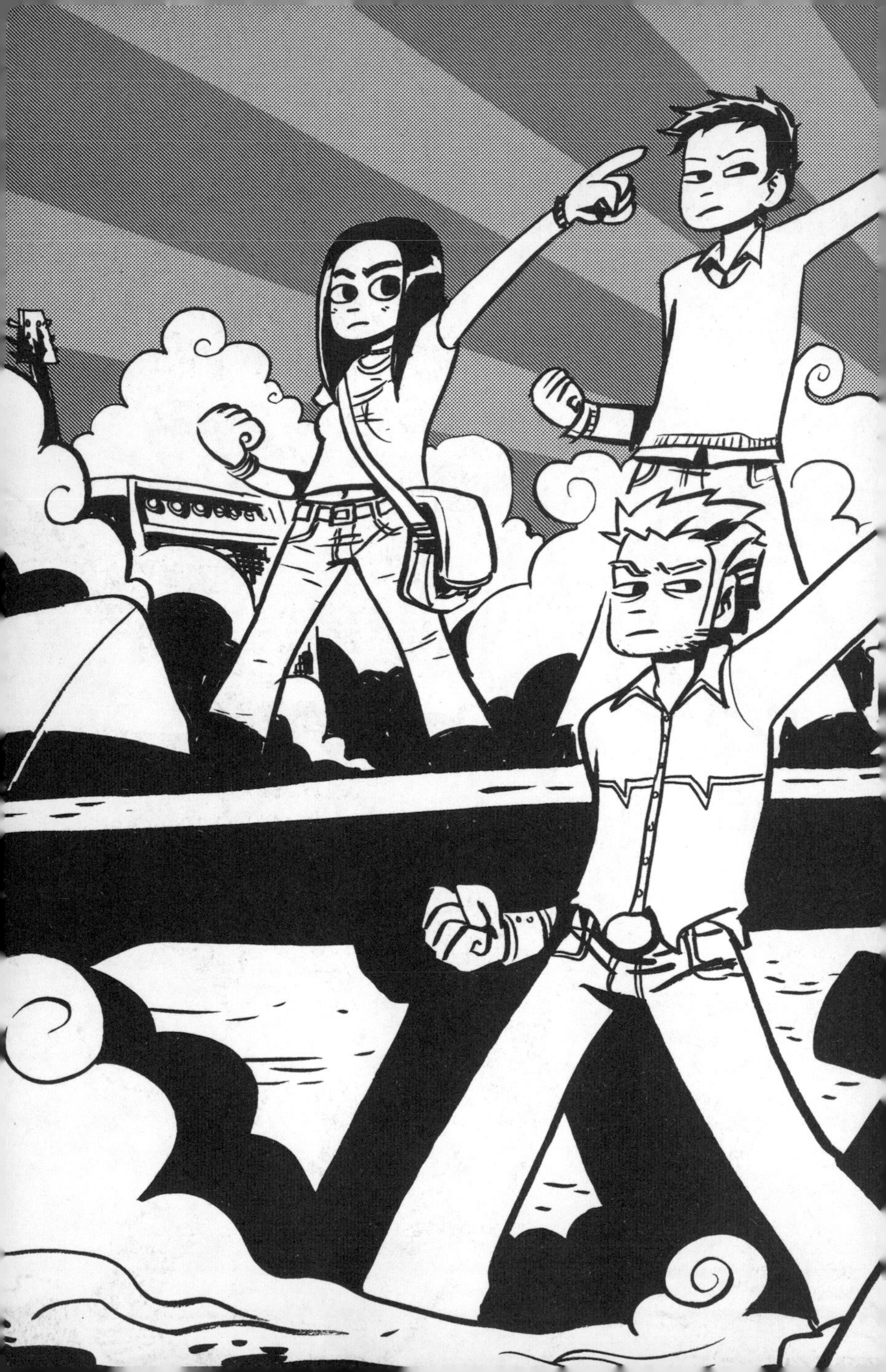

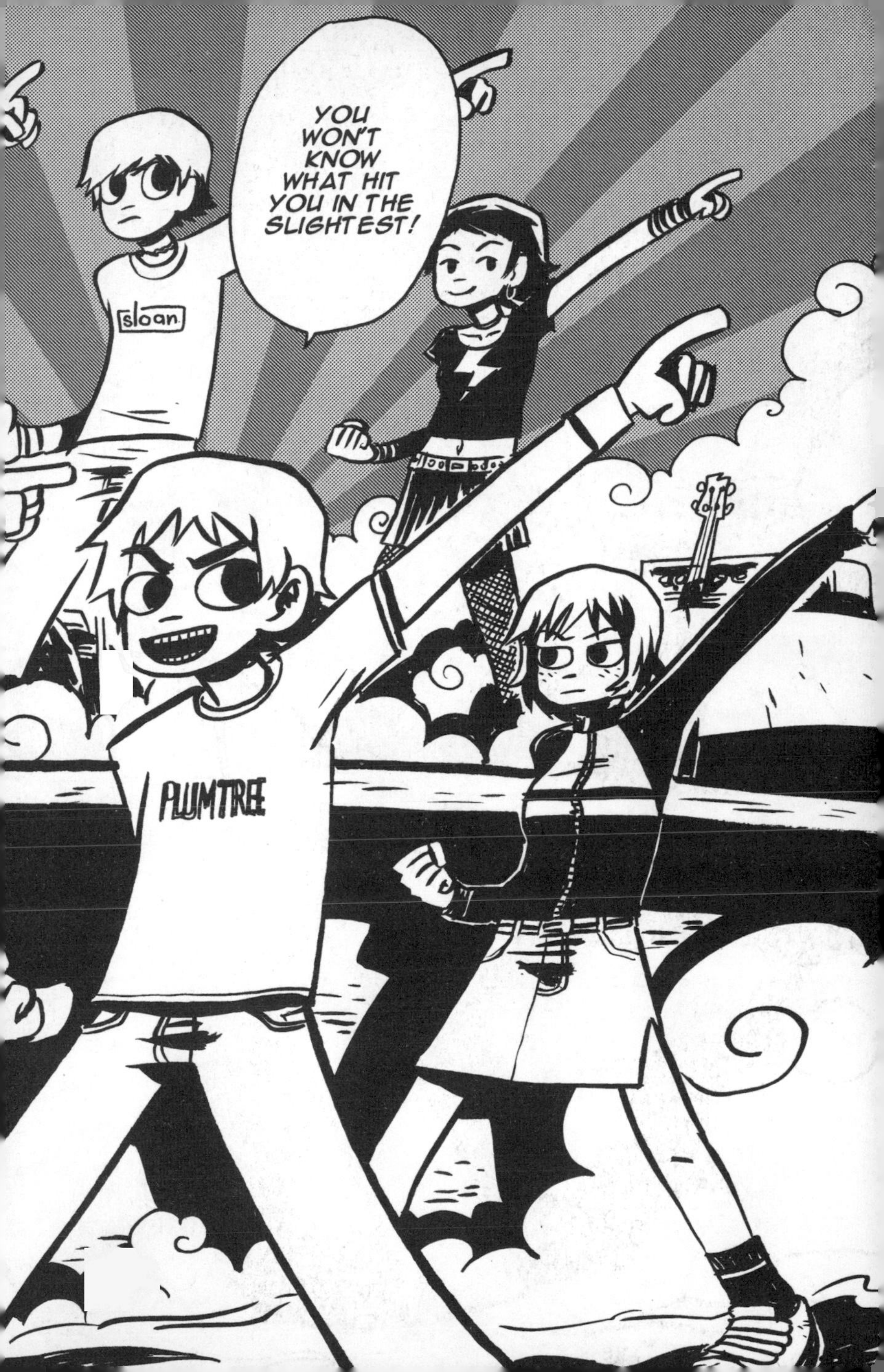
YOU WON'T KNOW WHAT HIT YOU IN THE SLIGHTEST!
sloan
PLUMTREE

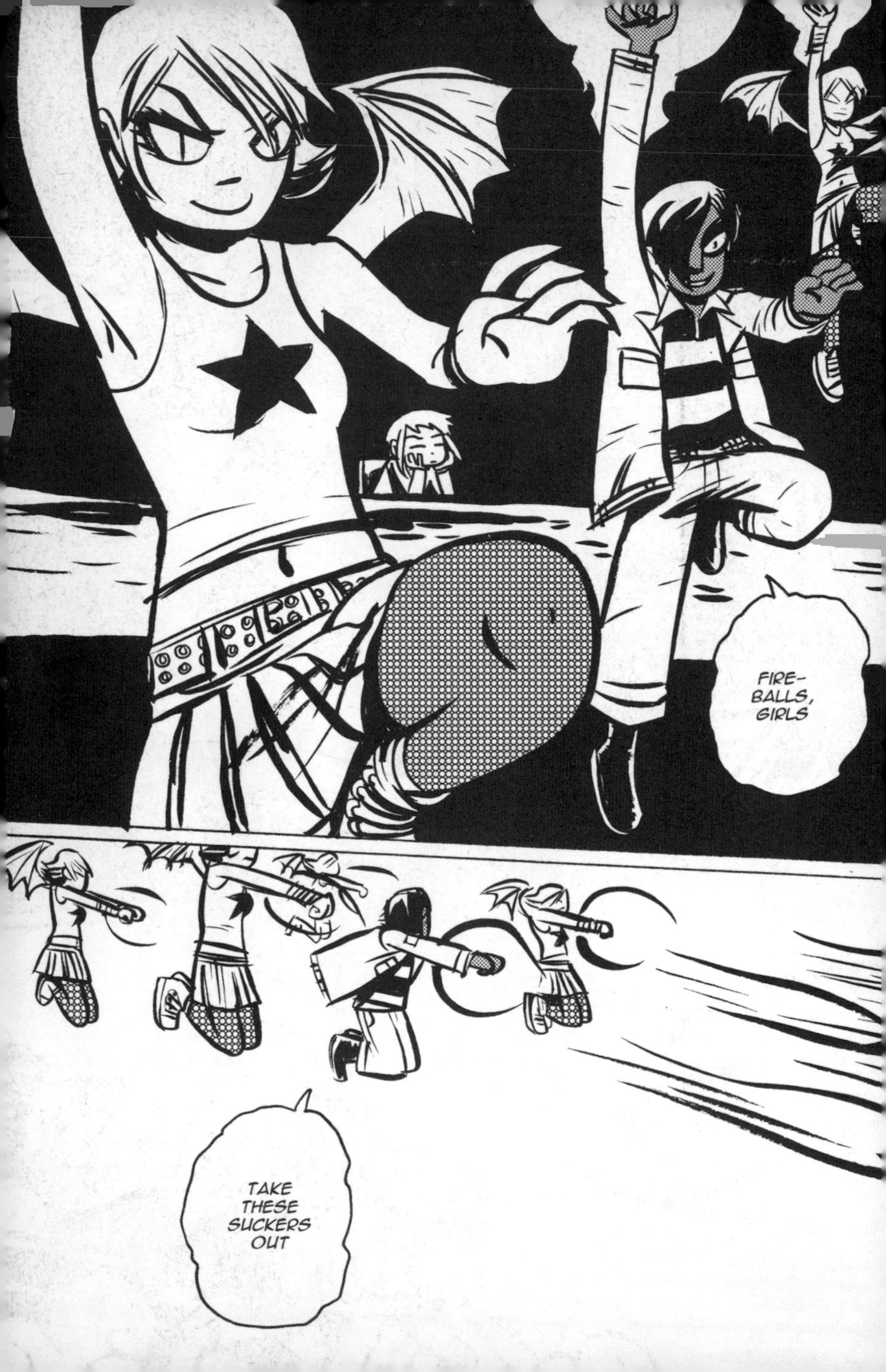
FIRE-BALLS, GIRLS
TAKE THESE SUCKERS OUT

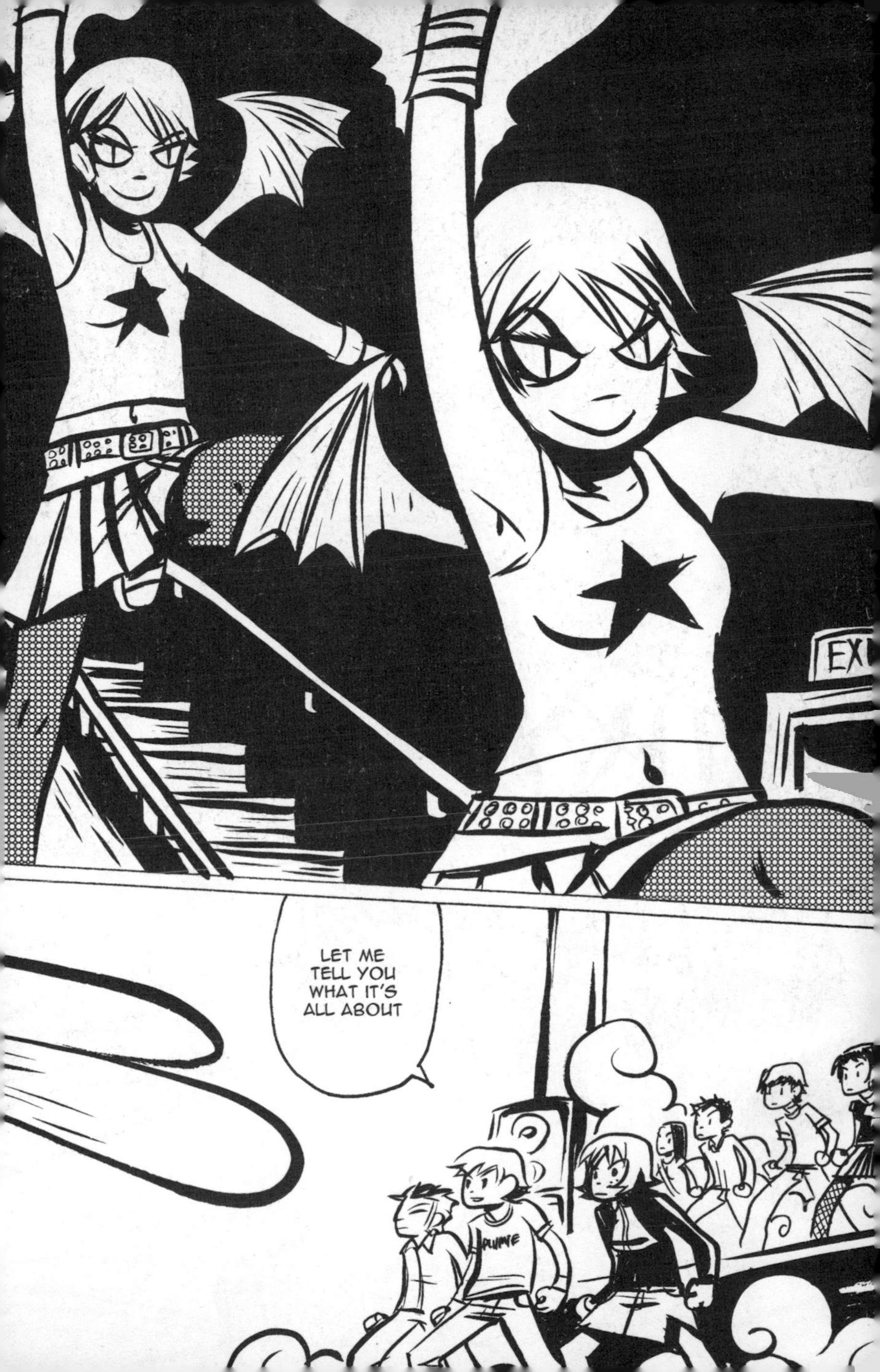
LET ME TELL YOU WHAT IT'S ALL ABOUT

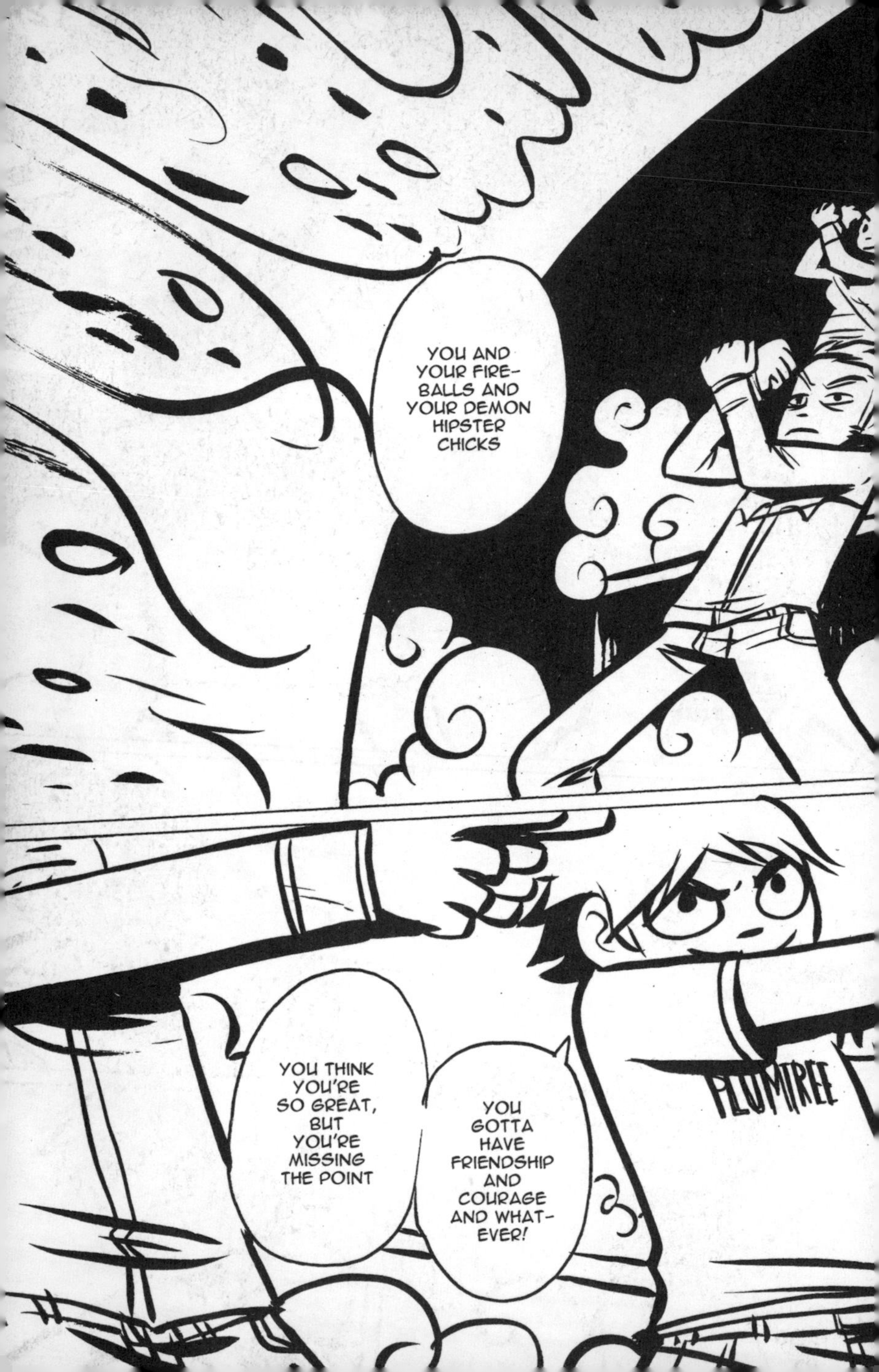
YOU AND YOUR FIRE-BALLS AND YOUR DEMON HIPSTER CHICKS
YOU THINK YOU'RE SO GREAT, BUT YOU'RE MISSING THE POINT
YOU GOTTA HAVE FRIENDSHIP AND COURAGE AND WHAT-EVER!
PLUMTREE

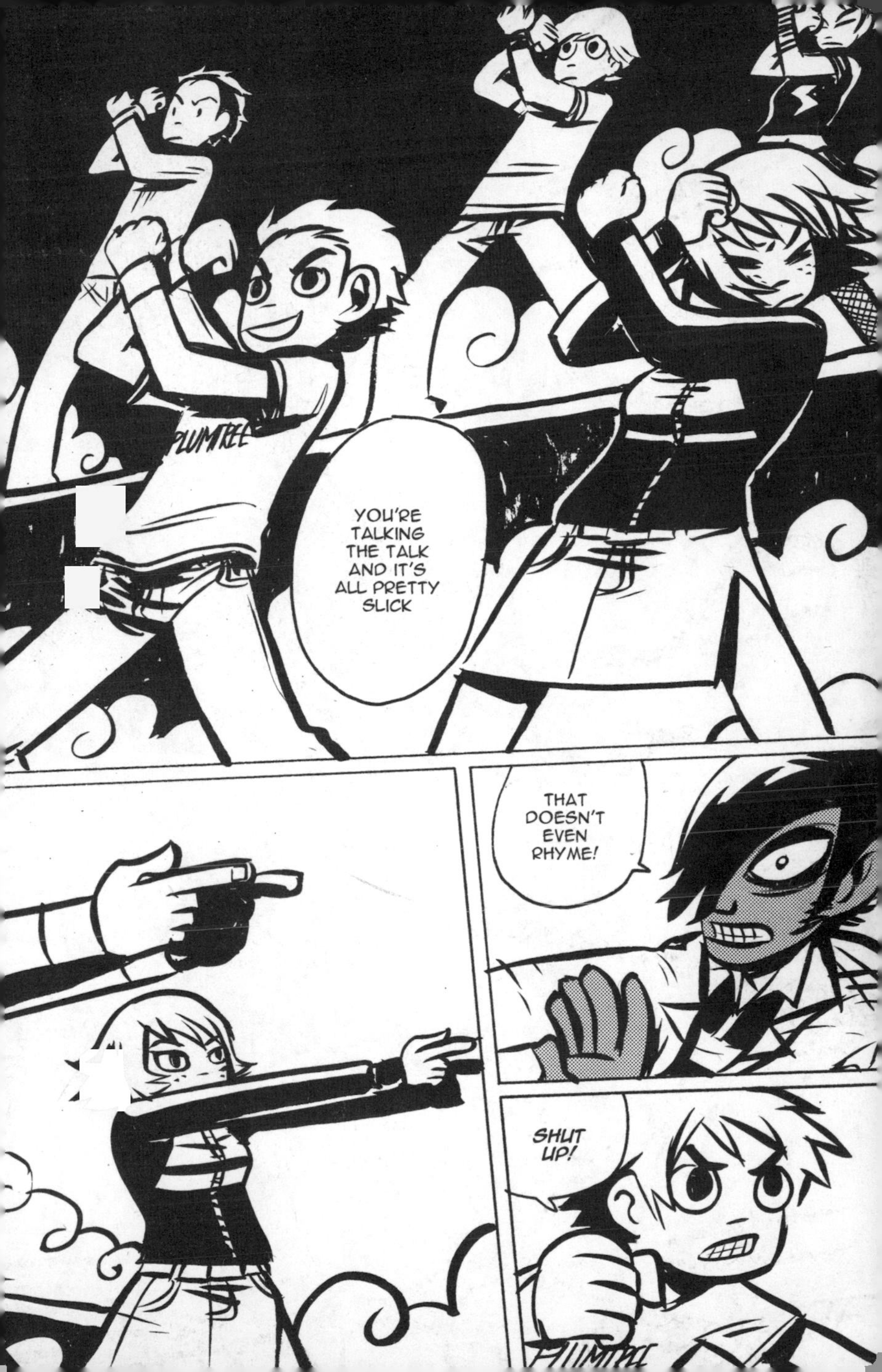
PLUMTREE
YOU'RE TALKING THE TALK AND IT'S ALL PRETTY SLICK
THAT DOESN'T EVEN RHYME!
SHUT UP!
PLUMTREE

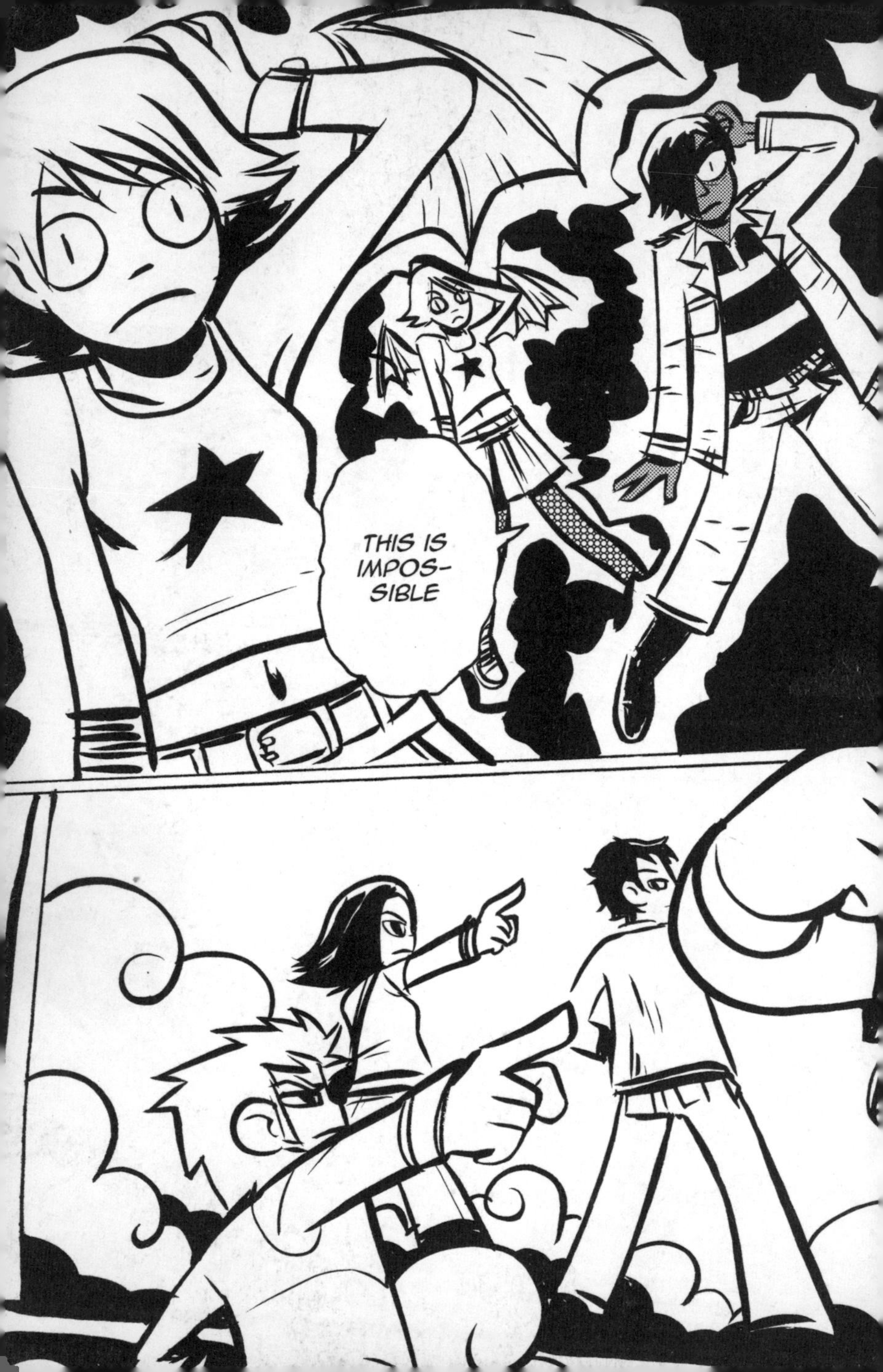
THIS IS IMPOS- SIBLE

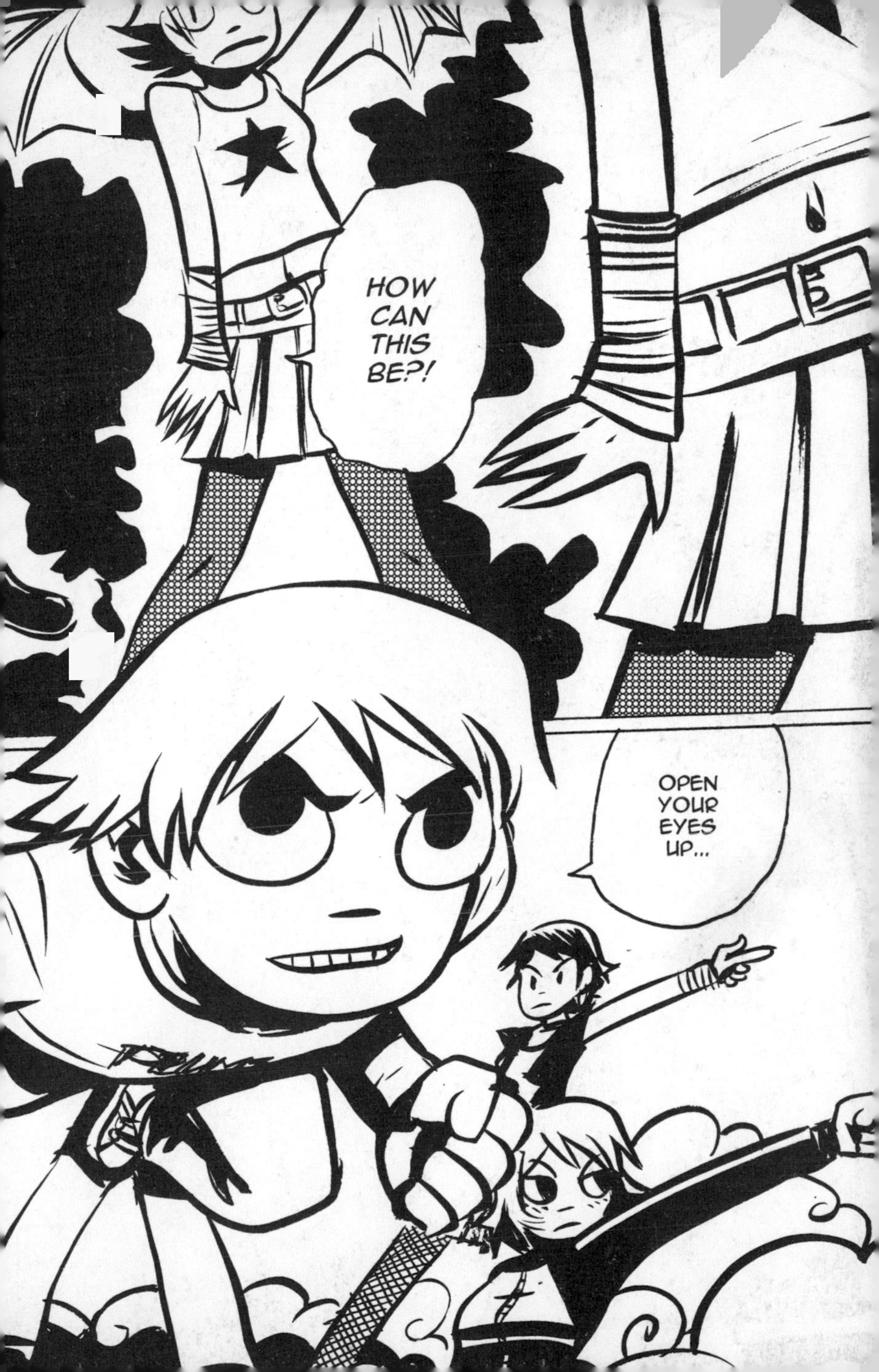
HOW CAN THIS BE?!
OPEN YOUR EYES UP...

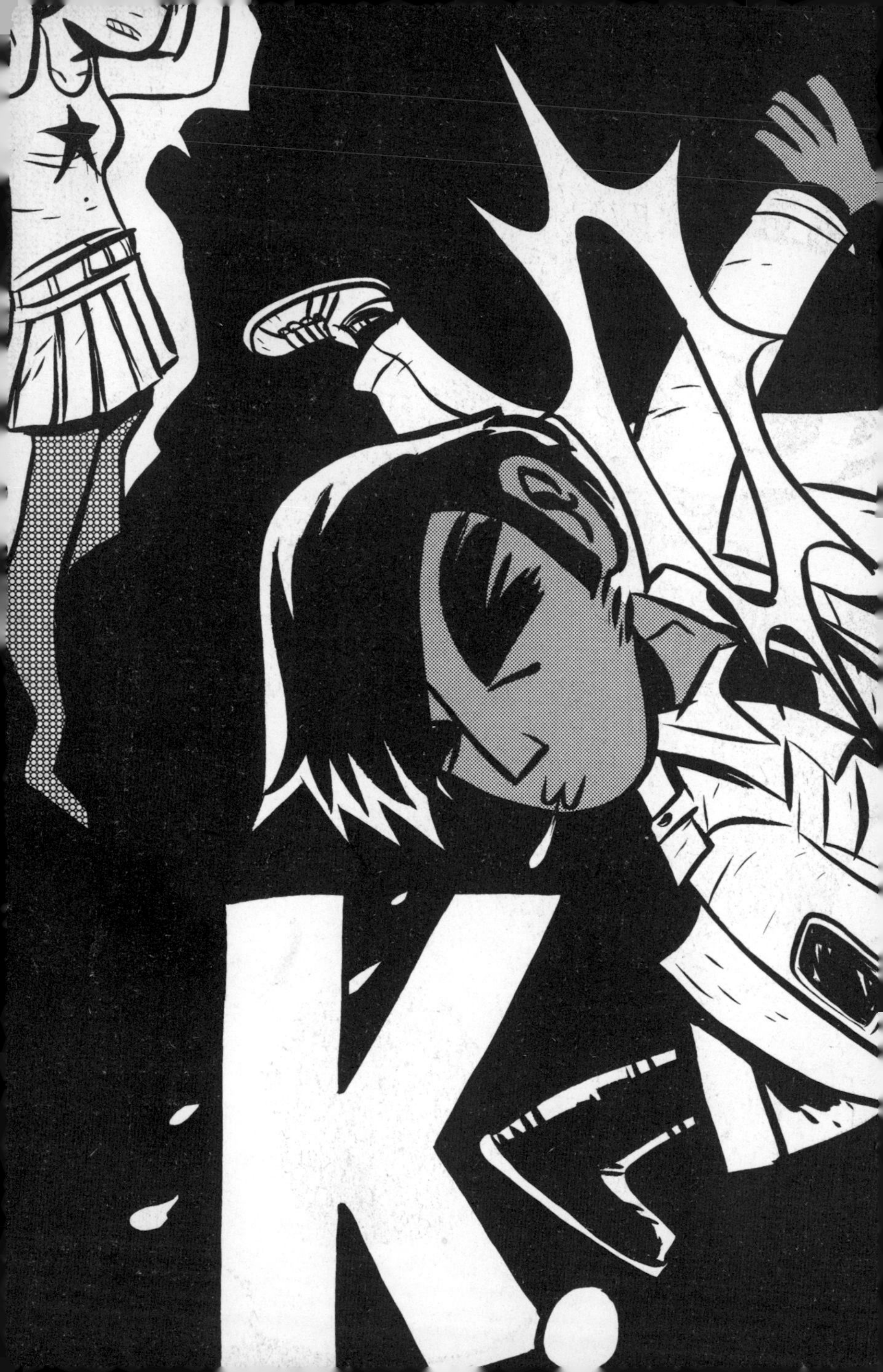
K.

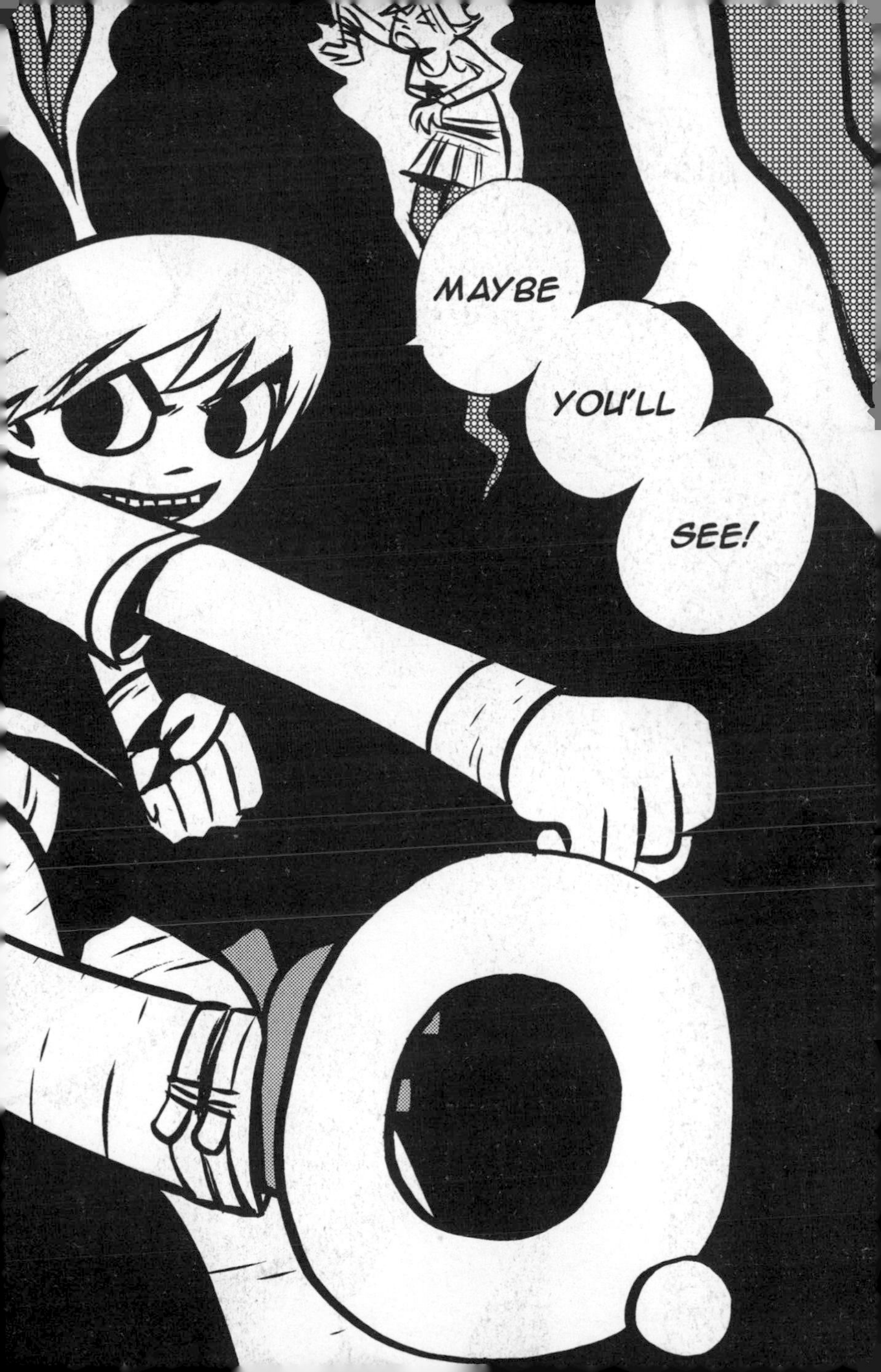
MAYBE
YOU'LL
SEE!

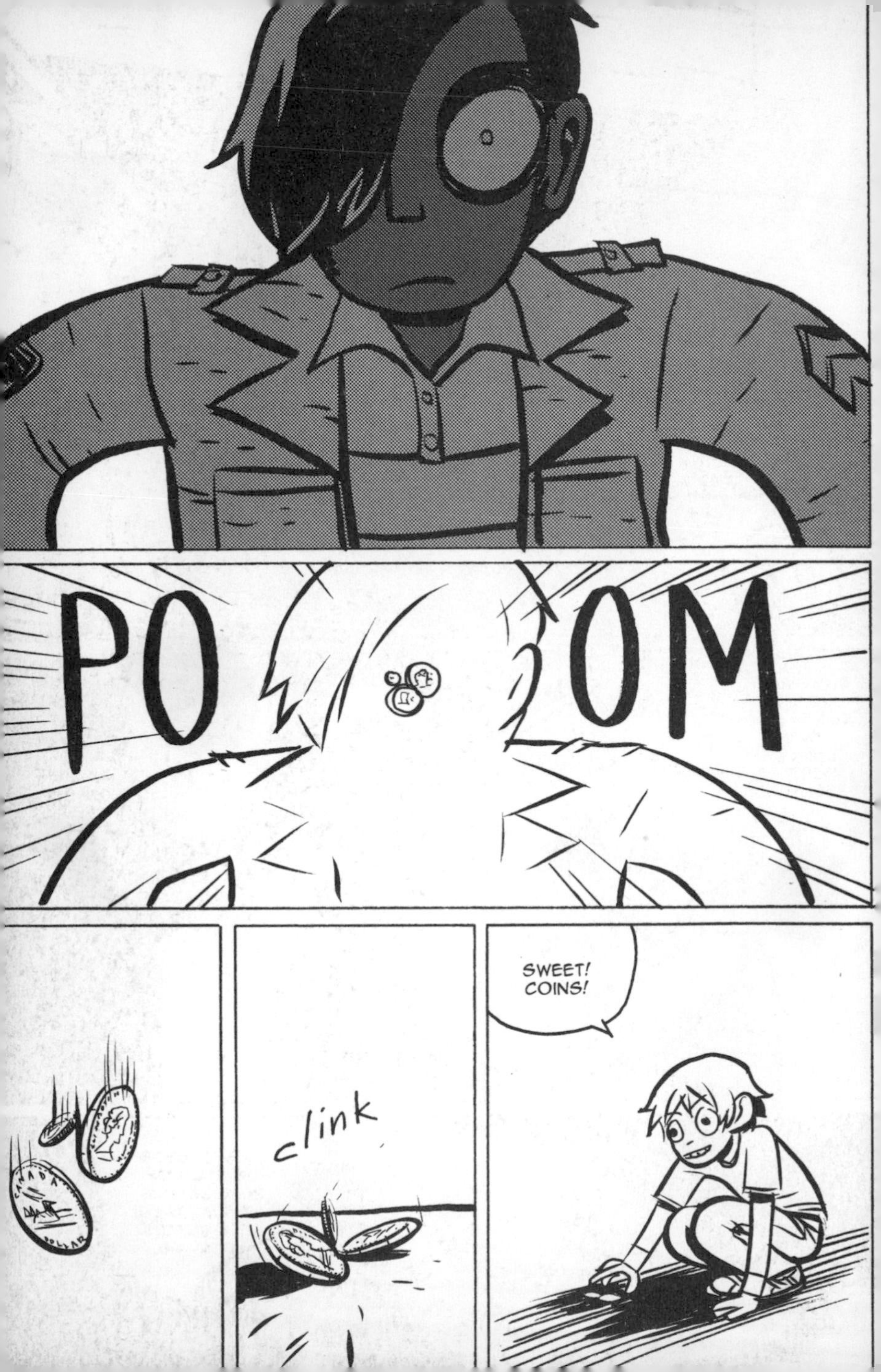
POOM
SWEET! COINS!
clink
CANADA
DOLLAR

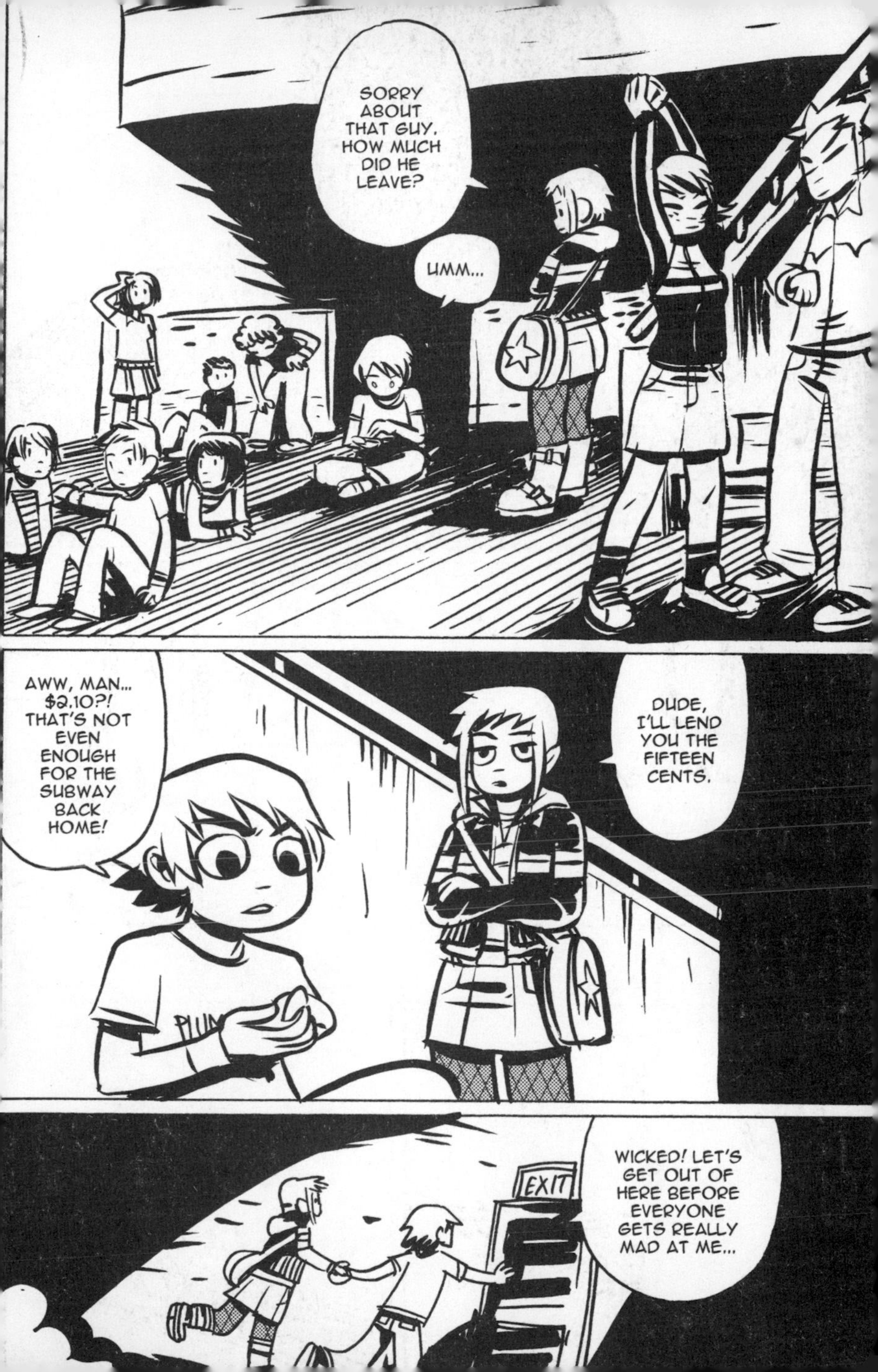
SORRY ABOUT THAT GUY. HOW MUCH DID HE LEAVE?
UMM...
AWW, MAN... $2.10?! THAT'S NOT EVEN ENOUGH FOR THE SUBWAY BACK HOME!
DUDE, I'LL LEND YOU THE FIFTEEN CENTS.
EXIT
WICKED! LET'S GET OUT OF HERE BEFORE EVERYONE GETS REALLY MAD AT ME...

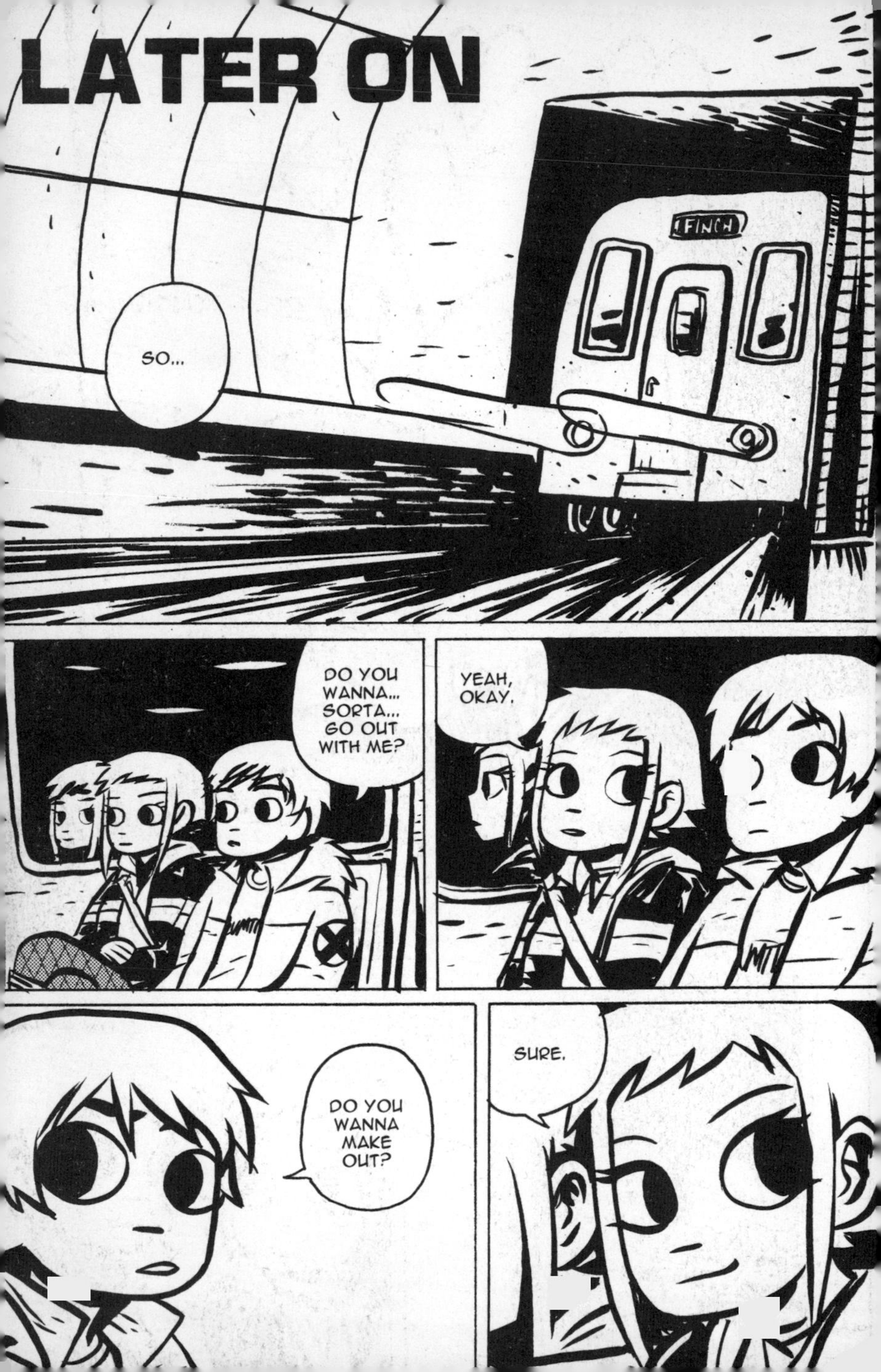
LATER ON
FINCH
SO...
DO YOU WANNA... SORTA... GO OUT WITH ME?
YEAH, OKAY.
DO YOU WANNA MAKE OUT?
SURE.

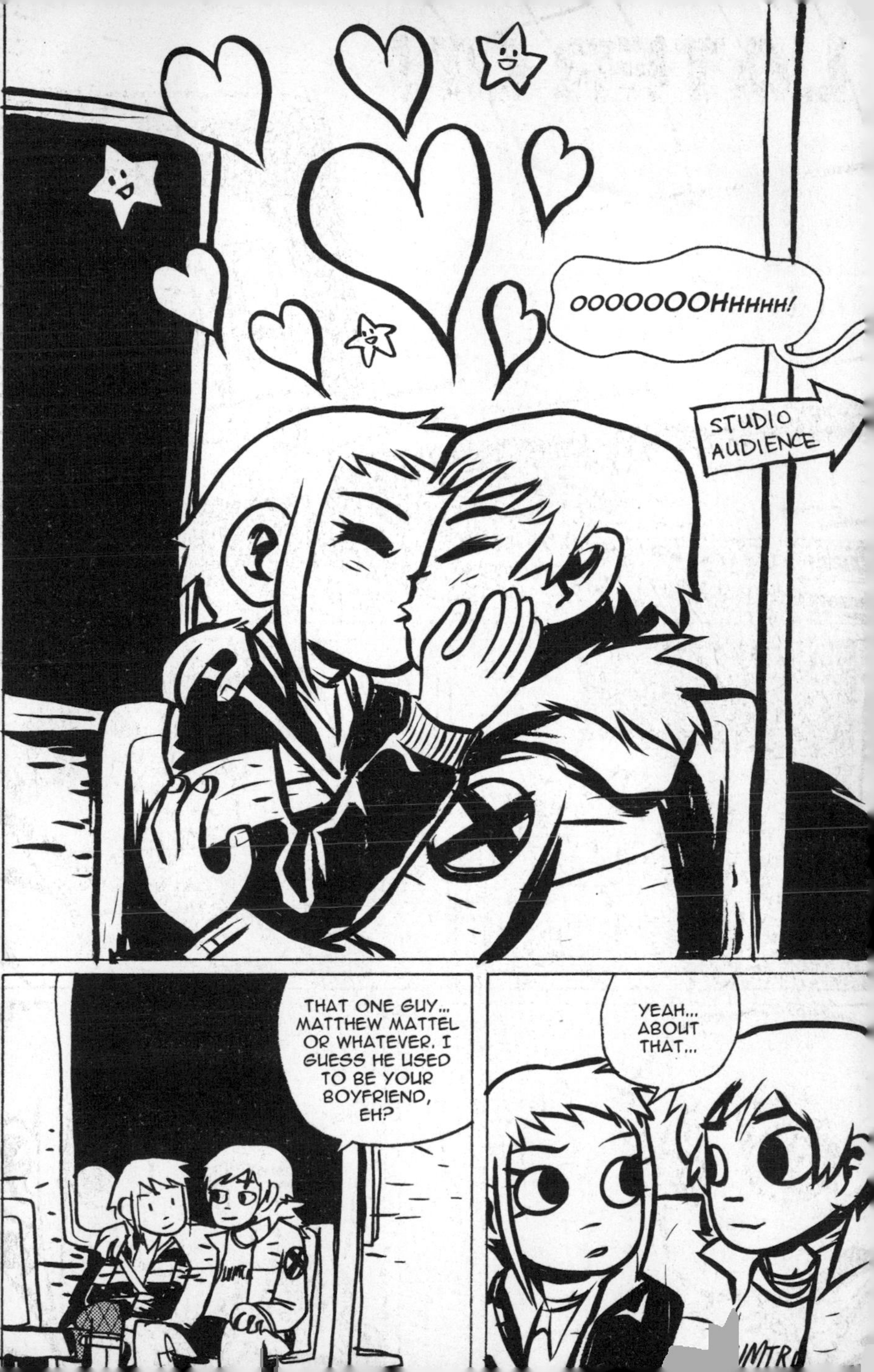
OOOOOOOHHHHH!
STUDIO AUDIENCE
THAT ONE GUY... MATTHEW MATTEL OR WHATEVER. I GUESS HE USED TO BE YOUR BOYFRIEND, EH?
YEAH... ABOUT THAT...

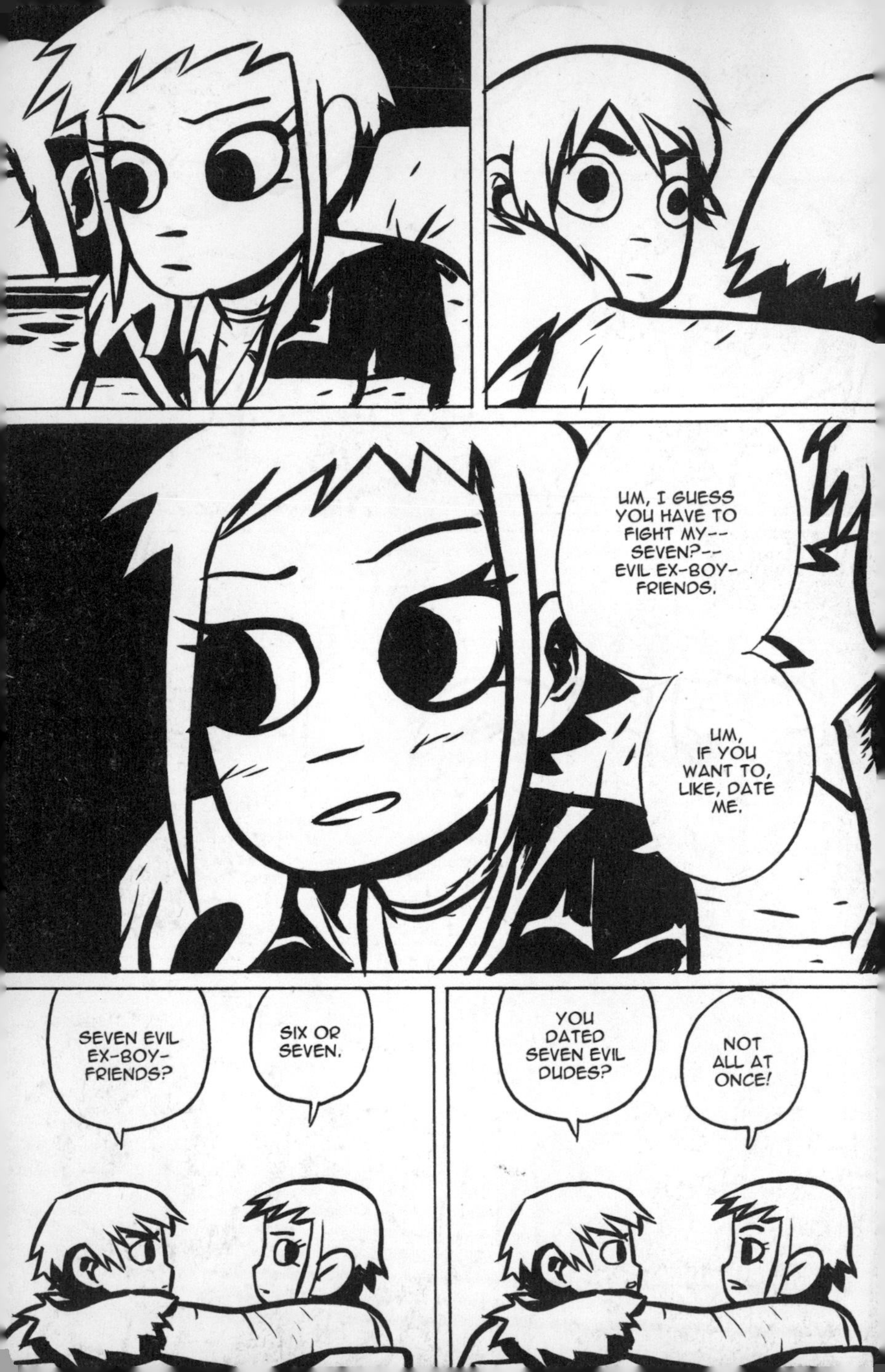
UM, I GUESS YOU HAVE TO FIGHT MY-- SEVEN?-- EVIL EX-BOY-FRIENDS.
UM, IF YOU WANT TO, LIKE, DATE ME.
SEVEN EVIL EX-BOY-FRIENDS?
SIX OR SEVEN.
YOU DATED SEVEN EVIL DUDES?
NOT ALL AT ONCE!

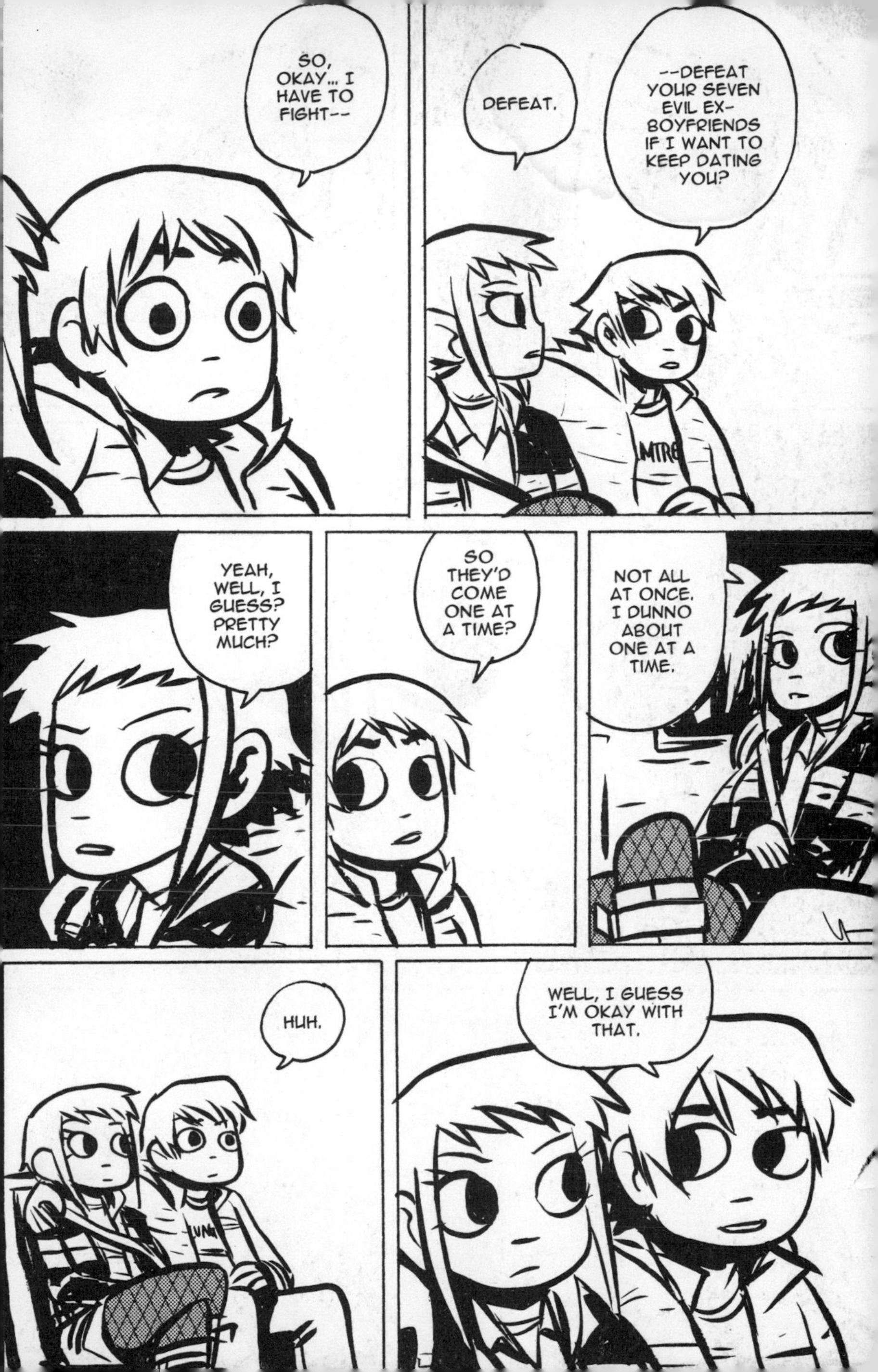
SO, OKAY... I HAVE TO FIGHT--
DEFEAT.
--DEFEAT YOUR SEVEN EVIL EX-BOYFRIENDS IF I WANT TO KEEP DATING YOU?
MTRE
YEAH, WELL, I GUESS? PRETTY MUCH?
SO THEY'D COME ONE AT A TIME?
NOT ALL AT ONCE. I DUNNO ABOUT ONE AT A TIME.
HUH.
WELL, I GUESS I'M OKAY WITH THAT.

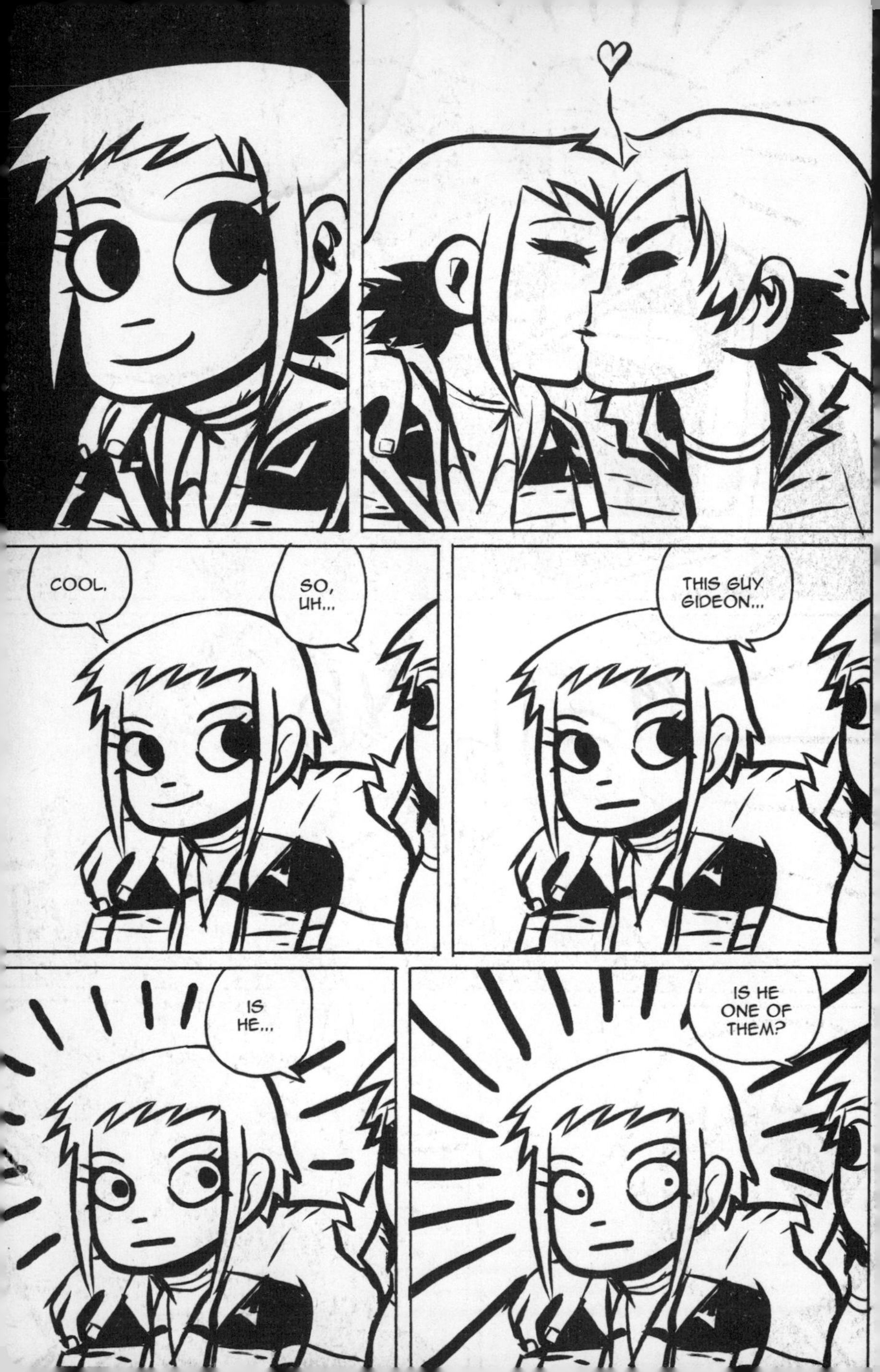
COOL.
SO, UH...
THIS GUY GIDEON...
IS HE...
IS HE ONE OF THEM?

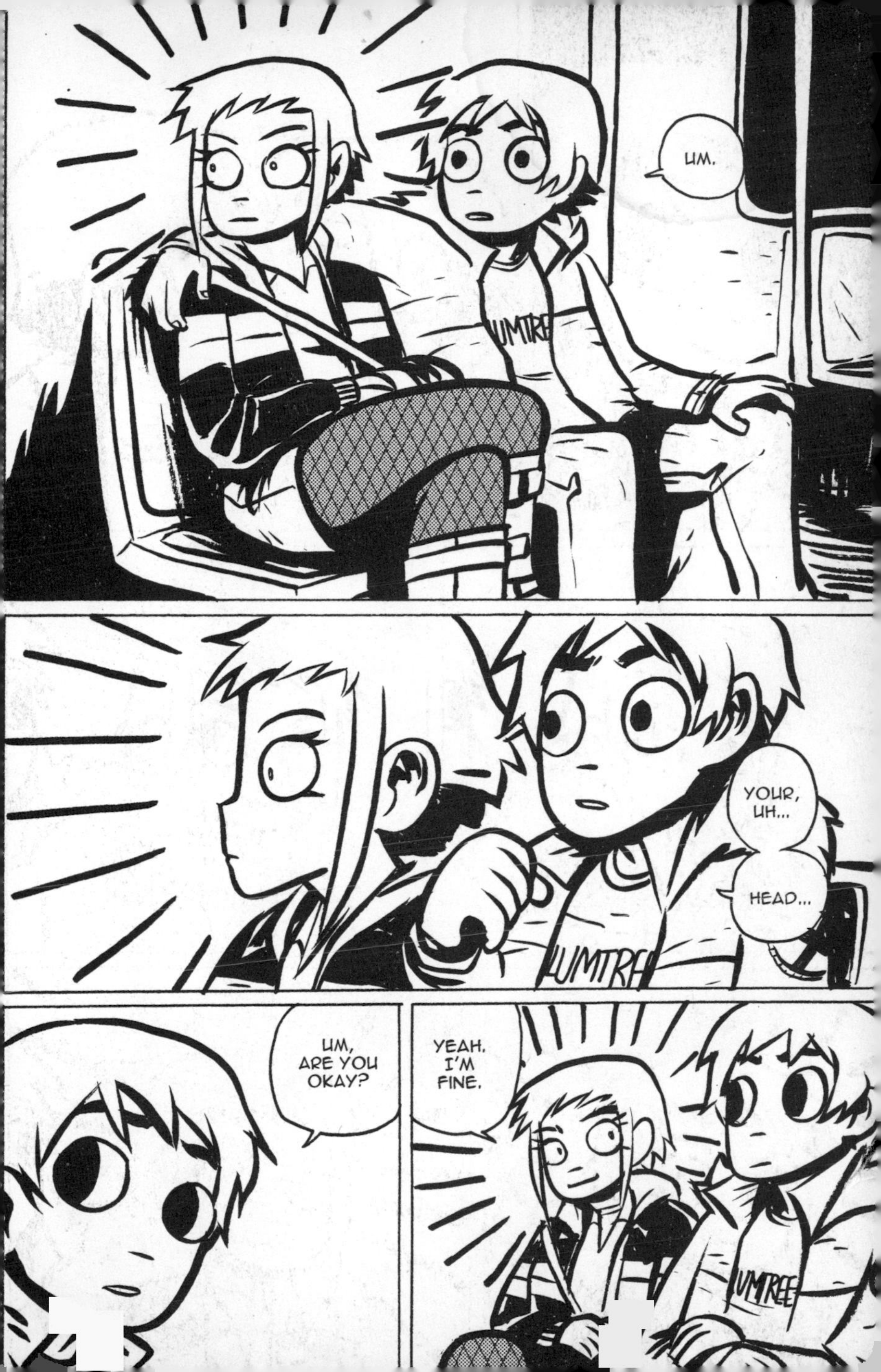
UM.
YOUR, UH...
HEAD...
UM, ARE YOU OKAY?
YEAH. I'M FINE.

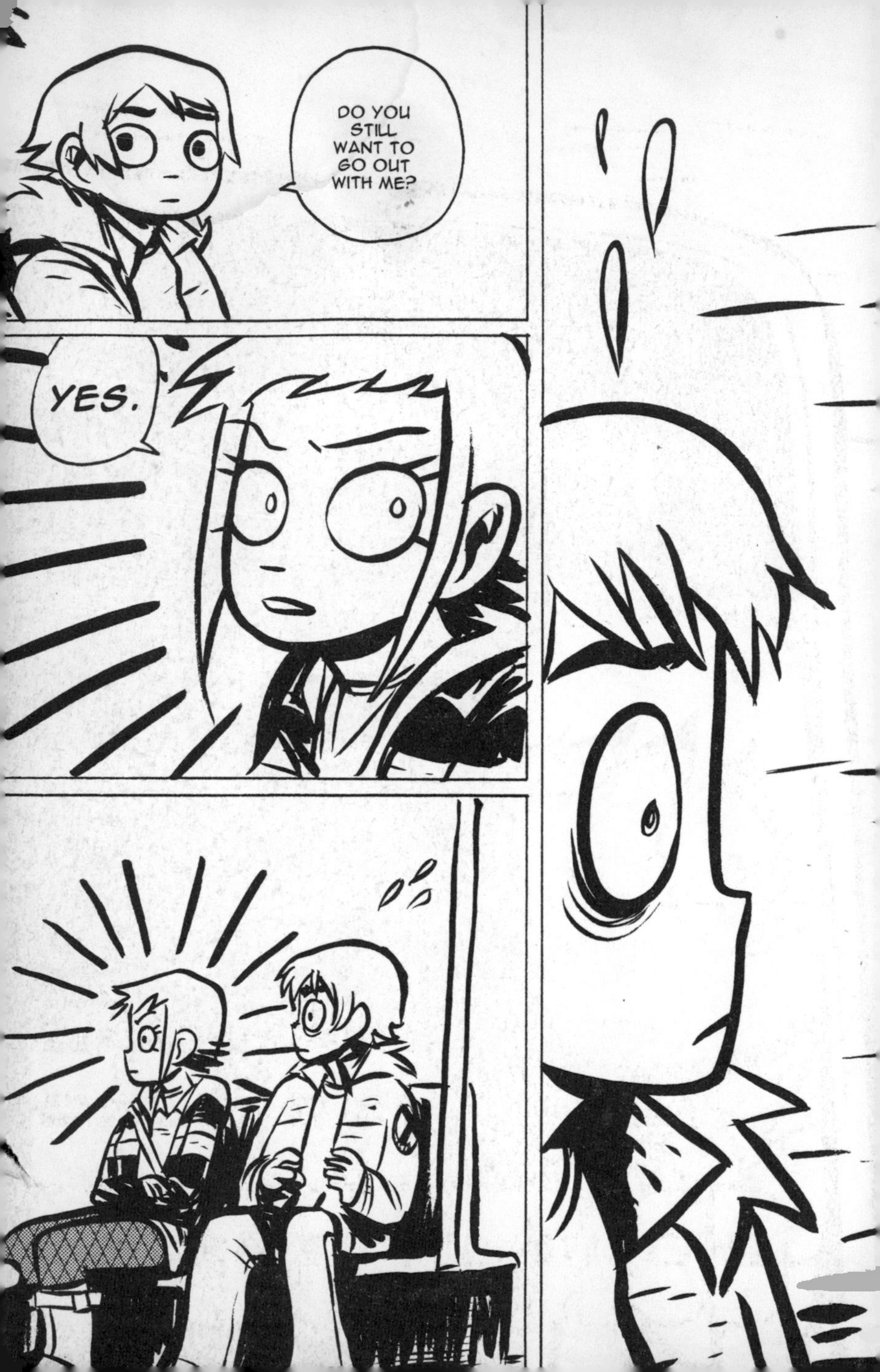
DO YOU STILL WANT TO GO OUT WITH ME?
YES.

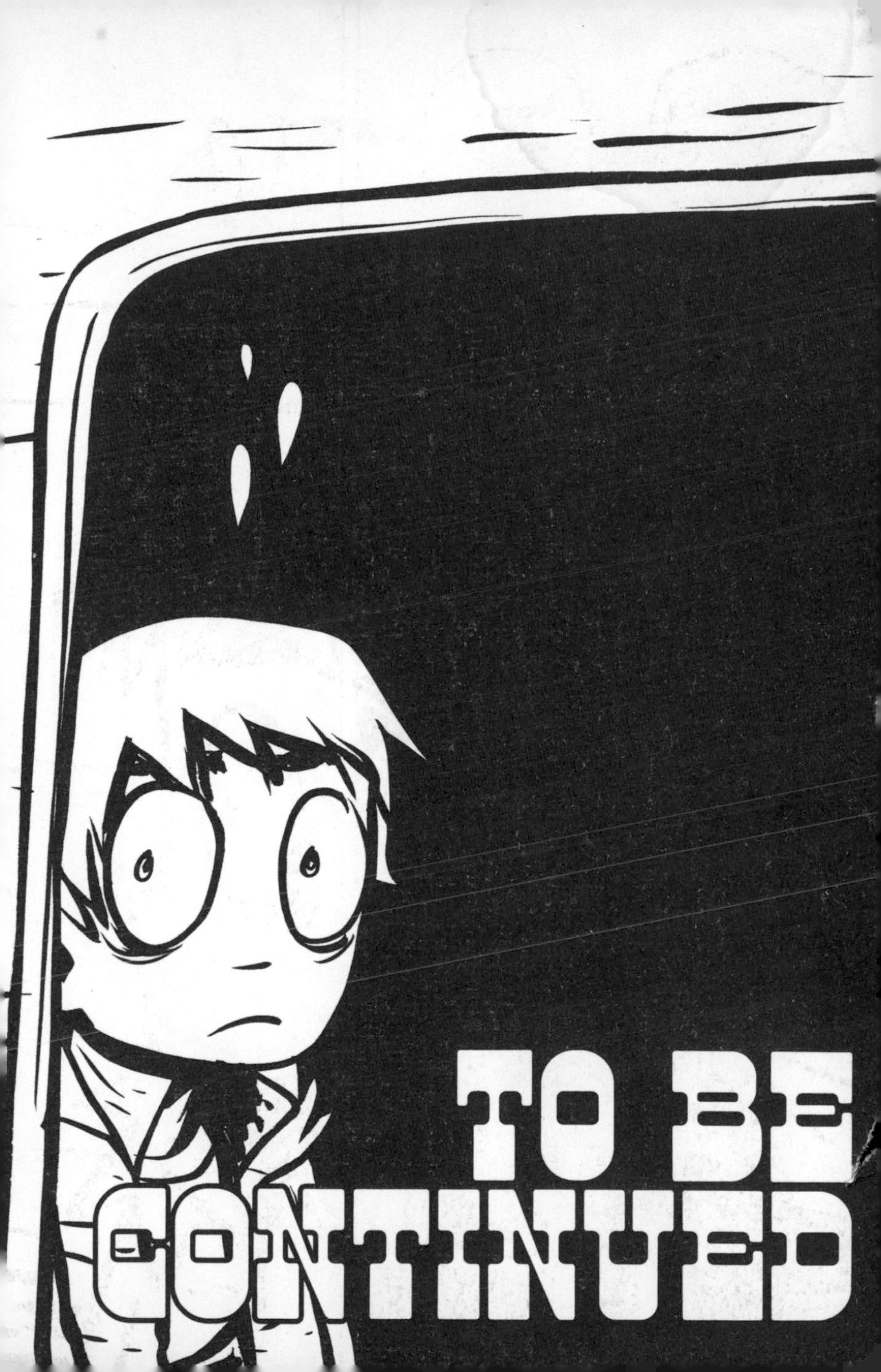
TO BE
CONTINUED

COMING IN EARLY 2005!

Does Scott & Ramona's burgeoning relationship have a future? Isn't Scott still supposedly dating Knives Chau? Who is Ramona's second evil ex-boyfriend, and why is he in Toronto? Who are The Clash At Demonhead, and what kind of bizarre art-punky music do they play? Who's their hot girl keyboardist, and what's her relation to Scott? Why are they Knives Chau's new favorite band? Fights! Drama! Secrets revealed! The answers to all these questions and more! It's all coming in...

SCOTT PILGRIM
VERSUS THE WORLD